Sweet As Candy

West University Book 2

Jess Carpener

To all the individuals, especially my friends, who get daily troll comments on our platforms. May we rise above so we can crush* the trolls under our influence.**

*I'm joking
**Sike, definitely not kidding

Contents

Chapter One - Candy

@candydeleon: Happy New Year, east coast people.
And to all those in Washington, D.C., remember,
we're coming for you. #MakeLoveNotWalls

My Twitter followers hear everything—the good, bad, and ugly. I have over a million followers, and Queen Candy's reign is only just beginning (dedos cruzados). Being a political influencer isn't always glamorous, but as I post my latest tweet and take a video of myself at the in-pool bar drinking a piña colada to story on Instagram, it feels pretty great.

New Year's Eve in Cancún. Lights sparkle in the night all around the pool and bars, glittering like stars against the dark sky. Music pulses in the background as I take a deep breath of saltwater air.

Every year, *mi familia* takes a vacation to Mexico to visit *mi papi's* family. It's been ten days of amazing drinks, gorgeous sun, and crazy fun. It's only ten here in Cancún, but my New Year's goals have been set for weeks.

Same pink hair, new and stronger me.

This is the year that we will kick out all the racists in the senate. Or, at least in California. It's a lofty goal. California's former governor, Joanna Marx, is the worst of them all. She ran for a special election last year and narrowly lost. But California's senate positions are up at the end of this next year. She's gonna run again.

1

And I'm going to make sure she runs herself right into the freaking ground like the cockroach she is.

Because that's what I do. And nothing is going to distract me from my goals this year.

My new year is about to start with an interview for Mitú in just one week. They're going to feature me, my activism, and have a personal interview tell-all where I'll talk about my upcoming plans for this year. And let's just say, I'm about to crush social media and make it my bi—

"Itchy sand," my best friend, Les, groans. She shakes her body and scratches at her elbow. "Why am I so itchy?"

I laugh. "Just hop in the pool."

She inches her way in, and I set my piña colada down to step out of the water, finding the seat with my towel.

Les follows after me, wringing out her blond hair as she sings, "We're gonna party, like it's your birthday. But it's really New Year's," to a random beat she just made up.

"White people." I roll my eyes.

Grabbing a bottle of water, Les stands on her tiptoes and looks through the crowded area. Probably looking for her boyfriend, AKA my twin, Carter. "Where'd your parents go?"

"Ah, they crashed an hour ago," I reply.

She nods. "I'm so excited for this year. It's going to be so fun."

"*Sí.* I'm excited for you to move in with *me* not *mi hermano.*"

Les grabs her towel and wraps it around herself. "It's gonna be a blast. Think of the pranks we can pull on Carter."

She waves across the courtyard to my brother, and I groan.

Of course, Carter is not alone. Because each year, *Mami y Papi* lets us invite someone on the family vacation. I chose Les. Carter…well, he chose *his* best friend. Who just happens to be my ex-boyfriend of five years.

"Please don't make them come over here."

Les clucks her tongue. "It's not my fault Carter invited

Tom on the family vacay."

I groan.

"You guys have kept it drama free. What's the deal?"

"The *deal* is that I know I look sexy." I glance toward Carter and Tom walking our way. "And my *ex* looks more full-time model than college baseball player, okay? This past week, seeing him in those tiny little trunks?" I pout. "My body is saying yes, and my brain is saying no. So why don't we start with the pranks now and run. *Adios, amiga.*" I move to walk away.

She grabs my arm and gives me a chastising look with her lips pursed and brow furrowed.

Ugh. "Okay, fine. *Está bien.* I can handle him. He's just a dude." Cracking my neck, I get ready for the screaming my heart and body are about to give my brain.

But then I glance that way and see the deep V that leads into his swim trunks. Pulling Les toward me, I say, "I need you to stick by my side. I can't fall into his lap. I mean trap."

I pull out my phone to tweet as a distraction.

Les snatches it out of my hand. "Oh, come on, Candy. It's a nice lap. You yourself say you're 'saving Tom for later.' It's New Year's Eve. Don't ever repeat this to Carter, but dang, Tom's been hitting the gym. He's lookin' like a snack."

I slap her arm.

She laughs. "We're in Cancún. Isn't it time for 'later?'"

I wrestle my phone out of her grip. "That's the great thing about later. It doesn't come with a specified date. And stop being thirsty over my ex."

"Believe me, Carter satiates my thirst very well." She takes a sip of her drink. "Look, this drunk woman at the pool was telling me that the man you kiss at midnight in this hotel is the man you'll marry."

I roll my eyes. "The drunk woman is my mom, huh. *Está loca.*"

Les shrugs. "I mean...she *did* marry your dad after kissing him on New Year's here. So, if you won't use Tom, then find one of these hot Latinos and kiss 'em!" She points out random people. And because she's hot and busty, every single guy she points to looks her up and down.

"*¡Párate!* You already have a midnight make out." And speaking of which, Carter sneaks up behind us and pinches my arm. I shove his hand away, and he chuckles.

"Tom and I just won the cornhole tournament. *Mira.*" He holds up a piñata keychain.

Tom follows, swinging a small piñata keychain, but I refuse to look at him. "We got keychains." His deep voice echoes in my stupid stomach as if he just asked me to go back to his room.

I clear my throat. Is there anything more suburban-dad-like than cornhole? Talk about nerds. "*Felicidades, hombres.* You're officially gringos. You should be so proud."

"Ha ha, very funny." Carter wraps his arms around Les's waist and kisses her cheek.

I glance at my phone, pretending to be enthralled with my lock screen. But I can feel Tom staring at me. We've been broken up for two years now, but every once in a while, I have a *teeny tiny* moment of weakness. Tonight, is *not* one of those nights. I won't even look at the tall, Black, and handsome that he is.

Way too much flavor in one man, lemme tell ya.

Ignore the muscles. *No mires su sonrisa perfecta.* Forget that he's too sweet for his own good. I repeat these in my mind like they are life-sustaining words.

Les and Carter are in their own little world, I'm silently repeating my mantras, and Tom comes up behind me with a, "Hey, can we talk?"

And I know it's immature, but I just can't. Because even his voice is giving me little shocks of turn-me-on. I look over at him. "*No hablo inglés.*"

"Come on, Candy." He bites his lip and runs his hand through his hair. It's grown out a bit longer than usual. He has it shorn short on the sides with loose, dark brown curls on top, and a few of them spill onto his forehead.

Me gusta.

Shoot. *No me gusta.* I can't like anything on him. Repeat it with me: *No. Me. Gusta.*

But he quirks his lips, so I know he's caught me dreamin'.

"*¿Podemos hablar?*" he asks, and the mofo *winks*. He knows what Spanish does to me. Stupid ladies' man. Licking his lips, he says, "You've avoided me this whole night. You should let me make things right."

Did he notice he just rhymed? Doubt it. He rubs his hands together while looking me up and down, and oh no, he's doing that thing. The thing that makes me want to dart out of everyone's eyesight and into a dark room with him.

But fool me once, shame on you. Fool me twice, shame on me. And I, Candy Ariana Maria DeLeón, do not like being made a fool. So Imma go with the rhyming route as well. "You know what? You're right. I should go get a Sprite. *Gracias* for reminding me, Tom, have a great night."

I speed off into the crowd, and for once, I'm thankful I'm short. It makes it easy to hide amongst everyone else. The DJ switches songs to a remixed Christmas song, announcing that there's a rooftop party tonight after the New Year's countdown.

I hold my towel around me and sit down at the above-pool bar. (There's about twenty bars within looking distance. Can you say paradise?) The counter is lined with blue tiles and the leather barstools are broken in and comfy. I sink down into one.

"*Bueno,*" I say to the bartender. "*Quiero un* Sprite, *por favor.*"

As the bartender readies my drink, I eavesdrop on the conversation next to me. Without even looking that way, I can tell the girl is about to get it. And by 'it' I mean *la chancla.* She's all over this guy, and it's clear he's not having any of her.

I glance at the two of them and stifle a laugh. The guy is staring at her like she's moldy bread. He glances my way, mouths *help me*, and turns back toward her.

Already avoided my own disaster. So isn't it in karma's rules that I help someone else avoid theirs? I place my hand on his shoulder. "She's so perfect, babe. Let's take her back to our room."

He raises a brow in my direction before sobering and nods. "I knew you'd love her." Holding out his hand for the other girl, he asks, "You ready?"

Her face goes from a smile with perfect white teeth to a grimace with a triple chin in a matter of a second. "Um, no thanks. I'm not interested in...whatever this is." She picks up her glass and runs away.

As soon as she's rounded the corner near the bathrooms, he exhales. "Thanks for the help."

The bartender hands me my Sprite, and I hand him a five. "*Gracias*. And you're welcome. Avoiding people is sort of my specialty. I'm Candy."

He points at my bright pink hair. "I'm not so sure about that." Taking my hand, he shakes it. "I'm Jake."

I take a sip of my drink. "What're you doin' here all alone, Jake?"

"Nursing a heartbreak." He holds up his drink and mock-cheers.

"Jake nursing a heartbreak." What is up with all the rhyming tonight? Feel like I'm in some middle-school musical. I pull my towel around me tighter. "Sorry, hon'. Well, I'll leave you to it."

Jake nods but then angles himself toward me. He's handsome. With wideset shoulders and a tank that shows off his muscles, it's clear he takes care of himself. His light brown hair is mussed as if he spent the night running his hand through it after playing in the ocean. Jake quirks his lips. "Unless you want to help me through it."

I lean in closer to him, putting my elbow on the bar counter. "What'd you have in mind?"

"Close the gap and find out."

I suck on my teeth and lean on my hand. "You first."

6

He chuckles and pulls back. "It was nice meeting you, Candy."

Looks like we're both too stubborn to make the first move.

"Ah, it always is." I wink. "You too, Jake. Enjoy *México*. Oh, and follow me on Twitter. Candy DeLeón. Maybe you can hit me up back in the states when that heartache is gone."

He rears his chin back, and his face sours. "Hold up a sec. I know you." He pulls out his phone and taps on the screen. "You're the 'make love not walls' chick."

Did he really just call me a 'chick'? I cock my eyebrow. "Oh, I'm sorry. You mean the *woman* who has started a whole movement against one of the most racist former-governors of California? Someone who has been interviewed by Vice, featured in Buzzfeed, and fought with a whopping total of 23 senators on Twitter? That's me. And you are?"

Jake puts his drink down and smiles, then slides his phone my way. "Speaking of governors...Jake Marx."

I pick up the phone, glance at the Twitter profile then back up at him.

No mames. Joanna Marx's son? How did I not smell the rat on him? Stupid me got clouded by blue eyes and a deep voice.

To be fair, we both should've recognized each other. But, we didn't. And now, we're in this comfortably awkward situation. I know he's attracted to me. And for him to be attracted to *me*? Well, that's a problem for his mommy.

I put the phone down a little too hard and step closer to him. Leaning down to whisper in his ear, I say, "It's a good thing we didn't close the gap, then, huh?"

Petty? Sure. But seeing the way his hands twitch against his thighs proves that I have a pull on him. So, it was worth it.

"Bye, Jake." I scurry off and nearly barf thinking about that encounter. I could have kissed Jake Marx—the son of one of the worst governors there ever was.

I pull out my phone and tweet:

@candydeleon: Funny seeing @jakemarx down in México. A

wall goes both ways. They can't come in. You can't leave. #Make-lovenotwalls

What a hypocrite.

I get back to my lounge chair, remove my towel, and put on my sheer black coverup. Goosebumps rise on my arm as a chilly wind blows through. Les, Carter, and Tom have disappeared, and I'm surrounded by people I don't know.

But I need to tell someone about Jake Marx. And if I'm being honest, I wanna tell Tom. Yeah, he's my ex, but he's also one of my best friends. While he might be one of the most talked about college baseball players at West University, he's also an activist and influencer like me. We go to a lot of protests together.

I head toward where the DJ is, and surprise surprise, Carter's trying to teach Les to *salsa*. I'd record it and make it go viral if I didn't love her so much.

"You need a good partner if you're going to succeed, Les. Move aside, Carter." I put my phone in my pocket and grab Les's hand and hip.

"You're, like, six inches shorter than me. How is this going to work?"

I clear my throat for my best Les valley-girl accent. "You're, like, six inches shorter than Carter. How did it work?"

She rolls her eyes, and I laugh. "Come on, *muchacha.* Let's dance."

We *salsa* for the next song and a half before Carter comes up and says, "It's time for me to have my girlfriend back. Get your own."

"Technically, I saw her first." I stand on my tiptoes and put an arm around Les.

She sighs. "Technically, you said you didn't like girls, so…"

I smack a kiss on her cheek. "I don't. Where's Tom?"

Carter turns his cap backwards and shrugs. "You mean the guy you keep running away from? Weird. Didn't think to keep tabs on him for you."

"Ha-ha, so funny. You should think about going into

standup." I glance at his wrist where a band of untanned skin lies. It's where his Apple Watch should be. He has type 1 diabetes, and he definitely shouldn't have his watch off. "Hey, you're manually testing your blood sugar, right? Put your watch back on. *Lo juro,* you're gonna be the death of me."

"Yes, *mami*." He puts his hands together as if he's praying.

Aight, Imma head out. Not gonna be mocked by my annoying twin. "B*adios*, Carter." It's what we've been saying since we were, like, three. Something about mixing our two languages, I guess.

"B*adios*."

"See you in the room, Can-Can," Les sings.

Walking backward, I shake my head. "I thought we agreed —we're not calling me that!"

I don't want to ruin their night. I'll tell them about Jake Marx tomorrow.

The stroll back to my room is quiet. A few hotel employees pass by, but that's it. I don't remember last New Year's. Probably because it was *una fiesta enorme.* But now, I'm gonna go back to my room, order some food, and watch the rerun of the ball drop while shoveling *queso* ice cream into my mouth.

Sounds pretty nice, actually.

I follow the little koi pond that trails between the different resort buildings. Yellow, orange, and white fish swim amongst the greenery and rocks. It leads straight down the middle of the first floor and leads me toward my room. When I finally glance up from the pond, I see him.

Tom's sitting on the concrete in front of his room—right next door to mine. His head is hung low, swimsuit riding up his thighs, and a cut muscle tee shows off his abs from my angle. His mahogany skin is tanned from the sun, and his long lashes can be seen curling against his cheekbones as he focuses on his phone.

So focused, I could pretend like I never saw him. But my heart flutters at his handsome self, and now I remember why I shouldn't want to see him. He's. A. Trap.

9

Apparently, I'm the mouse dumb enough to go after the peanut butter.

I swing my arms as I slowly walk toward him and clear my throat. "You good?"

He flinches as he drops his phone. "Uh, yeah. Yeah, I'm good. Just locked out." He throws his thumb over his shoulder toward the door.

"Right." I look both ways, really just to avoid his gaze. Thought I wanted to see him earlier, but I don't think I can do those hazel eyes right now. "Do you want me to go get Carter?"

"Nah. I can do things myself."

I point at him. "You, sitting on the ground in front of your room, would say otherwise."

He pulls up his knees and places his elbows on them. "Yeah, well, I was wanting to talk to you, alright?"

"I actually was looking for you too." I gently kick the toe of his shoe. "But you were just gonna wait out here all night? What if I came back to my room with another *chico*?"

"Another guy, huh?" He waves that off. "Then I woulda got my answer."

Sitting on the concrete can't be comfortable. Plus, our room's adjoining doors were left unlocked, so he can just go to his room from mine. I step aside and take my room key from my back pocket. Sliding it into the door, I say, "You coming?"

He scrambles up and brushes off his shorts. "If you don't lock me out first," he mumbles.

Drama king. I open the door, head to my bed, flop down on my stomach, and grab for the remote. It's not hard to find the channel with the New Year's countdown, so once I do, I grab the iPad to order room service.

Tom sits next to me, but he's on the very edge of the bed as if he's scared I may bite his head or *cajones* off. Which is ridiculous because avoiding him doesn't mean I'm suddenly a danger for him to be around.

"Do you want dessert? Gelato? Apple pie?" I scroll down the list. "*Ooh la la,* brownie with hot fudge?" I stop and look up at him.

He leans back on his hands and his gaze is full of melted caramel. "I don't want dessert, Candy. Unless it's you."

My arms break out in goosebumps, and I clear my throat. Couldn't the man just have said *yeah, sure, I'll take a brownie*?

"*Bien*. No dessert then."

Licking his lips, he shrugs a shoulder. "Give me one reason why I can't lay you on this bed right now and make you mine again."

A fire burns in my stomach. Not the acid reflux kind. But the kind that makes you do stupid things. I sigh. He knows why I can't be his. "You know why."

He trails his hand down my arm, and I nearly drop the iPad. *Danger! Danger!* is going off in my head. Frowning, he says, "It's a new year. Come on, girl. Let's reset. Get rid of that old past of ours."

I cock a brow. "Why?"

"'Cause I'm hung up on you, of course." He winks.

My eyes fight an eyeroll. It's hard to believe he's hung up on me when I've seen a carousel of girls parading around our apartment. It's really fun living with *mi hermano* and three other college baseball players. "Hmm. No. You're hung up on many other women. By the way, tell them to stop leaving their underwear in the bathroom."

His head shake is full of annoyance. "Ah. That's a low blow. You know I still think about you as more than a friend."

That's laughable. So laughable that I scoff. "Yeah, okay. If you wanted to be more than friends, you wouldn't have left me in the freaking Scandinavian airport without so much as a phone call. I waited for you. *Te esperé*, and you didn't come. Instead, you were screwing someone back at West. So don't pull this 'more than friends' crap with me. I'm not your friend with benefits. Be glad we're *amigos* at all."

I drop the iPad and focus on Taylor Swift singing on the TV so I don't have to look at him. Because I know how this goes. I've known how it goes for the past year and a half. He plays some smooth game, I end up in his arms for the night, and the next day it's as if it didn't happen. He erases us the moment I leave his arms. *Es muy triste.*

Beyond physical touch, there's never an answer to his past actions. Never an explanation. Our interactions are empty—just like it was at the airport the night he was supposed to show.

He leans back on his hands. "Alright, alright. Don't bite into my ass. I'm sorry. Shouldn't have brought it up."

I look at him, and his eyes are glazed with who knows what. "*Yo sé.* I know you're sorry." I sit up and cross my legs. "But I'm not some chick you can just hit and quit."

"I'm not here to hit and quit. We both know that we want this. I've just been waiting on you." He reaches for me, but I pull back.

I cross my ankles and fidget them on the bed. "You haven't been waiting on me, Tom. *Dios mío.* And I never asked, nor wanted, you to. You have your women, I have mine. Or, men. Whatever."

He groans. "Yeah, I know. Listen, I wanted to talk to you about something."

"What?"

One side of his full lips downturns. "I'm gonna move out of the apartment."

Running my hand through my hair, I laugh. "Yeah, right."

He doesn't say anything, and the smile drops from my face. "Wait, you're serious?"

"It's been two years, Candy. It's awkward living with an ex, especially when I don't want to be your best friend. I *do* want more. And no, not just your body." He shakes his head. "I got a place with Ethan and a few friends from the basketball team on the other side of campus."

I gasp. "*Ay Dios mío,* you're for real? Tom, you don't have to leave the apartment because of me. Especially not for Ethan. Come on."

I'm trying to add some humor into the conversation.

Ethan is one of our best friends. But the joke lands flat.

I bite my cheek as he picks at the sheet on the bed. When he finally speaks, it's laced with dejection. "Listen, I'm an idiot. I didn't mean the more than friends comment. It's not just that. I like you, no cap. I think this week changed things for me. But if it didn't for you…"

Did he just say he has actual feelings for me? My fingers go cold, and I sit on them because I want to grab his cheeks and pull him to me. I like him, too. I want to yell and scream, cry and make up for the past two years. I want opposites, and don't opposites attract? But this is the problem. Bad things happen when we're together.

I lick my lips. We've kissed a few times since breaking up. We've messed around. But…we've never admitted to any feelings.

Is he lying? Just trying to get a New Year's Eve bedmate? His gaze simmers against mine, and I know him well enough to believe that he's telling the truth. No malice or game lies in his eyes. If anything, they show a glimmer of sadness.

Maybe his confession should make this easier. Maybe this is the moment in every *telenovela* where the man admits his feelings and our leading lady falls into his arms, finally getting back together. Maybe leaving the apartment is an ultimatum, and I'm supposed to beg him to stay.

It would be so easy to be with him again. I know my feelings still exist. We could be happily ever after, a second-chance romance that everyone ships. The "it" couple. We'd fit together like two puzzle pieces.

I should tell him I have feelings for him too, and I should forget our past and look forward to an easy, happy future with the two of us by each other's sides.

On the TV, Taylor Swift leaves the stage, and Niykee Heaton begins singing "Starting Over." It gives me a moment to think as she sings.

Nothing with Tom is ever as easy as it seems. My sigh comes out breathy, and my heartrate should not be fluttering like this. The problem with *telenovelas* and romcoms is that they aren't real life. He *hurt* me. One confession doesn't erase the past. So I skirt around the issue entirely. "That doesn't mean you have to move out."

We've had a ton of fun this week. But whenever I take a step forward, I make myself jump back. He broke my heart, and I don't want to be in that position ever again. He's the only guy who's ever made me feel less-than to someone else.

How can you put a time limit on getting over that? This isn't some show. There's not a crowd of people shouting at the TV for us to get back together. It's life, and I'm just not ready.

Tom scrubs at his face, rubbing his forehead and eyes. "Something has to change. I want to believe we'll find our way back together. But I don't think we can do it as roommates. And if it never happens, we—I—can finally move on."

We've lived in this comfortable in-between. More than regular friends, but not a relationship. We talk every day, dissect each other's lives, make plans and goals together, but never talk about us getting back together or moving on with other people. It's what we do.

Part of me wants to be mad that he's ruined this weird peace we've had by admitting feelings. Another part of me doesn't even believe him. He's been with so many other people...but...so have I. The last part of me wants to give into him, and the pain splashed on his face makes me cave in that direction.

I reach out and grab his hand, pulling it into mine. He scoots toward me, and I stare at the waistband of his swimsuit. His abs are on full display, and since I apparently love to make *Madre Maria* angry, I sit on his lap and straddle him. As friends, duh.

Throwing my arms around his neck, I breathe him in. He smells of ocean and chlorine, as if summer leaked onto him. With just our swimsuits separating us, I feel the warmth of his body pressed against mine in every spot. He hugs me back, and I relish in the feel of his hands on me.

I lean my cheek on his shoulder. "I'll miss you in the apartment, Tom. I'll miss getting and giving updates on our crazy lives. I'm gonna miss hearing about baseball and the protests that you've gone to. I'm just gonna miss having you around." Sighing, I say, "I wish we could just rewind the clock so none of our past ever happened."

His hands land on my thighs. "I don't. You're much prettier now. Especially tonight."

I pinch his side. "Whatever."

Pulling on a chunk of my hair, he quirks his lips. "What can I say? The pink suits you."

I move away from him a bit to look at his face. The tension has eased a little, and if I forget that he said he had feelings, and I pretend I'm not straddling him (as a friend), it could almost be like we're back to our weird normal.

His eyes shimmer with speckles of emerald and gold as he takes a deep breath. "I'm gonna miss you too, Candy." Rubbing at his nose, he says, "I should go. You sitting on me like this isn't helping the fact that I admitted my feelings to you and now feel dumb..."

I trail my hand down his arm. "If you insist."

The New Year's Eve countdown in the background begins, and they count down from thirty, waiting for the ball to drop.

We stare at each other. I go back and forth between his eyes and lips. *If we could just go back.* Just *una noche.* We could pretend for one night that nothing happened two years ago. That everything is normal between us. That we never broke up. That he never cheated on me. That he isn't moving out the second we get back to West.

Would it be the catalyst to making everything right again? Or would it be a barely spoken about night, one that we forget the moment we cross the border back into California?

Is it worth the risk either way?

Five...four...three...two...

"For old time's sake." Tom grasps my hair and pulls me into him, our lips crashing together.

It's been too long, too distant, and we meet in sweet re-membrance of the one thing that keeps us living. It races down me, making me feel alive again. It's something old and some-thing new, and I bring him closer with my arm around his neck.

His lips are soft and warm, and I'm too busy relishing in the rightness of it all that I forget to brand it as wrong. His hands brush softly through my curls, and I cup his cheek. We kiss as if there's nothing and everything between us. No wor-ries, no fights, no questions. Just passion, love, and familiarity.

The kiss lights up my lips and tongue, traveling to my very core.

He leans back on the bed, putting me on top of him so our bodies press together. My hands roam over his chest and down his sides, and Tom traces the strings of my bikini.

He moans, and I melt, but a second later, my ears perk up with a different sound. A whirring near the door, and then a, "Hey, we're back!" from Les.

I tear myself away from Tom, whose chest expands with a deep inhale. Les comes in from the hallway, Carter following behind her. She smiles. "Oh, hey, Tom. I didn't know you were here."

Carter raises his eyebrows. "You guys good?"

I clear my throat and sit up on the bed, putting a few feet of distance between us. "Yes. *Sí*. Uh, Tom was locked out. You're back kinda early. *¿Por qué?*"

He points to his arm. "Dexcom malfunctioned. I need to put a new sensor on."

His blood sugar monitor for type one diabetes. Right. "Oh, okay. Um, I actually just got a call from Mom and Dad. I've gotta go."

Slipping on my shoes, I dart around Carter and Les toward the door.

Tom gets up from the bed. "Candy, wait."

I wave him off. "*Hasta mañana*, Tom."

Before I freak out in front of all of them, I run out of the

16

room as fast as my *chanclas* let me. I don't stop until I'm at the elevators, where I lean back, close my eyes, and take a breath of non-Tom air.

What did I just do? He's leaving me, and we kiss? I can't send mixed signals like that. Not to him, and certainly not to me. Even if it did make me feel like the luckiest girl in the world.

Tom has a life beyond me. I have a life beyond Tom. And now? Our paths will hardly cross. He's really leaving me this time.

My eyes sting. Why does this feel like a breakup all over again? We've kissed a few times over the years. Was it the words he said? Or, is it the fact that maybe Tom has outgrown me and is moving on for good now?

Why does that scare me so bad?

"Nice tweet about me."

I startle and open my eyes. Jake Marx stands in front of me, a smug look on his face. He presses the up button on the elevators and waits.

We stare at each other, but I don't utter a word. My heart still pounds from the leftover ecstasy of Tom. A sick feeling crawls up my stomach, and I don't want to deal with the hangover of everything I wish I could have.

The elevator doors slide open with a whoosh, and Jake steps in, holding the door. "You coming?"

My parents' room is on the first floor in the opposite direction.

But, I nod. And as the elevator doors slide closed, I turn toward him.

He bites his lip. It's almost as if he's amused by all of this.

I need the memory of Tom gone, so I take a step in Jake's direction. "Close the gap."

His eyes travel across my face. He furrows his eyebrows and cocks his head.

I say it again. "Close the gap, Jake."

Maybe he finally realizes that I'm not kidding because he

reaches down to my waist, picks me up off the ground, and
kisses me.

Chapter Two - Tom

C andy leaves me staring at a white door, her pink hair burned into my retina like smoke on a mirror.

Carter slaps my back. "Dude, sorry if we interrupted anything."

I don't even look at him. My mind is solely on Candy, who left me five minutes after I said I had feelings for her. "It's fine. I'll catch you later."

It's not the smartest move in the book, but I rush into my adjoining room, grab my keycard, and head out to look for the girl who occupies too much of my headspace. The trip was supposed to be drama-free. I didn't even want to touch her.

I was fine hooking up with her every once in a while. Ask around. I was *over* Candy DeLeón. But a week in Mexico, watching her every move messed me up. It wasn't the skimpy bikinis—though those did something to me too—it was the way she acted.

Her *essence.*

And now I sound like some dumb guy on a CW show like the ones my sister, Kira, used to watch. It's embarrassing. My teammates would be in stitches if they knew I was chasing after Candy still.

But here I am, running through the hotel, skipping over the small creeks of fish, trying to find where the hell she went.

She's maybe 5'2" on a good day. No way she can outrun my 6'3", future MLB-star, body. Maybe she went in the other direction. Toward the ice cream? She's been all over that *queso fla-*

vor this week.

Short of asking around and sounding straight sus, I'm out of luck.

"Can I help you, Sir?" a hotel attendant with long black hair, a too tight shirt straining at the buttons, and a mouth that promises a fun night ahead, asks me. Her eyes sparkle against the leftover Christmas lights bordering the walls.

I pull at a few of the hairs in my beard. "Uh, nah, I'm good. Just roaming. *Gracias.*"

She smiles. "There's a *fiesta* for New Year's up on the rooftop terrace. I'll be there after my shift."

I nod and rub my hands together. I'm not in the mood, but I'll check it out. Got nothing else to do. Carter and Les are that vanilla couple who are already probably saying, "Hey, we haven't taken a shower since last year. Hey, we haven't touched each other since last year."

Not what I want to hear tonight.

"Cool, I'll check it out. See you there." I wave goodbye and head toward the elevators. My lips still taste like Candy's cherry lip gloss, and I scrub it off with my sleeve. As I round the corner, I see a flash of pink hair and do-me curves. Unsuspiciously as I can be, I jog to the elevators, getting there just as the metal doors begin to slide closed.

It's not the elevator décor that makes me stop in my tracks. It's the mirrors on all sides of the elevator, where Candy reflects. Eyes closed, legs wrapped around some pasty white guy's waist, and lips locked.

He makes some weird grunt, and I see him pull back just enough to slip his tongue into her mouth before the metal doors meet in the middle, making me lose my view of the mirrors inside.

I may have told everyone I was moving on, but what the hell was that? In no way, shape, or form is that alright.

That's *my* girl, kissing some other dude a moment after kissing me.

I'm not mad. I'm not even really that jealous. Let her have

some fun. But I'm not waving some white flag to surrender. No, mark my words. Candy DeLeón is gonna fall back in love with me if it's the last thing I do.

∞∞∞∞

Candy avoids me at the airport. She's dressed in these linen pants we bought at the market in Mexico and the shirt *I* picked out for her, but she sticks to her phone, never lifting her gaze to catch mine. I try not to stare, but all I can think about is her kissing that other guy last night.

It should've been me.

It *was* me, before she left for some white dude.

I clear my throat until Les looks up, and I move my thumbs in the air on a fake phone till she furrows her brow and nods.

Tom: *Wanna switch seats on the plane? You sit with Carter. I sit with Candy.*

Les glances at me and texts back.

Les: *Sure…Why do I feel like this is a bad idea? Are you gonna have my future roommate pissed at me?*

I don't respond.

As we board our flight, I talk to the DeLeóns. They're practically my second parents, and because Mr. DeLeón wasn't shouting down my ear at every baseball game like my dad was, we get along well.

We're going back and forth in Spanish about how the A's and Giants are playing. It's a nice arrangement we've got. He helps me learn Spanish by solely speaking to me in Spanish. I head over to his house once a week, and we toss a ball back and forth while talking.

We've kept it a secret for years.

It's helped me understand a lot more in Spanish, which is helpful considering I'll now need it to get Candy back.

She's a sucker for when I speak Spanish.

The flight attendants greet us, and Candy sits in her assigned seat. But when I sit next to her, she rears her chin back and snaps her fingers. She rubs at her brows as if I'm a toddler who won't leave her alone. "This is Les's seat."

"Was."

She groans. "*Lo que sea.*"

I buckle my seatbelt and spread my legs a bit, reaching into her space. "So, where'd you go last night?"

Her spine straightens, and she reaches into her pocket, pulling out her AirPods. "Nowhere *importante*, why?"

"Eh, your parents just said they didn't see you after dinner last night, so I figured you had to be wrapped up doing something else."

She hums. "Nope, just...roamed the hotel."

I lick my teeth and tamper down a chuckle. "Hmm, alright."

"What's that supposed to mean?"

Shrugging, I say, "Nothing. All I said was alright."

She glares, narrowing her emerald green eyes. "It sounded sus."

"Well, did you do anything sus last night that would make you think that?" I fold my arms and put on an innocent smile.

Her cheeks flame, and she clears her throat. "*Párate.*"

"Stop what?" I bicker. "I'm not doin' anything. All I asked was if you were wrapped up with something else considering you weren't wrapped up with me."

She finally looks at me, and our gazes meet for a mere half second before she stares forward again. "I'm exhausted, and—"

"I'm sure you are," I mumble.

"I'm putting in my AirPods and going to sleep."

The rest of the flight, she stares at the back of the seat, refusing to even acknowledge me. But an hour before we land back in California, she falls asleep, and her head lolls on my shoulder. I snap a picture for proof and relish in her. The cotton candy strands nuzzle against my face and smell like sugar. She sleeps soundly and safe resting on me, and it cements it for me.

I've got feelings for her. Feelings that I don't think ever went away.

∞∞∞

Silence.

The world is quiet around me until the clear sound of a ball hurtling through the air at eighty miles per hour perks up my ears. I thrust out my glove and catch the baseball, the impact pushing my arm backward.

In less than a second, I twist to the side and throw the ball toward third base. A freshman struggles to catch it and Head Coach, Josh Trucker, nods. "Better, Walker. Still seeing slight hesitation in your turns. We need to cut that time in half if you plan to make a name for yourself in the big leagues. Hell, even the small."

"Yeah, I know," I grunt out. We've been working at this for the past two hours. My energy is null. Feel like I'm finna pass out, but professional athletes don't get that privilege. And dreamers like me? Those who aren't professional yet? They don't even get to *think* about that. I'm moving out of my old apartment after this, and it's weighed on my mind all day. Hard to focus at my second practice of the day.

I'm grateful Coach works with me so much. I want to declare for the MLB draft this year, but all the talk of me going in the first round seems to have faded. I have to come back this season stronger than ever, and I've got three weeks before proving myself.

"Pack it up, boy." Coach snaps to one of his low-level assistants. "Schedule Walker for weight training sessions twice a week with Maldon. Have them work lats, biceps, chest, 'specially on their throwin' arms. Give 'em rest days, and don't double schedule over practice."

"Yes, sir," the assistant says, stomping off toward the athletic facility.

Coach assigns me to work out with the world's biggest douche, but what can you do? We're the only ones with half

23

a shot at the MLB. But Ben Maldon doesn't even need a shot. He's got the money to throw at whomever he needs to to get his foot in the door. He's your picture perfect rich white kid that's been playing baseball for years. A dozen of him are on each MLB team, and they get drafted year after year. Coaches don't broaden their horizons. Baseball's an expensive sport, and right now, the pros are dominated by white men.

I'm gonna change that.

I roll out my aching shoulders and cross my throwing arm over my chest. "Anything else, Coach?"

He makes some sort of harrumph sound and shakes his head. "See you at five AM practice."

"Sure thing." I finger salute him and grab my gear before heading out to my Jeep and planning how to get everything over to my friend Ethan's place before it gets dark in two hours.

Notifications buzz on my phone, so I open up Instagram and see the newest comments on my carousel of pictures from Mexico. The first snap is Carter and I hanging off of each other, surrounded by the blue water of Cancún, drinks spilling over their cups as Carter leans on me, knocking me off balance. The next picture is of Candy, Carter, Les, and me at some fancy dinner, dressed in our best fits. The third picture is one Les took, and it's Candy and me looking at each other and laughing.

Her curvy figure is highlighted by the sun in the background. She's got on a hot pink bikini that's a sharp contrast against her golden skin. Bet she's pissed I posted it. She hates uploading any photos of us together.

It stirs up the "shippers."

We've been attending political rallies and protests together for years, and people have even started a hashtag #tandy.

No cap, I like it. But every interview she does, she drives home the fact that we're just friends. Out of respect for her, if people ask me, I say the same.

Still sucks, though.

I toss my phone into the passenger seat and drive one last

time to *my* apartment before it becomes *her* apartment.

Haven't talked much since I saw her sucking face with that other dude. The only other words she spoke to me were, "You're next," at customs in the Sacramento airport.

But if I had to guess, me not talking to her is driving her crazy. We've never gone this long without speaking. I know it's driving *me* crazy.

Whether she's mad at me for moving out, or hiding so she doesn't have to admit the feelings written across her face, it's anybody's guess. Only problem is she forgets that I know her. Did I screw up two years ago? Yeah. Did I want to make it better? At first. Then we got comfortable. I figured I'd give her some space, she'd give me some. It never bothered me much. You make your bed, you lie in sort of thing. But the itching feeling I got while seeing her wrapped up in someone else's arms?

That ain't comfortable.

I shouldn't care. Shouldn't even be focusing on her right now. This is the most important year of my life. Day one dream has always been the MLB. I shouldn't let anything occupy my mind outside of baseball and building my reputation as an activist. I want to be an example other kids can follow.

I've got big plans this year for both—and neither of those things can take a back seat to my confused feelings over a girl.

That's what my main head thinks. But my second one?

Not so much. It's calling out for Candy like an addict needs a drug.

Thinking about that smooth skin, the small freckle she has right below her belly button, her tiny waist, and the way she's easy to hold no matter where we're at is getting me stupid-excited. I gotta stop these feelings—now.

But I find myself driving over the speed limit, vibing to "Come & Go," ready to see her as I move out.

For the last time, I pull into my assigned spot and use the key fob to open the door. I race to our apartment to try and save daylight.

Carter, Rykard, and Jared sit on the couch. They jump up with various forms of, "Hurry up, let's go. Practice is early tomorrow."

I curse under my breath. Where the hell is she? Slapping Carter on the shoulder, I whisper, "Bruh, where's your sis?"

"Uh, Les had to close out her lease and grab a few last-minute things before the official move-in. Then I think they were headed to that one chick from game night's house." He types something on his phone. "Can't remember her name. You know, the one you kicked me out of my own bedroom for a month ago?"

"Erin? I didn't kick you out. You willingly grabbed your stuff and went over to Les' place. Damn, I thought Candy would be here."

Carter shakes a hand through his hair. "Sorry, *amigo*."

Just a girl, I convince myself. You've got more important things to focus on. *So focus on them, idiot.*

But damn, that girl's messed me up in the head.

I think about everything I hate about Candy to try and escape her grip: The way she leaves half-eaten granola bars on the counter. How she sheds hair like a pink golden retriever. How she can't write a single Instagram caption or tweet without at least three emojis.

Carter's on my heels as I head to our room to survey the boxes littering my side. "Your bed's gonna look lonely in here when I'm gone," I quip.

He slaps me on the back and chuckles. "Nah, I'm 'bout to get a queen. Gotta convince *mi novia* to move into *my* room rather than Candy's."

I swallow what feels like needles at the mention of her name. "Good luck with that."

It's been too long since I've been with someone else. That's the problem. After leaving here, I'm heading to West's dating app and swiping. Candy's just a girl.

I can find hundreds of those with a few minutes of swiping.

We transfer the boxes to the car, but I can't get those big

green eyes out of my mind. I'm so frustrated I could throw a ninety-mile-per-hour ball without a second thought. Is she still talking to the guy from Mexico?

Does she even remember *our* kiss?

But the real question is why do I even care? She rejected me. If I come at her like some desperate Casanova, she'll head to the hills faster than I can blink.

I'm not gonna simp for Candy DeLeón.

And to prove it, I do something I know will piss her off. On a post-it note, I write:

You were gone when I said goodbye to everyone.

See ya around.

-Tom

She'll be mad I didn't call her. She'll be mad I didn't say goodbye to her. She'll analyze the cryptic letter. Or, I hope she does.

Because being upfront and honest didn't get the girl. So maybe it's time I play unattainable.

As I hand my keys over to Carter and drive away from the apartment, I try to push Candy out of my mind.

She leaves her shoes in a pile by the door, and never cares to organize them. Her hair plasters the shower wall like an abstract piece of art. She eats pizza with a fork. Her beauty routine is high maintenance.

I can list a thousand things I hate about Candy DeLeón.

But the real thing I hate is I don't mean any of them at all.

Chapter Three - Candy

My tan from Mexico is slowly fading. Today is the day for my Mitú interview. And even though it's a Face-time interview with a woman named Gloria, I get fully ready and leave my apartment, crumpling the sorry excuse of a goodbye letter that Tom left me a week ago. It's been sitting on my dresser for days, driving me freaking nuts. I toss it in the trashcan before heading to the library.

It's too loud at our place to conduct any kind of interview. Living with a bunch of guys isn't always what I thought it'd be.

You have Les shouting at Rykard to pick up his shaved chest hairs in the bathroom, Jared shouting at Rykard for not being a good roommate (those two are like fire and gasoline), and Carter yelling at Rykard for pissing off his girlfriend. Not to mention *me* shouting at Rykard because he's mean to Jared, who simps for Rykard like no other.

It's really just everyone shouting at Rykard, the world's most annoying roommate.

I've booked ahead a study room alone for the interview, and though I've done this before (like with Vice last year), I still can't help but feel nervous. Let's chock it up to human nature.

Estás bien, Candy. I'm fine. I'm strong and beautiful. I am cool, calm, and collected.

Whew, I got this.

I close the door to the study room and open the blinds so that the lighting is good. Everyone likes looking pretty.

Right on cue, my phone begins ringing, and I blow a raspberry to clear my throat. Then I answer. "*¡Hola!* You must be Gloria."

The woman on the other end has long dark hair, a hoop nose piercing, and brown eyes that are lined with blue liquid eyeliner. My type of girl. She smiles with straight teeth that have a slight gap in the center. "*Hola Candy.* I'm a huge fan of your work. Wish we could be doing this interview in person, but the holidays are always hard to plan around."

She's walking outside, and a door opens and closes as she enters into some sort of shop.

"*Está bien,* Gloria. I know it's a busy time for all of us." My foot taps against the floor under the table.

"Alright, let's get started." She sits down at a table and puts AirPods in. "This will all be screen recorded, and then I'll transcribe it later before publishing."

"Cool, I'm ready when you are."

"First of all, I'm a huge fan. Let's talk a bit about your platform and what makes you different."

I cross my legs and let out a sigh of relief for already having the answer rehearsed. "*Por supuesto.* I mean, besides my pink hair..."

Gloria winks. "Remember when it was green? I was looking at your photos last night."

My nose crinkles. "Ugh, that was my Billie Eilish phase." I laugh. "But back to my platform...I'd have to say a lot of things. First, I'm biracial. My mom is American and white, and my father is Mexican and Hispanic. Growing up in the U.S., there were definitely a fair share of comments about my skin color or the way I talked in elementary school. So even though I'm American, it didn't always feel that way. It was like I wasn't American enough, but not Mexican enough either. I didn't want there to be this disconnect between the two. *Yo soy Americana y Mexicana, pero* it's equal. I'm so proud of my Latina heritage, just as I'm proud of my American heritage. Which is why I created my platform to show that these two things coexist and make America a better place because of them. Immigrants have created this beautiful place."

She nods and shuffles some papers. "Great answer. Now, you were popular before, but the riot against Joanna Marx at West last year really grew your platform these past several months. Why do you think that is?"

"That's when my movement really became well-known. A photo I snapped of *mi hermano* and his girlfriend made headlines across the nation, and my hashtag behind it #makelovenotwalls, started taking off. It was liked on Twitter a million times, and the protest was the first of its kind from WU. Now, I run the student organization, Equal Treatment For Equal People, which focuses on providing minority students with the resources that they need to succeed."

I take a sip of water from my Hydro Flask. "Joanna Marx is well known as a former governor, was running during the special election, and my platform gave the protest and image the momentum it needed to become what it's known as today."

Gloria looks down at something I can't see. "Awesome. So...We wanted to get your response to Jake Marx's recent comment about you."

My stomach drops. What is she talking about? *"Lo siento,* what comment?"

Gloria holds up a piece of paper in frame and reads, "Jake Marx was at the Venice Beach pro-immigration reform rally supporting his mother in her senate campaign. There was a group organized by you holding signs with the hashtag *make love not walls.* When asked about what him and his mother thought of your campaign against her, Jake Marx responded with, and this is a direct quote, 'I personally know Candy DeLeón, and all I'll say is she has quite a mouth on her. Thank you.'"

I gulp and run through everything I can think of in my mind. If I say no comment, that's just weird. His comment could have meant anything. Deep down, I know he's playing with me. He thinks this is some game of cat and mouse. He's been DMing me constantly since we got back. No one even knows who he is. He's definitely the least-popular Marx son. I just need to play it off. Give Gloria something to shut this down.

She's much more likely to be on my side. I clear my throat. "He's referring to a tweet where I called him out on his mother's border policies while he was vacationing in Mexico last week. Though Mr. Marx and I may not see eye to eye on everything, I will say that he's correct. I do have quite a mouth on me, and I'm going to use it by protesting their asinine desire to promote racism while advocating for the millions of Latinx individuals who are being discriminated against because of them."

"Thanks, Candy. Sorry to put you on the spot like this. I mean, if you ask me, he seems like a real piece of work."

"Mmm," I add in what is hopefully a non-committal answer.

"Do you anticipate coming into contact with him again this year?"

I nearly choke on the straw. "*Ay Dios mío,* no," I mutter under my breath. Kill me now. Then with a smile, I add, "I don't plan to, no. I want to focus on the policies I'm trying to change rather than the drama of opposing political sides fighting."

"Smart, girl. Very smart." She points at the screen and nods.

I wave her off while my insides crawl with cockroaches. "Thanks."

She puts the paper down and looks up out of the frame, waving to someone. When she glances back into the camera, her face breaks into a grin. "Sorry, one of my coworkers. This isn't the first time you've been mentioned in the media. There've been a lot of positive interactions and also a few negative."

I shrug. "With a big platform, that's to be expected."

"People seem to not take you seriously because you, and this is once again a quote, 'looks like she should be heading up a fashion blog rather than making a political name for herself.'"

Goosebumps break out over my skin as I sigh. Why do I feel like I'm playing defense this whole interview? I take a deep breath and smile, plastering on my schmoozing face. "Why can't I be both? The problem with many politicians is that they believe everyone has to fit in their mold. My platform is *meant* to break the mold. Their criticism of me is laughable, and it goes to show that they've missed the point of me altogether. A woman shouldn't have to be boxed in. I can love fashion, dye my hair every color of the rainbow, and still know more about politics than anyone you know."

She laughs. "*Bien.* I'm glad to see the criticism doesn't bring you down. *Mi mama* would say you embody the saying '*al mal tiempo, buena cara.*'"

Her mom would be right. I do put on a brave face through bad times. I'm positive. I have hope that things will get better. If I didn't, I wouldn't be trying so hard to fight for change in my community. "*Sí, mi papi* would hopefully say the same."

Gloria asks me a few more questions about my political career and what I hope to achieve. We talk about the kids who are currently staying in ICE facilities. How many of them will experience malnutrition, physical abuse, mental abuse, and sexual abuse. And when the U.S. is done ruining them, they send them back to their respective countries, broken in a way that they weren't before. These kids are growing up in horrible conditions, often taking care of younger siblings or kids they don't even know.

Plus, with DACA always seeming to be threatened, that puts so many at risk…like my older sister, Carlotta. When I use the hashtag make love, not walls, I truly believe it. I want love to be more prominent than the walls separating our countries and cultures.

The passion flows through me, and I can only hope I'm conveying how much I care through Facetime. This is just a step in the career I hope to have. She probably thinks I'm rambling, and who knows how long I just talked without letting Gloria respond. My bad.

I shrug and heave out a little laugh as I finish speaking. "Obviously, I can't change the world. But I do hope to change enough hearts to make a difference."

Gloria sets down her drink and cocks her head to the side. "I like that."

A blush creeps into my cheeks, and I avert my gaze. "*Gracias.*"

Thankfully, the interview takes a swift turn, and she starts asking me lifestyle questions, like who my favorite Latino actor is and what I enjoy doing for fun. We talk about the few months that I traveled, and my favorite country I visited. Let's just say this: Definitely not Scandinavia where Tom left me waiting for him in the airport. He never even got on the plane. I waited and waited, but nothing. All the things I had planned for us, I went and did alone.

Gloria scratches at her nose. "Why'd you come home from traveling? Was it always supposed to just be temporary?"

The real reason I came home? Because my brother almost died from type one diabetes. Six weeks after Tom left me waiting in the airport, I got a frantic phone call from him. I was in Ireland, and I'll never forget the pain in his voice. It was the first time I'd heard his voice or answered a call from him since he ditched me.

But he wasn't calling to beg for me back. He called because of Carter. Carter had passed out at a game, collapsing in his own vomit. I know someone was looking out for me that day. Because normally, I never would've answered a phone call from Tom. But *something*, or someone, made me pick it up.

I caught the first plane back and vowed to bury all the drama with Tom, committed to making sure Carter was okay.

"Candy?" Gloria prompts.

"Sorry." I swallow. "Someone close to me got really sick. I wanted to make sure I was home in case something went wrong again." I rub my lips together, but there's no lip gloss left and they feel dry. "I hope I haven't been speaking too much for your interview. Think you can piece all of these random answers together?"

My palms sweat, and I try anything to distract me from how I'm suddenly feeling.

Maybe she can sense that something is off, because a little wrinkle appears between her perfectly waxed brows, and then Gloria smiles. "No worries at all. You're doing great. We're almost done."

I nearly sigh in relief.

"So, a girl like you, at college, let's ask what all of your followers are dying to know. Are you single?"

Cue the full-on blush. "Yep. Livin' the *vida loca*. Just exploring what college has to offer me."

"Who college has to offer you." She winks.

"That too, I suppose." I laugh it off, but deep down, I'm feeling a little overwhelmed. I don't like personal lifestyle questions. It only gives the hateful DMers more ammo to hit me with. *Let's hurry this up, por favor.*

"I've seen you have some people hoping for you and the college baseball star Tom Walker to get together. Anything between the two of you?"

I shudder and pray to *Madre María* I'm not blushing. Tom is not on my good list right now. He left without saying goodbye, and we haven't spoken in a week. "Uh, Tom Walker is an ex of mine. We're really good friends now, but no, nothing between us. We've helped each other build our platforms, and though he's a great baseball player, he's also an amazing activist. So, I think people just hope two activists will get together." My legs won't quit bouncing underneath the table. I'm full of nerves, especially because I've never had an interview go so personal. I know the site is geared to a lot of women, but *mierda*, this is a little heavy-hitting.

Gloria clucks. "An ex, huh? Everyone likes a second chance story."

I smile, but don't say anything else.

Gloria reaches for her iced tea. "I think that's all I have for you. You answered everything *perfectamente*."

I give her a thumbs up. "Hopefully that wasn't too boring for you. I really appreciate it."

She nods. "Of course. If you're ever in LA, please call me. We can hang out, set up a meet and greet sponsored by Mitú, show you around. We'd love to have you."

"*Gracias, amiga.* I'll definitely consider it when the holidays die down. *Déjame saber si necesitas algo más.*"

"Have a good day, girl! I'll have the interview up in the next few days for you." She waves.

"*Adios*, Gloria. *Tenga un buen día.*"

She ends the call, and I slink back into my chair and let out a shaky inhale. I haven't talked to Tom since Mexico, and the flight back was weird. He kept saying stuff to me as if he knew what I had done with Jake.

I'm probably overthinking it because of that comment Jake made. But now with both Jake and Tom being mentioned in the interview, you can never be too cautious. The cancel culture is strong these days. I should give Tom a heads up about the interview for his own platform.

He's not huge into social media, but he still has a fair amount of followers—pretty much a hundred thousand ball chasers. The girls are straight embarassing on his feed. So many thirsty comments happen on each photo he uploads. Everyone wants their shot with him since he'll probably make it to the MLB.

With a curse to the Universe, I break the week-long vow of silence.

Candy: *Hey, I had an interview with Mitú and they asked about you. Not sure if it will make it into the interview, but wanted to let you know just in case.*

A few moments later, my phone buzzes.

Tom: *Thanks.*

That's it. He's moved out, moved on, we haven't talked in a week, and he responds with *thanks*. Well, *genial*.

I grab my backpack and push him out of my thoughts. But it doesn't work because all I can see is Tom's stupid smug face on the plane ride home from Mexico.

Chapter Four - Candy

Halfway to my Law, Politics, and Justice class, I run into Ethan, the guy who Tom moved in with and one of my best friends. He holds out his arms for me as if we haven't seen each other in months.

I run and jump into them, and he easily lifts me. Perks of being a tall basketball player. He's adorable, in an all-American boy type way. Sandy blond hair, emerald eyes, goofy, and a dunk that always makes it onto ESPN's highlights. He's the jock everyone's watching. Easily one of the most popular athletes at West. It's a shame I'm not into all-American boys.

"How's my favorite girl doing?"

"Fine. How're you? You still coming to game night tonight?" I ask, unraveling myself from him.

"Wouldn't miss it. It's been too long. I can't even remember who won last time." He walks to class with his arm around my shoulders.

"Les won. That girl is a Christmas fiend."

He laughs. "Ah, yeah. How could I forget your bro's heart eyes toward her all night."

"Blech. They're sickening...ly cute."

I hold open the door for him, and he mocks flipping long hair while batting his eyelashes. "And they say chivalry is dead."

"Not here. I am a class-A gentleman." I beam.

"Just like Cher," he points out.

I cover my eyes and cackle. "*Dios*, your sisters are my idols. They raised you so good."

He winks. "I'm good at a lot of things. If you ever let me into your bed, I'll show you."

I playfully slap him. "Carter would castrate you."

Chuckling, he concedes, "Tom, too."

We settle into our seats as class gets started. Since we're both poli-sci majors, we've been in a ton of classes together. Our specialty is writing notes to each other about stupid stuff. Most of his have to with animals, and he always doodles these strange looking animal combos. The guy is weird, but I love him.

Our professor is telling us about our next assignment, which is a twelve-page paper about any Supreme Court case ruling we'd like. This is only our third class session this semester, but no rest for the wicked (students), I guess.

We're going straight from holiday break into full-fledged hell. Ethan chooses this moment to slide a doodle to me of a cat and a walrus mixture that says *you're toothfully cute.* I snort and crinkle my nose.

"What the hell is that?" I whisper.

Ethan smiles on one side of his mouth. "I call him Mr. Walter."

The professor clears his throat and points at us.

Mr. All American Boy grins. "Sorry, P-Man. I was just helping Candy. She doesn't know much about politics." He salutes our professor, who rolls his eyes. Ethan gets away with everything because he's good at basketball.

The athletes at this school, I swear.

"Miss DeLeón, try to keep up. I can have the TA help out if needed."

I bite back a laugh and soberly nod. "I'll pay very close attention."

When the professor looks away, Ethan taps his pencil on my desk and nudges me with his knee. "You should try to know a bit more about politics, Candy," he whispers.

I push his pencil off my desk as he laughs. "One day, I'm going to get you back for all this."

Ethan just winks.

Our professor goes into talking about different Supreme Court cases, and brings up a few immigration ones. It's pretty close to my heart.

My dad got his citizenship two years ago, but before that, he came to America after marrying my mom, a blonde bombshell who now isn't afraid to use her *chancla* if we act up. She also makes a mean *tamale*, but my *abuela* won't ever admit that.

Had my dad been deported before becoming a citizen, I don't know what I would've done.

The professor wraps up his discussion, reminds us of the homework, and excuses us from class.

Ethan sidles up next to me. "So, whatcha gonna write about?"

I blow some hair out of my eyes and rub my hands together as we step out into the cold. "Probably Tinker versus Des Moines. About student freedom of speech. You?"

He shrugs. "Honestly, the only one I know is that Roe versus Wade case."

I laugh. "Oh yeah? You gonna write about women's reproductive rights? *Pobrecito*, I'm sure that case has really affected you personally."

Slinging his backpack on his shoulder, he says, "Yeah, yeah, whatever. Hey, I need to swing by your apartment to pick something up from the guys. You heading home?"

"Uh, I wasn't planning on it." I glance at my phone and the different notifications I have. My DMs are flooded. There are a few people telling me I suck (only an hourly occurrence), others telling me to lose or gain a few pounds (apparently everyone has an opinion on my body), and then come the DMs with the racial slurs. I'm honestly amazed that people have enough time in the day. I get my fair share of commentary. With my not-always-contained personality, I'm not your average advocate. Believe me, I get told that on a daily basis. I wiggle my phone. "I've got work to do."

Ethan shakes his head. "If only everyone was so lucky to work on their phone."

I blow him a kiss. "One day, *chico*. You too will have enough followers to make some money thanks to your basketball skills. Or for your hot bod."

"Yeah, yeah." He waves me off. "Well, it's time to go home. I need a ride to your place, so tough luck, sweetheart."

Did he seriously just say tough luck? He's hardly the pushy type. "Why can't you just take your truck?"

He shrugs. "It's in the shop."

I groan. "*Bien*. I'll take you."

He has a shit-eating grin on his face, so I push him, but he barely moves. We walk back toward my car, my mind on the huge pile of work I have waiting for me.

It sounds like a dream to be a social media influencer, but when you're more than style and fashion, when you have strong political views, you get a lot of hate. I have a filter on my messages, and still, I get hundreds each day. I have to find the legit DMs from the spam ones, so I don't miss any business offers. Thankfully, most people email me. I check that too and see that I have twelve business emails too.

I have offers from an energy drink company, a cruelty-free hair dye company, and then an offer from a human rights campaign. Now that's one I'm interested in.

Granted, I'll probably do the energy drink and hair dye company too. A girl has to make money somehow. Problem is, I have to vet those companies. At this point, I've basically become a private investigator. If anyone in those companies have made donations to a campaign that goes against my beliefs, I have to turn them down. The one thing I don't want to do is be crucified on social media.

With many followers comes many social justice keyboard warriors. I've seen what they've done to some of my influencer friends. I'd like to avoid that at all costs.

"Earth to Candy." Ethan waves his hand in front of my face.

I slap his arm. "*Lo siento*, I'm multi-tasking."

Unlocking the door, I shove my phone in my backpack. Ethan gets in and buckles his seatbelt as I find a suitable Spotify playlist and back out of the lot. I drive the short distance to my apartment as Ethan scrolls on his phone.

My thoughts trail back to Tom and his stupid *thanks*. I can't wait to rant about it later to Les. Now that she lives with me, it's like a slumber party every night with the two of us. Pretty sure we drive Carter mad, but we're a package deal.

The situation with Tom just pisses me off. He drops the bomb of moving, and then we don't say a word to each other after our kiss. Yes, I ran off when I had the opportunity to, but all of a sudden we're not friends anymore either?

Embustero.

I get out of the car and Ethan trails behind me. "You need a ride back to campus too?"

"Uh," he scratches his chin, "I think Jared is heading back up, so he can probably take me."

Holding the key fob up to the door, I give a, "Mmm, okay," in response.

Two seconds later, I hear, "'Sup, sis?"

I turn to find Carter holding five boxes of tampons. "Hold the door, *por favor*."

I glance at him. I could've sworn Les and I's cycles had synced...and I am so not on my period right now. "Whatcha got there, *hermano?*"

His face looks blanched, and it's clear he was struggling wherever he came from. "Les said she needed tampons. I didn't know what type she uses, so I just grabbed like five kinds." The boxes are stacked like Jenga in the crook of his arm.

I hold the door open for him, and he walks on through. Ethan nods. "If I had a nickel for every time my two sisters made me go get them tampons growing up, I'd be rolling in the dough."

Carter chuckles. "Yeah, well, usually Candy just throws tampons at me and says to carry them for her. She's never made me actually pick them out. Did you know there are flavors?"

I face palm, and Ethan's brows pinch. "I think those are just different colors and sizes, my man."

Carter cocks an eyebrow. "That makes more sense."

"*Los hombres serán nuestra muerte.*" I march ahead.

Carter swears under his breath in Spanish, and I just shake my head.

We get to our apartment 13666, and I fish around my backpack for my keys. Some may say our apartment is satanic, but I think it's just one more thing that will convince my parents I'm practicing *brujería*.

Before I can find my key, the door opens impossibly fast, and a bunch of people scream, "SURPRISE!" as they jump out from behind the couches and tables. One of the baseball guys knocks into my roommate Rykard, and they both groan and hold their heads.

Carter drops his jaw...and all the tampons as Ethan cheers behind me.

Chaos, like always.

I'm surprised all right. "What is this?" I cackle, gesturing at the rest of the people.

Les comes out from behind the door. "Surprise!"

"I think you're about three seconds too late, *amiga*." I wink.

She runs and hugs me, then moves to Carter and gives him a quick kiss before picking up the tampon boxes. "Happy birthday, you guys! Great job, Ethan. You did perfect."

Ethan gives her a side hug and moves into the apartment to talk to everyone else.

"Our birthday's next week," Carter and I say at the time.

Les smiles and claps her hands. "Yeah, but we have your family party then, and the rest of us wanted to celebrate with you. All the roomies and our game night crew are here. Plus the rest of the baseball team. Besides Ben, of course," she mumbles. "We're doing a birthday breakfast. Look at all we made..."

Her voice fades out as I turn to say hey to everyone and see Tom front and center. He's dressed in a coral short sleeve that hugs his chest and biceps, and my eyes pause on the muscles that beg that shirt to break. With acid-washed jeans that have rips running down them and white Nikes, everything on him is sculpted to his body. The same body I've been dreaming about since we kissed on New Year's. My hormones need to freaking relax.

I guess I'm staring too long because he nods, and his tight smile doesn't reach his molten hazel eyes.

I look away, but not before seeing Erin loop her arm around him. Her and I aren't friends, and now? We never will be, that's for sure. He sends me a cryptic note, a cryptic text, and now he's hooking up with *Erin* again?

Pathetic.

"Happy birthday, babe!" Jared plants a kiss on my cheek, his blond hair flopping into his eyes. Pretty sure he's my favorite roommate ever. Clean, funny, super-hot, and totally not into women.

"Thanks, boo. *Te amo.*"

He leans down and whispers in my ear, "You want me to stick by you? I saw Tom over there." He fake-gags. "I've never been a fan of him."

I push him away. Tom is one of his best friends. "Stop it, weirdo. *Estoy bien.*"

"You know I don't speak Spanish. I'm gonna say that was a cry for help. Fine, I will stick by you." He puts his hand over his heart and bats his eyelashes.

"Whatever. You're probably just trying to avoid Isaac. Or Rykard. We never know with you two," I mumble and pan around the room. "Ah, but there's Isaac, right over in that corner. Knew it." I shake my head then tuck my hair behind my ear.

Jared shoots me a knowing look. "Hurry, let's get some cinnamon rolls before you force us all to play Cards Against Humanity."

"Not my fault I always beat you." I pop out my butt and hit his waist.

We grab paper plates, and Jared lets me go first. I grab the biggest cinnamon roll on the baking sheet, scoop some fruit salad, and some of the *chilaquiles* that Les must have picked up somewhere.

I'm about to sit down when Jared gets pulled away with a, "Hey, can we talk?" from Isaac. I've seen him here in the apartment a bit, so maybe Jared is actually branching out from our idiot roommate. He mouths *help me,* but I grimace and hold my food up.

Ah, and karma is a cruel, cruel *perra.*

"How was your interview?" Tom's deep voice wraps around me like a hug, heat pooling in my core.

I can suddenly breathe normal, as if he's the boost of oxygen that I need to continue on. And that's why the entire situation between us sucks so bad. "Uh, it was good. Good, good, good."

Dios mío, what is wrong with me? Why am I sweating? It's one voice. It's one dude. A dude that I've seen in his most tired state. A man who hasn't talked to me since our last heated kiss in Mexico over a week ago. A guy who's farted in front of me countless times.

You don't get sweaty around a guy who rips one in front of you like you're one of the bros. If anything, *he* should be awkward, not me.

And yet, here we are. *Maldito* sweat glands.

He sits next to me on the kitchen table's bench, only a few inches between our thighs, and I swear, I can feel the heat coming off of him. That must be why I'm sweating. He's running a fever. Sort of irresponsible of him to be here, honestly.

I desperately want to fan myself, but I'm not about to let him see his effect on me.

I don't get what he's doing. You don't ignore a person for a week and then pretend like everything is fine just because we're here with other people. "Why are you suddenly talking to me?"

He takes a bite of cinnamon roll, and some of the icing gets stuck on the corner of his lip. "What do you mean? I've just been busy getting settled in at my new place."

I reach out and swipe the frosting off his lip with my finger.

Both of us freeze. His fork is lifted halfway to his mouth for another bite. My finger is casually pointing like I'm saying *E.T. phone home.* Our gazes are locked, and his gaze moves back and forth as if he's switching between which eye of mine he stares at.

I toss a glance at his lips, full and smooth, and I can almost taste the Burt's Bees chapstick he wears. To make matter worse, I don't have a napkin, so I bring my finger to my mouth and suck off the icing.

If I didn't know any better, I'd say he's biting his lip because he's turned on. But really, he's probably just trying to hold back a laugh.

A glass clatters in the kitchen, breaking the trance.

I clear my throat. "*Sí,* well it's just a bit strange that you don't talk to me for a week and then suddenly care how my interview went. Is it just because you're possibly in it?"

He shakes his head slowly as if he thinks I'm crazy.

Genial! Fine! He can think I'm crazy all he wants.

"Uh, no? We've always celebrated each other's accomplishments?" He sticks a bite of cinnamon roll in his mouth, sucking on the fork longer than I personally think is necessary.

Oh. I mean, he's not wrong. We have. I pick around my food, but don't respond. I'm acting insane. But this is what he does to me. I feel like I'm back in middle school whenever he's around.

"Right. My bad."

When he sets his fork down, his elbow bumps into my arm, and the warmth of it overwhelms me. It crawls up my arm like ivy and right into my heart, taking control. He doesn't seem affected at all when he says, "I bet the interview

45

will be fire, Candy. Mitú is a big accomplishment. I'm pumped to read."

"You're gonna read my girly interview about my favorite *Latino* actor and whether I'm single?"

He flashes a sideways smile in my direction. "Hey, gotta keep on ya somehow, you feel me?"

I cross my arms, swinging one leg over the bench so I'm straddling it. "Why are you trying to keep up with me?"

Our stares could burn anything in their path. My nerves pulse, whispering that it would be in our best interest to take Tom to our room and give his body some attention.

Tom licks his lips, and I drop my gaze to watch it. He brings up his hand and touches his lips, and I can't. I know those lips and those hands. I remember the rough callouses skirting over me, the softness of his mouth kissing it all better. The taste of him has been on my tongue for weeks, and another guy still couldn't get it gone.

I scoot closer to him, barely conscious of the effort it's taking to resist him. Seconds pass where all he does is look at me. He doesn't respond to my question, nor does he respond to what I'm sure are *do-me* eyes staring back at him.

He opens his mouth and closes it, and then says, "Regardless of what we are, I'll always keep up with you. I'm sure there's more in that interview than your favorite actor. Don't downplay your accomplishments. It's not a good look on you."

My chin rears back as I draw up my mouth in confusion. "That's not what—"

"Happy birthday, Candy," he says, picking up his plate and standing up.

"Uh, *gracias*," I reply, but he's already throwing his full plate away and heading out the door. I don't care that other people are around and that I might look like an idiot. I call out, "Wait. Will you be at my family's *fiesta*?"

He rubs the palm of his hand on the side of his head where the hair's shorn short. "Nah, you know I've got a few more months left on my ban." With a self-deprecating smile, he leaves.

Tom's right—I did know he still has a few more months on my *abuela*'s ban. He nearly burned the house down two Christmases ago by lighting a tree on fire. *Mi abuela* kicked him out for two and a half years. Asking him was just my excuse to talk to him for a second longer.

Why does he get me all out of sorts? Making me feel like I need him. I don't *need* anyone. *But you want someone,* my heart whispers.

Suck it up, Candy. Or, on the flip side, don't simp. Do something about it.

I get up and throw my plate away, rushing out the door toward Tom. "Hey!" I shout.

He turns around with his hands in his pockets, eyes saying *what the hell are you doing?*

And really, I didn't have a plan, so spontaneity it is. "You wanna go somewhere?"

"Where you wanna go?"

I shrug. "Um, snowboarding?"

Toms deadpans. "You wanna go snowboarding?"

"Yes." I nod.

"You hate snowboarding."

Crossing my arms, I say, "That is...okay, fine, that's absolutely true."

He cracks a smile, and it boomerangs over to me, and we're both cheesing at each other in the hallway. I laugh. "How about sledding?"

His gaze travels over my jeans and long-sleeve cropped shirt, pausing around my mid-section before stopping at my face. "You gon' change before we go?"

I glance down. "I'll be right back."

Chapter Five – Tom

C andy runs back down the hallway faster than I've seen her move in months. Sledding is not part of the "play hard to get" game that I had planned out. I should've said no. But as soon as her lichen eyes landed on me, I teleported back to freshman year of high school, simping like no other.

No wonder why my sister hates her. Candy makes me weak.

I'm mulling over ways to get out of spending a full day with Candy when she sprints out the door, hands full with snow clothes, slips on the carpet, trips over her feet, rights herself back up, and runs toward me. The clumsiness distracts me, and before I can utter the words that I have other plans, she shouts, "¡Vamos! Let's go!"

I grab the snow clothes from her and bunch them up under my arm.

"Gracias, T. You ready to crush some sledding?"

Tampering down the burst of energy that claws its way up my throat as she brushes against my arm, I hum a quick response and open the door for her, willing her to step away from me.

Raindrops outside begin falling, and Candy runs out of the building and to my Jeep, banging on the door with her hand. "It's cold, it's cold, it's cold. Open it!"

She bounces up and down, the pink strands looking like fairy dust, and the show is entertaining as her curves send my blood south.

I'm still under the overhang, grateful to be away from the sweet smell of her perfume. But I'm about to be stuck inside a warm car with her for an hour as smells of cotton candy sugar pushes into my nostrils.

Why did I agree to such an asinine request?

I pull the keys from my pocket and unlock the car, running and scrambling to get in as well. Cranking the engine, cool air comes through the vents, not yet warmed up. The rain screwed with my hair, and it's gonna be frizzy later. I quickly muss it before buckling my seatbelt.

"So," I put the car in reverse, "you have an actual plan?"

She snorts, which *should* be unattractive. Yeah, I'm tripping on the should, too. Damn, I have to get laid soon if I'm thinking snorts are cute.

"Do I look like I have an actual plan? No. I'm gonna google while you drive." She wiggles her phone out from her pocket and types in her password.

"Classic Candy," I mumble, focusing on the road again.

"You love it, though," she sing-songs.

"I dooo," I mimic in a high-pitched voice that sounds like her. "Come on, *cariña,* tell me where to."

Since playing hard to get isn't going to work on a full-day event, I gotta lay it on thick. And Candy gets excited whenever I speak Spanish. It's why I've been working with her dad to try and get to fluent status. It'll be another few years, I'm sure. Especially with us hanging out less. Usually, she'll say stuff in Spanish, knowing I can't understand it.

Call it toxic masculinity or the fact I hate being left out, but it pisses me off. Figured I better learn Spanish. And it works, 'cause she quickly glances out the window and shifts in her seat, something she does whenever she's turned on.

I resist rubbing my hands together as if I'm some villain. Get 'er to be putty in your hands, man, that's all you need. "*Qué linda eres.*"

She makes a strangled squeaking sound. "Don't say that."

"I'll say what I want," I quip.

49

"Your accent is getting better and better, though, I'll give you that," she mutters.

"*Lo intento.*"

"*Tal vez algún día aprendas cuando te estoy llamando un cerdo fastidioso.*"

Hmm, I'm further along in the language than she thinks. Looks like I can use it to my advantage. I know she just called me an annoying pig. Not much of an insult though. The stoplight ahead changes from yellow to red, and I slowly turn my head toward her. "I know what you just said."

"Doubt it, bruh," she replies. Her phone calls out directions. "Turn left up here."

I hop onto the freeway, and Candy turns on an old playlist we used to add songs to. Been awhile since I've added any songs, and I'm sure it has been for her too. "Losses" by Lil Tjay plays, and we meld into a mixture of comfortable conversation and silence through the drive. It's been over a week since we last talked, and while it didn't seem to do much for her, it sucked for me. I wanted to call her up, complain about the extra practices I've been doing, claim her as mine, and just spoon. Okay? I'll admit it. I wanted to be around her. But this is a long game. It's not a home run.

Hanging out with her all day wasn't in the plan, but I'd be lying if I said I wasn't a little relieved. I did a thing—a stupid thing—and this prolongs her finding the idiotic thing. Chicks are supposed to be crawling all over the college athletes. They are, actually. But most of 'em are jersey chasers and get old after an hour. All I know is it's not supposed to be *me* falling for a girl I thought I was possibly over.

The gold chain around my neck feels warmer, and heat travels into my cheeks. She's gonna hate the locket I got her.

It's basically a declaration of a relationship. Aight, not "basically." It's a definite declaration. Problem is, I bought it two years ago, and I planned to give it to her back in Scandinavia. My chain matches the locket, and a small golden key makes up the clasp, which unlocks her locket.

That's my only saving grace. At least she can't see what I had engraved in there when I was a stupid 19-year-old.

"So, how's Kira?" Candy casually asks a half-hour into the drive.

"Mmm, I'm sure you really wanna know," I respond, switching lanes so the black truck behind me can pass.

Candy and my sister, Kira, are fire and gasoline. The two of them can't be within twenty feet of each other without me feeling like I'll die.

"I was trying to be nice," she mumbles, looking out the window.

I chuckle, and she gives me a mischievous grin. The smile hits me straight in the gut. Things feel a little too comfortable. As if we didn't go a week without talking. As if she didn't dry hump me two weeks ago. I clear my throat and glance away from her, willing the feelings to go away.

Why is it so hard for me to get through my head that she rejected me?

Candy begins going on about her interview with Mitú, and I'm grateful for the distraction. As if she knows I'm in my head and pissed off, she doesn't miss a beat and switches topics when she's through discussing all the questions she answered. She goes from random topic to random topic, never pausing between then.

"Do you think dinosaurs actually looked like fat chickens?"

I give her side eye and shake my head. "You're weird. But yeah, probably."

She laughs without a care, and the sound flits through the car as gentle as the window chime my grandma used to keep on her porch.

When she isn't looking, I steal glances of her. The way her nose curves upwards, or how her lips look like pillows against her tan skin. I want to reach out and touch them—touch *her*, but I refrain. Instead, I grip the steering wheel with more force than I should. Coach would be yelling at me and the fact I could compromise my "magic hands."

Things seem normal between Candy and I, but that's just 'cause we aren't touching on the deep stuff. I don't mention seeing her feeling up some white man and she doesn't mention the fact I told her I still had feelings for her. We keep it light and friendly, which seems to be where we shine.

By the time I pull into the parking lot with the sledding hill, I'm feeling a little more relaxed. Probably due to the energy drink we stopped and grabbed a few miles back, but also a little bit because of the mountain air.

Snowboarding is something I love to do. But the DeLeón twins have never been too keen on it.

I grab the snow pants and jacket Candy brought me from the back. Thankfully, Carter is close enough to my size that they fit. She slips her snow clothes on over her shirt and jeans, looking like a bundled marshmallow.

The attendant is a young snowboarder bum, and he greets us as I pay for the tickets.

"I've got it," Candy interjects, reaching down the front of her snow pants for her wallet.

The young ticket guy stares at her crotch with his mouth agape.

I snap at him. "Bruh."

He glances back at me, grimacing once he realizes I've got six inches on him. Sighing, I pull her arm out of her pants. "Nah, it's almost your birthday. I got it."

She shrugs. "Fine, but this isn't a date."

I rear my head back. "Um, definitely not. You wish."

The look on her face and fake-steam coming out of her ears is worth it. Seems like she believes what I say too, which is one point for me in the playing-hard-to-get game.

We head in line and wait behind a few other people, mostly kids with one adult, until it's time for us to get on the ski lift.

The closer we get to the lift, the more my heart hammers. Not sure what it is, but these things freak me out. That's the only downside to snowboarding.

I let out a shaky exhale and lean against the steel pole as the slope attendant signals us to step up to the loading zone.

Candy grabs my gloved hand and squeezes. "I forgot you're afraid of heights."

Hold up, that's a *sympathy* grab? Hell no. I wave her off and stare straight into her grass-colored eyes. "Not afraid of anything."

"Tom, we have known each other for ten years. You are afraid of heights." She grabs my hand again and pulls me toward the loading zone, and two seconds later, the ski lift chair sweeps underneath us, pushing us back into the seat.

"Okay, fine! I'm afraid of heights. Put the safety bar down!" I gasp, scooting as far back into the seat as I can.

She rolls her eyes and laughs. *Laughs*.

I realize that was not a panty-dropping move. But it was instinctual. Like an idiotic cave man. I'm preserving my life here.

She pats my knee like I'm her nephew. "Better?"

"Not really, no."

"Calm down, *güey*. You're not going to die." She pulls out her phone and snaps a picture of us with me mean-mugging the camera.

"I mean, I might! These lifts be shady as hell."

"And you say I'm dramatic," she mutters. "*Los hombres son unos mentirosos.*"

"You are, and you know it."

"Least I'm not scared of heights," she retorts.

I ignore her and grip the safety bar as if my life truly depends on it.

As we slow down, I might be hyperventilating. All my bumbling has probably put me firmly back in the friend zone. Ya know...if I ever left.

The snow landing is coming up quick, but I refuse to lift the safety bar.

The chick beside me has other plans, apparently. Candy

throws the safety bar up and pushes me off the seat and into the snow where we're supposed to *casually* step off.

Her impulsivity got the best of her though, and she forgets that I have a vise grip on her, so I pull her, and we collapse into the fresh powder in a mangled heap of limbs. Her chest rises and falls against me, then she lifts her head from the snow and glances at me.

Candy's brows pinch and her mouth downturns. But as I bite my lip to keep from laughing at the snowflakes covering her eyelashes, her frown mellows into a straight line. Slowly, it climbs upward.

The lift operator cranks the chairs to a halt, and we break out into maniacal laughter, faces covered in crystals that slowly melt against the heat of our skin. Candy's makeup runs down her cheeks slightly, but even the yelling of the lift operator can't get us to stop cackling.

I reach out and wipe the dripping mascara, and that's what finally quiets us. Clearing my throat and pulling my hand away, I move to stand and help her up. "I'll be better the next ride," I promise.

She shakes her head. "I highly doubt that. You might be a one-run-man, bro."

As she hooks her arm around mine, I give a solemn apology to the lift operator before running away.

Clear tubes tower at the top of the hill like stacked donuts, and I grab a two-person tube. We stomp over to the line of people waiting to go sledding. Candy brushes off some of the leftover snow crystals from her hot pink coat. "When was the last time you went sledding?"

I run my hand through my hair, shaking the snow from it. "Hell, freshman year of high school?"

"You mean..."

"Yep." The words come out strained.

That was the night of our first kiss. We'd snuck away and hid in the trees away from everyone else. I'd learned just enough Spanish to tell her she was beautiful. My nerves were through the roof that night. Pretty sure I kissed her teeth 'cause I had taken her by surprise. But the kiss after that? Yeah, that's gonna replay in my mind for the rest of my life.

She squeaks some weird noise and points ahead. "Looks like we're next."

The attendant grabs the tube from me and places it flat on the snow. "Smallest in the front. So if you just want to sit down and have her sort of back up against you, that's probably best."

"Aight, thanks, man." I sit in the tube, and my pants are already tight from wearing two layers. But the fact that she's 'bout to back up into me? Not helping my situation.

She sits down and nestles into my chest, and her hair tickles my chin. Like her name, she smells of candy and sugar, and all I really want is to yank on her hair until her lips touch mine.

"What're you doing?" she deadpans.

Uh, crap. So caught up in my dirty thoughts of her, I don't even realize my hands have landed on her hips and are slowly crawling up her body. I yank them away and hold onto the handles of the tube, my entire core heating from my thoughts.

"You ready?" the attendant asks.

"Yep," we both respond, and it sounds like her voice is as strained as mine.

But she's not gonna give into me.

With a gentle push, we're sent flying down the hill.

Snow kicks up, spraying Candy in the face, and she sputters against the onslaught of cold. But she leans against me even harder. Can she hear my heartbeat through all these layers? Damn, even I can hear it.

As we hit a bump, I laugh as Candy lets out a high-pitched scream.

Another bump sends our tube a foot into the air, and the squeal I release is one I'm glad no one else will ever hear.

I choke as snow flies right into my screaming mouth and shout, "We're going too fast! We're gonna crash, dude. I'm not playin'. How do we stop?"

Candy shakes her head. "We don—"

Being the man here, I know I have to do something so we don't die.

I put my foot down into the snow, knocking the tube off-balance. Candy screams and scrubs at her face.

I lift my foot, sending us straight for a group of trees.

"Stop!" Candy yells. "This is how the chick from *Parent Trap* died!"

"Jesus better take the wheel," I mutter as I slam both feet into the snow. It catapults us forward. Candy goes somewhere else entirely, and my body is thrown a few feet in the air. Pine trees flash by me, and I cover my head with my arms as if that might replace the need for a helmet.

"Nooo!" Candy screams, but it seems to come out warbled and in slow motion.

My body hits the snow, and I roll a few times, ice pushing its way down my mouth and nostrils. Landing on my back, I cough up as much of the snow as I'm able.

Candy.

I lift my head enough that I see pink hair sprawled out against the white background a few feet away.

"You good?" I groan out.

Her head pops up out of the snow, and she glares. "Two strikes, yer out, sir."

I give her a thumbs up "It's three strikes, but I'll let you off the hook this time."

After falling into the snow twice, our clothes underneath have to be soaked.

Candy gets up on all fours and crawls over to me. She stares at me for a few seconds too long, and I wonder what it is she sees. From my perspective, her nose is tinged with pink, dark lashes rim her bright green eyes, and her pouty lips are nearly purple. But damn, if you'd told me I died and went to heaven, I'd believe you. Because against all this white, she looks like a freaking angel.

Until she talks.

"*Puta madre.* How does an almost-pro baseball player cause such chaos because he's scared of heights and scared of going *too fast*? How are those your fears?" She slaps my chest and calls me an idiot in Spanish.

"What're you talking about? I did it to help you! I was tryna save us."

She guffaws. "Don't make me call your mama. You were scared AF out there. Don't be lyin' on me. You...were...scared," she claps out. "So, I'm asking, *why* were you so scared?"

Ugh. I cross my forearm over my eyes so I don't have to see the stupid smug expression on her face. "I don't know. God has a sense of humor, I guess. You gon' help me up or will I have to do it myself?"

She curses under her breath in Spanish, but holds out a hand. Candy tries, key word: *tries,* to pull me up, but my barely-there grip is still stronger than hers, and she crashes on top of me. She lands on top of me, chest to chest, waist to waist. Her legs straddle me, and heat crawls up my body even though I'm lying in ice.

"You're hurt," she whispers.

"I'm fine."

Her hair dangles over my face like spun cotton candy. I brush the strands back and tuck them behind her ear. Her full lips part as my gaze drops, and I trail back up her face until we're staring at each other.

I'm asking for permission, or a sign to stop this, because hard-to-get my ass. I have to have her. Right here. Right now.

Her breaths come out short and she leans in a centimeter closer until the tips of our noses touch.

As I inhale, my head moves slightly upward until our lips skim by each other. Electricity laces through me as she lets out a heady sigh.

I moan, ready to explore her more.

A whistle blows, breaking our trance before we can kiss.

"Whoa! Are you guys okay?" a man dressed in red medic snow clothes with a cross on his jacket asks, barreling into the secluded grove of trees.

Dude has the absolute worst timing.

Candy tries to get off of me, but I grip her hips against mine. Two layers of clothing or not, "I'm gonna need a second before I can get up."

"We better get you checked out, bud." The medic signals someone from up the hill.

Candy gets off of me and averts her gaze anywhere but my lap. "You can check me out first."

The medic does a quick look over, but says she's fine. When the other guy arrives, the medic and him help me up and have me sit on a log.

"I'm fine," I grumble.

"Sir, your face says otherwise," the medic replies.

They flash a mirror my way. Right above my brow is a thin cut that gushes blood down my temple. I touch it and wince. And here I was thinking it was just my blue balls that hurt.

Twenty minutes later, I'm bandaged up and Candy and I are soaking wet as we peel off our snow clothes in the parking lot. I turn on our seat heaters and relish in the heat as we sit in the parking lot trying to defrost.

I look in the rearview mirror at the butterflied cut on my forehead. You can barely see it now that they've bandaged it, but because all butterfly bandages are the "nude" color of white people, it stands out like a sore thumb. "You have bad ideas."

Candy laughs. "Whatever. You know it was kinda fun."

I smile back at her. "Only because I got you on top of me."

She rolls her eyes. "Let's go home."

It comes out easily, and I see the moment her spine goes rigid.

"I meant, like, back to West's campus."

Because we don't live together anymore. We don't have a *home*. And I'd be lying if I said it didn't suck. If today reminded me of anything, it's that feelings aside, I miss this girl.

I don't want to play games.

I just wish she'd give me another chance.

Chapter Six – Candy

The drive back from sledding is quiet as dusk sets in. Or maybe it's because of something I said. We stop at an In-N-Out and grab hot chocolates, burgers, and fries, eating as we make our way toward West.

I wipe my hands off on the napkin. "I know it was a little spontaneous—"

"Your brand," he cuts in.

"—but I really did have a lot of fun. Thanks for taking me." I reach out and grab his hand, squeezing it twice before trying to let go.

He squeezes back and shakes his head, not giving it up. "Anytime. I, uh, I miss our adventures."

His face screams of past sorrows and regret. I sigh. "Let's not—"

"I'm not doing anything. I'm saying I miss our adventures, no matter what we got goin' on." He shrugs. "That's it. Don't get your panties in a bunch."

"*Ay Dios mío*, don't say panties." I look out the window as a blush crawls up my neck.

"Why? It turns you on, huh? Does it? Huh? Huh?" He annoyingly mocks, letting go of my hand to squeeze my thigh.

I gasp and turn toward him. "You *know* that's my spot. You know I'm ticklish there!"

He winks. "I know a lot of things about you, *mi amor*."

"You do not." I scoff, but as I see him pull into my apartment complex, something gnaws at me. I don't want our day to end. It's dark outside, stars shine above through the sunroof, and in this big vast world, he's going home to a different house. One that doesn't include me anymore.

Tom stops at the curb a few feet away from the building's entrance. I fish around in my bag for the key fob and move to open the door. I glance back at him. "For the record, *yo también extraño nuestras aventuras.*"

Part of me hopes he doesn't understand what I just said, because deep down, everything in me is saying I'm getting too deep. This feels too good, too natural, and if I give into it, Tom could break my heart in a way that would make it never recover. I can't do that again. Being friends is really what's best for us.

I wave. "*Gracias,* Tom. It was fun."

He parts his lips, but then closes his mouth and nods. I leave the car and head indoors to the warm hallways that lead to my apartment.

Once inside, I get ready to take a shower. It's been a long day, and next week's party at *mi familia*'s house is going to be even longer. I'm gonna need all the rest I can get if I want to beat Carter at the *baile.* Plus, I've got some schoolwork to catch up on. All welcome distractions from my own unresolved feelings.

My phone buzzes in my pocket, so I grab it out.

Ethan*: I feel like I need props for getting you to the surprise party.*

Candy: *Fine. I'll give you props.*

Three dots appear on the screen within seconds.

Ethan: *Enough that you'll volunteer to team up for our Supreme Court paper?*

Ethan: *Turns out I don't know shit about Roe v. Wade and yours sounds better.*

I laugh as I round the corner of the hallway into my room. He's typing another message, so I lean against the door and wait.

"Ooh, who are you texting?"

I jump at Les's voice and pull the phone toward my chest.

"No one. Just Ethan."

"You were cheesin' pretty big," she sing-songs on the bed, lying on her stomach and typing away on her laptop. "You gonna tap that or what? We both know he has a mega crush on you."

I hum and make my way toward my bed. "*No, porque* the boy is like all guys."

"*Idiotas,*" Les and I say at the same time. We look at each other and laugh.

"Thanks for the party, babe." I sit on my bed and pick up a box about the size of my palm, wrapped in glitter paper with a bow. "Is this from you?"

She sits up and her brows draw together. "No, I saved my present for the *fiesta*. Although in hindsight, now you have me worried. Maybe I should give you and Carter your presents here, away from the eyes of your parents."

I wipe away some of the glitter that's fallen from the gift onto my bed. "Unless it's lingerie, I'm sure it's fine."

"Well, I don't want to be banned from parties like Tom is. Y'all have me watching my back like no other." She chews her lip, seemingly lost in thought.

"Just don't set a Christmas tree on fire in *mi abuela*'s house, and you'll be fine," I mumble, untying the bow on the present.

"Where have you been?" she asks.

"Uh, I went sledding." Glitter falls off the package with every slight movement, but at least it's pink and matches my comforter. I lift the top off of the box, and a small letter lies on top.

Figured it was time you had this. -T

I'd recognize Tom's handwriting anywhere, but I'm not sure what the note means.

As I lift the tissue paper, my breath catches. A delicate heart locket, no bigger than my thumbnail (minus my fake nail, of course), sits on cotton. It's gold with a petite amethyst in the center. I pick up the locket to see what's inside. But with my long nails, it makes it nearly impossible to open.

I glance at Les. "Can you help me open this? I want to see the inside."

She gets up from the bed and sits down next to me, delicately grabbing the necklace. "This is so pretty," she whispers. "Who's it from?"

"Tom," I mutter, ignoring the look she gives me.

Putting her nails at the seam, she tries to pry it open. She lifts it up near her eyes and squints. "I think it's locked."

"Or broken." I hold my hand out.

She shakes her head. "No, it's locked. See this?"

I glance where her finger points.

"It needs a key or something." She shrugs. "Who cares? The outside is pretty by itself. Maybe it doesn't actually open, and the seam is just for looks. Let me put it on you."

"*Bien.*" I hold my hair up off my neck and she slips the necklace around and clasps it. When she finishes, I put it between my thumb and finger, rubbing the cool metal. It sits right beneath the hollow of my neck. "*Me encanta.*"

Les laughs. "Me too. Almost makes up for the past week of no talking, right?" She squeezes my shoulder and goes back over to her bed.

"Maybe." But I say it absentmindedly because I'm already dialing his number as I head into the bathroom. As the phone rings, I start the shower.

It continues ringing. And ringing, and ringing, and ringing, until, "Hey, you got Tom. You know what to do." He was just here, he's probably still driving, so why isn't he answering?

Not wanting to say thanks over a voicemail, I sigh and hang up. Stepping into the shower, I hold the locket between my fingers the whole time.

Chapter Seven - Candy

I wake up still dressed in my clothes from the night before when I celebrated the Mitú article being published. I got a little too confident with teaching everyone how to make jello shots in celebration. Thankfully, the whole Jake Marx mouth comment got one line and that was it. Tom's name was mentioned too, but just the part where I said we were friends.

People have shared the article, talked about future activism efforts, and it's been a great talking point the last few days.

Except for Tom, apparently. Because I still haven't been able to get ahold of him to thank him for my necklace. He didn't even come to the celebration last night. Regardless, it was a good night. Tiring, but good.

When I roll toward the other side of the room to glance at Les's bed, no one is there. Like each morning, I reach for my phone, but it's not on my nightstand. Crap. Probably left it out in the living room last night.

Rubbing my eyes as I walk, I flinch when I get into the living room and see Les, Carter, Jared, and Rykard huddled around the kitchen island whispering.

They're usually up much later than I am. "*Holaaaa*, what's up?"

Everyone stops talking. Suspicious, much?

I blow a raspberry. "Please tell me this isn't some sort of surprise again."

Les tucks her hair behind her ear. "Um, no. Have you checked Twitter this morning?"

Rykard mumbles, "Or Instagram, or any gossip site."

I rub the sleep from my eyes. What is going on? "No, I left my phone out here last night." I glance into the living room and move to grab it.

Carter runs and snatches it a second before I can get to it. "*Espere.*"

Did something happen? Did someone die or something? "What's going on?"

"Uh," he grimaces, "*no sé.* I mean, Les, maybe?"

Panic seeps into every nook of my soul. "Tell me what's going on right now."

She groans and looks toward the ceiling. "Okay, don't freak out, Candy."

I throw my hands up, which begin to shake. "Oh, *genial.* That's what every girl wants to hear the second they wake up."

Jared throws his arm around me. "It's probably no big deal."

Sympathy already? I don't even know what's going on. "*¡Cállate!*"

He pulls me closer to his side. "I can't understand Spanish, remember? So I'm just gonna have to assume, and I love you, too, babe."

I roll my eyes. "Les, spill it. Otherwise, I'll make Rykard do it."

He puts down his spoon of yogurt. "Alright, so basically —"

"No!" Les holds out her hand. "I'll do it. Crap. Uh, um, someone like leaked a photo of you. And it's...Well, um, let's just say it doesn't really look good." She taps on her phone screen and holds out a picture.

My profile is smashed against another guy's, and my signature pink hair gives me away, with mirrors on all four sides of the elevator. Someone's hand cups my face, and my legs are wrapped around the guy's waist. The guy is handsome, biceps showing clearly as he holds me.

We look like some love-sick couple.

But we are absolutely not.

"*Voy a matarlo.*" It's a photo of me and Jake freaking Marx. Two people who are supposed to be enemies. And I know exactly when it was taken. "*Chingao,* this looks so bad."

Carter stares at me, and his eyes are full of disappointment. "So, is what they're saying true?"

The gravity of Carter being disappointed with me is not lost. Guilt entraps me like a snake. "What're they saying about it?" I snap.

He rubs the back of his neck. "That, uh, that you two are going behind everyone's back in some secret relationship."

Everything begins to sound like I'm underwater as the pulse in my ears roar. I scoff. "Absolutely not. I *hate* the guy."

OMG, how did someone even get this? It's so violating and creepy. "I need to talk to Jake."

Rykard's mouth is full, but it doesn't stop him from saying, "Sounds pretty couple-y to me."

"*Cállate la boca,* Rykard. This isn't some stupid college drama. This is my freaking career we're talking about." I brush the hair from my forehead and hold my hand out to Carter. "Phone. *Ahora.*"

There's going to be so much damage control to do. Carter opens his mouth, glances toward Les, and his head shakes just barely. "Candy, that's not all."

I lean against the counter. "How could this possibly get any worse?" I groan. "What? *¿Qué pasó?*"

Les gets between the two of us and shows me her phone. It's a video of Jake Marx. "Um, this was taken a few hours ago on the East Coast."

Great, so he got to it before I did. She clicks on the video.

Jake walks, shielding part of his face. The camera shakes, and his mother's arm is hooked in the crook of his elbow. A girl voice asks, "Governor Marx, what do you think about your son sleeping with the enemy?"

She keeps her head down, but her knuckles whiten as she tightens her hand into a fist.

A few other people move into the camera frame, snickering

and pointing. "Jake! What about you?" another guy asks. "You together with Candy DeLeón?"

He turns toward where the small crowd is, and they hold up their iPhones. "I am dedicated to my mother's senate campaign. Any relationship I had with Candy is over."

The girl holding the camera laughs. "So are you confirming a relationship?"

He shakes his head. "I'm not confirming or denying anything. Get out of here, I'm trying to go to breakfast."

His mother pulls him away, but halfway up the stairs, he looks back toward the camera and bites his lip.

The video stops. He's not confirming or denying anything? He has nothing to confirm or deny! The picture is completely taken out of context. I take a deep breath. "Is that on TikTok? What're they saying about me?"

"No, Twitter." Les bites her lip. "I think you need to lay low for a while."

My throat tightens. If it was on TikTok, I'd maybe get lucky, but on Twitter? Everyone knows me. "But I didn't do anything wrong."

Rykard barks out a laugh. We all whip our heads toward him. He shrinks into his shoulders. "Sorry. Funny meme." He lifts his phone then continues scrolling. But then his eyes grow even bigger. "Oh, shit. That's not good."

He glances at me, back at the phone, angles his head, lifts the phone up to me, squints an eye, and nods. "Yeah, this isn't good." He slides the phone across the counter.

I pick it up, glance at the photo, and slam it back down. "*Tienes que estar bromeando.*"

Carter snatches the phone and sighs. "*Mierda,* Candy. What were you thinking?"

I glare at him. "*Claro,* I wasn't."

Les tries to smile. "It's gonna be okay. We'll fix this."

I huff out a laugh, but it borders on a sob. Not gonna cry. This has to be fixable. It *has* to be. But doubt wields its mighty sword. "How are we going to fix *that*?"

I point at the picture of Jake leaning against an open door, his hands gripping my thighs, my eyes closed, head thrown back, and his mouth sucking on my neck. I've fought against the Marx family for years. And now, these pictures tell a story. One painting me as the ultimate hypocrite. I screwed up. Big time.

And my generation? We don't forgive hypocrites easily. Especially not on Twitter.

"Give me my phone." I close my eyes, willing the warmth and wetness in my eyes to stay in my tear ducts.

"Candy," Carter starts.

I'm gonna break, and I can't do that before figuring out a plan. For everything, I always have a plan. So why am I coming up empty? "Just give me the phone, Carter! This isn't your business. Let me handle it!" I shatter, yelling at him.

Everyone goes silent, and it's as if my voice echoes through the kitchen. "*Now.*"

We don't yell at each other. It's not something we do.

Carter throws my phone to me and crosses his arms. "I'm trying to help, Candy," he spits my name. "Good luck," he mumbles and trucks down the hallway.

Les draws up her lips and gives me an awkward smile before chasing after him. I take one long breath, steeling myself for what's to come. Even as I do it, my phone vibrates nearly non-stop with notifications.

I head back to my room, slam the door, and flop onto my bed. I open Twitter and go straight to my messages. Heading to Jake's DM thread where he tried to proposition another hookup with me a week ago, I think of what to say before deciding on:

@candydeleon: *This affects both of us. Before saying anything to those people, and 'confirming or denying', the first thing you should've done was reach out to me.*

Then I read through some of the other DMs that have come through. *You're a slut,* one of them says. *Just another dirty, skanky ho who always needs someone in her pants,* another one proclaims. *Watch her abort his baby,* one pipes in. *If you wanted to f**k a conservative, you could've just contacted me,* some of the others proposition. And the fourth category? Racial slurs every other message.

Every DM reads *thot, slut, ho, perra, whore,* and the list goes on. Every comment, the same. If people are out there defending me, they're lost in translation. The overwhelming consensus is: I'm canceled.

Everything I've been working on for two and a half years is gone. I'm left with unsolicited crotch pics and slurs. They're degrading, they're hurtful, and...I deserve them. Because no one forced me into this. I made this choice, and it was stupid.

One mistake. One night. And my life is...gone. My chest tightens, but I choke back any sobs. I can't cry yet. It feels as if I've swallowed knives as acid burns my stomach, and my fingers go white as I shake, a coldness passing over me.

My hands tremble as I get out of Twitter and open Instagram.

I always knew she was a slut. Just look at her hair color. No self-respecting girl dyes her hair pink.

We all knew those pouty lips weren't solely for talking.

How do you think she became so popular? It wasn't her brain, that's for sure.

With a body like that, she never belonged in politics, anyhow... unless it was as a bed warmer.

The comments keep coming in every second. They pile on top of each other so fast, I can't keep up with the notifications. A hundred DMs are unread, but after glancing at the first one, calling me a psychotic prostitute who doesn't deserve Jake's attention, I exit that app too.

It's everywhere. Instagram notifications chime Twitter ones swoosh. My email dings. It's a symphony of chaos, and I debate throwing my phone away. Pain encircles my head, and my heart aches with a physical pain. My breaths come out quickly. Is this a panic attack? I don't have anxiety. I never get tripped up. But this is something new, and it's as if a hoard of ants are crawling on every part of my body. I hurry to my phone's settings to turn off my notifications completely.

I'm never going to recover from this. And that realization shatters me. *Me arrepiento de todo.*

My body shivers, and the tears come hot and fast. I collapse face down onto my pillow, bawling with everything left in me. I'm so pissed off. My phone vibrates with a call, but the screen shows me a number I don't recognize.

I turn it on silent and wrack my brain with what I can do to fix this. Can anything get me out of this? The pictures are damning.

Estoy arruinada.

I cry, choking back the sobs. The pillow soaks up the tears, but the more I think about it, the worse it gets.

∞∞∞

Hours later, I'm stuck firmly in the first stage of grief: Denial. Surely, my career isn't ruined. People have problems like this all the time. How many YouTube apology videos have been made by influencers in the past? The majority of them have risen from the ashes. I mean, let's be honest, everyone doesn't actually really like them anymore, but...okay, yeah this isn't helping.

I pull out my phone again, prepared to at least glance at the ruins once more. *Está bien.*

First email is from a friend, actually. *Bueno,* this can't be too bad. I open it.

To: Candy
From: Brandon
Subject: Best of Luck
Hello Candy,
Due to recent events, we cannot in good conscience have you preside over Equal Treatment for Equal People. Though we do not take a stance on your personal matters, our club

cannot have such a public figure and the attention that comes with that to lead our activism. We wish you the best in your future endeavors.

Brandon Porter
Interim President, Equal Treatment for Equal People

No puede ser! I founded the school club. How do you remove the founder? Is that even legal? Funny how they're so willing to have a public figure lead their group when it benefits them. But suddenly, I'm in the hot seat, and they drop me. *Culeros.*

The next email is from a t-shirt brand that I rep.

To: Candy
From: Mindy
Subject: Terminating Contract
Candy DeLeón,
In light of recent events, we regret to inform you that we are terminating our working contract with you. For questions, please see attached Section IIV, part B of our signed contract.
Mindy, CEO

I delete the message. I've lost my school club. Now I've lost one of my sponsorships. I scroll through the rest of my emails.

Subject: Violation of Terms
Subject: Breach of Contract
Subject: Misaligned Values
Subject: Termination of Sponsorship

Every single one except three. And those three? Teacher announcements sent through Canvas about class. I stare at my phone screen, dumbfounded, until it goes black. I have to do something, but what?

FML. I'm gonna have to make an influencer apology video. Is there a script for these types of things or...? I glance in the mirror only to find leftover makeup and crazy hair. But maybe that's better than getting all glammed up. Looks more legit. My eyes well with tears, but I blink until they go away.

Puedo hacer esto.

With one last shaky breath, I go to Instagram and press Live, holding my phone up to my face.

"Hey, everyone. *Soy yo.* I know matters of my personal life have been leaked to the media, and I want to apologize to each and every one of you."

Comments begin flooding at the bottom of the screen, but I close my eyes for a second before continuing and ignoring them.

"I first want to say that Jake Marx and I have zero relationship. We met in Mexico, and an incident occurred. However, nothing has happened like that again. I know as a public figure, I have a responsibility for the people who look to me for advice. And while I don't believe you need to be with someone that has your exact values, I've ran a campaign against the Marx family for quite some time, and getting involved with Jake was a conflict of interest on multiple levels. One I regret beyond measure. And I can understand what it looks like from the outside, to all the people who follow me."

"*Por mi Latinas* that look up to me, *lo siento mucho. Cometí un error al involucrarme en todo esto.* I'm sorry for disappointing you. I understand so many of you are confused and questioning where I stand. I promise you, my heart and spirit have been and always will be in these causes that I'm fighting for. I'm still human, I'm still me, and I still do things that are imperfect. I take full responsibility for everything that I did."

I lick my lips. "*He cometido un error y tengo que asumir las consecuencias.* To everyone out there who has supported me, to the brands that have partnered with me, I apologize again. What happened in my personal life was an error in judgement on my part, but it has never impacted the work that I've done, am doing, or will continue to do. It was one night, and I made a huge error. Please don't let my mistakes take away from everything that's going on in the world. I will still fight for minorities. I will still fight for the voiceless. And I hope someday we can fight together again."

I end Live and sink back onto my bed. What the hell do I do now?

Chapter Eight - Candy

I wake up to a dark bedroom with dried slobber on my cheek. I groan and check the time. It's just past six, which means I'll probably be up all night long thanks to my afternoon nap. We're heading to the second stage of grief: Anger.

Do I still plan rallies, reach out to my contacts, and try to continue my work? Anything I do now is just going to draw attention, and most likely, draw attention *away* from the issues I'm fighting for.

A knock sounds on my door.

"Come in," I croak. My voice is thick from sleep, and my throat is scratchy from crying.

Les opens the door. "Hey."

I sit up on my bed and turn on my bedside light. "Why'd you knock?"

She shrugs. "I don't know. I'm awkward. This is awkward. Carter's pissed, and I'm not, obviously. But, like, also like whaaaat?" She laughs once and clears her throat. "But, um, yeah." Her gaze wanders everywhere but my face.

So that's her way of saying she *is* pissed at me, let's be honest. Her family has some sort of history with the Marx family, so it makes sense. I rub at my eyes. "You can say you're mad at me. But honestly, I'm at a loss for words right now. *Lo siento.* I'm gonna be apologizing for the rest of my life." My eyes well up again, but I blink the tears away.

She sits beside me and hugs me. "I'm not mad. But I do have to say I'm confused. When did you even find the time to hook up with Jake in Mexico?"

I bury my face in my hands and tell her everything—from the elevator to the club. I don't hold back on the details, and I own the stupid things I did. "It was such a dumb decision. If I could go back and change it, I would, *tú sabes*."

Les twists her lips up and furrows her brow. "But why'd you do it?"

I half-groan and half-laugh as I collapse on the bed. "I don't know. I just couldn't handle things with Tom. He told me he liked me."

She shifts on the bed and looks over her shoulder toward the door. "Well, did you say it back?"

"No. Remember when you and Carter came in the room? We had just kissed, so I took my opportunity to get away from my feelings, and I ran. Except, my run ran right into Jake's arms. I don't know. It didn't mean anything. I just wanted the taste of Tom gone. Wanted to replace him." Even as I explain, I know how stupid and immature it sounds. *Soy una idiota.*

Les rolls her eyes, which is a bit rude, but whatever. "Girl, you need to figure your stuff out with Tom. I love you, you know I do. But, you literally just ruined your career because you won't face your past with Tom. If this isn't some wake up call, I don't know what is."

"*Genial*, Les. You're making me feel so much better."

She stands up and crosses her arms. "Look, when all the crap happened with me and my mom last year, did I blame you for putting the photo out there of me and Carter? No, I didn't. I had to face the music. Did I handle it great? Nope. But, I still handled it. Eventually." She waves me off. "We're not talking about me. We're talking about *you*. A public figure. Gen Z's angel. You're gonna have to handle it. I love you, but something between you and Tom has to change."

"I did handle it! Did you not see my apology? *Por el amor de Dios*, I'm trying but I don't know what to do! Everyone is mad at me, Les. Even *you're* mad, whether you want to say it or not. I screwed up, I get it. Stop rubbing it in." I put my pillow over my head. What does everyone want from me? I'm tired of this already.

I can't see her, but I know her footsteps, and she's stomping across the room, basically huffing and puffing. She snatches the pillow off of my face and stares at me. "You're upset, fine. You deserve to be upset. But don't freaking take it out on me. Lay low for a while, and since you won't be on your phone twenty-four-seven, figure out your feelings for Tom. It's been two years, Candy. Like, you might be able to recover from this mistake. But another one in the future? Not gonna happen." She tosses the pillow on the bed and tucks some clothes under her arm. "I'm staying in Carter's room tonight."

"Wow! Such a threat! You stay in there every night!" I yell as she slams the door shut.

I shake my head. Now I'm fighting with my best friend. *¡Qué bien!*

Another knock sounds on the door, and it's so ridiculous because this is her room too. Les doesn't have to freaking knock. "*¿Que podrías necesitar?* Did you forget your charger?"

The door opens, but it's not Les.

I stare at Tom, who stands in my doorway with a flat expression on his face. I sigh. "Not you, too. If you're here to yell at me, I've had enough of it today."

He smirks, tilting those full lips upward. "Have I ever yelled at you?"

I deadpan. "You literally just yelled at me when we went sledding."

Shaking his head, he laughs. "Nah, girl. That was more a shout if anything."

My mouth threatens a smile, but I glance at my hands instead. "Why are you here?"

From behind his back, he brings out a box of cinnamon rolls. "Figured you could use some carbs with all the blubbering everyone's been sayin' you've done."

My jaw drops. "I. Do. Not. Blubber."

"You want the rolls or nah?" His eyes sparkle with mischief.

How is he not pissed at me? I'd be pissed at me if I were him. I grab my locket and twist it between my fingertips. Patting the bed, I say, "Of course I want the cinnamon rolls."

He chuckles. "I've got you all figured out."

I roll my eyes. "It's cinnamon rolls, Tom. Everyone loves cinnamon rolls. *¿Por qué me has estado evitando?*"

"I've been busy," he mumbles, but doesn't look me in the eyes. "It's not like I've been avoiding you on purpose."

When he sits down next to me, we scoot so our backs are against the wall, feet hanging off of my mattress. He opens the box and hands me a cinnamon roll with pink sprinkles and chopped pecans. It's so extra.

Me encanta.

I hold up the cinnamon roll. "Well, thanks. And *gracias* for my necklace. That's why I've been calling."

His eyes land on my collarbone. "I'm glad you're wearing it."

We eat in silence. Whether it's because the cinnamon rolls taste *tan rico* or because I don't know what to say, who knows.

He breaks the silence with a, "So, you wanna talk about it?"

I shrug. "I feel like shit, so no, not really."

His arms brushes against mine as he readjusts himself on the bed. "So you wanna talk about it."

"Rant about it, *sí*." I laugh. "I-I just hate myself for it all. I'd do anything to go back and change it." (Ah, third stage of grief: Bargaining. See, Intro to Psych freshman year wasn't a complete waste.)

Tom nods. "Or just not got caught. Sometimes I think that social media and activism can't go hand-in-hand."

I slap his arm. "You also think lotion is a conspiracy, so excuse me if I don't agree."

"Do you *feel* this buttery skin? It's 'cause it's never seen lotion." He holds out his arm.

I rub it. "Yes, your skin is soft. But for the record, I think Vaseline still counts as lotion if you're gonna slather it on like *un bebé.*"

"So, what's up? Heard the news that some photos of you were leaked. You slingin' nudes, girl?" He winks.

I sigh. "*Ojalá.* That would probably be easier to play off than the fact that I, uh, got caught with Jake Marx, Joanna's son."

He crosses his ankles and stares at the wall across from us. "Shit, Candy. Why would you get involved with someone like him?"

"*No.* It's not like that, I swear. I made one bad decision, that's it. Or, a few bad decisions that led to one big mistake, but there's nothing going on between me and him. He's acting like there was something there, and the insta baddies ate it up. So, everyone's crucified me now. *Soy* canceled."

He doesn't say anything. Maybe he's disappointed like Carter, and for a few moments, we're silent until I speak again. "I'm just at a loss of what to do. I apologized and logged off. I don't know what they're saying to my apology, but I can't imagine it's anything good. Maybe I shouldn't have said anything, but if I didn't say anything, they would've been talking bad anyhow. I'm ready to do anything to get my career back, but I think the devil is on a holiday or something because no one's offered to take my soul or allow a blood sacrifice even though our apartment is 13666. It's the perfect place for demons."

Tom lets out a soft laugh before sobering. "Imma be honest, if something that damning is out there, I don't know how you recover."

I sigh. "You see my Live?"

He shakes his head. "No, I've been at practice all day. Why'd you go Live so fast? You should've thought about it longer."

My voice shakes. "Nothing I do is gonna be right, anyhow. It's like everything I did before this one night was all a waste. How does one mistake erase years of work?"

My mind thinks of all the protests, all the different connections, brands, and friendships that I've made in the process of my activism. I had gotten my dream, and now I've turned it into a nightmare.

Tom looks at me, something unknown darkening his hazel eyes, and barely quirks his lips. "I ask myself that every damn day."

If hearts could cry, mine would be sobbing, because for a moment, just a moment, I finally understand the gravity of making a stupid mistake that you can't take back. A mistake like Tom made two years ago. "What answer do you get?"

He shrugs. "I don't know. Haven't gotten it yet."

I swallow through the lump in my throat. "I don't know what to do. Even you think it's bad, and you're usually the voice of reason. And it all happened because...Well, Les thinks we need to, and I quote, 'Figure out our stuff.'"

"Ah, Les crazy." He grabs at the back of his neck and moves his head side to side. "Why'd she say that?"

My fingers go cold as I pick up a dropped sprinkle on my bed. This is the heavy crap that gets us into trouble. We thrive in superficial days, we love in passing, and we bloom on the surface of it all. "It happened in Mexico."

Tom stills. "Hold up...*that* was the white man I saw you in the elevator with?"

"You saw me? Wait, what are you talking about?" If he saw me...then Jake and I weren't the only ones who knew. That means... "Did you leak the photos?"

He flinches as if I've slapped him on the cheek. "How can you even *ask* that? *¿Estás bromeando,* Candy? I would *never* sabotage your career like that. Never. No matter what happened between us. I don't even know what those photos look like. I haven't been on Instagram today."

Part of me believes him, but another part of me thinks he's lying. What benefit would Jake get from leaking the photos?

He looks just as dumb as I do.

But Tom? He has motive. He said he had feelings for me that night, and I rejected him. And he *saw* me in the elevator with Jake. Maybe releasing the pictures was his way to get revenge.

Tom runs his hand down his face and laughs. "This is a joke. You for real think I could've had a hand in this?"

I bite my lip. No, he wouldn't do this to me.

But I also never thought he'd cheat on me.

"I don't know," I whisper.

He hops off the bed and shakes his head. "Let me make one thing clear, Candy. I may have hurt you in the past, and I owned up to that. But I wouldn't *ever* do something that would jeopardize the career you've worked so hard for. Just like I've always trusted you'd never do anything to mess up my MLB dreams." With a broken glare on his face, he mumbles, "You're fighting with Les, you're fighting with Carter, and now you're picking a fight with me. See a pattern? I'm here when you need me, but I'm not gonna sit here and be berated by you."

Before I can organize my thoughts, he slams the door behind him, and I'm once again left alone.

Chapter Nine – Tom

I head to the gym. Trying to do something nice for Candy didn't get me anywhere. Instead, she blamed me for her problems. How can she even think that I uploaded those photos of her and Jake? Just 'cause I saw them in the elevator doesn't mean I'd do anything like that.

I get she's pissed, but that was out of pocket of her. Yeah, it's stereotypical of me to hit the gym, but there's nothing that the stale smell of sweat and premium cleaner can't fix.

The gym is filled with weights, machines, and a few college athletes. But nothing like that is calling my name. I've got pent up energy that needs to get out, and it's either run sprints or do something with my hands. So, it's the punching bag that beckons.

But I get one punch in, relishing in the pain of it, before a voice drawls, "Coach will not like that."

I push on my brow as if I can wish him away. "Why are you here, Maldon?"

Ben, the only teammate who can give me a run for my money, walks in front of me and grabs hold of the punching bag. His light brown hair is plastered to his forehead as if he's spent the last couple hours here. "Same reason as you. The desire to get in the major leagues."

I chuckle and step back, crossing my arms. "What happened to those medical school dreams of yours?"

He shrugs. "That was all Les. Baseball is my life."

"Being a playboy is your life, Ben." Everyone knows it. He got chewed apart on the field by two girls within three days last year. One being Les Watkins, Carter's girlfriend. Maldon's a big TikTok influencer, and so was the other girl he was dating, Alice, so the drama is just now starting to die down.

Ben trails a hand down the punching bag. "No one else left to play. So here I am. But a punching bag that could ruin our hands? The same ones we throw with? Now, I wouldn't ever be so stupid."

I grab a towel and wipe my hands. "Stay out of my business."

"*Your* business? I'm just looking out for my teammate." Ben smiles, but it's more of a twisted grimace.

He takes two steps closer to me, so we're nearly chest to chest. "But if you want to ruin your hands, I won't stand in your way. Less competition for me. If you can even call yourself my competition."

I shove him, and his back hits the punching bag with a thud. "You're not looking out for shit." I grab the collar of his shirt, and he laughs. "I don't want anything to do with you. Off the field, stay away from me."

Ben opens his mouth just as another voice booms, "What the hell is going on here?"

I drop his shirt and flinch away as Assistant Coach Johnson steps in front of us. "Tom, what're you doing here? Our private session is tomorrow."

Ben looks at me from the corner of his eye, and I see a smirk lining his face. My anger only gets worse staring at him. He knew that would happen. He just wanted to get a rise out of me so our coach would see. Can't he see I'm already at a disadvantage when it comes to playing? Some MLB teams don't even have one Black man on their rosters. They've got three dozen of Ben, though.

I clear my throat and the anger with it to try and look respectful. "Just came for an extra workout, Coach."

Coach Johnson searches the area, and points to the punching bag. "No. Head to the track and work long distance sprints. Then head home and get a good night's rest, you hear?"

"Yes, Sir." I nod. When Coach Johnson mutters something

while crossing the room to grab his timer, I turn to Maldon and hiss, "You're not worth shit, rich boy. The only one signing with a scout here is *me*."

Ben sucks in his cheek and grins. "Have a nice night, Tom."

I don't know if I'm more pissed because of Candy or because Ben is an ass, but my head is hot as I jog to the outdoor track. The weather is cool and bites at my nose. At least it's not raining. I set my water, phone, and gym bag on the side of the field where the turf meets the track and quickly stretch my arms and legs before retying my shoes. This is the outdoor football practice facility, but they hardly ever use it. Instead, it's mostly just the rest of us student athletes using the field for sprints or pick-up games.

The cold air filters through my nostrils and fills me with the calm feeling I get whenever I'm practicing. Counting down in my head, I kneel to the ground.

Three...two...one...

My legs catapult forward, and I take shallow breaths as I push for the end of the track. It's all I see as I sprint, heart pumping, chest tightening. As I cross the white line I was aiming for, I slow to a halt, my shoes grinding against the track and kicking up bits of rubber.

I give myself five seconds before repeating the sprint back to my starting point. My body cries for a release, muscles screaming we just had practice a few hours ago, but I push through the fatigue. I hear my dad shouting to keep going, keep pushing, and I hear fans yelling my name. When I close my eyes, a stadium of people boom as I sprint to take third base.

The opposing teams move to strike me, throwing a ball right at me, but I keep sprinting, faster than they can aim.

I sprint, and I run, and I imagine everything the future holds. Me in the MLB, wearing an A's jersey, and hitting a home run as my lucky charm cheers in the stands for me.

It's not until my twenty-third sprint in a row that my fantasy shatters because the stadium lights shine on a woman with pink hair, who stands at the fence near the end of the track. My feet falter, and I slow my run so I don't fall face-first to the rough rubber below me.

My gait slows, and I walk a few steps before stopping to put my hands on my knees, breathing as deep as my diaphragm will let me.

Candy holds out her arms. "Aren't you gonna ask how I found you?"

My face scrunches as the bright lights behind her seem to shine right in my eyes. "Nah."

Always one for dramatics. It's as if she internally frowns. Her face is straight, but her shoulders slump a bit. Candy raises her brows. "Well, I went by your apartment. You weren't there, and Ethan was with some girl. I checked Anna's, but there wasn't an order for five French toasts, so I knew you weren't there. You weren't at my apartment, so I figured you were either at the store or the gym."

She holds up a bag of Red Vines like an olive branch. "You weren't at the store. So…"

Getting up from my squat, I shake the lingering fatigue from my mind. I grab the Red Vines, tear them open, and chew on one. "What're you doin' here, Candy?"

For maybe the third time in our lives, I can tell she's nervous. She hops between her petite feet and bites on her bottom lip as if it's bubblegum. "I don't know."

Lifting the leftover licorice in a salute, I then turn around. "Let me know when you find out."

"Wait!" she calls out. "I have too much to figure out right now. I don't even know where to start with any of it. Especially not with you."

I turn back around. "Then let's not talk about it. You made it clear you thought I had something to do with your demise, so I don't really want to talk to you right now."

"I'm sorry, okay? I just…am overwhelmed. I got into this situation because of us. I know. It's messed up. I shouldn't have done it. But it's because I don't know what to do with us. You never even gave me an explanation about any of our breakup besides that you cheated on me."

Is she serious right now? No, she didn't get into her current situation because of us. She made a choice. A bad call. I blow out a breath. "You're not gonna blame *your* choices on our breakup that happened two years ago."

She shakes her head. "No, *yo sé*. This was my fault completely. But, I want to know. *Porque yo necesita saber y entender exactamente lo que pasó*. My fault or not, I ruined my career because I was scared of falling for you again, okay? I was freaking out in the hotel room because..."

She drops her gaze to the floor and then glances back up to me as if it's pained. "Because I like you too!"

"Then why'd you run away?" My voice comes out more gruff than I intended.

She shrugs and brushes the bangs off her face. "Because I was scared. You broke me when you left me waiting for you at the airport two years ago, Tom. You never even told me why you cheated on me. Was I that bad of a girlfriend? Did you just stop loving me? What is it?" Her voice rises, and it's thick with emotion. "Why'd you leave me waiting for you at the airport when you never got on the plane? Why'd you sleep with someone else knowing you were coming to see me? I loved you."

My lungs still burn from all my sprints, and my mouth is left with a now-bitter taste of cherry licorice. I glance across her face, eyes puffy and mascara streaked on her cheeks. She's never really asked why. And I've been the coward who didn't want to give up all the information. But she's right. She deserves an answer. So I swallow the sour taste climbing up my throat. "I was scared, Candy. I had just made the biggest mistake of my life. I knew the second I stepped off that plane, you'd see right through me."

She swipes at her cheek, and I'm not sure how she has any tears left in her after what I saw earlier tonight. "*Sí, claro*. But I still don't understand why you cheated in the first place."

If she thinks I understand why I cheated, she's not right. I'm as lost as she is. I take a deep breath and glance at my shoes. "I've said it before, and I'll spend the rest of forever saying it. I'm sorry. *Lo siento,* Candy. I never meant to hurt you."

She sniffs, and I look into her eyes like she deserves. Nodding her head, she says, "I know. But sorry doesn't change things. I don't want *sorry.* I want an explanation."

I chuckle once, a defeated laugh. "No cap, I know."

She begins crying for real this time, blubbering sobs that take over her body as she covers her face with her hands. I walk and throw my arms around her, and she leans into my chest.

A few seconds later, she rambles, "Did you sabotage the relationship on purpose? Did you change your mind about the gap year to travel? I don't get it. Because nothing was wrong with our relationship, Tom. *Habíamos estado juntos por cinco años.*"

I tuck her hair behind her ear. "Are you kidding me? I never would've sabotaged anything on purpose. I wanted to travel."

"Well you have a funny way of showing it," she mumbles.

I sighs and lace my fingers around her lower back. "I made a mistake. Like you said earlier, a few bad decisions led to one of the worst nights of my life. I don't even remember the girl's name."

She glances away from me, and her eyelashes are wet and clumped together. "I honestly think that might be worse. If you would've fallen for someone else, then fine. But you cheated on me with a nobody."

This is uncomfortable, but I know it needs to be talked about if she ever wants to move on from it. Even if it's not with me. "You'd been gone for six months at that point. It just, I don't know. I missed you, and we were hardly talking with the time difference. I stopped hanging around Carter. Got with a few different friends, became more popular with baseball, made a decision to go to a party with the new guys after a protest, had too much to drink, and hooked up with someone. There's no long, drawn out story. That's what happened, and it sucks. I regret it every day. You gotta believe me, the second I woke up and realized what I did, I freaked." I unlace my hands and run one through my hair, pulling at the top.

She barks out a laugh. "*Esperaba que te asustaras*. We'd been together five years at that point. Tom, *tú eres todo para mí*. Were. You *were* everything to me. The thought of hooking up with someone was never even on my mind while we were together."

Did she just say I'm everything to her in Spanish? I pull back far enough that I can see her face and search her eyes for the truth. "Mine either. I'm tellin' you, it meant *nothing*. And the consequences of it meant *everything*. I lost you. Pretty sure I got the raw end of the deal here."

She pulls out of my embrace completely and stomps away. I follow behind her because she's going in the direction of my stuff anyway.

Then she turns around and shouts, "Sure did! *Soy la mejor*."

"Humble, too," I say, raising my brows.

Her crying stops, and she just stares at me. With a blank expression on her face, Candy swipes at the tears on her face and a sort-of hiss comes out of her. But it turns into a chuckle, and then...an actual laugh.

And I'm afraid I need to google how to deal with a breakdown because now she's laughing. Full on, maniacal cackling in the silence of the night that surrounds us.

Between giggles, she says, "You...really did...get the raw end...of the deal. And I don't need to be humble with you."

You'd think she's white-girl-wasted right now, but she's clearly sober. Finally, after staring at her for too long, I begin chuckling too. "This is so weird," I mumble. But then I reply with, "I did. Look at you, you took your anger and traveled the world, started a platform based on what you loved, way outdid my own platform, and I struck out every game the rest of that season. Any MLB scouts that were watching me definitely stopped after that."

Which isn't true, but it *was* true for a little while.

"So you're saying both of our careers are ruined?" She laughs even harder. "How are you still on the team?"

I crack a smile. "You came back, and suddenly, I started hitting again."

"*Ay Dios mío.* We're a mess." She runs her fingers under her eyes, barely affecting the black underneath.

I lean down to grab my phone and bag, but end up sitting on the turf. "Don't think anyone would argue against that point."

Candy sits beside me and steals a Red Vine. We sit like that for a while, relishing in the silence of the outdoors. Just her and I on the track, crickets chirping in the background.

"I don't think I'll ever understand it, Tom," she breaks the silence.

If there's anything I've learned, it's that things happen every day that you'll never understand. It's life. If I could take it back, I would. I'd do anything for this girl.

I suck in my lips and try to turn the conversation back to why we started arguing in the first place. "Don't understand why you'd run to a white boy's arms after kissing this either, so I guess we're even."

She seems to mull that over for a minute before saying, "Trust me, it was a waste."

I squeeze her thigh. "Knew it. You can't get better than this," I say while pointing up and down my body.

Candy rolls her eyes. "Yeah, I know. Been chasing it for the past year."

She has not been chasing me. If anything, I'm the only one who's chased her. And I caught her a few times. But it never lasted more than a night. She'd always shut me out after. Not that we're here to discuss that. She's torn up about the leaked photos. I would be too.

"So, what now?" I ask.

She runs her hand through the turf, disrupting little black pieces of rubber that lie between the fake strands of grass. "Honestly? I couldn't guess for a million dollars. You should probably stay away from me, though. My name is only going to bring your own platform down."

Groaning, she says, "I just want to forget about all of it. My mistakes and my crushed career. I don't want to remember any of it."

Doesn't she realize I don't care about my platform? The only reason it grew was because my name started getting tossed around by scouts. People are constantly badgering me to get out of college and declare myself for the draft. Probably ten percent of my followers are activists, and most of those came from Candy. The rest are jersey chasers hoping to hitch a ride.

"You're not bringin' my platform down. Stop with that." I nudge her shoulder, but she looks down at her knees.

I hate seeing her like this. I hate that I could've caused some of it with the talk of my cheating years ago. I want to *fix* it, but I wouldn't even know where to start.

It's quiet enough that I can hear her breaths. The stadium light shut off at nine, so we're gonna have to leave here soon unless we want to sit in the dark.

Candy lets out a shaky exhale. "The difference between our one-night mistakes is that yours shattered my heart, and mine shattered my career."

I reach for my necklace and feel the warm metal between my fingers. It calms me enough to ask, "Which one is worse?"

"My career," she whispers. "Hearts recover. Careers rarely do."

Funny she says that 'cause I'm still waiting for my heart to recover. Probably isn't gonna. But isn't that typical? The girl moves on after the guy's mistakes, and the man is left broken-hearted years later, still pining after someone who's been gone for far too long.

She keeps going. "It's like I try to think of something else. *No puedo dejar de pensar en eso.* It nags at me like a bad itch. The more you ignore it, the worse it gets. I just want to feel something other than complete and total despair."

"Is that why you came here?"

Her chest rises and falls as she takes a breath. When she

glances at me, her eyes shift over my face as if she's studying my features. Makes me feel like something is on me. She dips her chin. "Even after all this time, I still think of you as my home. I-I don't know. I thought being here with you would make things better."

Her revelation scares me. It gets my hopes up, which is never good when it comes to Candy. Because as soon as she gives in, she ends up blocking me off even harder than before. I tread carefully as if I'm dealing with a scared animal. Shifting on my bottom, I plant my feet on the ground and circle my arms around my knees, resting my hands on top. "Well, did it?"

A ghost of a smile appears on her lips. "Maybe a little."

"A *little*? Ay, no, no, no lil' mami. We gotta pump those numbers *up*." I grab my bag, fish out my keys, and stand.

"*¿Qué estás haciendo?*" she clucks. "I was just getting comfortable out here."

I hold out my hand and she grasps it as I pull her up. "You said you wanted a distraction. Apparently, my sexy looks aren't doing it—"

"I said they were a little!"

"—so I'm taking you on an adventure." I beam.

"Fine," she mutters. "Please don't tell me this is gonna end badly for me."

I entwine our fingers, and she doesn't pull away. My hand beats with its own drum, and I feel the touch all the way to my stomach. It's inevitable. I'm a fool for her. I ignore the heat that trails up my arm as she moves her thumb across my pointer finger.

"Nah, it's not gonna end badly," I say, using my other hand to type out a text. "I've got the perfect plan. How do you feel about vandalism?"

She glares at me.

I wave her off. "Chill, *cariña*. It'll be mostly legal this time."

Chapter Ten – Candy

"Where are we going?" I grip my seat as the car bumps along.

Tom clucks his tongue. "Wouldn't you like to know?"

I pull at the blindfold, which he insisted on, and it's just some sweaty shirt of his. Feeling a little like some weird *365 DNI* stuff is happening. "*Claro.* Hence why I asked."

"Just a few more minutes," he says, and it sounds like he's distracted while he's driving. *Perfecto.*

I lay my head back against the seat, trying desperately to figure out where we could be going. It's been maybe twenty minutes, which could either be near our hometown or in the opposite direction. But considering it's pretty late, I doubt a lot of the shops will be open, and that's about all that there is away from home. "Are you going to get us arrested? Because that will definitely be the nail in the coffin of my career."

He pulls gently on my hair, and my thighs clench. Chuckling, he says, "No, we are going to be doing something perfectly legal."

"Since when is vandalism perfectly legal?" I mutter, not being able to tell if he's acting sarcastic or not. He turns, and the car bumps as if we're driving on a dirt road. I slap the air until I hit his arm and push. "Please tell me you did not bring me to my house. I cannot deal with my parents right now, I swear."

"Yeah, I thought, 'Let's take the girl right home to her

mom when she's grumpy. She could do this alone, but Imma blindfold her, put her in the car, drive to her house, and act like it's some cool surprise under the guise of vandalism. I be smooth like that.'"

"I can hear the eyeroll in your voice, *tonto*."

I imagine him shrugging, a little smile pulling at his lips as he winks at me. "Well, stupid questions get stupid answers."

"*La gente estúpida recibe preguntas estúpidas*." I mock him in Spanish.

"I know what you said."

I mumble, "Maybe taking Spanish classes was a bad idea." The car comes to a halting stop, and I fly forward and gasp. "Oh, so it be like that, eh? *Está bien, chico.* Just wait until I blindfold you. *Pasarás por mucho peor.*"

My door opens.

"Don't threaten me with a good time," he whispers right in my ear, and my lady friend is gettin' a lil' too excited.

He unties the blindfold, and I pull it off. All around me is literal junk. We're in some sort of...bulk trash place? Stadium lights shine down, illuminating the place where old cars, piles of tables, chairs, and broken couches are packed high and scattered around. Glass windows, old window frames, minivans that have seen better days, trucks that look like they're more rust than metal, and tire rims lie all around us.

"Where are we?" Thankfully, it's not a landfill because it doesn't smell like trash. Just looks like it.

Toms closes the door once I get out of the car. "Remember my cousin Mike?"

I squint an eye. "The one who tried hitting on me when he was drunk at Thanksgiving?"

He glares at me. "Yes. Well, because of that, he owed me a favor. I finally called it in."

I cock an eyebrow. "Yeah, not following."

Tom walks to the trunk of his Jeep and pops it open. A sledgehammer, crowbar, safety glasses, boots, spray paint, and plastic suits sit in a small heap.

"You do realize had we gotten pulled over with all of this crap in the car, we probably would've been arrested, right?"

He deadpans. "*Sí, chica.* I know I'm Black. Thank you for pointing that out."

"I'm just saying," I mumble. "Anyway, what is all this stuff?"

"Mike owns this junkyard. We're gonna destroy some property. Get our anger out."

I gasp. "Like my business idea!" A few years back, I had an idea to open a warehouse where you could go to smash things. From what I recall, Tom said the idea was *slightly concerning,* so...

"What can I say? I make dreams come true." He raises his brows twice.

"*Dios mío. Tú quisieras.*" I grab the sledgehammer, but it's heavier than I think, and it drops to the ground, narrowly missing my toe. *Genial,* so we'll work up to that one. Had I known what we were doing, I would've gotten out of my sweat-shorts and Tory Burch sandals.

Tom hands me a plastic suit, boots, and safety goggles. We get suited up, and he grabs all of the tools. I follow behind him as he goes to the nearest car, a beat up Toyota missing all four doors and seats. The windshield is intact, but the trunk and hood of the car are rusted so badly there are holes in the metal.

"You wanna do the honors?" He holds out a hammer.

I grab it and inhale. "*Chingate,* Jake Marx!" I yell, slamming the hammer into the glass windshield. It cracks and shatters, but stays in the frame. "Screw you, judgmental people!" I hit it again, and a fist sized hole appears as the glass falls into the car.

Kicking the tire, I scream, "I hate you *jalena68! Vete a la chingada, ericspartanspam!*" I list off the other usernames I remember, the ones who hurled racial slurs at me. "No offense, Tom, but screw you and the girl you cheated on me with. Screw Erin who was all over you at *my* party. Screw our screwed up past!" I hit the metal of the car over and over, until sweat beads down my forehead.

Tom claps and shouts, "Hell yeah!" never trying to stop me as I get all the anger out.

Putting the hammer on the ground, I step back and admire my handiwork. I imitate a chef's kiss. "*Es una de las cosas más increíbles que he visto.*" I toss a glance at Tom, and he shakes his head and chuckles. I wink. "You want to try?"

He nods toward a minivan and holds up the sledgehammer. "I got my eye on that beauty over there."

"Yeah? What're you angry about?" I walk behind him.

"You think I'm never angry?" He zips up his plastic suit.

I shrug. "No. I know you get angry. So what's it about?"

He winks. "Screw the scouts that stopped watching me. Screw Eric Girk." I'm not sure who that is, but Tom slams the sledgehammer into the minivan's door, leaving a softball-sized dent, so he's obviously a big deal. "Screw my two strikes from Saturday. Screw the keyboard warriors on your case." He shatters the side window. "Screw *everyone* who is saying shit about you." He knocks the side mirror off, and it clatters to the ground, stirring up dust.

"Alright, I see you. Let me get in on the action." I try to lift the sledgehammer. "*Bien, necesito ayuda.*"

Standing behind me, he holds the sledgehammer between my hands. I think about what else I could be angry about. "Got it. Screw that dude freshman year of high school who got us suspended for making out behind the bleachers."

We slam the hammer into the car. Tom laughs. "Screw Mr. Shafto and his creepy remarks."

"Yassss!" I squeal, shattering the front windshield.

We cackle as we get the spray paint and write on the cars and wooden tables. I write *thot, ho, hypocrite,* and everything else people have said about me in the last couple of days. Tom writes a few different names, *MLB,* and the other things that he fights for on a daily basis. He has a soft spot for turtles, so he even writes plastic straws in spray paint, and I have to choke back a giggle.

It briefly reminds me of a moment in our past that I've

spent so long pushing down. But I blink it away and focus on the present instead.

I glance toward Tom, and he bites his lip and nods. I cackle and reach the hammer up high before swinging, bashing the wood, splitting it apart. He does the same, shattering the table into a ton of parts. We keep going like unhinged maniacs, destroying everything that people say about us. Preconceived notions, unfair judgements, and everything on our minds.

With a final shout, I throw the hammer into the pile, and it disappears from sight. My arms feel like jelly, and I sit down on the dirt, breathing hard, taking off the safety goggles and plastic suit.

Tom sits next to me, does the same, and place his elbows on his knees. "Feel better?"

I sigh. "Told you it was a genius business idea."

He smiles, knocking his shoulder into mine. Against the bright lights, his eyes shine, and he licks his lips before biting into them.

I miss this. I miss him.

We don't say a word, but my gaze crawls over him. The thin gold chain dipping below his shirt. The button up baseball practice jersey where his biceps flex against the sleeves. The chest I've run my hands over a million times but can't remember the feel or exact sensation.

Maybe we're just meant to be friends. The thought crawls up my spine, making me itchy.

I don't want to be friends.

I want to remember.

Remember the feel of his body on mine, remember what it feels like to be loved by him. Remember the little moments, like snuggling while watching movies or going on late night adventures. I don't want to be his friend. I want him. All of him.

The realization doesn't scare me. It fills me with a bubbling need. I crawl toward him, and his brow furrows. "Uh, what're you doing, Candy?"

"Something I should've done a long time ago." I straddle him and bring his face to mine. "*La pregunta es, ¿estás lista para probar algo diferente?* Would you still be down if my reputation is forever ruined?"

Our lips barely brush, but the sensation makes me flinch against his waist. He grabs my hips and pushes me down in his lap. "Yeah. But are *you* sure?"

"Only thing I'm sure about right now." I place my hands on his cheeks, rubbing my thumbs across his lips.

He rips my hands from his face and grips my chin, forcing the space between us to disappear. Our lips collide in fragmented desire and splintered hope. Gripping my thighs, he stands, holding me through our frantic breaths and kisses. My hands explore his arms and chest as his tongue opens my mouth.

I let him in and he moans, fire and heat trailing into my core. He opens the car door and lays me down in the back seat, pressing the button on his key to automatically start the car.

The radio blares, picking up where we left off on my playlist. "Lasting Lover" by James Arthur pulses through the car.

"I...don't...think you'll fit back here," I breathe out as he trails kisses from my belly button to my throat.

This isn't a small stolen kiss like all the other times. It's heat and want in its primal form. It's taking a step into territory that's different and new, something that will change *us* for the future. But with the uncertainty surrounding me everywhere else, this is the only thing I feel right about. I'm done fighting against it.

I can only hope that it'll last for more than a night this time.

I don't want to be remembered for my mistake, so why should I keeping hold his against him?

He chuckles against my neck. "Guess it's time for a truck."

I whimper as he bites the sensitive skin on my shoulder up to my mouth. "Make yourself fit."

His lips swallow my growl, and I pull him on top of me.

Reaching under his shirt, I touch each hard muscle, relishing in the heat of him.

The kiss grows frenetic and frenzied as my nerves fire at an all-time high. Only he can make me feel like this, alive and excited in a crappy junkyard. The smell of him caresses me, and I want to drown in the ocean scent. I'm overwhelmed and underappreciated by his lips all at the same time.

I need more. Breaking our kiss, I say, "Get all the way in here, *y cierra la puerta.*"

With a heated glare, he obeys.

Chapter Eleven - Candy

I wake up with a smile on my face. My phone's only notification is a text from Tom saying good morning, and though I'm sure there are thousands of nasty things awaiting me on social media, I choose to pretend like I'm a nobody. I text Tom as I get ready, and each time my phone clatters against the counter, I curl my toes.

I'm a little hesitant to get excited over this, but at the same time, I've missed being with him. Who knows where it might lead? I'm done overthinking. Enough drama surrounds my new circumstances.

Which reminds me, there's a different relationship I need to check in on.

I knock on Carter's bedroom door, fidgeting on my feet in the hallway.

"Come in," he says, and I can *feel* his exasperation through the wall. I shouldn't have yelled at him when he was trying to help.

He sits on his bed, Les next to him with her feet draped across his lap. I stand there awkwardly, but no one says anything, so I lift my hand in greeting. "*Lo siento,* guys. I don't want to fight with either of you. I was just stressed out, and I shouldn't have yelled at both of you."

Carter leans back on the bed and gives me an impassive stare. Les nudges him. "Don't be rude, babe."

He rolls his eyes. "I'm not. We're working this out the only way we know how."

Staring contest. I sigh and stare at him. Some weird twin

telepathy is telling me that he's confused, thinks I'm weird, and also hates the shirt I'm wearing. I hope my stare is telling him that I'm also confused, that I'm sorry for everything, and *love* the shirt he's wearing (since I bought it for him as a Christmas gift last year).

When I cock my head, he nods, and I know we're good.

I make my way over to the bed, sitting between Les and him, forcing her to put her legs down, and put my arms around their necks. "We're the three amigos, yeah? You can't stay mad at me."

Carter leans his head against mine. "Not mad, *hermana.* Don't get it, but not mad. Rest of the world sure is, though."

I blow a raspberry. "*Gracias for reminding me.* Les?"

She shakes her head and smiles. "I love you. A girl's gotta get some no matter who he is, right?"

"Oh, no." I groan. "That is not what it is, I could've gotten some many other places."

She winks. "Kidding. At least tell me, was it worth it? 'Cause if it was like the best ever, I can understand a little more. Maybe even tell me in detail. I think I need detail."

Carter whips his head toward her. "Whatchu talkin' bout, *señorita?* Nuh-uh. Candy, do not tell her details. *Especially* if it was the best ever. Gosh, woman, are you not satisfied?"

"Nope." I stand. "Not talking about this. Gotta get to studying. *¡Te amo! ¡Adios!*"

Their laughs echo as I race out of the room and grab my bag, but it's not fast enough because I can hear Les say, "Oh, I'm very satisfied," and lemme just barf.

On my way out, I pull out my phone and click Twitter out of habit, clicking on my DMs. And look who finally replied to my message.

@Jakemarx: *I told them to leave me alone. But what would you have wanted? Our pictures are plastered all over.*

I groan, stomping through the hallway and typing back.

@candydeleon: *And how did those pictures get leaked, Jake? Because on my end, the only people who knew were me, you, and the* *surveillance cameras in Mexico. So has someone been running that little mouth of theirs?*

I get in my car and slam my hand against the steering wheel a few times. "Stupid freaking men!" I shout it as my mantra. "Gahhh!"

A shrimpy dude chooses that exact moment to walk by my car, staring at me as if he's ready to call the police. So I cuss him out in Spanish. "Mind your own business, *puto.*"

He speed walks away, and I pull out of my spot and head to West's library. I'm supposed to meet Ethan to work on the final edits for our paper. And by 'our,' I mean mine. But I'll help him out because he's a friend. One that apparently doesn't hate me right now, so he's winning in my book.

I pull into the closest parking lot to the library and text him that I'm on my way in. As I get out of my car and gather my bags, I hear whispering behind me. I turn and cock a brow, ready to throw some hands (or words) if needed.

Two white chicks sit there glancing at me from between cars.

"*Hola, perras.* I couldn't quite hear you. Speak a little louder!" I give them a peace sign and walk away. They're not worth it. But it still irks me. People are quick to be my friend when they think they can use me for my platform, but the second I screw up, they're ready to crucify me.

I get halfway to the library when I pass the large fountain in the center of West's campus. Another girl glances my way. Auburn hair down to her waist, a West soccer sweater that's cut into a crop top, and high-waisted black leggings. She looks somewhat familiar, but not sure why.

She smiles as if I'm fresh meat and races over to me.

Dios mío, I don't do petty girl drama. Isn't being canceled online enough?

Waving, she says, "Hey! You're Candy DeLeón, right?"

I keep walking, hoping it will deter her, but she walks right along beside me. I give her a tight smile. "Yep, that's me. What's up?"

She holds out her hand. "Grace."

I shake it and stop strolling. "Nice to meet you."

"So, I run West's *Jaguar Paper*, and wanted to see if you'd be interested in an interview?"

She seems somewhat genuine, but no. "Yeah, right now isn't really a good time for me."

Grace nods. "I know. Hence the interview. I don't think what's happening to you is fair. I'd love to sit down and talk about it."

I tuck hair behind my ear and glance to the side. "Well, you'd be in the minority. I'm not ready for that right now. *Gracias*, Grace. It was nice meeting you."

I wave and begin walking away.

"If you change your mind, let me know. The offer is open ended."

Nodding, I turn around and head the rest of the way to the library. Ethan waits for me in the foyer, backpack slung onto one shoulder. Dressed in basketball shorts and a long tee, he towers above me and breaks into a grin when he sees me. "The woman of the hour."

I bow. "Yes, hello, it is I."

He bops me on the head, and I look up to him. Why are basketball players always so tall? Laughing, he says, "I think I need to call you tiny little shrimp."

My face pinches. "Say what now?"

"Yeah, 'cause you're short. But also pink hair. Tiny lil' shrimp."

I shake my head. Is he for real? What is with this man and animals? "*Chico, te voy a golpear tan rápido.*"

He shrugs. "Don't have a clue what you just said."

I just said I'd knock him out, which to be fair, I probably couldn't. But if I could, I would. "That was the point, bruh. Come on, let's grab a table."

I stomp ahead of him, trying to be as unlike a shrimp as possible. Tiny freaking shrimp. I swear, men are so dumb.

We grab an empty table, and I get out my laptop as Ethan

scrolls on his phone. Knocking it out of his hand, I say, "Get your laptop out now, *muchacho.* You're not just piggy-backing off of my paper."

"But the professor said we could partner up," Ethan whines. "Come on, do your friend a favor. Remember how I did most of the group project for History of Rock and Roll?"

"Please tell me you're joking, Ethan. I swear, you are gonna get on my nerves, dude."

His jaw drops. "I wrote that entire jingle and you know it."

I cross my legs underneath the table. "Which is why we got a C! Get your white ass outta here. I swear, you make me crazy."

He laughs. "I never said I did it *well.* I just said I did it."

Ignoring him, I type in the password to my laptop and get to work. After being annoying AF and waving his hand in front of my face for a full minute, I sigh and look at him. "Are you ready to be serious for once in your life?"

He guffaws. "I am not un-serious. I'm having fun. But sure, I am ready to listen, Professor Candy."

I roll my eyes, but he *does* get to work, and he prepped by doing research beforehand, so he's not totally useless. After compiling all of our data, we write and polish a buddy-paper that I'm praying will get us an A. If I have no career to look forward to, at least my degree will be nice padding for a backup plan.

He closes his laptop and leans back against the wall, hands behind his head. "Let's grab dinner."

I cock an eyebrow at him.

"As friends," he laments.

I give him a face that says *uh huh, sure.*

He holds his hands up in surrender. "I swear. I know your boyfriend would beat my ass."

I pull out my phone and see a text from Tom saying he's studying but can meet up later. My stomach skips thinking about kissing him again. Which is embarrassing, honestly, 'cause it makes me feel like I'm sixteen again. I glance at Ethan.

"Don't have a boyfriend. And you're *always* flirting with me."

"Hey, you know we would never. It's friendly banter," he says in an English accent.

I laugh. "You been onto *Love Island* again?"

"Always. And I'm fancying a new bird."

"Well, good. I'm glad. You know I hated Rachel."

He shrugs. "So did I. But man, did that hate express itself well." Biting his lip, he chuckles.

I slap his arm. "I'm gonna pass on dinner. I don't know if you've heard, but I'm sorta on social media death row right now. I should probably check in."

And because karma's a *perra*, I get a text from Gloria asking if we can talk.

Ethan packs up the rest of his belongings in his bag and zips it shut. "Ooh, yeah. I saw some of that. Don't really think it's a big deal, but you're catching major heat from it."

"Yeah, well, that's because you're not in the world of politics."

He winks and stands halfway, inching out of the booth we're sitting at. "Won't need to be when I'm in the NBA."

I hold out my hands. "Um, no, everyone needs to be into politics." I roll my eyes. "Have fun at dinner. Can't wait to hear more about these feelings you be catching in class next week."

Ethan flips me off and chuckles, walking away and out of the library. I press Gloria's contact and take a few calming breaths while it rings.

The call connects with a, "*Hola, Candy. ¿Estás bien?*" Before I can respond, she continues, "I guess that's a stupid question to ask right now."

I laugh awkwardly. "Uh, yeah. No, I'm holding up as well as I can, obviously."

It sounds like her heels clack against a tile floor. "I'm calling because my boss asked me to. We're not going to pull the article. To quiet any *Latina* voice right now would be a mistake, especially with how much yours has helped."

My body goes numb. Did she really just say they're keeping my interview posted? That's...that's huge. They have to be catching heat because of it. "*Ay Dios mío, muchas gracias,* Gloria."

"We do, however, want to ask for a follow-up comment. Jake Marx's publicist wanted the article corrected to show that there had once been a relationship between the two of you. We've added his disclaimer to the bottom of the article and wanted to give you the chance to respond as well," Gloria explains.

I groan. "Off the record, Gloria, we spent a few hours together, that was it. But on the record? I'm not really sure how to respond. Um, just say that I continue to deny any allegations of a relationship between the two of us."

"Okay. *Gracias,* Candy. Regardless of everything, I do feel bad for you. I hope things get better."

I scratch my side and sigh. "Yeah, same. Thanks for checkin' in. *Adios,* Gloria."

"Bye."

The phone call disconnects, and a swirl of emotions occur. On one hand, I'm glad that Gloria sympathizes with me, no matter how small. Maybe that means there are others out there like her and...the girl from earlier today...Grace?

But hope is dangerous. It beguiles you, and often, hope is pointless. Careers don't recover. It's like a pro-ball player getting surgery. They rarely, if ever, come back stronger. Instead, they're cast away to the sidelines.

I pull out my phone and go to Twitter. Jake responded to my earlier message. Oh, joy.

@Jakemarx: *I haven't been 'running my mouth.' I'm offended you'd even think that. This is exactly what I would expect from someone like you. What would I get by doing that? We're both being blown up here.*

So, yeah, that's a lie. I click on his profile. His first few tweets are retweets.

Looks like @candydeleon was making a little too much love and not enough walls.

Jake, I live in California too. Hit me up the next time you want a little flavor in your life.

Imagine being so hot that you get a left extremist in your bed.

Is...he...joking right now? Nuh-uh. He's not going to act all nice guy to me while pulling this crap. Stupid white boys and their stupid egos.

I go back to our DM thread.

@candydeleon: *Are you serious right now? Look at your retweets. I just talked to Mitú and you had a publicist try and change the article. There was one sentence in there about you. One! You're a freaking clout chaser. No one knew your name before this, Jake. You think these five minutes of fame are going to do anything for you? Gtfo, puto.*

His following count is up to a hundred thousand, which is far more than he used to have. I roll my eyes and go to my own profile. Eight hundred thousand on Twitter. Which means that I lost four hundred thousand followers over this stupid crap. *Estoy furiosa.*

I go to Instagram, where my DMs have tripled. I give them a minute glance, but after seeing the word *perra* and *ho* five too many times, I exit out of that app too. My emails are radio silent, so that's cool. I suppose that means there are zero sponsorships left to ditch me.

Guess I'll give it a few more days. Problem is, I don't know what I did wrong. (I mean, obviously, yes, I do.) But, like, if you make a mistake that's offensive to someone else, you can educate yourself. But me? I didn't do anything *wrong*, I'm just a hypocrite. And you can't fix this type of hypocrisy with education.

Nothing I do can take back what I did, and I'm obviously not going to do it again in the future. So, we're just at a standstill here. Is this acceptance? Am I at the end of the stages of grief? When does the whole 'get a swift kick in the ass and actually do something' stage start?

Never? My Live seemed to make things worse, so I'm not sure where to go from here.

I grab my bag and slide off of the bench to stand. As I head out of the library, I see the back of someone's head that I would recognize anywhere. Tom has his AirPods in and a baseball cap on backwards. His laptop is open, and he types away on a document. I slide into the booth with him, and he flinches as he glances to the side.

"Damn, girl, you scared me." Tom pulls out one of his Air-Pods. "What're you doing here?"

"I had to study with Ethan for our poli-sci paper. What're you working on?"

His gaze shifts to the table where his phone sits. "Uh, yeah, sis. I'll call you back, aight? No, it's not that I don't want to—Okay, yeah, I'll call later. Candy just got here and—Yeah, hopefully so. No, I know. Alright, Kira, I'm in the library, I can't do this right now…Yes, I promise. Okay. *Alright!* Stop. Fine, okay, talk to you later, bye."

He double taps the AirPod, and his phone's lock screen lights up as the call ends. It's a picture of Carter and him in Mexico doing handstands on the beach. "Sorry, Kira had just called a few minutes ago, so I was talking to her while working on this business calc assignment."

The mention of Kira makes me want to roll my eyes, but I refrain. "Cool. What's she up to?"

Tom gives me side eye as he takes out his other AirPod and puts both of them back in their case. "Don't play."

I hold my hands up and wink. "*Bien.* But don't say I didn't try."

"How much more do you need to study?" He clicks out of his assignment and goes to his email.

"I'm done. I could finish a few other things if you wanted company, but otherwise I'm good to go home."

A few students pass by, chatting way too loud. Clearly, they're freshmen. Tom waits until they're just out of earshot before he slides a hand under the table and squeezes my thigh. "Oh, I want some company alright."

"You wanna get out of here?"

He nods. "Yeah, I actually had a question for ya."

"Mmm?" I fiddle with the strap on my bag, still mildly distracted from his fingers on my thigh.

"What're you doing for Valentine's Day?"

I can feel the smile break on my face, and when he winks, I laugh. "Nothing, why?"

"'Cause we're going to Disneyland with Les and Carter."

My jaw drops. "I totally forgot that she bought him tickets for Christmas! Let's do it. Think they'll care that we're crashing?"

Tom throws his head back and laughs. "Nah. Imagine a girl like Les in a place like Disneyland. Trust me, Carter will be grateful."

I lay my head on his shoulder. "*Cierto.* Let's go get dinner."

His hand skirts up my thigh, and he raises his brows. "As long as you're dessert."

Chapter Twelve – Tom

The weights clatter as I set them down. Sweat drips down my forehead, and I swipe it with my forearm. "You Got It" by Vedo plays in the background of the student athlete gym, and the night sky shines with a full moon beyond the floor-to-ceiling windows.

Assistant Coach Johnson writes on an iPad, glancing at Ben Maldon and me in between his notetaking. When he sees I'm finished with the set, he clears his throat and swipes on the screen. "I'll be right back. Gonna grab the bands for y'all to work out with."

I lean back on a column, and Ben finishes his set. After setting the weights down, he stretches his arms above his head. "Got a scout coming to opening game for me."

Seriously? My stats are better than his are, but no scouts are coming for me as far as I'm concerned. He knows this. But this is what Ben does. Always bragging about himself. His Tik-Tok platform, his money, his everything. The guy has it all. Of course he's gonna try to take an MLB position from me as well.

If I get angry, it's just gonna make him happier. But damn, that stings. "Cool, man. Congrats."

Shrugging, he says, "Don't worry. If he's there for me, he could still watch you play too."

"Thanks, how generous of you to bring that up." Sarcasm coats my voice. "What team is he coming from?" I tread carefully, not wanting Ben to know I even care.

"Angels."

Alright, whatever. Fine by me. Any team is a good team,

but I've always planned for the A's. Still, my shoulders tighten when I see his satisfied smirk. "Nice. Well, good luck. Don't hesitate on first base like you do in practice."

Ben whips his head toward me. "I don't hesitate."

A chuckle threatens to escape, but I raise my brows and poke my tongue in my cheek instead. "Yeah, bro, you do."

His face twists up in a scowl, but it silences him for the rest of our extra practice. After working out for another thirty minutes, I get up to leave, and I hear Ben ask Coach Johnson if there's any tape he can watch from practice. I got in his head, and the smile that slides on my face is pure ecstasy.

That scout *should* be for me. It pisses me off, and it's not fair. Why does Ben get scouts coming to opening games when I don't?

I know the answer. Because Ben is the All-American boy they want. Which is why I'm fighting for the future of Black players. Crap like this is ridiculous. I deserve a spot in the MLB, and I'm gonna have to double down to get it. It'll be worth it though. It *has* to be.

My muscles are fatigued, but as I head out of the gym, I scroll Instagram in the parking lot. I've got a few DMs, so I read through and respond. In the corner of the screen, I see a DM request. Half of them are always nude photos from dudes and girls, but I check in case it's legit. The account has no profile picture, which screams scam. I click the message, and two videos were sent with the message, "Do with it what you will."

I accept the request since I can clearly see Jake Marx's face in the videos. But before I can play them, an incoming call from Candy pops up on the top of the screen.

I press accept and her soft voice comes through the line with an, "Oh, *perfecto*. I was worried you were still at practice. Would you like to go on an adventure?"

Her sweet essence settles my stomach, and a smile grows on my face. "Will it require me to change out of sweaty clothes?"

She giggles, and I'll be damned if it doesn't charge my

battery like I run on pure Candy energy. "No," she says. "The sweatier, the better."

"Give me five minutes, and I'll be outside your apartment." Hanging up, I run to my car. Every step is easy, as if I haven't spent four hours working out today between my practice and extra training session.

Haven't broached the girlfriend subject with Candy, but this feels good. I want to call her mine, but who knows if she'll randomly decide I'm no longer worth her time. Every night I was with her after we broke up, it took one wrong word before she'd shutter herself.

I've been holding on for too long for that to happen again. I want to be hers, I want to save her from every heartache, and I've known it since I was thirteen. Just waiting for her to let me.

As I drive to her place, I know I'm simping. Just have to hope it's worth it.

Candy's waiting outside when I pull into the parking lot, and she's dressed in a skimpy tank and booty shorts. My core heats with the desire to park the car, grab her, and take her straight to her bed. To hell with the adventure. Let's have an adventure in bed.

But she opens the door and flashes a light in my face, shattering my fantasy. I throw my hands up in front of my eyes. "Whoa, what the hell are you doing?"

She flicks the light off. "Just making sure we're set."

"Set for what?"

"Don't be mad."

I lay my head on the steering wheel. "What have I gotten myself into?"

Candy lifts my head and kisses me, smushing my cheeks together. "We're going to Rainbow Bridge."

Wrestling out of her grip, I say, "What part of your boyfriend being scared of heights don't you understand?"

The word slips out, so this is a test, I guess.

Candy kicks her feet up on the dash and buckles her seat.

"Ah, I don't have a boyfriend, so…"

And, test failed. Cool. So, I'm her hookup? Friend with benefits? Exactly what she said she didn't want on New Year's? Funny how the tables have turned.

Before I can respond, she squeals. "It's gonna be fun, *te lo prometo.*"

My breath whooshes out of me. Damn, I'm whipped. I put the car back in drive and head toward Folsom where Rainbow Bridge is. "So, what's the plan?"

She shrugs. "I don't know. That's the point of being spontaneous."

"I don't even got a swimsuit to jump in."

Waving me off, she replies, "Boxers will be fine."

"Dude," I groan out. "I just worked out. I'm wearing sliders."

She stops scrolling on her phone and glances at me, raising a brow. "Good. Those are way too tight." Licking her lips, she reaches over to my lap and places her hand there, giving me a quick peck on the cheek before pulling back. "You'll be fine."

∞ ∞ ∞

I am not fine.

We hiked up the arch underneath where the cars race, and I'm staring at the slow moving river below Rainbow Bridge. A few cars pass by above us, their lights illuminating the sky a bit, but we're the only idiots on the underside of the bridge. Not only is it still winter, so the water is going to be freezing, but a light, misty rain begins to fall.

"Candy, this is not a good idea," I say, feet threatening to slip off the bottom curve of the bridge. The water churns maybe twenty feet below us, and I'm struggling to breathe normally. I freaking hate heights. "Why did you want to do this?"

She takes off her shorts and throws them to the rocks off

to the side. Next comes the tank, and she's shivering in a thong bikini. Candy is looking too good in that. I took my clothes off before climbing, so I'm just thankful it's dark out.

Or, I was, until Candy decided to shine the flashlight right at my shorts. "Nice," she whispers, and I wrestle the flashlight out of her grip.

I shine the light on her, roving over her goosebump-speckled skin. The bikini cuts above her waist, narrowing where her hips dip to the space between her thighs. It looks as if I could tear the material without thinking twice, and the need to have her on me, under me, or beside me is so strong that I take a step closer to her despite my wobbly knees.

Candy softly laughs. "I wanted to do this because…I don't know. I want to feel in control of something when everything else seems out of my control."

I circle my arm around one of the bridge columns and pull her toward me with my other. She hasn't really mentioned how she's felt. She's talked to me about her career, but every time we're together, she glosses over her feelings. If someone leaked photos of me mid-hook up with someone, I'd be pissed. It's creepy. "Candy, are you okay?"

She lays her cheek on my chest. "I'm fine."

"Are you though? 'Cause I wouldn't be—"

"I said I'm fine!" she snaps and tries to pull away from me, but I squeeze her tighter. "I just want to forget about it for a moment, okay? I want to jump off a bridge with a guy and just be a girl. I need that. *Necesito sentirme normal por un momento.* So please, don't mention it again tonight."

Her body feels warm against the cold of the night, and I take a deep breath against her neck. "Okay. Alright." And I do what she wants. I change the subject. "Mmm, you smell so damn good."

She pulls at my hair. "Sooner you jump, the sooner you can have me."

I glance at the water below. It's not really that far, I guess. Just a quick swim, and Candy will reward me. I try to give myself a toxic masculinity pep talk. Things like, *grow some balls, dude. Don't let a girl see you scared, bro. Show her how tough you are, fam.*

It's not working.

Candy looks at me with her big green eyes and a pouty expression. "Please jump with me, babe."

Her calling me babe cuts the last of my resistance. Ridiculous, I know. "Will you at least hold my hand?" I grumble out.

She nods. "Yes. On the count of three, okay?"

"Alright," I bite out, shivering as the rain picks up and begins to pelt us. "It's gonna be freezing. You know that, right?"

"Then you get to warm me up." Candy kisses my cheek and laces our fingers together. "One...two...three!"

She jumps, pulling me along with her. We fall, and I squeal like a girl while thinking *please, don't let me die. Take the crazy woman who made me do this and not me.*

My feet slap against the water, and ice crawls up my body as we plunge into the river. The force of the water tears my hand away from Candy, and I'm momentarily stunned from the cold.

A second later, I pop out of the water, gasping against the ice that crawls through my veins. Candy comes up laughing, and we swim as fast as we can to the rocks on the side of the river. I pull myself out of the river and onto the rocks, holding out a hand for Candy to come out as well. She collapses on top of me, still giggling.

"Happy?" I ask, pushing the wet hair off of her face.

Rain pitter-patters off of the water and stones, but her body shivering against mine is warm. "Very," she whispers before pressing her lips to mine.

And even though it's cold and rainy, rocks are pushing into my back, and I'm pretty sure we lost the flashlight, my heart beats at double time. "I really like you, Candy. You know that, right?" I ask against her mouth.

"*Sí.*" She kisses me again. "I like you, too, Tom."

But I can't help myself from asking, will that be enough to keep her?

Chapter Thirteen - Candy

The next week goes by in a blur of nothingness. I try reaching out to West's student engagement presidency in hopes of getting back into my club, Equal Treatment For Equal People. I mean, I founded the organization, and we had big plans this year. Even if they don't want me there, it's not fair I'm being excluded from the events we planned. But the presidency said they couldn't help. Apparently, club activity is at the discretion of the club, unless it's illegal. Annoying.

A new photo comes out of Jake and me, sipping on drinks at the bar in Mexico. Not scandalous, but people have still been talking. It's like I'm an object. Everyone picks me apart as if I'm not a person. They talk about my body, my hair, the words I've spoken, the words I haven't spoken, my morality, and things they know nothing about. They may as well have stomped on my soul, leaving dirty footprints behind with all their opinions. I've been trending on Twitter off and on for a couple weeks now. I haven't posted anything on Instagram, and I've temporarily turned off comments and my Twitter DMs. I can't handle it.

The only platform that people have yet to crucify me on is TikTok, but I've kept off of that too.

Maybe today will change my sour mood. It should be a good day. It's my birthday.

"I thought we said no big party this year," Carter says, pulling me from my thoughts as we drive into our childhood home, a modest house sitting atop two acres of land with a giant barn in the back that's used solely for parties.

I link my arm around his, leaning over the center console. "I think this is the small party, bro."

"*Están locos.* You ready for the *baile*?" He glances in the rearview mirror as he backs into the driveway.

"*Sí.* I'm more excited to see what havoc Mateo and Adrian cook up tonight. Ten bucks they break some form of glass at the party." I snicker at the thought of our hellish nephews creating chaos for our sister, Carlotta. Plus, she's ready to have their third baby, a girl, in two short months. So she can't chase them quite as well as she used to.

Carter snorts. "Yeah, no. *No soy un idiota.* I'm not buying into that bet. They're definitely breaking something."

"*Bien,*" I huff. "You think of something for the birthday bet, then. *Me acabaron las ideas.*"

He turns off the car and leans his head against the headrest. "Uh, how about ten bucks that Les gets me a better gift than she gets you?"

I give him side eye. "Boy, please. I'm her best friend. My gift will definitely be better."

"You forget who she sleeps with," he says, shrugging as he exits the car.

"Um," I hop out of his truck, "me! She sleeps with me! We share a room."

He winks. "But we share a bed. And believe me, I keep her *muy, muy, muy contenta.*"

I retch. "Boo you whore."

His eyes widen as he stares at someone behind me. *Mierda,* someone just heard me. Should I run? Is *la chancla* coming for me?

"Don't talk to your brother like that!" my mom shouts.

I flinch and turn toward her voice. She glares at me. This calls for holding my hands up in surrender. "*Estoy bromeando.* It's just a joke, chill."

She ushers me into a hug and kisses the top of my head. "*Ay,* your *papi* would not be happy with that answer. Happy birthday, loves. *Te amo mucho, mucho, mucho!*"

"Thanks. Love you too, Mom." I pull back. "Where's everyone else?"

"Inside!" she calls as she pulls Carter into a hug. He towers above her, but she still fawns over him.

I pass the house to our backyard and head inside the barn, where soft music plays in the background. The inside is decorated in pale coral décor, with balloons covering the back wall behind the cake, a happy birthday sign next to it, and a dozen tables that cover half of the barn floor. The rest of it has the DJ stand and a concrete dance floor. We've been holding parties here since I was little. *Mexicanos saben festejar.*

My extended family huddles in smaller groups, laughing and talking. The energy is contagious, and despite the crappy things I'm going through, the party is enough to make me genuinely smile. "*Hola,* party people!"

A chorus of, "Birthday girl! *¡La reina! ¡Mi amor!*" rings out from Carlotta, *mi abuelita,* and one of my aunts. We talk as the guys finish setting the food up, small chit chat about who's coming, or who *isn't* coming, my *sad, sad* love life (according to my aunt, who I don't care to tell about the recent Tom developments), and my job that *mi abuela* doesn't seem to understand. (So you just talk about immigrants all day? You don't actually do anything? You're just a pretty face? Ya know, comments like that.) And it's yet another topic I avoid because *ha ha,* I don't have a job anymore. But what am I supposed to tell them? The internet canceled me? They simply won't understand. Plus, I don't want to talk about it.

Carlotta sits on my lap, and I *gently* push her because she's a million years pregnant and all up in my business.

Mi abuela clucks. "Keep making that face *y se te va quedar así.*"

I manage to get out from under Carlotta and groan. "My face is not going to stay that way. Even if it did, my face is gorgeous. So who cares?"

My aunt snickers, and *mi abuela* crosses her arms and gestures to the other side of the barn to Carter, who picks up a pineapple Jarritos and makes his way over to us. "*Hola, Abuelita. ¿Qué pasa?*"

My uncle Arturo gets up to the DJ stand at the back of the barn and finishes setting up a few speakers. "Me Gusta" blares, and I cover my ears against the loud music.

Abuela throws her cane. "*Dile que le baje la pinche música.* I can hear it even without my hearing aids."

Carter yells to Arturo, who waves him off.

I laugh. "I don't think it's possible for Arturo to turn it down. You know how he works. *Todo tiene que ser ruidoso.*"

She rolls her eyes, reaches out, and pats mine and Carter's cheeks. "I love you both. But when I was your age, I was married and already had *dos bebés.*"

"Yep, not happening." I shake my head. "Babies are far off."

Carter shrugs. "If it helps, I've been thinking of adopting a puppy."

Abuela slaps his wrist. "*No, idiota. No ayuda.*"

"*Te amo, Abuela.*" I give her a kiss on her forehead, and stand up, eyeing the chocolate fountain that my cousin and dad just finished setting up, along with the food.

"*Espere,* Candy," she says, grabbing onto my hand.

"Mmm?" I raise my brows.

She takes a deep breath, which leads to a cough. "*Generalmente no hago esto, pero,* the ban on Tom is lifted."

I rub my lips together, tasting some of my gloss. "*Gracias, Abuela.* That is...unexpected."

"*Lo sé.*" She has this knowing little smirk on her face, and I don't like it. *Mi abuela* is up to something, and that's never good.

Les pops in through the side barndoor, looking as frazzled as they come. Adrian and Mateo swarm behind, pulling her arms in opposite directions. She played with them one time, and now? They're obsessed with her.

"Les, I want to dance!" Mateo shouts.

"No, let's play tag!" Adrian puts on his best pouty eyes.

She pats their heads. "Okay, boys. Sure! Um, let me just find Carter first." Our gazes lock, and she heaves a sigh. "Want to play with *Tia* Candy?"

"No," they both whine. "*Tia* Candy sucks."

I pull the boys toward me. "Excuse me? *No necesito una chancla,* do I? 'Cause I'll go get your mom right now and tell her you said the 's' word."

They shake their heads in tandem. Freaking twins. I suppress a smile, but hold onto them by the back of their shirts. "You just get here?" I ask Les.

"Uh, no. We've been outside playing tag. Hence the hair." She picks a leaf out of a clump of strands.

"*Amiga,* you need to grow a backbone and say no sometimes. They're children."

"I heard that," Adrian grumbles.

Les laughs, and I lead the three of them toward the arch of balloons that Carter waits underneath. Then, I give the twins to Carlotta before going to grab some dinner. With a plate full of tamales and cupcakes, I head to one of the tables, watching the *fiesta* happening around me. I pull out my phone, record a bit of the party, but mostly just watch. Not like I have anywhere to post the footage anyway.

I catch up with some of my relatives I haven't talked to in a while, and soon enough, my uncle is announcing over the mic that it's time for the dance off between Carter and me. It's been a yearly tradition ever since I can remember. Our families put money in boxes labeled with our names. Whoever gets the most money wins. We're fiercely competitive, and Carter won last year. Not letting that happen this year.

My bro can dance, I'll admit it. But I'm more creative, so he usually runs out of moves before me.

"What song do you choose, Candy? It is your turn, right?" Tio Arturo asks.

Carter and I stand facing each other, smiling like little kids. I'm staring up at him, but I still manage a menacing glare. "*Yo Perreo Sola.*"

He laughs. "Mom's gonna kill you."

I grin too. "That's why I did it."

Sure enough, I hear the groans of my mom *and* my dad in the background. Carlotta tells her husband, Antonio, to distract the kids with *dulces* and shakes her head.

Bad Bunny's song comes blaring through the speakers, and I can't help but giggle at my twin. He does the same, and soon we're wiping tears from our eyes as we dance. I leave all modesty out the window as I shake and dance. It's a welcome distraction from everything on my mind.

Carter unbuttons his shirt, and I glance at Les, who legit chokes on her water. He winks in her direction, and it just fuels me to dance better than he does even though I don't have a reason to…other than that I want the money.

It's a little unfair that he can strip down to show the nips and I can't. Free the nip and all that. But this is also a family function, so I go *aggressively* family-friendly. I hit the crowd with some old fashioned sprinklers and scubas—even though the song definitely doesn't warrant that.

Antonio and Carlotta uncover Adrian and Mateo's eyes, but keep their ears covered.

When we get to the last thirty seconds of the song, I bow, holding my hand out for Carter to grab.

"Truce?"

He nods. "Truce."

We dance together like we did when we were little, just a mess of tangled limbs and laughter. He twirls me. I try to twirl him, but he's way too tall.

Carter's eyes light up as if he's five. "*Dirty Dancing*?"

I shake my head. "No way. We haven't done that move in years."

"DIRTY DANCING!" he shouts, garnering cheers from everyone else.

"*Esto no va a ser bueno.*" I back up from him, covering my cheeks. This will be fine. Carter can hold me. We've done this a thousand times. Sure, it's been five years, but everything will be fine. *Está bien.*

He holds up his fingers, counting down from three...two... one.

I run toward him and jump, and he hoists me up in the air.

I'm wobbling. "Don't drop me!"

"You're fine," he groans out. "Use your core!"

My arms flap like wings. "What core? Don't—"

His left arm shakes, and his hand dips a fraction of an inch. But it's enough for me to start kicking. "OMG, put me down! Put me down! Carter, *te voy a matar!*"

"*Estás bien.* Chill!"

But I do not chill. "I'll kill—"

His hand slips from my waist right as the music ends. My foot collides with Carter's face as I fall, screaming, "Ah! I'm gonna—"

Someone grabs me around my waist from behind, and I heave. I open my eyes, staring at the ground a foot away from me. I reach out and touch it. I'm alive.

I'm folded up like an upside down V with the person holding me so my butt is against their waist. But Carter is on the floor, too, so it's not him who caught me. Their hold is making me nauseous, and I'll probably barf if they don't let me go. I place my hands flat on the floor. "Thanks for catching me. You can release me now."

The person unwinds their hold from my waist, but my feet hit the floor harder than expected, and my arms buckle. My forehead slams against the cement floor. "Ouch," I mumble into the ground.

I flip over so I'm lying on my back and heave a breath before opening my eyes.

Tom's worried gaze stares back at me. "Crap. Are you okay?"

I blink because I might have a concussion after all. "Tom?"

He glances to my dad and mumbles something I don't hear. When he leans down, he brushes my hair from my face. "Yeah. You've got quite the bruise."

Carter sits talking to Les, who pampers him. I groan. "Probably would've been worse had you not caught me."

"Oh, it definitely would've. You're welcome, by the way." He grins full lips and winks.

I groan. "Always so arrogant."

He tucks some hair behind my ear. "I'm kidding."

My family swarms, people clucking and cooing over me and Carter. It's absolute chaos, and Tom speaks in Spanish to them all as if he's been speaking it since he was little. Lowkey getting me turned on, so that concussion is probably for real.

He helps me up, and I brush invisible dust and dirt from the shirt I'm wearing. Carter is now sitting a few feet away, muttering to Les while he covers his eye. Half of the relatives are shouting at him for being *tonto* and suggesting the move, which I hope makes everyone give me more money in my box.

A few minutes later, most of them disperse, and I tower above Carter, who's still sitting. "I accept zero responsibility for that stupid idea of yours."

He deadpans and glares up at me. "If you didn't freak out, we would've been fine."

My mom points at him. "*Ay, ay, ay, Carter. Asumir algo de responsabilidad.*"

"No, I'm not taking responsibility for *mi hermana*'s stupid freak out mid-air."

Les holds her hands up. "I didn't see it. Too busy with the tamales."

Tom chuckles. "I'd say the blame should be split pretty evenly. I saw the arm wobble, bro. And you," he throws an arm around my shoulders, "were kicking like it was no one's business."

Carter and I both scowl.

"Be nice," Les chastises. "*Both* of you."

My mom nods and hugs Les. "So smart, this one. You okay Candy?"

"*Sí, Mami.* Now tell Arturo to put the music back on. I don't want all the attention on me."

"Take care of her for me, Tom? Because if she doesn't want attention, she must've *really* hit her head hard," my mom says. She turns around and tells everyone I'm fine and to resume the party shenanigans.

"What're you even doing here?" I mutter to Tom, but he knows I'm just fake-glowering.

Tom squeezes me into his side. "Your *abuela* called and told me I could come. And I couldn't miss my friend-with-benefits' birthday party," he whispers in my ear.

I roll my eyes.

He pulls away and speaks normally. "But she said *¡Te voy a dar una cachetada!* if I even look at a Sterno can the wrong way." He laughs. "That one had to go into Google Translate for me to get it. And I still don't think I fully understand. But she said it threateningly enough that I ain't even going near the buffet."

I smile at him before glaring toward *mi hermanito*. "All I know is you almost killed me, Carter, so Imma be pissed if I don't get all that money in your box." I nod toward where our dance off boxes sit on the table, people already putting bills into each one.

He shrugs. "I'm going to have a black eye, so I think I deserve something. Tom pretty much saved you."

"Yeah, but then he dropped me." I point to the top of my forehead. "Hence this."

"*La reina* of drama," Carter mumbles as he gets up and holds Les's hand.

She touches his eye. "Let's go get you some ice, boo thang."

As they walk away, I chuckle, "At least we never call each other weird names like that."

Tom raises a brow. "I'm down for it, *boo thang.*"

I pretend to gag. "Don't, *por favor.*"

His arm is around me still, and I grin up at him. "I'm happy you're here. Wanna get out of here?"

"Not so fast." He arm slides down to my waist and he turns me into him. "You still have presents. Let's dance."

It's been so long since we've danced. Probably way back in

high school long. But with his heated stare making me blush, I agree, knowing that everyone on my family tree is staring at me. They're obsessed with Tom.

"Okay," I concede.

He moves his hand to grab mine, intertwining our fingers. "You look hot."

His clothes hug every chiseled muscle, and the white shirt he's wearing makes his hazel eyes seem to glow. I draw a finger from his chest to the waistband of his jeans. "You too. Talk about a flavor overload," I whisper, winking at him.

We head out to the dance floor, going from *salsa* to hip-hop moves to everything in between. When a slow song comes on, we dance then too. I inhale the scent of him, clean and fresh like the ocean, but my gaze is right where his nipple probably lies beneath his shirt. Awkward, but at the same time, he needs to take his shirt off right now so I can confirm if that's where my stare is.

I can feel the heat of him, and it makes me squirmy. Change the subject, Candy. "So," I drawl, "how's your new place? You wanna take your friend with benefits there?"

Internally, I cringe at the name. But, I don't know what he's thinking. The last thing I want to do is get together and have people say bad things about him because of me...if he even wants to be together like that.

Taking things slow is best.

He twirls me before bringing me back to him. "Yeah, it's good. I like it a lot. Tristan and Scott are a riot, and it's always nice hanging with Ethan."

"I bet it's a party over there every night. Tristan and Scott are such players."

"Sure 'nough." He doesn't say anything else, and I let my eyes wander through the rest of the party.

Everyone seems to be slowing down. *Abuelita* is sitting in a chair, cane laid across her lap. Even my crazy uncle Rodrigo is rubbing at his eyes. My family can party hard, but when it's over, we tire quickly.

I tap Tom's shoulder. "When this ends, how about you show me your new place?"

He nods. "Yeah, I'd like that. I, uh, I need to talk to you about something, too. I got a weird DM—"

"One sec," I interrupt as the song trails out, and I signal across the room to Carter saying *let's get to presents and end this.* He gives me a thumbs up and comes my way. "Sorry, what were you saying?"

Tom forces a smile. "Nothing. It's nothing."

I want to ask what's wrong, but Carter grabs me and pulls me toward the gifts, and the party follows like we're magnets. Tradition wins, and Carter and I open up our money boxes. It *looks* like it's split evenly, but… "*Mira,* that's a hundo on top of mine, bro," I whisper and stick my tongue out.

"Whatever," he grumbles. "It's probably from creepy cousin Alma."

We spend the next hour opening up gifts. My favorites include a pair of boots from *mi tia* Arianna, a promise of free hair touch ups from my cousin Ana who colors and cuts my do, and surprisingly, the gift from Les. She got Carter and me skydiving certificates, so we both hand each other a ten dollar bill and call the bet we made earlier even. It's a pretty great gift.

I go around and thank everyone, hugging each person. By the end, I'm still alight with energy. Tom waves at me from across the room. He puts his hands in his pockets and bites his lip. And I'll be honest, I want to bite *his* lip. Hard. Shaking the thoughts from my mind, I skip over to him. "Let's get out of here."

"Say no more, my girl."

∞∞∞

Tom and I are three songs deep when *"Quiero Más"* by Ozuna comes on the playlist. Knowing what the words say in Spanish, I figure we better change it if we're gonna make it to his place.

"Talk about a throwback." I *ha-ha* awkwardly, reaching for the next button on the screen.

Tom raises a brow. "Don't change it. I've been memorizing it in Spanish."

My neck itches, and I'm about to roll the window down because it's suddenly hot in here. "Do you happen to know what the lyrics say?"

The stoplight we're approaching turns from yellow to red, and Tom brakes. He looks me straight in the eyes and nods. "Yeah, I do," he says with way too much husky than should be allowed.

Ay, this man is going to be the death of me. I gulp. *"Bien.* Cool, cool."

Problem is, then he starts singing those words in Spanish, and I have to clench my thighs. He should not be allowed to speak *español.* And the sexy fool *knows.* He knows what he's doing to me. I catch him sending little showy smirks toward me, and I growl lowly. "You're such a tease."

His eyes twinkle against the street lamps as he drives, and the car is stuffy—with the scent of his delicious cologne. I've gotta get out of here. I'm about an inch from hopping out of the car because my body can't handle sitting in here with this hot guy giving me zingy feelings.

I'm white-knuckling the center console, and when *"Quiero Más"* ends, another Spanish one comes on, and the man knows *that one too.*

"¡No mames!" I groan, debating whether it would be inappropriate to cover my ears so I don't have to hear him sing.

He laughs. For the next three minutes, I pretend I'm at some luxury resort doing beachside yoga. *Breathe in, breathe out. Estoy bien. Estoy bien.* You're zen, baby. You've got this. Settle the FREAK DOWN, kitten.

"You good?" His voice rumbles through my beachside fantasy.

"Estoy bien!" I shout too loudly, and even I cringe.

But he just chuckles again as he pulls into a new apartment complex on West's north side of the campus. I nearly jump out of his car and run.

The car shuts off. "You don't even know which room it is!" he shouts.

I run back to him and hop into his arms. He grabs my thighs and chuckles. "Happy birthday, Candy. You're a little crazy tonight, aren't ya?"

"Just hurry up and carry me across your door's threshold."

He pinches my side. "I thought only married couples do that."

I nuzzle into his neck. "Do you not see these heels I'm wearing? I don't want to walk another foot if I don't have to."

"You don't have to," he whispers into my ear, making my skin break out in goosebumps.

That's it. I lift my head and kiss him as he walks up the complex stairs to wherever his apartment is. Our mouths take time exploring each other, getting to know what we've missed for so long. His kiss is more than enough as it lights a fire in my stomach, reaching out to every part of my body.

He's hot and hard as stone thanks to his grueling college athlete schedule, and I let my fingers discover every part of him as he reaches into his back pocket for the keys. He leans away to put the key in, holding me up with just one arm. I kiss his neck, trailing from his collarbone to his ear, biting his most sensitive spot.

He groans and fumbles the key, and the second he gets it open, he yanks the key from the lock and nudges the door open with his hip, going in backwards.

His lips find mine in the dark, and I briefly hear Ethan whoop from the living room couch, "Get it!"

I laugh against Tom's mouth, but he swallows the sound and turns down a hallway. We get into his room, and he throws me on the bed. "Candy, my room. My room, Candy. You two are gonna be seeing a lot of each other."

Then he dives back to find me, putting his weight on top

of me and kissing from my stomach to my mouth. With each caress, I feel myself falling. This time, I can only hope that Tom will catch me.

Chapter Fourteen – Tom

W e're on the way to Disneyland when my phone buzzes with a text from my Dad.

Dad: *Played good your last game. Coach says you've been having two extra practices a week. Heard from any scouts coming to your games?*

Tom: *Still nothing.*

Dad: *What about the A's?*

Tom: *Scouts for them have been silent.*

Signing with the Oakland A's has been a dream of mine since I was a kid. I'd do anything to start in their minor leagues. The scouts reached out to me after high school, but I went to West instead of declaring for the draft. I know they watched my freshman year. But after striking out five games in a row, everything went radio silent from them. It's been two years, and I still haven't redeemed myself, apparently.

I've got this season, and maybe next year to catch their eye if I don't declare for the draft. My parents are more than supportive on the baseball front, but my momma would kill me if I didn't get my degree first. The chances of a professional athlete succeeding are slim, and minor league players make little to nothing in terms of contract.

But if I have to use the business degree I'm graduating in, I don't have a clue what I'll do. Heaven knows my activism isn't paying anything either.

I send a quick email to Coach asking for an update on scouts coming to games. Even if they're there for Ben Maldon, they'll still be watching the other players. My masculinity shrivels at the thought I'm grasping for second place after Maldon.

I put my phone away and glance out the window as we pass through Stockton.

Candy plays Among Us on her iPhone, but as the game ends, I see a moment of hesitation. She closes it out, clicks on Instagram, and then quickly exits out before notifications can register.

Tapping her on the shoulder, I nod toward her phone. "You good?"

She guffaws. "*Sí*, duh. Why wouldn't I be?"

I shrug and adjust myself in Carter's truck, which isn't as comfortable as it looks. "You haven't mentioned much since the whole bridge jumping thing."

The DMs I still haven't told her about linger on my mind. I finally watched them last night, and I don't have a clue what to do with them. With how happy Candy was at her birthday, I didn't want to mention it. And now...I'm scared to.

She tucks her feet underneath her and pulls her seatbelt looser. "What's there to mention? Still canceled. Still hated."

"So that's it? You just gonna sit back and watch as the career you built burns to the ground?"

Carter coughs. "Abort, dude." He coughs again.

Candy rolls her eyes. "I'm so sorry, Tom. What would you have me do since you seem to have a perfect opinion on *my* life?"

Les turns around and wiggles her phone. "Let's turn on some music! What're you in the mood for?"

"No." Candy holds her hand up to her.

Les visibly shrinks. But apparently she's grown a bit while living with Candy because she continues on in a high-pitched whisper, "Please, don't make me sit in the car while people fight. It's so awkward." Her voice holds the last syllable for two beats too long.

Little does she know, Candy and I thrive in confrontation.

And it's time for her to get out of this funk. I see her. She puts on a brave face, acting like it's fine her world has imploded on her, but it ain't fine. It's messed up.

"I'd screw the haters and get on with life," I say.

Carter snorts. "Technically, she already screwed the hater."

Candy bops him on the back of his head, and he leans forward toward the steering wheel while simultaneously cursing at her in Spanish.

Les kicks her feet on the dash, and Disney music begins playing in the background. Not quite the soundtrack I'd want for a heated discussion with me and my hot friend-with-benefits, but whatever.

"Tom," Candy smiles sweetly, "I appreciate the input, and it is *duly* noted. *Pero, es estúpido.* I made a Live, which then got me in more trouble. I'm being called a slut on an hourly, if not minute-ly basis. Another photo was released, which stirred it all up again. So let me hide in some Disney and Valentine's Day fog, and I'll figure it out when we get home."

The sarcasm is dripping off her tongue, but I humor her for a moment. "Promise? 'Cause you can't jump bridges for the rest of your life, babe."

She crosses her arms and scoffs, looking out the window and away from me. "*Sí papa, prometo que voy a mejorar este mundo.*"

She did not just call me her dad and act as if I've been grilling her for the past few weeks. I've stayed silent and supportive.

"The drama with you, I swear." I pull her toward me, loosening her seatbelt more so I can throw my arm around her.

Candy fights it and elbows me in the side, but I just chuckle and kiss the side of her head. She relents and snuggles against me. An hour later, we stop so the girls can take their *third* bathroom break this trip.

"Why they gotta pee so much?" I groan. "It's gonna take forever to get there like this."

Carter lays his head against the headrest. "You're saying. I'm the one who's driving," he mumbles as he pulls out his phone to check his blood sugar.

"You want me to drive? I don't mind taking a turn."

His phone beeps, and he grabs his insulin pump manager and presses a few buttons. "Nah, I'm fine. Glad you're coming with us, though. Heard anything from Coach about last game?"

Ben's scout was there, but it would've been nice had the scout noticed me as well. "Nothin'," I huff.

"Ah, that sucks. *Lo siento,* man." He scratches at the back of his neck. "Look, I don't want to put you on the spot or whatever, but you're in it with Candy, eh?"

"What do you mean?"

He taps on the steering wheel, and it's almost as if a blush crawls up his neck. "Just don't hurt her, alright? Last time, it took a while before she was back to her normal self. If some shit happens like that again, especially after everything with her career, I'm gonna have to throw hands."

I sputter into laughter thinking of Carter going up against me. He glares, and I quiet down knowing this is an important conversation to him. He flips me off. "Tom, I'm serious."

Solemnly nodding, I say, "Yeah, man. I hear you loud and clear. Don't worry, I'm not gonna hurt her again. Honestly, I keep waiting for her to freak and leave me. You know how flighty she is with me."

He shrugs. "*¿Sí, pero, esas son todas las chicas, no?* I mean, look at Les. Once she committed, she was committed. I think Candy is the same. I see it in the two of you. You look like love-sick puppies."

I hope not, because *that* knowledge would definitely make Candy leave. "Yeah, let's not repeat that to your sister. She's always makin' fun of y'all, and the last thing I need is her thinking we're like the two of you. No offense."

"That was out of pocket. Damn," he sings.

I chuckle as I see the girls walk out of the gas station. "Yeah, well, again, don't go around repeating that."

Candy laughs at something Les says, and her hair bounces as she walks back toward the car. She looks more carefree than I've seen her in the past few weeks, and I realize *I* was out of pocket for even bringing up the shattered remains of her reputation.

Whatever she chooses to do with that is up to her, not me. I want to keep that smile on those full mocha-lipstick-colored lips if it's the last thing I do. So when she gets into the car, I don't say a word. Instead, I grab her by her hips and pull her in backwards till she hits my chest.

An *oomph* leaves her, but I kiss the top of her head then buckle her into her seatbelt.

"Sorry about earlier," I whisper in her ear.

She grazes her hand over my chin, and her brow furrows. With a quick kiss, she says, "It's all good, *amor.*"

Chapter Fifteen - Candy

When we said Disneyland for Valentine's Day, I forgot what I was damning myself to with my best friend.

The mirror shows my reflection, light purple crop top, mermaid-patterned green booty skirt, and purple Minnie Mouse ears on top of my head. Who knew that Les likes crafting so much? She made me a mermaid skirt for this occasion. I feel sort of bad saying no. But… "I look ridiculous."

Les coos. "You look beautiful. You're the perfect Ariel."

I readjust my sleeveless top, lifting my boobs up in the process. "No. I really don't. How will I even ride the roller-coasters in this? I already have revealing photos of me online. I really don't need anymore."

She holds up a pair of black shorts. "Wear this underneath. Trust me, Tom is gonna love that top. Totes hot."

"Totes hot," I mumble under my breath.

"What'd you say?" She turns back around with a big grin on her face, naïve as always.

"Nothing. I'll put on the shorts. Thanks."

I walk out of the bathroom, well aware of how I look, and Tom sucks his lips in the moment he sees me.

"*No digas ninguna palabra.*" I glare at him.

He bites back a laugh, and I roll my eyes as I sit on the bed. Sitting next to me as I lace up my Nikes, he mimes toward where Carter is standing in front of a floor-length mirror.

Carter dons a red shirt, black shorts, and is currently scowling at a pair of ears. "She's crazy if she thinks I'm putting

these on," he mumbles, probably more to himself than anything.

Tom gets up and slaps him on the back. "Come on, Mickey.
Hot-diggity-dog, let's go!" he says in a near-perfect copy of the
mouse himself.

I grab my phone and snap a picture. People will eat this
up on Twitter. Opening the app, different captions pass across
my mind. *Wear ears to stifle girlfriend's tears. Date a Disney lover,
they said.* I chuckle to myself until...

Reality drops like Gatorade on the winning-game's
coach's head. Nothing to upload unless I want to feel like I just
stepped into a wasp nest.

Well, this sucks.

Les comes storming out of the bathroom, discarded curling iron in her hand, and a smile on her face. She jumps on
Carter's back and squeals. "You look perfect. Just put on the
ears and we'll go!"

Tom gives me wide eyes from behind the two, and I cover
my face in embarrassment for Carter. My twin telepathy con-
nection is burning, and he's sending me major SOS signals. But
I love Les, and frankly, I also love seeing my brother get tor-
tured. So I ignore the tingling brain cells.

Carter takes a deep breath. "Babe, I've got the shirt and
pants. I'm not wearing these mouse ears."

∞∞∞

He wore the mouse ears.

And, unfortunately, he's now the brunt of the inside jokes
Tom and I keep cracking to distract us from the long line to get
into Disneyland.

Tom flicks one of the ears. "Bro, there was a famous baseball player named Mickey. Now you look just like him, no
cap."

Les laughs. "Stop," she says. But it sounds more like

stawwwwwp. "He looks cute."

Holding up her phone, she shows us the picture I just took of them a few moments ago. "Everyone in the comments agrees, so you two can suck it."

Tom shields his eyes from the sun. "I would, but now that he's wearing those, I'm afraid of what I'd be sucking."

I snort as a breathless laugh comes out of me. "No, Les is right. We should get you a pair too, Tom."

"Nah, no way in hell, *boo thang*." Tom winks, and it only elicits more laughter out of the two of us.

Thankfully, Les and Carter are fairly good sports. I glance down at the cement tiles we're standing on and read the different names to pass the time. Families purchase them with little messages or pictures, and they're placed into the ground. It's always been one of my favorite things about Disneyland. Like these families are a part of the park, and for some weird reason, I get sentimental each time I see one.

The line is mostly made up of young kids too eager to get in to see the characters, and their parents who look like they could use one of my jello shots...or five. As we wait, I entwine my fingers with Tom's.

We're only about twenty feet from the entrance when I hear a family speaking Spanish behind me. I turn around, and a few people down the line is a lady kneeling down, adjusting a little girl's princess crown. She looks like she's probably three, and is decked out in Elsa gear. They look alike, so I'm guessing it's a mom and daughter.

It's adorable, really. But...wait, hold on.

The lady stands and says something to the person in front of her, but I can't hear it.

The response, though, comes loud and clear. "I can't understand you. Speak English!" the woman shouts.

A man walks up to the mom and picks up the little girl, who immediately wraps her arms around his neck, as a white woman throws out her hand. The little Elsa glances toward the woman speaking, then nuzzles her head into the man's shoulder, who looks to be the dad.

Tom nudges me. "What's going on?"

I don't glance away from the family. "I'm not sure."

The white woman readjusts her fanny pack. "We are in the United States of *America. Here,* we speak English. And your husband just cut the line!"

My feet move before I even realize it.

Tom mutters, "Come on, let's follow her," to Les and Carter, so I assume they're behind me as I walk over to the Hispanic mom and raise my brows to the white woman. "Is there a problem here?" I ask.

White Woman crosses her arms and glares at the Hispanic family. "Oh good, you're an employee? There's no line-cutting here. She can't wait in line and save a spot either. It's not allowed. I would know, I've been a patron of Disneyland for over twenty years. I'm trying to educate them. But they don't speak a word of English."

I roll my eyes at her idiocy. "Yeah, no. Not an employee here. But, you're standing in front of them. Him joining them has no effect on you. You're not educating, you're trying to cause a scene."

The white dude with Cruella De Vil, decked out with head-to-toe Goofy gear, plants a slimy gaze that stays on my chest for too long. Then he pops in with, "The rules are there for a reason, miss. We'd be able to tell them that if they spoke English. They're breaking rules."

Are they serious right now? This is so not about rules. This is solely because the family behind them isn't white. It doesn't affect them in any way, shape, or form.

The mom of the little girl taps me on the shoulder and whispers, "*Está bien. Vamos al otro lado.*"

I shake my head and squeeze her arm. "*No, no. Quédate dónde estás y no te muevas.*" They shouldn't have to move anywhere. Glancing back at the white woman, I say, "Over 40 million people in the *Estados Unidos* speak *español.* So maybe it's *you* who needs to get with the times, not them."

Grimy Goofy holds up a hand as if he's trying to silence me. "We aren't going to be harassed by you. Janet," he hisses to the white woman, "go get an employee. This is ridiculous."

A laugh bursts out of me. "Aw, Janet, you don't want to do that. If you step out of line, your great husband here can't save your spot. And then you'd be right in the same position as the beautiful family beside me. So I guess we're at a standstill here, aren't we?"

Janet licks her lips and frowns. "Bert, call someone! I'm not going to have my day at Disney ruined because these..." she throws out racial slurs like they're not big deal.

I see red and forget anything else she says. Call me a ho, call me a slut, but you do *not* get to call me that.

"Excuse me?" My voice raises, and a few people in front of Bert and Janet turn their heads to watch. "You think it's okay to use a racial slur? Who the hell do you think you are?" I snap my fingers in her husband's face. "Call someone, Bert! Let me tell them about the hate speech your *perra* of a wife just used on me."

Janet doesn't back down. She takes a step toward me and waggles her finger in my face. "I'm sick and tired of you all coming in here and making *us* the enemies when it's been you people all along!" She points to the family beside me, who are wide-eyed. "This family committed a crime, and they can't get away with it."

I push her hand away from my face. "They saved a spot in a line at Disneyland. That's not a crime, *Janet*." Her name comes out of my mouth as if it's a cuss word.

Les taps me on the shoulder. She stands, fidgeting with her hands. "I told the ticket counter what happened. They're sending someone over."

I clap my hands. "Hallelujah! I doubt Disney wants racist idiots in their park. Care to bargain?"

Janet's face turns my favorite shade of red: The exact color of the Mexican flag. Karma is a bitch, Janet.

"This is an outrage! You—"

I wave her off. The family beside me is still clearly confused. I'm sure the fact that Janet and I got in each other's faces while loudly exchanging words showed them we weren't up to any good. I turn toward them and hold out my hand. *"Lo siento mucho."*

The dad shakes my hand and hands their princess over to her mom. *"¿Qué pasó?"*

I wave them off. *"La mujer hizo comentarios despectivos. Un empleado de Disney viene a ayudar ahora mismo. ¿Podemos quedar en línea contigo hasta entonces?"*

He nods.

"¿Cómo se llama su hija?"

"Liliana."

"Que linda." I smile and hold out my hand, and Liliana high fives me.

Right then, a Disney security employee walks up in a sweater vest and paperboy hat, a somber look on his face. He asks Janet and Bert to leave, saying, "We have no tolerance for hate toward other guests, cast members, or individuals. We'll need you to come in to make a report…"

Janet and Bert protest until the Disney employee waves to security behind him. They agree to walk away, still mumbling remarks as they go. As they continue walking away, the rest gets muffled by the people around us.

Tom sidles up next to me and slings an arm around my shoulders. "Mmm, that was kinda hot."

Ah, someone's got a social justice kink. I push his face away from my ear. "We're at a children's park. Cool it, *amor*."

But what I really mean is save it for later.

I say goodbye to the family and tell them to enjoy Disney before we get back in our own spot in line, a few families ahead. And *shocker*, the people ahead and behind of us saved our spot and had zero problem letting us in after seeing that racism is alive and well as always.

My hands itch with an unforgotten desire to tweet, record, and keep the receipts. Not for clout, but to raise awareness. It's a little sad that Twitter has become like a cut-off limb, still tingling as if alive. But nope, it's a goner.

Because the *chisme* is in, and I'm still canceled.

But, canceled or not, cameras on or off, what Tom said in the car yesterday grates on me. I can't sit around and do nothing. I'm not going to stop fighting for what I believe in.

The realization lights a match in my soul. Not enough for a fire, but a flicker in the darkness. Just because social media has torn me up, down, and across, doesn't mean I'm done. I'm still here. Still a fighter.

And if that means only helping one family or just righting the wrongs that I personally witness, is that so bad?

Alright, let's be honest, it sucks. But it's better than nothing. And I think right now, I need little steps. I can't trust anyone, not after what Jake did to me.

Tom smiles. "Think someone got that on video?"

I cringe. "I hope not. I don't want to see a recorded video of myself, or a video, or a picture, for that matter, about myself for quite some time."

He stiffens, and I can only guess that it's because of everything he said in the car. But by the time we scan our tickets, he's back to cracking jokes with Carter.

I lean into Tom's side as we enter the park and walk down Main Street toward the castle. Sweet smells of ice cream cones and waffles flood my senses, and I wiggle my hips in anticipation.

Families with strollers and diaper bags too big for their bodies march toward the castle, leaving no child behind. They're quick and determined, and I'd rather not be caught in the crossfire of their snacks and sticky fingers. I pull Tom's arm and motion to the sidewalks in front of one of the gift shops. He follows, along with Carter, who has taken on the role of suburban dad and has the Disney app pulled up on his phone, zooming in on the map to check out the attraction wait times. "*Bien, entonces,* what should we do first?"

Les pops up beside him (lowkey didn't even see her disappear) with cotton candy. These two are straight out of a basic influencer Instagram account, I swear. Tom sighs and snaps a picture as Les smiles and feeds Carter a bite of cotton candy.

I glance at him with a *wtf are you doing* face. He shrugs. "She's got that white girl drip. Had to capture the moment for the two."

My head shakes of its own accord. "You gonna simp for them next?"

Pointing to his phone, he says, "Think I passed that point already."

We bust out laughing, and I snake my arms around his waist. "I stan a supportive king." I smack his butt. "Especially when he's got cake."

He steps out of my hug. "Get outta here with that nonsense."

Les holds out her half-eaten cotton candy. "Uh, hello? You two are in your own little world. We literally just asked what you want to do."

I grab a piece of the cotton candy. "Pirates?"

Carter taps on his screen. "Twenty-minute wait."

"Bruh, let's do Space Mountain!" Tom nearly squeals, and I look at him like he's really lost his mind.

"Dude, no, it's like an hour wait."

"Hmm," Les says. "Matterhorn?"

He taps a few times. "Ten minutes."

"Let's do it!" Tom booms, putting his hands around his mouth. He slaps Carter on the back, and they walk ahead, making dumb jokes that are only funny to guys.

Les and I follow behind them, finishing off the cotton candy. She throws the stick in a trashcan without stopping. "You know, I always liked the two of you as friends, but I have to say you and him in a relationship are next level. You guys are, like, actually really cute."

I playfully smack her. "You thought we'd be different? Girl, please. The only difference is physical. *Gracias,* though. I'm glad you ship."

"I'd ship you with anyone, you know that. But whew, the way Tom looks at you makes even *me* blush." She fans herself.

"*Te sonrojas por todo.*"

Les closes one eye and draws up her lips. "Not sure what you said."

I walk on my tiptoes and sling an arm around her, watching her blush, which just proves my point. She blushes at everything. "*Si, ya se.*"

She readjusts her mouse ears. "Once I learn Spanish, it's over for you *perras.*"

I cackle loud enough that Tom turns around and winks. "Oh, Les, we'll still have to work on that accent of yours."

Chapter Sixteen – Tom

As the sun sets on the Disneyland castle, it catches in Candy's hair, lighting up the strands in a show of sunset red. Her hair's a little tousled from the rollercoasters, and my curls are destroyed as well. Now, we're relaxing before the parade and firework show. She dips her spoon into the Dole Whip and sucks it off while staring right at me.

This girl.

Half her makeup is gone, but it only makes her look more beautiful, and my fingers tingle with the desire to pull her into me and never let her go. I saw the fire in her eyes when she defended that family today. If there's anything Candy loves, it's bringing people down who deserve it. And oh, did she bring those racists down.

But that DM? The one I've been trying to tell her about? It's a video. *About* her. And she said she didn't want any videos about her posted. So, even if I think it could help her, I'm gonna let her do this herself. I know this is a phase. She's gonna get that career back and be stronger than ever.

As she laughs up at me, a wide smile gracing her face and hitting me in the feels, I know it in my soul. She's gonna change the world.

Maybe it's dumb, but a part of me saw her defending that family, and the way she cooed over the little girl dressed as Elsa, and I caught feelings. Not just feelings that she'll be an icon. But big, personal feelings. Feelings I thought that the 19-year-old me had buried after I cheated on her.

It reminds me of the locket sitting against her collarbone,

and my own chain seems to burn my skin. We've laughed more today than we have in a long time, and I can't help but watch her as she relishes in her surroundings, seemingly without a care in the world.

I wish I could always make her this happy.

She leans her head against my side, 'cause everyone know she can't reach my shoulder, and says, "You want to go on one more ride before the firework show?"

"Hmm," I grab the Dole Whip from her and take a bite of the pineapple soft serve, "whatchu got in mind?"

The nearby rides to choose from are a rollercoaster, drivable fake cars, or teacups. She moves in front of me and grins with the eagerness of a mischievous child. "Teacups."

A traumatic memory fires through my mind, and I glare at her. "Bad choice."

"No, I don't think it is. Teacups, Tom!"

I've got a sickening (literally) feeling that this is not a good idea. At all. But she looks so happy that I feel bad saying no. "Date the crazy ones, they say. It'll give you a life time of adventure," I groan out.

She yanks on my arm and skips to the teacups' short line, her skirt flying up to show her black booty shorts beneath. "Toss the Dole Whip!"

"This is a bad idea." I sigh but listen to her and throw the empty plastic cup into the recycle bin. I shudder as we get close to the front of the line. "I know you remember the state fair in eighth grade."

"That was *years* ago, Tom. *Calmate.*" She waves me off as if the incident in mention didn't almost make me stop being her friend.

The ride operator is a small girl with red hair and freckles. She has on giant glasses and owns the world's tiniest waist. She looks like that one TikTok famous chick from our school. Her voice is mousy as she calls us into the teacup arena.

Lights sparkle from where they're strung up around the exterior of the ride. Now that dusk is upon us, it begins to look like a magical ride rather than one that's giving me bad anxiety of what's to come. Candy points to the pink one, that's the exact shade of her hair, with swirling blue curls. So, like the gentleman I am, I open the teacup door for her, still shaking my head.

She secures her small purse around her shoulder and hops in, gripping the teacup wheel. My body is too big for this ride, but Imma make myself fit, even if my knees barely clear the wheel in the center. Now I give her my best parental stare. "Promise you'll go slow."

And this woman decides to roll her annoying eyes. "Yes, daddy. *Ay, ay, ay.* We haven't even had dinner yet. It's gonna be fine."

The 'daddy' I can get behind. But the eyeroll? Nah. I glance at my new Jordans. "I'm just saying, these are new shoes."

The operator checks that our door is secured and makes her way around the rest of the teacups. Rules are spoken in both English and Spanish through the loud speakers, and then the ride begins. The teacups slowly begin to turn, and Candy rubs her hands together before placing them on the steering wheel like some Disney villain.

I've got a half a mind to stop her from trying to spin us. She pulls at the wheel until it begins to turn toward her but then pouts. "Come on, Mr. Muscle. Help me out here."

Instead, I fish out my phone and point it right at her. "Nah, I'm recording for video proof that you went against my wishes. Should've known you'd wait until Carter was gone to suggest this ride."

She struggles with the wheel, her small biceps flexing as she goes at it from a different angle. "Gen Z and their stupid receipts," she huffs out.

It seems she's determined to make a scene with or without my help. A few moments of struggle later, I move my foot away from the wheel where I'd successfully slowed her efforts with my toe. She squeals as it becomes easier to turn, and she doesn't give up, spinning us as fast as she can.

I don't drop the phone, but our eyes meet above it as if it's not there.

Her smile lights up the surrounding area, and everything behind her is a blur as we twirl. We're in our own world, and I'll admit that it's a little peaceful just being able to see her.

I'm even excited to see what my phone captures. Will the video be as blurry and exhilarating as it feels now?

Despite everything that's happened between us in our past, here in the present, it's perfection. I scoot closer toward her. She scoots closer to me, and turns the wheel one more time. Then, she reaches up to my cheeks and pulls me into her.

She tastes like pineapple and sugar. I tuck her hair behind her ear and grip her face. Parting her lips with my tongue, I forget about our surroundings and make out with her, not caring if anyone sees. When I finally break away and wrap an arm around her shoulders, she scowls at me.

"Well, fine. I'll keep kissing—"

She folds in half and spews throw up all over my shoes. Everything, and I mean literally everything, she's eaten today seems to come out.

"Shoot!" I yell and grab her hair, pulling it back. She keeps barfing, so I rub her back as our teacup continues to spin, albeit slowed a little.

When she finally stops, the ride does too. Candy puts her hands to her forehead. "Don't. Say. A. Word."

I grab a water bottle from the backpack I've been carrying around and hand it to her. Signaling to the ride attendant that we need help, I mutter, "I'm trying, Candy. Swear. But..."

"*Lo siento mucho,*" she whines.

I nod, solemn, but also a little annoyed. "Bro, I told you so. You plus spinning rides don't mix."

She groans. When I glance around, I find Les and Carter standing on the other side of the teacup ride's gate, oblivious to what's happening here. They smile and wave. I hold up a hand and probably grimace. Not gonna lie, throw up smell plus *me* don't mix. I'm feeling queasy sitting in it, but the attendant is taking her sweet time with everyone else.

"*Sí,* I made a bad call," Candy agrees.

When she holds out the water bottle, I take it from her and dump the rest of it onto my shoes, washing away the yellow throw up and chunks. Despite it all, I'm already over being pissed at her. "Just be glad I love you," I mumble.

It slips out. My hands still with the empty water bottle mid-air. Shit. I wasn't supposed to say that. I didn't even know I *felt* that. Again? Still? Maybe I've always been in love with her.

Seeing her today, watching her unguarded expressions and the pure happiness that she exuded, it transported me to earlier times. *No*, it reminded me of earlier times. But now that I finally have her back, the feelings are even stronger.

I want her. All of her. The sad days, the happy days, the days where I want nothing more than to hate her, because no matter what the days bring, no matter what happens from here on out, I'm still gonna love her.

Candy DeLeón is always going to be it for me.

So I'm not gonna regret saying it. How could I? My feelings have existed all this time. I thought in Mexico that seeing her and being with her again brought back small feelings. Thought I'd caught another crush. Thought I'd liked her. But it's always been more than that. My feelings have lived just beneath the surface, waiting to be jumpstarted since the night we broke up two years ago.

So despite the fact that she just upchucked on me, I breathe out the insecurities of the past and say it again. "I love you."

She looks up at me with big green eyes, her face pale and eyebrows raised. Then, a smile creeps up her face as if it's been waiting to appear. "*Te amo,* Tom."

Chapter Seventeen - Candy

As my professor drones on about the structure of the political system in America versus the rest of the world, I swipe through the week-old photos of Disneyland on my phone. It's weird having photos for no other reason than to preserve memories. I'm so used to getting the best photo so I can post it to Instagram and Twitter. But now?

These photos exist for the sole purpose of showing me how much fun I had.

I still itch to get back online. At what point is my silence worse than what I did in the first place?

I've checked Instagram and Twitter a bit. Jake Marx never responded to my last message calling him a clout chaser. It does seem like the messages have slowed. Same with comments and everything else. Granted, that could be due to the fact that I turned off comments.

Not sure if that means I'm truly canceled or if the keyboard warriors have moved onto someone else. Maybe I should test the waters. Post something on my story?

Nothing about myself. But...a new report came in about an ICE detention center in Arizona. Children and adults alike are being slowly poisoned due to the chemicals they're using to clean the facilities. Reports of burns, irritated eyes, and worse have come through.

I find the article and upload it to my stories, linking the signup form for People Power, an organization that helps prevent family separation. Fear burns in the cavern of my soul, and I quickly exit out of the app and try to focus on class for the remaining ten minutes.

My phone buzzes against my thigh.

Les: *You're back! I saw your story. Love it. Great intro back into insta, I think.*

Candy: *Meh, we'll see what everyone else thinks. Crossing my fingers.*

The professor dismisses us, and as I head out of the classroom, I glance at my email. A few different assignment notifications, an email from our landlord saying rent is due, and...

A new email pops up.

To: Candy DeLeón

From: Grace Brooks

Subject: Interview

I know you said you weren't ready for an interview. But, hoping this might change your mind.

Attached to the email is an article with a photo of Jake Marx with a woman on his arm. The title reads: *America's Sweetheart Details How He Got A Liberal Under Him*

It's a trashy site I've never heard of, but seriously? How is this okay? I click the link.

Los Angeles, CA – Rumors began nearly one month ago about political activist Candy DeLeón and son of Joanna Marx. Since then, both parties have remained quiet, neither speaking to media outlets or posting on social media other than retweets or comments. Now, Jake Marx is speaking out about the forbidden relationship that took place between him and DeLeón.

My footsteps slap against the concrete, and I pocket the phone before heading into West's library. The smell of coffee and frothed milk hits me the second I pass through the door, but it doesn't calm me down.

If anything, it makes me more mad. The room is nearly empty, so I throw my stuff on the nearest tabletop and sit down in a beanbag before scanning the rest of the article. According to Jake, we were in a secret relationship, but it ended badly in January. He even details how I was open to hearing his thoughts and views on political issues. And the best part? I just couldn't resist his sweet gestures, but in the end, nice guys truly finish last, and he's just trying to move on.

All of it is as real as freaking *Frozen*. Problem is? *Frozen* is still the Disney movie everyone talks about, and I can't just *let it go*.

I collapse deeper into the beanbag and text Tom, Les, and Carter the link.

Tom: *You need to make a statement.*

Les: *What a douche!!!!!*

Les: *Screw him!*

Carter: **disliked Screw him!**

Carter: *Please don't, that'd only lead to more problems.*

I roll my eyes. Carter's why I never include these three in group texts.

Candy: *What do I even say?*

Tom: *Where you at?*

Candy: *Library.*

Tom: *Be there in five.*

Carter: *I've got an appointment with the team doc. ¿Estás bien?*

Candy: *Sí. See you at home.*

Les: *I'm at my internship, but I'll see you ASAP.*

Grace's email started all of this. First, she corners me after the two catty girls. Now, she sends me this cryptic email. Gotta respect the hustle of a future journalist, but *damn*.

Now my first post after this scandal is going to be, yet again, another apology. How many times can you apologize for the same thing?

According to Tom, a million. Speaking of him, Tom peeks his head over the top of my beanbag and kisses my temple. "'Sup, girlfriend?"

I raise my brows. "Girlfriend, eh? I don't remember you asking me *that*."

His face pinches as his eyes roll. "Bet. You said you love me. So...girlfriend."

I tap the brown bean bag in front of me with my foot, and

he sits down, laying his backpack across his lap. "Alright, *mi novio*. Let's plan this statement out."

I begin typing on my Notes app until there is a full paragraph. Shoving it in Tom's face, he snatches the phone away, takes one glance, and tosses it back toward me. Shaking his head, he says, "Maybe without so many cusswords."

"They're in Spanish. Jake Marx wouldn't even know what they mean."

Tom flattens his lips and gives me a chastising look. "Google translate, girl."

I wave him off. "It's wrong like eighty-five percent of the time," I mumble, but delete the statement and start typing something new.

In light of recent events, I'd like to speak out about the allegations of a long-term romantic relationship between me and Jake Marx. In no way, shape, or form is this allegation correct. I have never had a romantic relationship with Jake Marx, and do not plan to ever have one. I only met Jake Marx once, and while I regret the events that transpired between us, we have not—

I glance up from my phone. "You think I can put up screenshots of mine and Jake's DMs on Twitter? I called him a clout chaser and told him not to talk to me. Also, he sent me multiple messages trying to hook up with me again when we got back from Mexico."

Tom picks at his bottom lip and slowly cocks his head side to side. "Eh, screenshots can still be photoshopped. I don't know if you wanna bring attention onto it more, ya know?"

Nodding, I finish typing.

--not been in contact since that night. I apologize again for the hurt that my actions have caused and—

What else can I say? I can't "educate" myself on not hooking up with douches.

--and hope that we can step away from this issue and look to the future of helping minorities and immigrants together once again.

Tom taps his foot to some invisible beat while staring up at the glass ceiling where an overcast sky shines through. I clear my throat, and he glances at me.

He reaches for my phone and scans the screen, face unreadable the whole time. Nodding, he says, "That'll do."

Sighing, I grab it back. Then, I type the same statement in Spanish and screenshot the note. I twist my legs underneath me and sit higher in the beanbag. My face is in a perpetual state of cringe as I upload the picture to my Instagram without a caption. Talk about a ruined aesthetic.

This is the...what? Third stage of grief? Fourth? Or maybe we've just nestled into acceptance at this point. My career is no longer a career.

I will forever hold the ~~relationship~~ hook up with Jake Marx on my shoulders. Why isn't anyone wondering who released these photos? I know I am. But no, there hasn't been one article about who slandered my career.

Waiting until the first notifications roll in, I go to Tom's profile, which I haven't seen in...a month now? And whew, child, he has some new pictures—and he broke the hundred thousand follower mark. When I did that, we threw a party at our apartment with Carter, Rykard, Jared, and a few others. Tom got me cake and number balloons that spelled out "100K," and then he and Carter shoved my face into the cake as I blew out the candles.

The picture broke a new like record on my profile.

But Tom didn't even mention that he broke that milestone. I would've done something for him—canceled career or not. I look up, and he dances while tapping his foot as he stares at his phone.

My fingers itch to take a picture of him, but I settle for stalking his new pictures instead. The first one is of him on the baseball field, biting his lip and winking.

Freaking flirt.

I suck my teeth and subtly screenshot the picture because that one will definitely get use later. The next post is him at Disneyland. But it's a carousel of photos. I scroll through them. A picture of him with a Mickey Bar, another of him standing in front of the castle (looking like a snack), and a picture of his stained white high tops. From my barf. How endearing.

My finger swipes across the screen to the last picture. I gasp, then disguise it as a choking cough because I don't want Tom asking why I'm gasping. The last picture is of him. With me. Arms wrapped around his neck in a piggy back, hands covering his eyes, and sticking my tongue out.

Why didn't he say anything?

I glance up, and of course, he's still oblivious.

Because men.

I tap on the comments and it pulls up the most popular ones amongst the two thousand of them.

Um, anyone else peep that last pic?

Looks like fun! Hope y'all enjoyed it! (This is from a mutual activist friend, so doesn't count.)

Is #tandy fr happening right now?

Dw, we know our mans is smarter than to get with her again.

They're just friends. I saw it in an interview with her.

So we just gonna ignore the fact homegirl jumped from the right to the left in a matter of weeks?

Unpopular opinion: I think they're cute. I'm here for it.

Are...are we un-canceling her?

If they're together, imma lose it. Cut the cameras...deadass.

I NEED TEA.

Someone drop the chisme.

"What're you over there buggin' out for?" Tom's voice makes me flinch.

I put the phone screen down on my leg and flip my hair off my shoulder. "Nothing. Anyway, um, wanna head to our...I mean...my house and hang out?"

He uploaded a photo of me. That's definitely DTR territory. *No, no nos estábamos besando.* But it's not like a kiss has to be uploaded to show two people are together.

Does he *want* his career over? What the hell was he thinking? It's one thing to call me his girlfriend. It's another to publicly post it.

He stands up and stretches before slinging his backpack on his shoulder. Holding out his hand, he shakes his head. "Nah, I've got a better idea."

I grab his hand, and he pulls me up. Leaning down to grab my bag, I say, "What's your idea this time?"

He shrugs. "You trust me?"

After he uploads a picture of us and declares his love for me in the only way Gen Z knows how to, *sí, por supuesto.* Plus, the last time I trusted him led to us making out in a junkyard, so my answer is a resounding, "*Sí.*"

For whatever reason, saying yes to him makes my stomach feel like it just became home to those jumping beans my dad used to buy me whenever he went on a business trip. Half my life knowing Tom, and *siento mariposas en mi estómago.*

Lacing our fingers together, he marches ahead, pulling me along with him.

My chest dances with a bubbly feeling as we nearly run through the bottom floor of the library, but I tamper down any laughs since everyone in here is studying. As we round the corner and Tom pushes the door open into the brisk winter air, I shiver in my long sleeve. It may not be *cold cold,* but it's California cold, and I should've brought a jacket.

I skip to his side, still holding his hand. He rubs his thumb over my pointer finger, and a little trail of lightning follows the movement. I squeeze his hand as two guys rush past us, throwing a football.

"Don't they know football season is over?" Tom mumbles, turning his head to look at them again.

"Baseball is king now." I give him a little rawr with my claw nails. "Especially Black baseball kings."

He nods and lets go of my hand to mimic placing a crown on his head, which (for whatever reason) makes me want to grip his hair and pull him on top of me. But we're walking in the middle of campus, so it'll have to wait.

Try telling that to my body, though.

"Don't you forget it." His tongue moves across his teeth as

he opens his mouth, and I really hope whatever he's planned includes me, him, and his bedroom with no roommates home.

"If I forget, will you punish me?" Now my toes are curling in my Doc Martens. Heeeelllllp.

We step down off the sidewalk and into the parking lot. His Jeep sits a few spots in on the left, and as I move to the passenger side, Tom comes up from behind and gently pushes me up against the door with my cheek resting on the glass. He sweeps my hair off my back, trails his finger across the necklace he gave me, the one I haven't taken off since, and leans into me from behind, whispering, "No, I won't punish you." His mouth captures my ear lobe, and his teeth play with my earring. "I'll just remind you of what really makes me a king."

When he gets off of me, I crave the weight of his body. The breath I didn't know I held whooshes out of me, and now my body is even more upset. Like I said, me, Tom, *y su cama.*

My knees may be jelly, but I manage to open the door and hop in, immediately connecting my phone to the Bluetooth. Putting on Taylor Swift's new album, I buckle in and turn up "Exile."

I'm vibing as he starts the car and pulls out of the lot, but then...

"Uh, why are you turning right, *mi amado*?" I snap my fingers near his ear.

Tom's wearing this little grin that I don't like. Nah, he actin' weird.

Silence. He licks his lips, but doesn't say a word. I fold my arms and stick my legs up on the dash. "You better be taking me up to make out hill, *idiota.*"

His deep chuckle reverberates through me. "*Cojelo suave.*"

I slap his arm and laugh. "Do not adopt that from Carter. Just because we went to Puerto Rico senior year does not mean you guys get to say that. It sounds freaking dirty."

He shrugs and places his elbow on the center console, tilting his head toward me as we slow to a stop at the light. "Even better."

Saltwater and spice wraps around me, so I lean in and kiss him, pulling at the collar of his shirt. His slim gold chain tickles my finger. I bite his lip as I pull away. "Take me to *su casa por favor, amor.*"

A car honks behind us. The light is green, so Tom guns it and switches lanes once through the intersection. We're headed toward Downtown Sacramento, which is near my parents' house. So...why?

"Can't take you home just yet. But, how 'bout this? We do what I have planned, and then I'll take you back to your place. It's game night, if you forgot."

"I didn't forget." I snort in disbelief. But yeah, I totally forgot.

He cocks a brow, and I raise my hands to say *what're you looking at?*

"Anyway," he continues. "We do what I got planned, head to game night, and we can watch a movie together or something, yeah?"

I groan. "Are we in high school? Grab the chocolate sauce and whipped cream, and we'll head back to *your* place. Right now. Forgo your plans and game night. Deal?" I give him my Instagram-worthy smile and frame my face with my hands.

He draws his lips in a pout. "Tempting, but no. Candy Ariana Maria DeLeón, I need your help."

I glance out the window. Freeway passes by, trees and cars blurring. "Help with what?"

"Hey." He snatches my hand and makes me look at him. "Do you trust me?"

"Ehhh," I say, wiggling my hand in the air.

He laughs as he takes the nearest freeway exit. It's been a few months since I've been down in good ol' Sac Town, so not sure where we'd be going.

I look at the tall buildings ahead, across the Sacramento River. We drive on Tower Bridge as we head into the middle of Downtown. He turns right and heads to Southside Park. I sigh. "Can you just tell me where we're going? Why are we here?"

"Eh, where's the fun in that?" He grins.

I let out a half-groan, half-scream as he pulls into some paid parking lot. Glancing across the street as he parks, I freeze.

A group of people walk together, and I'd recognize their type anywhere.

I lock the car and shake my head. "Absolutely *not. ¿Eres estúpido?* Take me back to West, *ahora mismo.*"

He leans his forehead against the steering wheel. "Nah, can't do that."

I'm about to go full Latina on him. Tom Walker just brought me to a freaking protest. What on earth was he *thinking?*

Chapter Eighteen - Tom

Candy crosses her arms and stares out of the car window at the different people passing by.

I knew she'd put up a fight, just not this much. Turning toward her, I place my hands on her shoulders. "It's small. No one will even notice you're there."

She shakes me off like I'm a barbed hook. "That's the biggest cap I've ever heard. Everyone will know!"

"How will they know?"

"Thanks to you and that Instagram photo you uploaded of us, people are already on high alert. Not to mention the apology I *just* posted. Plus, you're going to be there. Everyone loves you. *El hombre perfecto*," she mocks.

But my mind is elsewhere. She saw the picture I uploaded of her? Good. I wanted to upload even more. "You saw the picture?"

"Yeah. Today." She pulls out her phone.

I snatch it from her. "People liked it, Candy. People like *you*. People like *me*. They like us *together. Cuando estamos...*" I close one eye to think how to best say this without freaking her out. "*Cuando estamos juntos, todo es...todo es más fácil.*"

She better know I'm getting serious if I'm speaking Spanish to her.

She sighs, which sounds more like a whimper. "You're the only one who thinks being together makes things easier. Everyone in the world hates me right now, Tom."

"That ain't true."

"It is." She brushes the hair from her forehead.

Another group of five pass by us, posters in hand. Yeah, I brought her to a protest. I let her go easy at Disneyland, and I didn't push the conversation any more after the car ride. But now? We've been home for a week, and it's time she gets back into her activism. People need her. *I* need her.

"Who's to say that Joanna and Jake Marx won't be here? She's running for senate." Candy's lip sticks out in a cute pout. "Tom, I can't."

I lift her chin and kiss her forehead. "Please. It's not the same when you're not here with me. We won't stay long. If things get out of hand, we leave. I got a game tomorrow, and you don't need any bad attention your way. We'll stay for a couple hours, and we'll bounce if we see them. I swear."

She closes her eyes, and I watch as her throat bobs. "This protest is about that boy who was shot? He's fine, right?"

I lean back against the door and nod. "Yeah, but a journalist went through public records and found that people are dying under the police chief's command. *Black* people."

"This isn't even what I usually protest, Tom. It's going to look weird that I'm here." She bites her thumbnail, but we came all this way, so I'm not going down without a fight.

I toss her phone back and scowl. "So you can fight for immigrants but not Black rights? That's how it's gonna be?"

"*¿Qué chingados?* You know that's not why." She huffs, but I know my plan is working. "Why would you even say that?"

I clench my jaw and look away from her, rolling my eyes in the process. "If the shoe fits."

"It doesn't freaking fit. I just told you that's not why. *Mentiroso.*" She laces up her Doc Martens and opens the door. "Get the hell out of the car. You want my help? Fine. But you're dealing with the aftermath when the protest turns from being about police brutality to the whore that just showed up." She slams the door and exhales forcefully.

Mussing my hair, I take a few deep breaths, clench my fist in satisfaction, and get out of the car. As I round the corner, she inhales quickly and gasps. "You just said all that crap to get me out of the car, didn't you?"

I pull her into me. "It worked, didn't it?" I give her a quick kiss before unlocking the trunk. "And don't call my girlfriend a whore."

She shrugs. "*¿Por qué no?* It's what everyone else calls me."

Nah, she's not about to think that's okay. I stop the trunk in mid-air. "*I* don't. Les doesn't. Carter doesn't. Jared doesn't. Ethan doesn't. Rykard, the man with the most body count of all of us, doesn't even refer to himself as that. Erase the word from your mind. For real, I don't want to hear you say that again. I love you, and I'm not gonna stand back as you call yourself a whore."

She waves me off. "What're you going to do?"

I give her a hard stare. "Bet."

Rolling her eyes, she concedes. "Whatever."

Grabbing the posters from the trunk, I shake my head in defeat. She's gotta stop referring to herself like that. People are going to do it as long as she allows it to happen.

Candy glares at the posters as if they're a living, breathing representation of Hell. Her gaze flits to me, and she chews on her full lower lip like bubblegum.

A notification pops up on my Apple Watch from a friend asking where I'm at, but I ignore it and step toward Candy. Placing an arm around her waist, I squeeze her toward me. She stands up on her tiptoes and laces her arms around my neck, pulling me into her. Our lips softly touch, and when I hear a small gasp, I take the opportunity to part her lips with my tongue and softly tickle her back.

She giggles into my mouth, so I push against her hips until she backs up into the trunk of my Jeep. I snake my hand around her hips and downward to the crease of her thighs. Just when I know I'm about to have her as putty in my hands, I pull away, leaving her wanting more.

Her cheeks are flushed as she drops her chin.

Smiling like Lucifer himself, I say, "Finish the protest, and we can finish this."

She busts out laughing. "*Ay Dios mío,* you're cheesy."

Strike one to my ego. Girls are ruthless. I wipe pretend dust off of my shoulders. "That was sexy, whatchu mean?"

"Grab the posters, and let's go," she mutters.

It's the satisfaction of knowing that I won, for me.

With arms full of poster board, we walk toward the capitol, passing fellow protesters along the way. A few of my friends stop me, and I introduce Candy and chat for a few minutes before moving on. It's been a while since Candy and I have been to a protest together. Though she may have gotten me started in this, it's something I'm passionate about without her too. The MLB has always been the end goal, but if I can use my position in the MLB to speak out against abuse or unfair treatment of Blacks and other minorities, why wouldn't I? It just makes me want to reach the MLB even more.

With each step, I see the nerves coiling around Candy. Usually, protests are her happy place. She's completely herself and at ease. But, now? She's jumpy. I find her flinching when we pass any tall white dude, and her fingers are red, not from the cold, but from wringing them as we walk. She laces her hand through mine and takes a calming breath. "I like watching you like this."

I chuckle. "Me? What do you mean?"

"Just the way you interact with everyone. It's admirable. All-encompassing. Definitely a turn on," she says, winking as she draws up her lips in a kiss.

Her words are sincere, but I can tell she feels awkward. A cool breeze blows through as we wait at a crosswalk. I mull over the thoughts in my head before responding, "I think that's how people used to look at you, too, Candy."

She smiles and glances to the ground.

I trace her cheek with my finger. "They'll still look at you like that. You just have to get back out there."

Her gaze is unsure. "Let's just focus on the protest, okay? I don't want to draw any attention toward me."

I nod and respect her wishes, despite what I want. The crosswalk turns to walk, and we head across the street to the capitol. Meeting up with the other people in my protest group, I hand out some of the signs we brought. Everyone holds their signs peacefully, some chanting "Fire the chief."

I hand Candy the sign that says NO GOOD COPS EXIST UNDER A RACIST CHIEF and hold one of my own.

The energy is somber but infectious, and we link arms, chant, dance, and hold posters demanding that Eric Girk be investigated and fired. Too much pain and heartache has been caused under his intolerant reign.

Though the recent shooting didn't cause a death, it was grossly negligible, and now the young man is in the hospital with a shattered femur. He cooperated, and he was still shot.

A few people manage to walk in and out of the Capitol, glancing at the protesters before they shield their faces. News cameras point toward us to film, and it seems some networks are live-streaming everything with reporters that narrate what's going on.

We stand tall, listening to those who speak out on megaphones, holding our signs and chanting for change. Candy still flinches whenever someone calls her name, so I place my hand against her back, which seems to calm her for a second or two.

She talks to some people she knows, and also makes friends with a few others. No one mentions the scandal, but I see the trepidation on her face whenever someone strikes up a conversation.

An hour in, a reporter comes up to me. "We're interviewing some of the protestors. Would you be interested?"

I glance toward Candy, and she nods encouragingly. Worry is traced in her irises, but when I give her a questioning face, she shakes her head and waves me along.

Turning back to the reporter, I agree. "Yeah, absolutely. I'd love to."

"Great. What's your name?"

I clear my throat. "Tom. Tom Walker."

"Nice to meet you, Tom. I'm Nancy. Are you a student at a local university?"

"Yeah, I'm a baseball player over at West U."

We talk for a few moments about why I'm here and what I've done in the past before the cameraman signals we're about to go live on air. She holds a microphone in front of her, smiling at the camera. The cameraman puts up his hand and counts down from three...two...one.

Her voice comes out smooth and strong. "I'm Nancy Farrow. We're here in Downtown Sacramento, live, as the protest against Eric Girk and the recent shooting of Paul White occurs. For the better half of the day, individuals of all backgrounds and ages have been chanting, singing, and holding signs, demanding for Eric Girk to be fired as police chief." She turns toward me and gestures. "Here, we have West U student, Tom Walker, who has led a group of students here at the protest. Tom, why are you all out at the protest today, and what do you hope the outcome will be?"

I rub my hands together. It's a little nerve-wracking being on TV. "Yeah, Nancy, we're here today because everyone is tired of what's happened under Chief Girk's leadership. With the recent shooting of Paul White, it's impossible for us to stay silent. We're not going to stand down, and we hope that the city understands that something has to change. We want Eric Girk fired and for his past judgments to be looked at again to free the incarcerated men and women who could be innocent."

Nancy nods along, her blonde hair bouncing. "What would you say about how the protests are going thus far?"

"They've gone great. Everyone's been calm and collected, and it's been a peaceful, but direct protest. I'm really optimistic that the city will put the desires of the Black community at the forefront of their operations. This isn't political. It's about basic human rights. Paul was innocent, and I know there are others who were hurt or killed under Girk's leadership that are innocent as well. We're just hoping to draw attention and demand the change we all deserve."

Nancy smiles. "Well, you heard it live. We've been watching the protests around surrounding cities, but this one at the capitol is clearly the largest. Despite the many people here, there's been no misconduct..."

Two voices break through my focus.

"What the hell are you doing here?" one says.

"Look who crawled out of her witch cave. Nice to see you, Kira."

Candy and my sister. You've got to be kidding me.

I'm on edge as Nancy continues talking, gesturing to me. I'm sure I look like a deer in headlights, but it's live TV, and I can't do anything.

They continue bickering in the background. Two of the fiercest personalities I know, battling just a few feet away as the news stations record the protest.

I silently beg God to end this interview before Nancy captures their dispute, further ruining Candy's career.

Chapter Nineteen – Candy

My stomach burns as I turn around and glance at Tom's sister, Kira. She stands half a foot taller than me, arms crossed, looking down her nose at me like I'm a stale McDonald's french fry forgotten between the seats of her car. Her skin is glowing bronze as if she just got a tan, her lips are perfectly puckered and shiny red, and her lashes reach her brows. She looks better than when I saw her last.

As a woman of fashion, I'll admit, she looks good. But as a woman of reason, I know she is not my friend, so I don't compliment her.

"Look who crawled out of her witch cave. Nice to see you, Kira." I nod, and try not to raise my voice because I don't want negative attention or the people filming to capture whatever it is she's gonna say to me. But I can feel the blood coming to my cheeks, and like a snake, I'm ready to strike.

She brushes her platinum and gray braids off of her shoulder. "Where's my brother?"

I point to a few cameras where the top of Tom's head pokes above. Within a few hours, it's as if he's grown even larger in my mind. Usually at protests, I'm so busy organizing things that I don't really pay attention to Tom. I pay attention to everyone as a whole, as a group of people, but individuals take a backseat. If I'm being honest, I can't even remember the last protest I went to with Tom when I wasn't the one who organized it.

But he's so much more than what I thought. He's not just a small activist who comes to the protests I throw. He cares, he believes, and he's working to change things—with or without me.

I've been so busy with myself that I lost sight of the individuals who make a difference, even without a platform like mine. Let's add a few more points to my vain-o-meter.

Makes me feel a little stupid, honestly.

So I'm not going to ruin his interview because his rude AF sister showed up. I cross my arms. "He's being interviewed. What're you doing here? Been a while since I saw you at a protest."

She scoffs. "What're you doing here? I thought your career was over."

"Aw, you're keeping tabs on me? How nice of you." I shake my head and glance to the side, not wanting to look at the face that's so similar to Tom's.

Why is she such a *perra?*

Kira laughs as if she's an uppity character from *Gossip Girl.* So *fresa.* "Only to be sure you stay the hell away from my brother."

I square my shoulders and stand taller. Granted, it doesn't help because I'm short AF, but it does boost my confidence. *¿Qué es su problema?* "Look, I'm not going anywhere. Things have changed between Tom and I. Maybe it's time we call a truce. I'm sorry I beat you at the middle school talent show. Time to get over it, love."

She takes a step toward me, too close, so I stumble backward. "*Ay Dios mío,* what're you doing?"

Is she tryna catch these hands? 'Cause I'll throw 'em up, *lo juro.*

As she leans toward me with a sneer on her lips, Tom grabs her bicep and yanks her backward. He looks at both of us, and his eyes are full of disappointment as he slowly shutters them. His fist rests on his nose and he heaves out a sigh. "I was trying to do something good. I'm over there, minding my own business, and I hear two petty ass chicks going at it."

His glare bounces between the two of us as if he's a dad.

When it lands on me, I give him a wobbly sideways smile. He squints, holds up a finger, then turns toward Kira. She flips him off, which to be honest, I could kinda respect.

If we didn't hate each other so much.

"I just saw you're here with Noah, so please behave," he groans. "And Candy, give me five minutes and we'll head out. I have to go talk to a few people. You better hope the cameras didn't pick up your conversation."

Now I feel a little bad, but as he walks away, I get a look at that booty and commit to making it up to him later.

Kira scans the crowd. "Try not to let your hoeing mess up my brother's career too, or we'll have more issues. Think you can do that?"

I bite my cheek and give her two slow blinks. "Bet, hon'."

She gives me one last eyeroll before she walks away. And it's just another one of our many exchanges over the years, but my stomach jumps. She's right. Not that she knows the whole situation, but I could mess up Tom's career.

So why doesn't he care?

I look over to where he chats with some of the other protesters. It comes so natural to him. He's an icon, the *guapo* man who's held my heart since high school.

He laughs at something they say and gestures to the reporter, who shakes hands with everyone. I'm sure they've finished recording or he wouldn't have come over to Kira and me, but it still looks as if he's camera ready. Everything about him is alluring, from the way his nose crinkles when he talks about something he's passionate about to the way he fumbles with his thin gold chain when he grabs the back of his neck.

I really do love him. So much so that my gut roils. I try to swallow down the nausea, but it doesn't help. The crowd seems to crawl inwards, so I weave my way through the bodies until I get closer to the front. Closer to open space where I can breathe.

It's been a peaceful protest, one that's well-documented and will hopefully get the result of firing police chief Eric Girk.

Still, a couple police officers stand beside the capitol's steps as if we're dangerous people.

I lick my dry lips and take a deep breath without everyone surrounding me. The hair on my neck stands up, and I get goosebumps on my arms. An eerie sense that I'm being watched washes over me like an ocean of dread. I blink and snap my head up, scanning the crowd for any danger.

My heart races, but I don't see anything amiss in front of me. Still, I arch my back as if someone might stab me and turn around. My breath becomes a sharp inhale as I catch gazes with Jake Marx, standing on the bottom capitol step as if he doesn't have a care in the world. A tailored jacket sits on top of a checkered suit shirt with perfectly pressed slacks. He looks as if he stepped off of an Armani ad.

I rub my arms and narrow my eyes, sending him all the hate in the world. Though we exchange no words, I can read it all in his stare.

Part of me never wants to speak to him again. The other part wants to strap him into an interrogation chair and ask how he did it. How'd he get the elevator footage? Because no one else could've. He was the *only* person who knew.

Except Tom, a dark voice whispers inside me.

But I won't entertain that. It *had* to be Jake. I itch to get my hands on him—to strangle him for everything he's put me through. *Pendejo.* He's the scum of the earth.

My eyes burn, and I feel as if I'm staring into the abyss of a canyon. So much space stretches between the two of us, but with each step he takes, it's a bullet to my heart. Just a few moments of my time made him popular while knocking me off of my pedestal.

But I won't give Jake the satisfaction of seeing me cry. I straighten my imaginary crown and hold his glare, not even daring to blink. It makes me feel hollow, broken, and quite frankly...used.

The worst part is no matter what I do, I don't even faze him. In fact, he rubs his thumb across his jaw and over his full lips, cocks a grin, and winks before coming within two feet of me. "Well, well, well, if it isn't the woman who blocked me on Twitter."

I shake my head. "If it isn't the man playing the victim card. Poor baby, were you that hurt when I didn't call?"

He chuckles, and the sound grates on my ears. "Why are you here, Candy?"

"Certainly not for you. I'm here for the protest."

Glancing over my shoulder, he combs the crowd. "Is your beard here, too?"

Ice fills my veins. "Excuse me?"

He lifts a shoulder. "The guy you hitched your bandwagon to. Saw the picture of you two on his page. Also got sent some video. Though, I have to say, it isn't doing much for your reputation, is it?"

The fact he thinks I'm using Tom makes me want to throw up. That's not what's going on, but I'm not going to waste my breath defending Tom to a Marx. "How'd you get the pictures, Jake? I deserve to know."

"You think I leaked them? Why would I do that?" His face is unreadable. But deep within me, *yo sé,* Jake planned this. All along, nothing was a coincidence. Call it *brujería* or call me a *curandera,* but it's never been more clear than now: It was never about me, and it was *always* about him. He's going to milk my reputation for everything it's worth.

I'm just the idiot that was willing to participate in my own downfall.

Trying to play it cool, I shrug. "No one else had reason to."

Jake smiles like the Cheshire cat. "Guess we'll never know. But, maybe you should look at your beard. From what I remember, he was in Mexico with us."

While shaking my head, I turn and step toward the crowd.

He calls out, "Hey."

I glance over my shoulder.

"You've got my number if you want a round two."

"Like I'd call for a measly minute and a half of fun," I reply.

I hear his deep chuckle behind me. "I'll see your beard at *Young Americans.* Let me know when you've decided to drop the act with him."

Now *that* is what guts me. Jake Marx was invited to *Young Americans Changing the World*? How? I was hoping for an invite. What has he possibly done to warrant an invitation? And Tom too? Why didn't he mention it? I don't respond. My feet carry me back through the crowd, but I don't even know where I'm going as I head to the middle of the crowd. My hands shake, and I wish we never came here.

Someone taps my shoulder, and I flinch away, covering my heart with my hands.

Tom's brow furrows, and he cocks his head. "*¿Estás bien?*"

His face slows my rapid heartbeat, and now all I want to do is snuggle and watch a movie, or be the little spoon as we doze off to sleep. I crave doing all these things with him so I can forget my problems and pretend that none of it ever happened. Tom's embrace does that.

He's the comfort I need. I'm just not the weight *he* needs.

Tom reaches for my hand and rubs a thumb over my palm. "Hey? What's going on? Are you okay?"

Instead of doing the right thing, despite what Kira said about ruining her brother's career, I barrel into his side to try and steady myself. Because for the first time in my life, I feel outmatched. And a creeping thought tells me this is just the beginning to a very bad situation with Jake Marx.

"No, not really," I say against his chest.

Even as I say that, I know something has to change. This protest reminded me of it today. I can't just sit on the sidelines as my career goes to crap. *Something* has to give. Because a snake like Jake Marx isn't going to take my spot in the activism world when he stands against everything that I believe in.

Americans need *me*, not him.

I've gotta get an invite to *Young Americans Changing the World.* It's a huge televised event that happens each year, and a bunch of schools from California bring their kids to listen to speakers, ask questions, and more. It's the holy grail of activism.

This was supposed to be my year. Jake Marx is *not* going to ruin it.

Without hesitation, Tom throws his arms around me. "I'm proud of you. I know today was a big step after everything that happened."

I nod, allowing him to think that it was the protest that got me upset. Little does he know, it felt good to get back to my roots. But I let him believe it because he doesn't need any more of my drama. There's no reason to pull him down with me and make him fear what I know is bound to happen. Jake Marx isn't going to stop until he destroys me, but I'm fighting back. I clear my throat and try to push the thoughts out of my mind. "I love you, Tom."

He kisses my forehead before grabbing my hand. "*Te amo*, Candy. Let's get out of here."

Chapter Twenty - Candy

Tom and I ride home from the protest in silence, but it's blanketed and warm. Hands entwined, his thumb rubs circles on the underside of my wrist in a comforting pulse of energy. My mind works out the details of everything Jake said.

I have to secure an invite to *Young Americans*. It's a few months away, but they're probably finalizing their lineup. Thinking back to the comment about Tom, I toss out, "Hey, were you invited to *Young Americans Changing the World?*"

Tom nods. "Yeah, I'm going to talk about the lack of Black college and MLB players. It's not for another few months though. Why?"

I shrug. "Could I have the contact of the event organizer who invited you? I'd like to…propose an idea."

"Totally." He reaches into the cupholder at a red light and grabs his phone. Tapping away, a few seconds later, my phone buzzes. "Just forwarded the email."

"*Gracias.*"

"Does this mean…" he trails off and breaks into a goofy grin.

"*Ay, don't give yourself so much credit.* I'm just sick of wallowing. Well, that's not true. I'm not sick of wallowing. I freaking lost 400,000 followers. But Jake Marx got invited to *Young Americans.* And I'm not gonna sit back as he freaking succeeds from this crap. Stupid clout chaser," I mumble, already typing out an email to Tom's contact.

"Okay, queen, I see you."

By the time we pull into his apartment's parking lot, I've typed out an email introducing myself. Hopefully it bordered on professional and not desperate, but who knows these days. I pocket my phone as we head up the stairs.

His house is empty, all roommates gone, and he leads me to his room. I lie down on the bed, and he lays his head in my lap, turning on his Spotify playlist. "Be Like That" by Swae Lee and Kane Brown plays in the background, and I close my eyes while resting against the headboard.

We don't say a word, and my heart beats happily to the rhythm of the music. Things suddenly feel very different than any other time.

As he nuzzles into my lap, emotion threatens to overwhelm me. I don't know if this feeling has been absent for two years and is now back in full force or if I never felt like this from the start and it's new.

It's as if I've jumped off a cliff but float instead of fall. Right here in Tom's arms, I'm happy, even with all the drama that's happened this year.

He turns toward me and smiles, just a gentle quirk of his lips. I run my hands against the side of his head and lay my arm across his face as I play with his ear. He places a hand on my waist. "What happened at the protest?"

I break our eye contact and glance where the Bluetooth speaker plays. Instinctively, I grab onto my locket and slide it back and forth on its chain. Shaking my head, I say, "I just ran into Jake Marx and he tried to get under my skin. But it's whatever."

"Shit. I'm sorry. I had no idea he'd be there. What does he even do? I'd never heard his name before the scandal with you."

I groan. "Don't call it a scandal."

He laughs. "My little scandalous nugget."

My face is saying *please don't ever call me a nugget again.* "Anyway, who knows what he does. Maybe run intermission between earth and hell?"

"Seems fitting." His lips purse and he reaches out to touch the locket. "I love that you wear this all the time."

The touch makes me shiver. "Yeah?"

He fiddles with the bottom of my shirt. "Yeah. Listen, I know I called you my girlfriend earlier, but if you're not okay with that, it's chill. Whenever you're ready, you let me know."

"Okay," I whisper. "But I'm pretty sure I'm okay with being the guy I love's girlfriend."

"Yeah?"

I nod. "Yes. More than yeah. If you're *not* my boyfriend right now, we have a problem."

"You became my girlfriend the second I saw you swinging that hammer at the junkyard."

I laugh and play with his hair.

He licks his lips and taps his fingers in a rhythmic motion against my thigh. It's almost as if he's nervous. "That goes for everything, by the way. I'm ready for it all, whenever you're ready."

I silently laugh. *"Bien. Bien. Like what?"*

His gaze is heated as he looks into my eyes. "You want your career back? I'll help. Want to ditch our separate places and move in together? I'm ready whenever you are. You want forever? Bet. Book a ticket to Vegas. I'm letting you call the shots here, so whenever you're ready, and for whatever it is you're ready for, I'll be right by your side, cheering you on and supporting you."

I've gone from self-proclaimed bruh girl to the please sir emoji. My eyes water, and I shake my head. "Ah, well, I do love Vegas."

Pushing up off my lap, he chuckles. "I memorized that speech in Spanish too. So whenever you're ready for that, I've got it."

A blush crawls up my face as I think of everything people have said. "I'm bad for your brand, babe. Some might even say I'm using you."

He rolls his eyes. "I could delete 'my brand' tomorrow and

be the same person as I am today. You know I don't do activism for clout. Screw the haters."

I lean into him and breathe his scent, reminding me of summer beach days in high school when we'd have bonfires with friends and camp at Bodega Bay.

His chin scrapes up my neck, tickling the sensitive parts of me. With it comes his hands, trailing from my hips to my shoulders. He kisses me, lips barely touching mine.

"It'll look bad if you suddenly start posting pictures of me." I edge closer to his lips again, but he pulls back and grins.

"Meh, I already have pictures of you." He pushes against me until I fall back onto the bed, and he lays on top of me.

A smile creeps up on my lips.

His nose moves across mine, and I feel like we're kids again, giving Eskimo kisses. I trail my finger along his gold chain. "Why'd you switch necklaces from your old one?"

Tom kisses my nose, lips, chin, neck, and trails down my body. "It's a secret."

When he gets to my stomach, I prop myself up on my elbows. "I like secrets. Tell me."

His lips move to my hipbones, and I hit his leg with my foot. He's trying to distract me. Resting his forehead against my waist, he sighs. "Got it when I got yours. We match."

Okay, wait, that's actually really cute. He wanted to *match* me? *Aww querido.* I toy with the locket on my neck. "Aww, you little softie. Hey, how do I get this open? I tried and —"

He crawls on top of me and plants a kiss on my lips, stealing the words from my mouth. "No more questions."

His lips are soft and warm, and his body weight comforts me. Our kiss could paint a masterpiece, our emotions a swirling design of sunshine. It bursts through every nerve of my body, warming me up from the inside out. Everything tingles as if his body awakens something dormant inside of me.

My toes curl as he tucks a strand of hair behind my ear and puts his hand behind my back. He tickles my neck when his tongue parts my lips.

"Dusk Till Dawn" blares in the background, and as the beat drops on the chorus, he lifts and twirls me until I'm on top. I move to explore every part of his body until he grasps my hair and yanks me back up to his mouth.

I snake my hands up his torso, touching all of him. His abs, chest, the small scar on his hipbone he got three years ago backflipping off a jet ski at Folsom Lake, the hard ridges of his sculpted body, and the roughness of his happy trail.

He moans as my finger skirts across the hem of his jeans, and I bite his lip before pulling back. We gaze at each other, exchanging a silent conversation of yesses. The song encompasses all of us, and as it echoes against the walls of the room, I know we both make a silent promise: This means something more than it ever has before, and we're not backing out.

He nods, and my lips quiver.

"I love you," he says, squeezing my hips.

"Show me," I whisper.

∞∞∞

I trace hearts on Tom's chest with my nails. He closes his eyes and takes a deep breath. It's the sound of serenity. Or it would be, if he would take a Claritin and stop sniffling from his pollen allergy.

But even with the runny nose, if I could spend forever in here, away from the world's criticism, I would. Paradise for some might be at the beach where sunshine spreads across their skin. But mine? Mine is here with him, in his arms, in some crappy college apartment with a plaid sheet wrapped around us.

"What time is it?" I ask, reaching for my phone. "Seven. Should we forget about game night?"

Tom lifts his forearms from his face. "Eh, it's up to you. You want someone dethroning you from What Do You

Meme?"

I'm *la reina* of the game. My memes are straight fire. "I mean...I would if you wanted to."

He kisses my temple and chuckles. "So that's a no." Stretching up his arms, he groans. "Aight, let's get going then."

"Les and Ethan are going down tonight. Do you ever feel like they're the same people?"

Tom sits up. "Ehh, no. Les is more like that dog from that Disney movie with the old guy and the boy scout kid. Ethan is basically the dog from *Air Bud*."

Ookay, he put way too much thought into that. I unlock my phone and go to Instagram. My DMs are insane, and I don't got time for that, so I go to my last post with my screenshotted apology to read a few of the comments. "Just give me *un momento, por favor, amor*."

Not that I agree with what she did, but Jake sure is capitalizing on it.

I'm over this. Can we get back to the regular content now?

If she thinks we're going to just forget that she slept with the enemy, ella es una tonta.

You know it's sad when you get excited that no one called you a slut or ho. But...the comments seem to be a little bit better? Maybe?

I exit Instagram and head to Twitter. Follower count is at 800,000, so at least I'm done bleeding followers. Then I check my email. I have a response from *Young Americans*.

Hi Candy! Thanks for reaching out. I'd love to hop on a phone call and talk a bit more about what we're looking for, and what we'd need from you. I also have a few questions. I've included the link to my calendar. Just schedule a time that will work for you, and I'll call then!

So, that's not an automatic no. A little spark of excitement lights up my body, but I don't want to get my hopes up. I put my phone down and twist the edge of my shirt.

Tom gets up from the bed and yanks open his dresser. He rifles through it and pulls out a tee and joggers.

My eyes don't leave the strong muscles of his back as he yanks the shirt over his head. He turns, catches me staring, and the right side of his lips quirk.

"Creeper."

I can't help but bite my lip. "*Ay papi,* let's skip game night after all. Let me love on that bod." I raise my brows and shake my booty on the bed.

He dips his chin and laughs. "*Ay mami, no,*" he mocks me. "Because I'll hear about it later, and you'll be pissed. Not risking it. I like my balls too much."

I pout but scoot to the edge of the bed so I can get ready to go. As I do, he messes with his hair and puts some cream on the small amount of facial hair he has lining his jawline.

The lamp on his nightstand shines right at him like a spotlight. He gives his hair one last muss and tosses his keys up in the air. Catching them, he does a little spin that he learned from TikTok.

"It's the self-satisfied smirk for me." I roll my eyes but hide a smile.

"Oh, whatever," he mutters. "Get a girlfriend, they say. Date a Latina, they say. It'll be fun, they say." His head shake could win an Oscar. "I try to be sexy. Lemme be your *papi chulo, pero noo.* You want to make fun of me." He snaps in front of his face and moves his head in a sweeping motion.

"Your sarcasm is sending me."

He deadpans. "Let's go, my dramatic little pop-tart."

What the...I break out into a breathless laugh. "You are so weird," I choke out, following him out of his apartment and down the steps.

Right when my foot hits the concrete, he says, "Race you to the car?"

Déjà vu has me cheesing like a kid. The first time he asked that was Freshman year of high school. Tom said, *if you win, I'll buy you a McFlurry. If I win, you'll go out on a date with me.* When he said *on your mark, get set, go,* I didn't even run. He got to the car and *then* I ran to him. I jumped into his arms and kissed him as if the whole school didn't exist.

That was our *second* kiss, and whew, anyone who says first kisses are the best clearly haven't had a second kiss.

From that day on, it became our thing. Every day after school, he'd challenge me. *If you win, I'll wear the suit you want for prom. If I win, I get control of the playlist in the car. If you win, I'll try surfing with you. If I win, you'll try snowboarding with me.*

"Candy?" His voice brings me back to the present.

I shake the past from my mind. "*Bien.* What's on the table this time?"

He leans against the stair railing. "If you win, I'll let you do that *thing* to me you asked to do."

Ah, he wants something bad then if he's offering that up. "*Tú eres un chico muy, muy travieso. ¿Qué quieres?*"

A gleaming smile breaks out on his face. "If *I* win, I get to upload a picture of you from the protest."

"Why would—"

He holds a finger up. "And you'll finally admit you're my *novia* to the haters."

"Tom—"

"And Imma give you a hickey."

Out of all things, that's what he would choose? I roll my eyes and laugh. "That's three things. You're taking advantage of me."

The only way I'll win is by cheating. Let's be honest. We have a 6'3" college athlete versus a 5'2" only-does-home-workouts-*chica*. But I'm not so sure I'm ready to give up my silence and our relationship's anonymity. Not because of me, but because Jake thought Tom was my "beard." Are others going to think that too?

I trust Tom, I do. Or, at least I think I do. But if something goes bad, especially when my reputation is up in the air, I'm not sure I'll recover—career-wise and heart-wise.

But I say no often. I tell people no all the time. Whether it's for work, school, romantic relationships, family commitments, everything. I'm always saying *no.*

So this time, I swallow the fear swirling up from my gut and nod. For once, I'm going to do what I truly want to do. As if I'm just some regular girl at a college campus that no one is watching. I'll say yes. "Well, who wouldn't want a hickey, right? Especially from a man who can't stop sniffling because he refuses to take an allergy pill."

He holds up his hands. "Because allergies are a conspiracy —"

"Not even going there. Okay, on your mark, get set..."

I take off running. Risk taker or not, I still have to cheat a little bit. Think of it as a head start because I'm not as privileged in the height area as him. My *chanclas* slap against the asphalt, and my gaze zeroes in on the car. Twenty feet, fifteen feet, ten feet...and I see a flash of black hair out my peripherals.

"*¡Despacito!*" I shout as he steps ahead of me.

He turns his head. "I'm not slowing down, boo!"

So instead, *I* slow down the moment he touches the car. Tom throws his hands in the air and shouts, "Suck it!"

I walk toward him, accentuating my curves. "Actually, you're gonna be the one sucking, Mr. Imma Give You A Hickey."

He grabs me by the hips and pulls me toward him. Angling his head down, he says, "Just wait until you see the photo I'm gon' upload you. You're looking like a bad ass Latina queen."

His hands travel up my body, lacing my arms with goosebumps. He grasps my chin and plants the gentlest of *besos* on my lips.

It shouldn't do anything to me, but it does. And when I pull back to gaze into his hazel eyes, a sense of excitement tingles my fingers. Fine, I'll admit it. I can't wait to shout it from the rooftops that *él es mío.*

Tom smiles. "Let me make good on the bet real quick."

Pulling out his phone, he winks at me. A few taps later, he shows the photo that he took of me at the protest.

There I stand at the golden hour, sun on my face, lighting up my wistful gaze. It makes my hair look more sunset than bubblegum-colored, and I stand holding a sign above my head.

It's good—*muy bien*. Like, I would've paid a ton for this photo in the past.

"Who said you could be a jack of all trades, huh? You're a good photographer." I glance up at him and he wears a smug smile. "Seriously, Tom. *Yo no sé lo que hiciste, pero estoy impresionado.*"

"My photos aren't the only thing you'll be impressed with," he counters.

I roll my eyes. "Do you think people are going to be angry with you posting that?"

He shrugs. "Honestly? I think you should post it. If you're not ready to go public with our relationship, *está bien*. But the world isn't going to be half as good as it should be without your activism in it. So, for real, I think you should post it."

My mind goes back to seeing Jake today. "I-I can't. Not yet, at least. *Pero, me veo muy bien en ésta.* Upload it for me. You won the bet fair and square."

Chapter Twenty One – Tom

Candy might not like the publicity from us announcing our relationship, but I couldn't care less. People liked the photo of Candy on my account. A few comments were salty, but most of them were cool.

It's straight embarrassing how much I love this girl. I've got like five minutes before class, but I decide to use them to stop at Candy's apartment. I'd say I'm simping 'cause of that body of hers, but I'd be lying. It's everything about her that I'm simping for.

I got an email from *Young Americans Changing the World*. They want both of us to do a Q&A about our activism together as a couple. I'm excited. But because it's together, I know Candy's about to put up the biggest fit in the world. She may have agreed to me uploading a photo of us a week ago, but with all the Jake Marx drama, I know she's gonna hate us having to do this.

I knock on her door—my old apartment's door—which is weird. But, I knock. A second later, the door flies open, and I glance down about a foot to a red-faced woman looking wildly rosy thanks to her pink hair as well.

"Absolutely not!" she shouts, slamming the door in my face.

I knock again, harder this time. "We are *doing it*. This is our first public appearance as a couple. Don't take this away from me! Let me show them how obsessed with you I am."

I hear her snort through the door.

"We each have our own separate interviews. I know

you're freaking over the photos. But so what if they got a few nasty comments? There were a bunch positive too. Face it— you'll have to get over it at some point!" I yell loudly through the door, and one of the neighbors comes out to give me a dirty look.

But it's my boy, Josh, who I used to let borrow my Xbox controller. "This your Romeo moment?"

"Yes, wherefore art thou Juliet or whatever."

He salutes me and goes back inside.

Candy opens the door again, crossing her arms over her chest. Pretty sure she isn't wearing a bra either, so she could probably convince me to ditch the Q&A together.

Focus, man. You came here to convince her.

I let out a breath and force my gaze upward. "I already replied saying we'd be there. Both of us. For the Q&A. No backing out now, *amor*."

She glares at me with her eyes squinted nearly closed. "You *replied* for me as if I'm some woman from the 1800s who can't talk for herself? *¡Tu eres un idiota! ¿Quién te crees que eres?*"

I lean against the doorframe as if I don't have a care in the world, but no cap, my heartrate is through the roof. She could rip my balls off just with words, no doubt. Not to mention her claw-tipped nails. The boys are shriveling from the thought. I swallow the lump in my throat. "I'm your boyfriend. These people want to see you. They want to talk to you. It's a bunch of high school kids who are looking up to activists like both of us. You really gonna deny the younger generation a hot *Latina* role model? Think of the children, Candy."

"Think of the children, *mi culo*," she replies.

I bite down a grin. "We're going. We've got weeks to prepare. Everything will be different then, I promise."

"Fine," she relents. "I mean…I'm excited I got an invite. Just didn't realize I'd have to do a 'couples Q&A.' I swear, one *damn* question about Jake Marx and I'm hightailing it out of there."

I nod. "They're not gonna do that when kids are present."

I give her a quick kiss. "They sent me all the meet up information. I gotta head to an extra baseball training. Wanna meet up tonight? I have some calc homework. We could have a study night."

"*Sí*, I suppose." Her arms stretch above her and she groans. "And we can watch *The Bachelor*. But first, I have to plan how I'm gonna punish you for replying *for me*."

Winking, I say, "Don't threaten me with a good time. I might miss practice."

∞∞∞

Sweat trails down the center of my back, no doubt pooling and soaking through the waistband of my pants. One more mile and I'm through. Both my endurance and sprints need work if I'm making it to the MLB. I've gotten out too many times after hitting. Coach has drilled that into me. No one wants a slow runner. I get it.

I hear my dad's voice shouting in my ear, telling me to keep going, the years of him being my coach still resonating in my mind. Kinda nice that my parents live in Temecula, hours away. Means he isn't at every game, pressuring me even more.

I block out the others and run, knowing I'll have to push myself harder than ever to be ready. Still nothing from the scouts. Whether I declare for the draft or not this year is still up in the air. But either way, I gotta be ready.

Lungs burning, chest straining, I finish the last lap and slow to a jog before walking half a mile to keep my legs from locking up. Waving at a few trainers, I head to the locker room to grab my stuff. A quick rinse of my body later, I wipe my face with a towel and pull out fresh sweats and a hoodie. My phone buzzes, so I fish it out of my bag.

Three missed calls from Kira, five texts, and a snap. I'd be worried someone died, but Kira's dramatic as they come. She's probably just trying to chew me out for what happened between her and Candy at the protest a week ago.

I'll never understand those two and why they hate each other. No cap, they kinda remind me of each other. Not that I'd ever tell them that.

Barely holding in a curse, I press Kira's contact.

It rings halfway, and she answers with a hurried, "Where the hell have you been?"

"Hold up, I've been training. Why you calling so many times, sis?" I shake out my hair and slip into my Nikes.

She sobs, and I can't deal with this today. But she doesn't give me a chance to hang up. "I know you're going to be so mad, and Mom and Pop are gonna hate me, but I don't know what to do. I've been sitting at my house all day, worried sick, or just sick in general, I don't even know. I'm finna die if y'all don't help me out, but you can't tell Mom. She'll kill me, I swear, Tom. It's just..." she continues to ramble, but no real words come out.

I head out the locker room and to my car. I'm half-listening to Kira's dramatics until I hear, "...maybe I'm pregnant."

"Wait, what? What in the actual hell, Kira? Are you out of your mind?" I unlock the Jeep and get in, slamming my hand on the wheel. "What were you thinking?"

"I wasn't!" she cries back.

"Clearly," I huff.

"I don't need a lecture from you of all people. Are you going to help your sister or not?" She sniffs, and a small part of me, an incredibly small and stupid part, cracks.

I'm supposed to be meeting up with Candy tonight. She'll understand, though. Even if I'd much rather be with her than helping Kira with this.

"Yeah, I guess. I got you." But in my mind, I'm cursing her out like no other. "I'll come over after I grab what you need."

She sighs. "Don't tell anyone."

"Aight." I rub at my eyes. Kira's right about one thing. Mom and Dad will kill her. It's one of the only things they drilled into her growing up. Tom's going to the MLB, so wrap it up.

Kira's becoming a lawyer, so pop your pills.

Kira's voice hardens. "And that means Candy, too. If I find out you told her, I'm not talking to you."

Because getting a break from my sister's incessant nagging is such a threat. My fist finds my forehead, and I breathe out a silent groan. "Yeah, alright. Noted, sis."

"I'm serious, Tom."

"Like I said...Noted."

"I still have that video, you know," she replies.

My hands still on the steering wheel. "What video?"

Trepidation lines my voice, and I already know what her answer is when she says, "You, Candy, senior year. The only video you'd never want getting out."

I run a hand through my hair as I try to fit this together in my mind. "So I'm bein' blackmailed by my sister now? Real cool, Kira. Real cool." But if that video of Candy and I senior year of high school gets out, not only does my reputation go down, so does Candy's. "Alright, whatever. Like I said, I won't tell Candy. It's not like she'd find out anyway."

"Just bring me what I need," she replies flippantly. "A few minutes, and we'll forget about this entire thing."

Chapter Twenty Two – Candy

As I go through the photos of Tom and I from the protest a few days ago, I get an email from Alyssa, the coordinator for Young Americans Changing the World. Enclosed are the two tickets for the event in LA at the beginning of April, the hotel reservation, and the itinerary for the event, including instructions for my interview and Q&A with Tom. It's a lot…but, I'm a little excited too.

My career is obviously not "fixed." Not by a longshot. But this event doesn't care about drama, and they're inviting me for my views and my activism. It's a step in the right direction. And this isn't some fairytale, it's real life. I won't have this miraculous event that will save my career. I'll just have to keep working hard to prove myself to everyone I let down. It's going to take time, I know.

But for once, I don't feel this overwhelming weight on my shoulders. Alyssa invited Tom and I as a couple, so there's no point in trying to hide anymore. If they think he's my beard to cover the Marx scandal, fine. They're wrong, and maybe it's time I start caring a little less about what others think of me. So, I'm gonna upload a picture of Tom and me.

And *this one* is perfect.

We stand next to each other, both holding protest signs, his arm wrapped around me while he kisses my hair. The sun shines behind us, barely putting us out of focus. But you can see my smile and read the words clearly on our posters.

Without a second thought, I upload it with a caption that leaves no one guessing whether we're together or not.

The likes and comments roll in, but I don't care. It's my platform, and if people have a problem with me, they can un-follow. The feeling is a little freeing. *¡Qué alivio!*

For the next few hours, I work on my school assignments and focus on upcoming events and protests. I'm still not en-tirely sure how I'll rebrand, but I need to come back stronger than ever...even if I feel weak.

For the first time since the whole incident happened, I wish I hadn't been kicked out of Equal Treatment for Equal People. When I started that club freshman year, it was my out-let. Just me and two other club members who would meet and plan ways to create a safer and more welcoming campus at West U. It'd grown to twenty members, and I considered a lot of them close friends.

If I were still in that club, I could brainstorm with them, figure out how we fight someone crazy like Jake Marx, and come up with a plan to kick some ass. But they dropped me as soon as a scandal came my way. It sucks.

I make my way to the kitchen for a study snack break and to get my mind off of being sad. Les and Carter are cozied to-gether, Les sitting on the counter and Carter standing against it, between her legs.

"*Galletas.*" Carter holds up a cookie and points.

"Guy-yet-uhs," Les repeats. Though *repeat* is a strong word for what she just did.

"*¡Dame un respiro!*" I shake my head. "Good luck, *chica.* That Spanish course has its work cut out for you."

I snatch a cookie and head back to my room, pulling my phone out on the way.

I check my phone while lying on the bed then grab my lap-top. I'm about to email my professor about making up a quiz, but as I pull up my email, I hear two voices mumbling sicken-ing words in Spanish, like *beso y amor,* amongst other things.

So you know what? I think I need to go to the store. Yep, maybe grab a donut or something before Tom and I meet up. Or, maybe some chocolate to melt on each other. My mind plays out a little fantasy of him sprawled out on the bed and me drizzling dark chocolate over his hard abs.

My body shivers, and it knocks me out of the dream. I've gotta get away from this apartment. Les and Carter's love talk is making me a romantic. I hightail it out of my room, slinging my purse over my shoulder, and wave my keys in goodbye. I love them. But I still don't want to hear them slobber on each other.

Once in my Kia, I exhale in relief against the soft cloth seat. This thing is a beater, I'll admit it. But, it's *my* beater, and I love all the memories that have happened in here. I drive toward the nearest Walmart, relishing in the scent of summer days with the windows down, shave ice, and my hand intertwined with Tom's. So many of our memories were made in this car before Tom got his Jeep. We took this thing off roading, got it stuck in the sand in Santa Cruz, illegally parked it in San Francisco, spent a few too many nights making out in the backseat, and took it on midnight In-N-Out runs when I'd sneak out of my house to go pick him up.

If *mi papi* knew about that, I'd be dead and gone.

Those were happy, happy times. I sigh, pulling into the *parqueadero* and finding a spot close to the doors. My phone buzzes with a text.

Tom: *Can't meet up tonight. Sorry. Let's plan for tomorrow.*

What the...? He was the one who asked to hang out. And what's this "can't meet up tonight" stuff. As if I'm a bro he can't hang out with? Nah.

I call him, but it rings twice and goes to voicemail.

Candy: *Uhhh why?*

Boyfriends should give more of an explanation than "can't meet up." Does he have diarrhea? Does he have to stay at practice longer? Is there a last-minute assignment he can't remember? It takes two seconds to explain.

Freaking men. Always doing the bare minimum.

I blow through my lips, casting the hair off of my forehead.

Well, that's a bummer. I was excited to see him. Looks like it's gonna be a personal night.

Easter is in a few weeks, so of course, the store is covered with too many bunnies, pastel colors, and treats. I roll my eyes and keep walking, but then backtrack because I see some chocolate truffles. Surely, you can't pass on chocolate truffles. It's basically a law. I don't want to go to jail.

Grabbing the five-pound box of chocolates, I tuck them underneath my arm in a football hold. I came for chocolate donuts and tampons. Might as well go big on the chocolate.

Students mill around, talking way louder than necessary. Some guys in their football jerseys are yelling at what I'm gonna assume are sorority girls, and someone yells, "Get more whiskey!"

I snort. Must be a frat party tonight.

A telltale gush happens between my legs, and I curse *Madre Maria* who must want to punish me for my earlier dream of pouring chocolate on Tom. Literally always the worst timing. You know how I know God is a man?

Women are the ones with periods.

Should I get ice cream? I check down the frozen aisle that's packed with people. Nah, forget the ice cream.

Three aisles over is the aptly named "feminine products" aisle. Heaven forbid you put "tampons and pads" like they slap on "beans and rice." But no, everyone is so sensitive with the word period. Oh, and the family planning of course. AKA, condoms in this college town.

I scan the contents on the shelves, looking for my favorite brand and size of tampons. And what would you know? They're on the top shelf.

A groan escapes me, and part of me wants to stomp my foot too, but I close my eyes and shake my head. I should really just switch to a cup, but this month's red river is already flowing, so I'll have to find a store attendant to grab them for me. I try one time, jumping and reaching for a box. If only they came down like snacks do in vending machines.

"Need some help?" A warm voice snakes down my spine and curls in my stomach.

A dark arm reaches across me, grabbing me a box of tampons.

I turn around and glance at Tom, holding a basket full of stuff. Laughing, I take the tampons. "Um, thanks. What's up with your text? You can't hang out tonight?" I tuck some hair behind my ear.

He glances to the side, and I see stubble on his jaw. Three lines are cut into the side of his hair where it's been shorn short. He must've gotten it faded today.

As he adjusts his basket, his bicep flexes, pulling at his shirt. Even after seeing him nearly every day, I can't help but stare. Damn, he's sexy.

Snap out of it, Candy.

"Nah, just got some stuff going on. You know, my calc is gonna take longer than I thought, so...But I saw you down here and wanted to say hey. Then when you started jumping, I figured you'd need help." He nods toward the chocolate. "You planning on sharing those with someone?"

"Well, I *was*. But said person now ditched me. So, looks like I'll have to find someone else to share it with." I try to act smug, lifting my chin as if I have a ton of prospects begging to share chocolate. "Unless you want to melt it on me."

Tom smirks, drawing up one side of his lips.

Now I can't focus. He smells like the coast, like saltwater air and spice. I glance down at his basket, but he puts it behind his back.

"Whatcha got there?" I ask, trying to peek.

He laughs. "Nothin'. Hey, tempting offer, but I for real gotta go. I'll catch you later."

Which is weird, because what? He doesn't say 'catch you later.' And if he had to grocery shop, we could've done it together. Unless he's sick of me. Is he second guessing uploading the photos of us?

Tom snakes around me, but I turn before he switches the

basket around and I see a slim box on top. I freeze. Is this a freaking joke?

I heave out the breath I automatically held. "What the hell is that?"

He turns. I take a step back, putting distance between us, and point at his basket. He furrows his brow and glances down.

"*¿Qué chingados es eso?*" I bite out. "What is it?"

His face goes gray, and he licks his lips. "Hold up. Nah, I can explain that."

My boyfriend. The guy I am in love with has a *pregnancy test* in his basket. This can't be real. This cannot be real. I am either the world's dumbest girl, or I'm a clown. But if there's one thing I'm not gonna succumb to, it's crying in a freaking grocery store. And now all I can think of is that old stupid "New York Summer" song from TikTok about fighting in a grocery store.

So I put on a steel exterior, which is probably just made up of spray painted cardboard, but will hopefully get me through the next two minutes.

"A pregnancy test, Tom?" I laugh so I don't cry. "I'm an idiot." But my voice wavers, and I'm not sure I can play it off like I don't care. Because I *do* care. And what the hell is my boyfriend doing buying a pregnancy test for someone else?

He tries to reach for my arm, but I step away and shake my head.

"Screw off, Tom. Seriously. I'm so done." My voice cracks on the last word.

I make my way past him and march down the aisle, but his hand lands on my shoulder, pulling me back.

"I swear, I can explain. It's not for me."

"Get your freaking hands off of me!" I grab his wrist and toss his arm toward him. "And obviously not. You can't get pregnant!" I look over my shoulder at him. "Don't you get it? I don't want your explanations. Nothing you say is going to make this better. You clearly think you can do whatever and

192

whoever you want with zero repercussions. But save me some time and drop the lies." I nod toward the test. "*Buena suerte* with that."

"Candy! Wait!"

I turn around and shrug. "Who's it for, Tom? Tell me her name."

He opens and closes his mouth. "I-I can't do that."

"That's what I thought."

He runs his hand through his hair, and for a second, a wild look flashes in his eyes. "You can't just erase us again. People know we're together. We have the event next month. As a *couple*. I-I love you."

All I see is him trying to figure out the best way to fool me again. It feels as if I'm being stabbed in the heart with a wooden stake because I love him too, and he just ruined us. I glance up, willing the tears to stay in my eyes until I can get out of the grocery store. "Yeah, well, you should've thought of that before you possibly knocked someone up. You're the only one here to blame, Tom. Goodnight," I whisper, hands shaking as I walk away.

Nearly running toward the self-checkout, rushing to get away from this store and from Tom, I can feel my fake steel exterior running out like an hourglass of sand. In a few minutes, the resolve will collapse into sorrow like Cinderella's façade at the stroke of midnight.

Everything Tom said was a joke. It was all a lie. That we'd find our way back together, that he needed to move out to give us space, that he believed in me, that he...loved me.

How is this happening to me *again*? I must be the stupidest freaking girl on the planet.

Tom's a liar.

I don't want to think about him wrapped up in some other girl's arms, her legs casually folded over his. I don't want to imagine him calling that girl beautiful or whispering sweet nothings in her ear. I don't want to picture the two of them happy, laughing and smiling, or even scared and anxious. I don't want to think about how he found the time, or why he cheated on me *again.*

I don't want to think about any of it.

But I do.

My phone buzzes, and I open a text from Les. *¿Qué chingados? ¿Es una broma?*

Kill me now.

Attached is a video from Twitter of Jake and me speaking at the protest. So, Tom's a liar, we get into an argument, and a video gets released. Maybe he lied about that too. Maybe Jake was telling the truth. Maybe Tom uploaded everything from the beginning.

I feel my soul crack, and it's all too much.

With my tampons in one arm and chocolate in the other, I walk out of the store, head held high but tears already dripping onto my shirt. Screw men. Screw exes. Screw periods and their perfect timing.

Chapter Twenty Three – Tom

I throw the pregnancy test on the table. "That's it, Kira. I'm done. Don't call me, don't text me. I'm done with your shit."

She throws her aqua-dipped braids over her shoulder. "Wow, I'm so sorry you had to buy your sister a pregnancy test. For your information, my antibiotic interfered with my birth control."

"That's—" I let out a pent up breath. "That's not why I'm mad. You *threatened* me and said I couldn't tell my girlfriend. And karma is obviously out for me 'cause she caught me in the store, and I couldn't tell her that the pregnancy test was for you. You know what she thought?"

Kira snorts. "That girl is so insecure. When are you gonna grow up and find yourself a woman who can handle you, bro?"

"Insecure?" I throw my hands up. "I cheated on her. I was the one who messed up, sis. And I could've told her. Candy wouldn't have judged or told another soul. But you blackmailed me for no good reason. And my girlfriend just broke up with me because of you. I can't even believe we're related. Piss off, Kira."

Snatching the keys off the table, I turn to leave.

Kira scrapes the chair across the tile and sits down. "All because of some girl?"

My anger hits its boiling point. I pull at an errant curl in my hair and walk toward the door. Turning the handle, I glance back at Kira one last time. "When are you going to realize that she's not just 'some girl' to me? She's *everything*—"

"You said you were over her!"

I slam my hand against the door. "I lied! Dammit, sis. You're clueless. I freaking lied. She's not just some girl. She's *never* gonna be just some girl. I'm in love with her." My voice cracks, and I shake my head. "I'm in love with her, and because of you, I just lost her."

I move to leave, bringing the door toward the frame. Kira walks toward me. "You'll thank me one day. You'll see!"

Refusing to talk more, I slam the door and leave. Everyone would call me a fool if they saw me right now, but I don't care. Tears fall angrily down my face, and I swipe them away before they drop onto my shirt. Everything I just said is more true than Kira will ever realize.

Everything I've done has all been for Candy. I may have fooled myself for a few years, but that's all it was. I've never been over Candy, and I never will be.

The second I get in my car, I dial her number. I don't know what I'm going to say, or how I'll get myself out of this, but I can't lose her again.

It rings once and goes to voicemail. I clear my throat so it doesn't sound like I've been bawling my sorry eyes out for the last few minutes. "Candy, please call me back. I just want five minutes. That's it. Please."

I call again. Same thing. Rings once and goes to voicemail.

I send a text.

Tom: *Please, just let me explain myself.*

Really, there's nothing to explain. If Kira released that video, both of our reputations shatter. No MLB teams will even look at me, and who knows, we could even get kicked out of school.

I rake my fingers across my scalp.

I think about sending another text, but...

That's weird. The message didn't deliver. I tap on the screen to try and send the message as an SMS. My iPhone won't let me. My text before this one shows a read notification, but this one doesn't show a delivered notification.

Oh, FFS. Candy's blocked my number.

I rest my forehead on the steering wheel and punch the dash before calling Carter.

It rings twice before he answers. "What's up, dude? My girlfriend was just ripped out of my arms in the middle of a very-heated make out session, so you've got five seconds to explain yourself."

My heartrate feels as if I just got done running sprints. "Shit, man. I don't even know what to say. Something happened, and it looks bad, but I swear it's not what it looks like."

Carter is silent for a moment. "That's not sus at all. Just answer me honestly. Should I be kicking your ass for Candy?"

My throat thickens. "What if I say yes *and* no?"

He sighs, and I don't know what to do or say. I'm stuck. I know I look like an asshole. I know what Candy is thinking. Carter will probably think so too if I tell him. But he's also my best friend.

"Aight, look, Candy caught me buying a pregnancy test—"

"*Chingao.* You told me you wouldn't hurt her."

"—but it's not what it looks like. It wasn't for someone I had sex with," I finish.

"Then who was it for?" Carter's voice sounds irritated, not that I can blame him.

"I can't say. But I swear on everything, man, I didn't cheat on your sister again. You have to believe me." I'm grasping for straws.

He doesn't respond, so I start my car and back out of Kira's parking lot.

"I've never lied to you. Please, Carter, I need your help. I..." My eyes begin to burn, and I rub them at a stoplight. "I can't lose her again. She's blocked my number, and I just need to talk to her."

Carter's probably the only guy who won't judge me for crying right now. A long moment goes by, and my gut feels as if I've drunk acid.

"I'm not conspiring with you. *She'd kill me.* But if you want to drop by unannounced, she's here."

I wipe my eyes and nod. "Yeah, okay. Thanks, man."

The call ends, and a tightness in my chest makes it feel as if someone just threw a fastball straight at my heart. I'll come clean to Candy. I have to.

Kira won't talk to me, and I'm fine with that. How will she even know if I tell Candy?

As if the devil whispers my thoughts aloud, a new text comes in.

Kira: *1 Attachment.*

Kira: *Is one secret worth your entire career?*

I toss the phone into the passenger seat and keep driving, ignoring the gnawing feeling in my insides. It's been a long time since that video was taken. We were seniors in high school. Minors. Meaning it'll be three years in just a few months, which is the statute of limitation on property damage in California.

But criminal charges or not, a video of us making a dumb, illegal decision at a late night protest will ruin our futures. I can't do that to myself, to my dreams, and I definitely can't do that to Candy.

Not after everything that's happened this year. Maybe, just maybe, my reputation would recover. But hers? It would shatter.

And in the long run, I know she'd rather her heart get shattered than her reputation. One of our past conversations echoes in my mind. *"Hearts recover,"* she said. *"Careers hardly do."*

The clouds hang above dark and dreary, mimicking how I feel. As rain splatters on my windshield, I don't bother wiping it away. Instead, I drive through it, with blurred lights shining back at me.

Tonight was supposed to be fun. I got her to agree to the interview with me. Plans were made. Figured we'd celebrate. Had I known that my entire life would turn into a flaming pile of crap just a few hours later, I would've skipped that extra practice. I would've stayed in, wrapped my arms around her, been the big spoon, and not complained one bit about watching *The Bachelor*.

Damn, who have I become? I sniff back the tears threatening to come again.

Pull yourself together, man.

I drive into Candy's apartment complex, hands shaking as if I'm a five-year-old getting ready to tell my dad I pissed in bed. I park and turn off the car, stalling.

Nothing I can say will fix this. Only the truth, which I can't give.

Grabbing my phone, I cough to clear my throat. I open the attachment and watch the video.

Candy and Erica, a girl from class, snicker off in the corner, leaning against the hood of a police car. People shout in the background, but I stand and stare at the girls, shaking my head.

Weston, a guy I haven't spoken to in years, holds up a can of spray paint and a homemade duct taped firework. With a short howl, he kicks at the car's windows. When that doesn't do anything, he smashes the metal part of the spray paint can against the glass until the window splinters.

"Whoa, what're you doing, Weston?" I push him back. "Are you dumb?"

"Are you trying to get us killed?" Candy hisses. "I don't want an arrest record."

Weston rolls his eyes and points to the camera that Kira holds. His red hair flops into his eyes. "The whole block's been cleared out from the protest. The security cameras are smashed. No one will know it's us. Come on, guys, don't you want to get a little payback?"

Candy bites her lip and looks toward me. I shrug and relent. "Fine, give me the spray paint."

Weston finishes breaking the window before handing it over. I spray paint some illegible words and toss it toward Candy. She hops back and forth on both feet before sighing. "Well, since you guys already ruined it."

She paints on the hood of the car, kicks the tire once, but it doesn't move, and tosses the spray paint to Erica. When Erica finishes with it, Weston glances at all of us.

"Should we light it up?"

I shake my head but laugh. "It's ruined anyhow."

Candy shrugs. "Light it up."

"Yes!" Erica shouts.

Weston lights his homemade firework, throws it into the cop car, and we sprint off. The car blows into pieces as we cover our ears. A few screams echo before the camera goes dark, and the video ends.

We were kids. Stupid and seventeen. Caught up in the moment, encouraged by someone who didn't have any skin in the fight, and made a mistake.

Which is why we haven't talked to Weston since that incident. Because the firework went off like a bomb, shattering the windows and blowing off one of the doors of the car. I still have a scar on my arm from a piece of the metal that blew off and cut open my bicep.

Our faces in the video are clear. Everyone would know what we did. I shake my head and respond to Kira.

Tom: *Candy won't care that you took a pregnancy test. Come on, sis. It's not a big deal.*

Immediately, three dots appear.

Kira: *If you get back with her, I'll know you told her. The video will take thirty seconds to upload on Reddit.*

Tom: *Why you doing this? I have public appearances to make with her. Me and her can't just break up.*

Kira: *Bet. And don't try any shady shit. I have my ways of finding out.*

I lean my head back against the headrest. That's it. She's crazy. Absolutely, batshit, crazy.

But Kira's a crazy person with evidence, which never turns out well. I get out of the car and stare at the building. What am I even doing here? Can't tell Candy the truth, and she thinks I'm the scum of the earth.

For whatever reason, maybe these Nikes are self-propelled, my feet start moving toward the complex's door. I type in the emergency code, since I don't have a key fob anymore, and head down to the old apartment I used to call home.

I knock twice and give my eyes one last rub. I'm hoping they make me look more high than sad. No one wants a blubbering man on their doorstep.

The door swings open, and Carter stands in front of me wide-eyed. "Yeah, right now might not be a good time," he whisper-hisses.

Yelling voices come from the back room. A few seconds later, my mind registers that the yelling voices are *singing*. "What the fu—"

"Ay, apparently, it's rage karaoke. Pretty sure Masha at the manager's office is going to get at least a hundred complaints from our neighbors." He rubs a hand down his face. "I'd say let me come with you and we'll ditch this, but I'm supposed to be the DJ? *No sé. Perras* be crazy."

Les and Candy sing a horrible version of "Because of You," and my ears ring with the off-key ballad.

"Will you just tell her I'm here?"

Carter's countenance legit collapses, and he looks so much like Candy in that moment, my eyes burn again. When he speaks, it looks as if it pains him. "*Amigo,* are you trying to end up on *Dateline?* I'm scared she'll murder *me* just for telling her you're here."

I clench and unclench my fists. "Fine. Can you give me some paper and a pen? I'll just write her a note."

He throws his hands up, but turns around and rummages through the kitchen with the door open. "What is this? The freaking 1800s?"

It sounds so much like what Candy said earlier today, just this morning, that my throat thickens with everything I've just lost. He thrusts the paper and pen into my hands just as I hear Les's whiny voice. "Carter, we're ready for the next one!"

Carter shudders. "Just slide it under the door when you're done, and I'll make sure she gets it. I gotta go. I'm being summoned by two *brujas*."

He slams the door, and I lean the paper against it and begin writing.

Candy, I wanted to talk in person, or at least over the phone, but yeah…Guess I'm blacklisted. Not that I blame you. I get it. I get that it looks bad.

I'm sorry. I'm so sorry, and I know it means nothing, but I swear, the pregnancy test had nothing to do with me. I'd tell you all about it if I could. And I hope one day I can, but until then, I promise, there's no one else. There's not gonna be anyone else. No matter how long it takes for you to trust me, I'll prove it. I'm all yours.

I love you, and I'm sorry I hurt you. You have no idea how sorry I feel.

I'm here for whatever you need, even if it's just as a friend.

Tom.

My face gets wet at the stupid last line, and I feel like an idiot for crying so much. But you know what? No, it's fine. Men can cry too.

I slip the letter under the door and pull out my phone as I head back to my car.

I open Instagram and slide into my front seat, looking at the photo she uploaded of us. The caption from yesterday reads: *Mi amor forever and always.*

The comments on her post still suck. People claim she jumped from Jake Marx to me, just to make her image look better. Others continue that theory and say she's using *me* for clout…even though her platform is more than triple the size of mine.

But the comments on my photo of her? Most of them are good. A few are rude, or confused, but a clear difference from my profile to hers shines through. People have been a lot harder on her than anyone else.

I head to Jake Marx's Instagram, and his newest photo is a picture of him winking at the camera, gripping some tiny model's hand as he pulls her across the street.

The comments talk about how girls can't get enough of

him. How he's the hero of the right, and plenty of other sickening things. A few comments say the model is another "snowflake liberal" he's brought to the right with his magical *eggplant emoji*.

No negative comments at all. The men are praising him, and his following has only grown.

It's not fair.

That old DM with the videos of Jake calls to me. I open up Instagram and head straight to it. They sent a third video, and this one has *Candy's* face in it.

I wasn't gonna take them up on the offer before, because I didn't want to cause more drama with the Jake Marx debacle. But…Candy's already not speaking to me. So, it's not like she can get mad at me. Plus, she won't know it's me. I'm not stupid.

Candy might hate me, and she might not take me back, but it's time we knock Jake down from the pedestal he's crawled upon.

As I watch the videos, I realize I might just have the key to getting her career back.

Maybe even the key to destroying Jake Marx in the process.

So, I make an anonymous TikTok account and get started.

Chapter Twenty Four - Candy

"Y ou're avoiding your boyfriend," Les says as she shoves string cheese in her mouth.

We're sitting outside the library at a picnic table where a large fountain cascades down two flights of stairs behind us, drowning out my sorrow with white noise.

I swipe through Tom's Instagram. "I am not avoiding my boyfriend. I do not have a boyfriend."

She takes a sip of her iced tea. The sun is shining, but it's still too cold for iced tea. "I get that it's only been a couple days, but I think you should talk to him. At least hear what he says. The two of you never get closure. Don't you think that could be part of the problem? If you're really done, make it for real this time."

My throat feels swollen. My eyes are puffy from the crying last night, and I've basically lost my voice from rage singing "I Hope" all night long.

"I don't have any interest in hearing what he has to say."

Les sighs. "Well, what're you going to do for *Young Americans*? I saw your Insta, girl. You kept the picture of him *with* the lovey-dovey caption."

I humph. "If I delete it, people will start talking, and I'll be branded as the slut who can't keep a guy."

"Stop that," Les chastises. "Life happens. Life sucks sometimes. People break up. No one is going to think that."

"Everyone is going to think that!" I whisper-screech, pulling at my hair. "*Ay Dios mío*, Les, even I think that right now, okay? And not seeing him *hurts*. My heart. Right now." I point to my chest. "It. Hurts. *Lo puedo sentir yo mismo, algo está mal en mi*. This whole situation is the worst. Not only do I feel stupid because I fell for him again, but I feel stupid for missing him."

She holds out her hand and squeezes mine. "Candy, that's totally normal. You love him. You've been in love with him for over five years. I would be more concerned if you *didn't* feel like that."

I crack my fingers and stare down at my phone. "I don't want to do this anymore."

"What do you mean?" Les types on her phone.

"I want to move to some nowhere town in Alaska where no one knows my name and just hide out for a year. I'm done. So freaking done with life right now." I fold my arms and lean back in the metal chair, feeling the coolness of it through my jacket.

"Aw, come on. Things are starting to look up in the career department, yeah? You got the event with those people, and that's a good step, right?" Les gives me a sympathetic look.

"People are still commenting rude stuff about me on all of my posts, so who knows. And Jake Marx is also invited to that event, so..."

"But eventually, people will forget, okay?" She toys with her straw, but her eyes are glazed over, probably thinking of her next exam.

I bury my head in my hands and groan.

She nudges my shoulder, and I prop myself back up. "I've gotta get to my next class. You're on break for a bit? Maybe think of what you're going to do for the upcoming weeks. Don't drop out of the event just because you have a Q&A with Tom. You can figure something out, and it's still weeks away. Focus on the short-term for now."

My phone buzzes, and I nod. "Yeah, I guess you're right, *amiga*. Good luck on your test. *Te amo*."

"Love you too." She crosses her fingers. "I'll see you to-night."

She leaves in a flurry of expensive perfume and happiness, and I wallow in my despair and unwashed hair as I open a new text.

Kira AKA *poop emoji*: *Hey, Tom just told me what happened. I know we're nowhere near friends, but I wanted to say I'm sorry. I've been cheated on before, and it sucks. Here's me waving a metaphorical white flag. My bro sucks. If you need anything, let me know.*

That is...probably the nicest exchange I've ever had with Kira? I guess bastards cheating really do bring people together.

Candy: *Gracias, girl. Just a lot of thoughts going on. I'm supposed to go to an event with him in April as a couple, and that's obviously not happening. But yeah...I just don't know what to do right now. Kinda stressed. But, thanks for reaching out. I appreciate it.*

I put in one of my AirPods and decide to scroll TikTok. My FYP is filled with humor that makes me laugh, and it always helps me get away from my problems. But the second I open up the app, my notifications explode.

Which is weird, because TikTok is my smallest platform, and I'm not even well known on the app. So what the hell could it be now? My gut clenches as if already knowing to prepare for something bad.

I click on my notifications and see my name being mentioned every few seconds. Do I even want to know what this is? From the small thumbnail, I can clearly see Jake Marx's side profile.

As I'm about to click on the video, someone shouts, "Candy!" and I jump a few inches off of my chair.

Glancing up, I see that Grace girl furiously heading toward me. Head of the paper at West or whatever. I lock my phone and tap the screen to see the time. Ugh, still thirty minutes until my next class, so I can't avoid her.

I try to hide my grimace as I wave. "Hey. Grace, right?"

She takes the empty seat, and I slide into my old professional-mode that I haven't used since the scandal broke.

"That's me. Did you get my email the other week?" She smiles, but it feels like it's laced with a lethal poison. If I wasn't terrified now that I'm about to be canceled on yet another app, she'd be my type of woman. Blunt, powerful, straight to the point, and just enough bitchiness in her eyes to make you fear her the slightest.

But right now? She's not exactly my favorite person.

"I did get it. Thanks for sending me Jake Marx's interview. He obviously lied about it all, but it was what helped me make my apology, so I appreciate it." I smile and start packing my things into my bag, hoping Grace will get the hint.

She bites her thumbnail, which is painted blue. "Sure. It's my job to keep up to date on this information. And you went to a protest after your apology, so you're back into your activism, right? Listen, I still want to interview you for West's paper. If you want, we can avoid the scandal altogether, though I think it'd be a great way to show how men and women are treated differently in today's society."

I cock a brow. "What do you mean?"

Grace purses her lips in what looks like she's hiding a smile. "You know, how his career has suddenly blown up for being with you and yours has sort of..." She bites her lip. "Imploded?"

Sí, es cierto. I lick my lips and taste the cinnamon lipstick I have on. "Yeah, I've noticed that too. But we still don't know who leaked that footage. So, I don't really feel comfortable talking about how Jake's benefited from something someone else did." And maybe a few days ago, I wanted to change things. But with the heartache of Tom, I feel like I'm drowning. "I don't think it's a good time to interview. Plus, we're probably in the minority with our beliefs."

She shrugs. "Hm, maybe. I'd like to think otherwise. Especially after those anonymous TikToks were leaked." Grace winks.

Before I can even respond, she stands and walks off, hips swaying with each step. That was weird.

I quickly unlock my phone and head back to TikTok, clicking on the first mention in my notifications. It pulls up a short video.

Jake laughs, shoulder bumping against some guy with dark, mussed hair. The beach is in the background. "Bagged a liberal, what's up."

"Some random?" the other guy asks.

Jake shakes his head. "Nah, that make love not walls chick. Candy DeLeón. Saw her posts a few days ago, and figured while we're down here, I'd stir up a lil' trouble, ya feel? How's that for the winning hit, Lewis?"

Lewis turns toward the camera and looks over it, as if he's staring at the person recording. "No way. I don't believe you."

"Bet." Jake pulls out his phone. "Got the security footage."

The person holding the camera, a woman, says, "Isn't that, like, illegal?" in a high-pitched voice.

Jake shrugs. "Nah, we're in Mexico. Nothing is illegal here."

Lewis zooms in on Jake's phone. "Shut up. This is...holy shit, I can't believe you did it. How?"

"She seemed kinda off. Maybe she was drunk or somethin'. Who knows. Let's just say, she fell into my lap."

The girl points the camera toward the ground, where perfectly painted red toes show. "You took her back to your room while she was drunk? What the hell?" she hisses.

"Relax," Jake says. "She definitely wanted it."

The camera shakes, showing the calves of the two guys. "How can you even know that if she was drunk?"

"Even better, right? She couldn't have said no then. But let me tell you, those curves, that hungry for a green card pus—"

The video ends there.

¿Qué chingados? I definitely was not drunk. Nowhere *near* drunk. But the fact that *he* thought I was, and he still went through with it is gross. And get the hell out with that green card crap. I was freaking born here.

I'm livid. The only emotion I feel is blinding rage. He somehow got the security footage, showed other people, and released photos. It's a complete and total violation of my privacy. And this just shows he really did plan it from the beginning.

That is so sick and twisted, not to mention, completely violating. He purposely used those photos against me, knowing how it would make me look. He used me, and he didn't even care if I could consent.

My rage turns into a creeping sense of doom. Who does something like that?

I scroll up to read the comments.

It's the lack of consent for me.

Let's just call this *rape*

People get offended by everything. She didn't look drunk in those photos.

She already admitted to it. Obvi wasn't drunk.

So he's a frat boy who never got enough attention.

He's canceled, but she still went through with it. So…

Someone really said it's lack of consent for me lmaoooo

Jake Marx screws drunk chicks. Must be a slow news week

Is anyone surprised by this info? Let's be honest

You ever just wanna *fist emoji, man emoji*

I head back to my notifications and scroll until I see a different thumbnail. Please, don't let this be more. I click on that first mention and watch.

I stand facing the racist couple at Disney, talking to the Latino family about what just happened. I go back and forth with Jan and Bert, or whatever their names were. I tell them off for the last time before the Disney employee pulls the couple away, and I shake my head as I turn toward Tom, Carter, and Les.

Les's face sours. "Those people were so rude!"

Carter laughs. "More than rude, but yeah, babe."

They walk away and Tom stares at me with a smile creeping up his face.

I wrap my arm around his and give him a quick kiss on the cheek.

Tom cocks an eyebrow and gives me a chastising pout. "What happened to being done with your activism?"

Laughing, I say, "Nah, I'll never stop calling out racists when I see them."

Without warning, Tom picks me up, and I gasp as he walks away with me in his arms, pressing kisses all around my cheeks and foreheads as I squeal.

The video ends with me laughing and him kissing me on the lips.

This video just makes me...sad. What was the point in this one even being uploaded? I swipe at my cheek as a trail of water forms from my dumb tear ducts. The comments on this one are different.

This called me single in seven languages
I don't even know her, but I like her
Isn't this that canceled twitter girl?
Wait, someone fill me in? Who is she and why's she canceled?
Who recorded this? lol
Here, sis, you dropped this *crown emoji*
Get them racists, queen

My phone buzzes with a text.

Unknown number: *Ready for that interview now? – Grace*

I didn't truly doubt Tom when he said he didn't upload the photos of me and Jake, but these last few days, I considered that maybe he did. Wouldn't be the first time he's lied to me. Now, I know for sure he didn't upload them. It was Jake.

Not that any of it matters anymore. What's done is done. I'm just left with a sick, oily feeling in my gut. Jake had planned this from the beginning. He wanted to exploit us getting together. I guess the confirmation is what really cements it for me. I feel so violated.

And now? I also feel heartbroken after the Disneyland video. I head to Instagram and go to the photo I uploaded of Tom and me. I'm looking up at him like I'm some Disney princess.

But in this story, the Disney princess gets burned. Because the prince was actually a villain who cheated, the princess was naïve, and a guy she barely knew took advantage of her for clout, so...

So much for this being my year. My relationship is gone and ruined. My career, if you can call it that, is hanging on by a thread, and I'll somehow have to carry on.

The past few years, without Tom, I had my career. Now, without Tom, it feels like I have nothing. I don't like it. I *need* my career. It fills me with happiness and a sense of surety that I'm doing the right thing. It is the only thing I am a hundred percent sure of. My life has always had the end goal of working in politics.

And politics are messy.

I can't run away anymore.

It's time I get my career back. Here's the thing...people like Jake? They always have skeletons in their closet. People like Jake get messy, and this video is proof. If he openly talked like that in front of his friends, there's no way that I'm the only one this has happened to.

He paid someone for the footage of us together. This definitely isn't his first rodeo. My mind works like a well-oiled detective machine. I know guys like Jake. I know how they work. And I'm willing to be my career that there is a whole hoard of girls who have been violated by Jake Marx. All I need to do is find them and expose his ass.

Grace is a future journalist. It's time to leverage her desire to help with my desire of revenge.

Candy: *I think it's time to think a little bigger. Wanna help me?*

Grace: *Let's set fire to the patriarchy. What do you have in mind?*

I plan to crush Jake Marx like the cockroach he is. It's time he gets a dose of his own medicine. I post the TikTok of Jake to Twitter and my Instagram stories with a new hashtag. First step into taking Jake Marx down: Starting another movement.

#Marxfamiscanceled

Chapter Twenty Five - Candy

L ife is busy, but as a twin, you show up.

It's why I'm here, at the baseball game, even though Tom is on the field with Carter.

Les is next to me, dressed as Carter's number one fan. She's got her hair in long blonde braids, wearing a West University sweatshirt with Carter's number on it, and a big fat smile on her face. She throws her arm around me and squeals.

I sigh. I mean, her energy is kind of contagious, but I can't focus. My parents sit next to me, chatting about different plays. Carter hasn't been pitching great, and I feel like it's somehow my fault. Like my mood is affecting his pitching through some weird twin telepathy.

Tomorrow is a big day. Behind the scenes, Grace and I have worked our asses off. My bet was right. Skeletons upon skeletons upon skeletons exist in Jake's closet. Stories so sick that I've been reeling the past few days with the weight of them all. What started out as getting revenge for him violating me has turned into so much more. I couldn't be prouder of everything Grace and I have set up. Now, it's time to start it all.

Tomorrow, I'm doing a photoshoot with West's paper, a tell-all with Grace for the Jaguar Paper, and we're making a video together announcing our future plans. It's a video that will damn Jake, if not get him arrested.

It's time to cancel Jake Marx for good.

But I wish I could stop coming to these baseball games. Seeing Tom play is bringing back our grocery store exchange.

It's the first time I've seen him since. Well, seen him out of the corner of my eye. I'm not gonna look at him more than that.

Carter's next pitch is his best one this game, and the batter strikes out. The teams switch, and Les's ex, Ben, is the first one up to bat. I secretly hope he strikes out.

He doesn't.

Rykard's up next, and Les and I shout, "Woo!"

He blows a kiss in our direction, and I slink deeper into my chair. This feels too normal, and if I'm being honest, my mood isn't up for it. I'm gonna feel unsettled until everything else is figured out with Grace.

I chew on a piece of popcorn. "What're you doing after the game?"

Les shrugs. "We were gonna go to Anna's."

It's a popular diner for WU students, and it's one of the restaurants I always third wheel to with her and Carter.

"You wanna come?"

"*Ay, probablemente.* Nothing else to do. Tomorrow's the big day, though." I quickly pull out my phone, looking through Grace's last texts to confirm the time. "I can swing it. It'll be good to hang out. I feel like I've been holed up in the house for the past week."

She steals some of my popcorn and leans back in her chair. "I know, if I haven't said it, I'm really proud of you. I'm excited to see the final video. I wish I could've been there more during your planning sessions. Now that Dr. Guilliod is back from her maternity leave, I've been dying with this semester's course load and the internship. In hindsight, I probably shouldn't have taken, like, twenty credits."

"*Sí,* that was a mistake." I grip my chair as Tom steps up to bat.

Les nudges my elbow and points a knowing glare toward my hands. "You're gonna break a nail, girlfriend."

"*No me importa.*" I cross my arms instead. "I hope he strikes out. He deserves it."

My mom whips her heard toward me and gives me a weird

look. I haven't told anyone about the breakup but Les, Carter, Jared, and Rykard. I smile sheepishly and mutter, "I was just kidding."

Tom hits a line drive down the third base line. By the time the left fielder runs the ball down, Tom has rounded first and sprints toward second base with long strides. He slides into the bag, narrowly beating the throw. Standing, he wipes dirt from his butt, which now faces me. I scoff.

Arder en el infierno, dude. And as if I said it out loud, he turns around, glances in our direction, then quickly looks away.

I pull out my phone again and stare at it the rest of the time he's in my field of view. West ends up winning by three, and the team celebrates, slapping each other's backs and cheering. We head down closer to the dugout so we can tell Carter congrats and good game.

When I see my twin's goofy grin, I can't help but smile too. I'm telling you, it's some weird twin telepathy. "*¡Mi hermanito!* You did good."

He rolls his eyes. "Not your little brother. Hey, *Mami.*" Carter hugs *Mami y Papi,* then talks to Les some more.

A bead of sweat drops down my back, despite that it's cold outside. It's a warning of what's about to come. I focus on my mom's soft hair cascading over her scarf, zoning in on the fabric as if it's the most intricate piece of art.

Out of my peripheral, I see Tom coming. He's basically family. My parents adore him. I knew he'd come say hello. I just didn't want to face him. And he shouldn't be coming up to us right now.

His grin breaks his face into the gleaming athlete that women fall for. It even gives *my* heart flutters, and I'm only staring at it out of the corner of my eye. "Well, well, well. What's goin' on, DeLeóns?"

Mi mami betrays me, giving him a big squeeze. With her movement, my gaze shifts, and Tom's face is right where it lands. His eyes close, his long lashes fluttering against his cheekbones. His full mauve lips tilt upwards, and for a moment, my eyes tear up.

I can feel the unguarded expression on my face, the lack of hardness in my gaze. And when he lets go of her, I glance down, afraid he might see me for who I really am.

He says hello to everyone but me, and when our gazes do finally meet, I'm prepared. I've buried the feelings inside of me, and my stare is ice. He dips his chin. "Candy."

I look at my freshly manicured, hot pink stiletto nails. "Tom," I mutter.

If *mi familia* knows what's going on, they don't say anything. It might as well be me and him in a small room rather than all of us at the ball field. I sigh. "I've gotta get home and study. I'll see you all when I get home."

Les rubs my arm. "But you said you were coming to Anna's with us."

I shake my head and widen my eyes. "No, I *said I had to study, remember?*"

"Psh." She cocks her head to the side, and her braids swing. "Duh. I totally forgot. Dumb blonde and all that. My bad, babe. I'll see you later."

I give my mom a kiss, squeeze Les's hand, and hug my dad goodbye. Les mouths *text me,* and I nod before racing out of the stadium. What I said isn't a lie, I *do* need to get home and study. But, I could've gone to dinner with them.

A little extra time to watch all the videos and go over what I'll say tomorrow with Grace is important. Probably gonna need to wash my hair with Overtone too so the pink is fresh. Don't want to look like I've completely let myself go.

I feel a little overwhelmed after everything that's happened, but I'm determined too. It's time to end this crappy year and get my place back on top of the Marx family.

Footsteps echo behind me. "Candy, hold up."

I lose my breath as if Tom's voice pushes me to the ground. I don't want to see him. "What?" I shout, turning around.

He runs a hand through his hair then scrapes his palm

across his newly-formed stubble. "Who have you told about the test?"

I glare at him. "*Vete a la chingada,* Tom. That's what you want to know?" I laugh, but there's no mirth behind it. "I didn't tell anyone."

One more step and he invades my space with his obnoxious scent. "I didn't get anyone pregnant."

Like that matters? He clearly thought he did when he bought the test. "*Genial.* Glad it came back negative. I have to go." I fish out my keys and unlock my car a few rows over. "Bye, Tom."

As I walk away, he yells, "So, this is how it's gon' be, huh? You avoid me, ignore me, act like you hate me? Come on, Candy, I know you better!"

He wants to have a screaming match in the parking lot of the baseball field? Blistering heat makes its way from my stomach to my head. I shake my head. "No, you really don't know me at all," I say as I sling my belongings into my car.

I don't need him.

"That's a lie, and you know it. Ask me, Candy. Ask me who it was for. I'm not gonna lie if you ask. I'm right here." He throws his arms out to the side. "I wouldn't do that to you."

I grip the top of my car door. "When are you gonna learn that everything you say that you're not gonna do, you do? Go screw around with whoever you want. Go knock someone up! *Puto, ¡me vale!* I think it's pretty clear that me and you are through."

He folds his arms. "That's the biggest cap I heard in a minute."

"*¡Párate!* I mean it. I'm done." My voice breaks, and I get into my car and slam the door.

My hands shake as I fire up my car and drive away. But when I pass Tom in the parking lot, he just stands there, hands by his side, tears rolling down his face.

It breaks my heart all over again.

Chapter Twenty Six – Tom

The video didn't change anything. Seeing us together, laughing, happy and carefree, it didn't affect Candy at all. But from her tweet and the trending hashtag, I guess one of the videos I uploaded worked, and as much as that sucks, I'm happy for her too.

As I walk into my apartment after the game, my heart is a kettlebell of despair. I gave her the opportunity to ask. Felt like if she *asked* me about the pregnancy test, then I couldn't lie. And then whatever fallout happened from Kira uploading the video, we'd handle together.

I was selfish.

But joke's on me because she didn't even ask.

She didn't even care.

My mood is firmly planted halfway between punching a hole through the door and throwing a blanket over my head for the next year.

Life post-Candy, post-cheating, was fine. I was enjoying it. I had a carousel of girls, I focused on my games, I went to protests, I was friends with Candy. No complaints.

But now post-Candy, post-I-love-you, yeah, there's some complaints. For one, I didn't know how dead my life was before. It may have seemed like I was having fun, but I was fooling myself.

I unlock the door and step inside where Ethan, Tristan, and Scott sit on the couch, cackling with a petite red-head as they watch a movie.

Ethan's got his arm around the girl, but he unwinds himself and stands when he sees me. Giving me our roomie hand-shake, he pats me on the back. "Nice game, man. How'd you feel about it?"

"Yeah, it was good. Good, good," I say, rubbing at my eye. "What're y'all up to?"

"Watching the new Kevin Hart movie. You wanna join in?" Tristan asks.

Scott is swiping on West's dating app, like always. Give it an hour and those two will be wrapped up in some girls' beds.

I glance at the TV. Ethan points to the red-head and says, "This is Grace, by the way. Grace, Tom. Tom, Grace."

"Nice to meet you." I quirk my lips and nod.

She looks at me as if she's studying my past, present, and future, and I'm not so sure I like it. "Likewise. As Ethan said, great game. We'll run an article on it in the paper. Are you de-claring for the draft this year?"

Ethan laughs. "Alright, reporter. Let the man breathe. He's not declaring for the draft. The draft is declaring for him, if you know what I mean."

She shakes her head. "I do not."

They bust into a fit of giggles, and I don't think I've ever seen a player get played so hard. The man's in trouble, and I have half a mind to knock him on the head and make the heart eyes fall from his face.

Ready to get into my room and sulk, I ramble, "The draft, I'm not so sure of. Guess we'll see the interest this year from scouts. Anyway, I'm gonna shower and catch an early night. It was good meeting you, Grace. Night guys."

I head to my bathroom and crank the shower as hot as it will go. It burns my skin as I step in, but I don't care enough to turn it down.

I'm a fool. It's not like I thought I'd upload two videos and Candy would come back into my arms. I did it to help her car-eer. To expose the slimy things Jake Marx has said and done, and to show that no matter what, Candy is still fighting for minorities everywhere. I still don't know who it was that sent me those videos in my DMs. It's an anonymous account, and even though I ignored the original Jake Marx one, the Disney one came a few weeks later.

Just figured the videos would've made her at least talk to me. Instead, all I got was a fight. The only thing I'm not blocked on is Instagram, but I'm not gonna blow her up on there.

She's only keeping me unblocked to save face, I'm sure. From what I can tell, no one knows we're broken up...besides her apartment. Candy kept the photos of us up on Instagram, and we still have our Q&A at *Young Americans*.

Whether she's still going or not, who knows.

This mess is already affecting me. Yeah, we pulled out a win today. But I wasn't playing my best. I was distracted. Got two strikes before hitting the fastball in the third, managed to screw up and didn't catch the ball on second. Mistakes that others might think are regular happenings. But my hitting average is high for a reason, so Coach noticed, and so did I.

Scouts will as well. The sad thing is I don't even know if I care. Let 'em watch my failures. Right now, my future seems as dark as when I close my eyes.

Ain't a thing to see.

The water beads off my hair and into my eyes. When I begin to sweat, I hop out and towel off.

My phone buzzes on the counter, illuminating the background of Candy sucking on a lollipop at Disneyland.

Guess it's time to change that.

It's a text from Coach.

Coach: Meeting on Thursday at 10AM. Had Coach Johnson film the two of you. We're gonna review after morning training.

I don't even have to question who the 'two' of us are. It's me and Ben Maldon, like freaking always. Beating him, making sure *I* sign with a scout and not him, is the only motivation that keeps me going.

Candy is done with me. Maybe it's time I'm done with her,

too.

∞∞∞

I finish training on Thursday only to find a text message waiting for me from Kira.

Kira: *You done pouting?*

Not even gonna deign to respond to her. She was out of pocket for the whole pregnancy test mess, but she was downright wrong for what happened with Candy and me. To threaten Candy, who she's always clashed with, is one thing. To threaten *me*?

That's a whole other thing.

We're supposed to be family. Family don't do shady shit like that.

I quickly pack my things and head to Coach's office to watch film. I know it wasn't my best work, but I guess watching will make me see just how bad I really was.

Ben stands outside the door, scrolling on his phone. "What's up, Tom?"

I stand beside him. "Not much, Maldon. Not much."

"Saw that TikTok of you and Candy." He glances up and raises his brows. "I commented."

"Cool, man." I scratch at my neck, not really sure where this is going.

"Seemed like the person who posted it wanted to get it viral. Figured a comment from someone verified might help the video make its rounds."

I hum and nod. "Alright, dude. I get it. You're a TikTok creator. Thanks, I guess? Whether it went viral or not doesn't affect me."

I'm playing it off, or I'm tryna, but I'm getting hot under his inspective gaze. Why's he so keen on getting in everyone's business? He used to be cool. Or...bearable. Now, I can't stand him.

Maybe it's just the competition between us. Our stats, build, and positions are all too similar. We're battling each other for a spot in MLB, whether we want to be or not.

Ben chuckles. "Sure, doesn't affect you." He scrolls on his phone once more as if dismissing my presence. "Just seemed like a real interesting video to appear on my for you page after I heard you and DeLeón screaming at each other in the parking lot."

He slips his phone into his pocket and holds up his hands. "Not my business of course—"

"Then stay out of it," I cut in.

"—but I am interested in why. What's a guy like you have to gain from uploading a video like that? Think you'd be a little more concerned with securing your spot in the leagues than a chick." He shrugs nonchalantly.

Because someone can't have more than one interest? He should know that's a lie considering he had a girlfriend, a side chick, a baseball career, and a supposed pre-med route calling his name. What the hell is his problem? And how does he know I uploaded it? It was completely anonymous. Not sure what his endgame is, but I'm over people holding stuff against me. No way am I admitting to him I did it. "Didn't upload it, so it doesn't matter."

Ben laughs. "Chill, dude. I'm not gonna tell anyone. I've got more important things to worry about. And after you missed that ball, seems like you should too."

All he's trying to do is get in my head. He's constantly doing this. And the annoying part is he knows it works. I'm about to show him exactly why he shouldn't mess with me. But the second I clench my fist, Coach's door swings open and he booms, "Get in here."

Ben plasters on his rich-boy grin and strolls into the office. I can't even fake it. I feel the scowl on my face, and Coach sees it too. "Get your attitude in order, Walker."

"Yes, Sir," I mumble, but my face still twists as I walk in front of him and sit down.

We spend the next hour reviewing footage, which is full of Ben getting praised and me getting dragged.

"You hesitated here, Tom. Why? You could've thrown to third and taken that kid out, but you didn't." He rewinds the footage and points to the screen. "And earlier, here, Maldon throws to second, and you don't even catch it. It's not a fast-ball, kid."

I scrape my hand down my face. "Yeah, I know. I-I don't know. Just got caught up and hesitated."

"Stop hesitating," he grinds out.

Enlightening, truly. I try to smile, but my lips aren't co-operating. "I'll watch my reaction time and stop hesitating."

Coach grunts, but doesn't say any more. Out of my peripheral, I see Ben grinning. It's a miracle I hold in my punch at this point.

Coach fast forwards to Ben's throw from third base to second, where I barely caught it. "Perfect arc here, Ben. Really well done."

"Thanks, Coach. The extra time we've been working has helped a lot."

Kiss ass.

Coach nods his head. "Good, kid. I'm glad. I'd say your biggest flaw is you play it too safe, and that won't cut it in the majors…or minors, quite frankly. You need speed like Tom."

It's shallow of me, I know, but a little satisfied grin finally overtakes my face. Ben's not as untouchable as he thinks. And I'm *faster*.

Ben twists in his seat, sending daggers my way. "Yes, Sir. I'll work on paying more attention and weighing my risks."

Coach seems to take that answer to heart and dismisses the both of us. Like a wounded puppy, Ben spits out, "Who's hesitating now, Walker?" the moment he passes the door.

I easily got criticized twenty times more than him, but it seems rich boy can't take a little heat on his own hide. "At least I've got speed on you, my man."

I chuckle to myself as I grab my phone from my backpack

and walk toward my next class. The weather is starting to warm up a bit now that we're in March. Flowers are even starting to bloom on the trees, making my allergies act up fierce.

Heading from the athletic building to the business one is about a fifteen-minute walk, so I scroll Instagram on the way. Some of the guys I've met from protests have the hashtag #Marxfamiscanceled in their stories. The video of Jake Marx talking to his friends has been reposted thousands of times, and the hashtag has been trending on twitter for over 24 hours.

I wonder what Candy thinks about this movement she's created.

An email notification pops up at the top of my screen, so I quickly hit it and then march up two flights of outdoor steps near the library.

Coach

Subject: Scout Interested

Tom,

Just got this email from Joseph Guildo – one of the A's scouts.

FWD: To: Coach Josh Trucker

Sent From: Joseph Guildo

Josh,

Great talking to you on Monday. Really interested in watching Tom Walker. Been hearing his name around, and want to check out a game. Heard he's great at second base. Is he planning to enter the draft this year or is he a senior draft? What about the home game against Cal Poly April 5th? Send over a confirmation, and I'll get it put in my schedule.

Talk soon,

Joe

I jump and punch the air, not caring that people turn and stare at me. A scout, *from the A's,* is watching me. Everything I've dreamed of and planned for could come true. Holy shit. This is huge. *Huge.*

I slap my hands together and feel the smile growing on

my face. Candy is gonna be pumped. Dad will be thrilled. My hands shake as I bite my lip to keep from having a full freak out on campus. Going to my phone's favorites, I press on Candy's number to tell her.

The realization hits me, and a sour breath bleeds out of me. The first person I want to tell isn't even here. She's blocked me. And it was my stupid choices that lead to it.

It doesn't take my happiness completely, but it does put a damper on it. Because together or not, she's been there for me every step of the way. As a girlfriend, as a friend, or as the girl I'm in love with. But now?

She doesn't even care. I try to push the thought of her out of my mind as I call my dad to tell him the news.

Halfway through the phone call, right in the middle of my dad's strict pep talk, the thoughts come barreling back.

'Cause right across the quad, standing in front of the large WU red block letters is Candy, posing for a photoshoot. She laughs at something the photographer says, and my heart pinches.

"Tom!" my Dad's voice cuts through my self-pity. "Did you hear me?"

I glance away from Candy and walk into the business building. "Yeah, Dad. I heard you. No distractions. And you don't have to worry about that from now on. All I've got left is baseball."

Chapter Twenty Seven – Candy

G race walks up to me as I'm posing with the photographer for our last shot. He's a sweet guy named Gus, who's on the basketball team.

Grace pats him on the back. "Looks good. You can head home, Gus. Thanks for doing this last minute."

"Anytime, Grace." He looks at me and breaks into a goofy grin. After just an hour together, it feels as if we've been friends for years. "See ya, Candy. Count me in for your next game night."

"Only if you bring this girl you've been telling me about," I reply.

He waves and walks away, looking over his camera as he strolls toward the parking lot.

Grace hands me an iced tea and swipes some condensation droplets off of her blazer. "I always like doing the photos first. Interviews have a way of causing awkwardness."

I hum nonchalantly. "You planning to ask awkward questions, Grace?"

She wraps her arm through mine and pulls me toward the Union building that holds small intimate rooms and beanbag chairs. "I'm gonna try really hard not to."

I tuck my hair behind my ears. "Well, thanks. I'm really excited about this. Thanks for getting it all worked out with the media team."

"Yeah, of course. But you got the lawyers, and that was the most important part."

"I'd argue the women are the most important part of all of

this. I'm just glad that you had the time to help me with this. I think it will be good for both of us. Question. Why'd you want to feed into my crazy idea in the first place? I mean, we hardly know each other."

Shrugging, she looks away from me, but doesn't stop our brisk pace. When we get to the building door, she unwinds her arm around mine and opens it for me. It's then she glances back. "Let's just say I have a thing for bringing down men who think women owe them something. It's sorta my MO, you could say."

It comes out genuine, and though I don't know her well, it's clear she's speaking from some sort of experience. I can only hope it's not the same type of experience that the other women we've gathered have had. Giving her a curt smile, I reply, "Then let's burn the patriarchy, eh?"

Grace leads me down a hallway and into one of the side rooms. It's glass-walled and looks over the quad area, where students mill around, laughing and studying. A small desk, two beanbag chairs, and a sleek office chair make up the room along with a trash can in the corner. A few math equations are left scrawled out on the glass in dry erase marker, leftover from whomever used the room before us.

Grace wipes the dry erase away before sitting in the beanbag closest to the desk. She rummages through her bag, pulling out her phone, a notebook, a ring light, and a camera. I may have read Grace wrong before. She's not so much filled with bitchiness as she is filled with passion. Plus, she got me an iced tea.

¡Ay carajo! I'm cheap these days. A couple bucks and I'm ready to be your friend.

"So, you ready to make a statement?" she asks, fiddling with the ring light.

I sit across from her and sink into the office chair. It's stiff, which sort of matches my personality right now. I'm nervous. So many women have trusted me with this, and I worry I won't do it right. That I can't give them the justice they deserve.

I let out a breath. "Yes. After seeing what he said about me on those videos, and now knowing everything we know now, it's time. Hopefully this will sort of end the whole thing."

She taps on her phone and slides it in the middle, between us. "I'm ready to knock Jake Marx off of his last peg. And you're gonna announce the new non-profit?"

Eso me gusta escuchar. It's not that I'm ready per se, as I know people will have their fair share of comments with anything I do these next few months. I'll be under more scrutiny now than if the photos with Jake Marx never occurred. But I think I've finally got to the point of hiding isn't an option. People are dying every day from racists like Jake Marx. It's time I care less about myself and more about helping those people. I still have a platform, even if it's shrunk in the last few months.

It's time to use it for good again.

And maybe that's the only good thing that's come out of this breakup with Tom. I don't have him to lean on. And now I have to make the choice: Do I wallow in self-pity and despair, hoping people don't talk about me? Or do I screw the haters and do the work I'm supposed to?

"Let's do this," I reply. What's a few more haters anyhow? I may have been kicked out of my Equal Treatment for Equal People club here on campus, but I'm about to blow them out of the water.

Grace and I have worked our butts off for days straight, staying up at nearly all hours of the night to come up with what I'm about to announce. Called in a few favors with other activists familiar with this territory, and I'm ready.

Grace sets up the camera. "It's ready whenever you are. Just start talking."

My hands are clammy, so I wipe them off on my jeans before speaking. "For those of you who don't know me, I'm Candy DeLeón, a student at West University and a political activist. I started the hashtag #makelovenotwalls, and recently, my personal life was thrust into the spotlight. You may have seen the photos of me and the former governor of California's son, Jake Marx. I made a mistake, so let me make one thing clear: I was not drunk, and I *did* consent to the event in question."

Grace quirks the side of her mouth and crosses her legs, nodding her head from the opposite side of the ring light, encouraging me to keep going.

"But I want to make one more thing clear. I did not consent to being recorded, nor did I consent to photos being taken, nor did I consent for those photos to be leaked. It was an incredible violation of my privacy, and I recognize that as a public figure, I don't have as much privacy as others. That being said, these photos weren't released from a third-party. They were released by Jake Marx, who had planned and orchestrated the whole event."

I take a deep breath and shake my head. "This egregious lack of disrespect for me, and for a woman in general, is absolutely not okay. Have I called out the Marx family before? Yes. Have I ever leaked footage like this to purposely end another person's career? No.

"The fact that Jake Marx was willing to orchestrate his plan whether or not I was coherent enough to consent is abominable. But perhaps the worst of it is that I wasn't the only one he's done this to. I'll be playing other women's stories at the end of my statement to show how Jake Marx has a history of cyberbullying, revenge porn, and violating women across all fronts. Which leads me to an announcement.

"Though this does not excuse my own actions, I want to show how a man like Jake profited off of my downfall. We ran a report on his different accounts, and this 'CEO'," I air-quote, "is far from the shining poster boy for the cancer non-profit that he runs. In fact, my colleague, Grace, looked into BC Warrior's non-profit finances, and Jake Marx is being paid a generous million a year salary."

My chest burns thinking of all the donations going to pay

for Jake Marx's partying and abuse. Smiling, I clasp my hands. "Jake Marx has hurt too many people—directly and indirectly. I'm creating a non-profit with West University's media team and law school, one that will provide legal counsel for women of sexual assault, harassment, and violence. Its name is Making Our Mark, and we're asking Oak and Trough, a company that has solely supported BC Warriors with a yearly four million dollar donation, to donate to Making Our Mark instead. We hope this will help reform BC Warriors while also supporting the foundation that we've created, specifically to help deal with Jake Marx and the pain his actions have caused. Making Our Mark's first clients will be any woman that Jake Marx has personally hurt."

Now, it's time to make sure I don't have to share my space with him any longer. "I'm also personally calling for all organizations that support Jake Marx, including *Young Americans Changing the World,* to drop your partnerships or scheduled interviews with him. It's my hope that after watching the stories of these women who have been hurt by Mr. Marx, that you'll rise up and take action with me. We have no room for men who hurt women in our activism. *Gracias.*"

Grace stops the camera, and nods. "That was perfect. So, so good. And I'm so excited to have this organization with you."

"Me too." I nod. "Let's decide on the order of women so we can edit, then we'll get to the West Paper interview."

She pulls up the different submissions I've gotten in my DMs the last couple of days. After one woman reached out to me about Jake Marx's past, I knew she couldn't be the only one. I asked her to help me find the others, and together through the hashtag #marxfamiscanceled, over fifty women came forward, some with texts and emails proving everything.

We go through the videos, which are sickening. One woman dated him in high school, and he leaked nude photos of her online when she was a minor. Another woman was nearly assaulted at a college party two years ago before a friend stepped in and stopped him. A few women say that they were drugged and date raped by him, and countless others say they were inappropriately recorded or photographed.

Grace puts the video together, and I get chills when the women come on camera and share their stories from all across the country. They're real, raw, and I know it's going to impact everyone else who sees it.

It *has* to.

Once we finish editing, Grace sends me the file to upload a few days from now. We have to be sure each woman feels protected when sharing their stories, and a few of them insisted on traveling elsewhere out of fear of revenge from the Marx family. So I'll wait patiently until I get the green light from all the victims.

I glance at Grace. "Don't you feel drained? After hearing all of those horrible stories, it makes me sick. I just feel...gross. Violated."

She nods. "Yeah, same. Honestly, those women are so brave. I can't even imagine going up against the Marx family like this. I mean, I'm happy to do it with our non-profit, but as a victim? I can't imagine. You too. You're all so strong."

Checking my watch, I realize just how long we've spent holed up in this study room. It's been nearly three hours. "We better get to the interview questions before it gets dark."

Grace grabs her notebook, pen, and a recorder. Putting it in the center of the table, she begins the recording and asks me to start from the beginning with Jake. I explain everything that happened, but this is a small part of the interview.

Moments later, she asks about our new organization, and I make a statement, telling her to add on whatever she thinks since she's one of the founding members on the media team.

We talk about how we have a group of local West Law School grads (all who are women) who are doing these cases pro-bono for those who can't afford legal counsel. It's for West students and more, and they'll help with any harassment, rape, assault, violence, or discrimination case. Our lawyers will help both men and women, but right now, they're creating a legal case against Jake Marx.

Grace and I chat like old friends, and I'm happy that she'll be a part of it all.

"So," Grace taps her pen on her notebook, "as long as *Young Americans* drops Jake Marx from the interview lineup, you'll be going, right?"

"*Sí*, absolutely. I want to inspire these young kids, but I also want to be sure that Jake Marx won't be there to sow dangerous ideology."

She leans forward as if she's about to tell me a secret. "How do you feel about the leaked TikTok videos?"

I swallow as flashes of them come across my mind. I hear Jake's words.

"Um," I blink and refocus.

How do I feel? Like a joke? Like I was a pawn in a game that I didn't get the instructions to? Used, naïve, and a little lost, honestly. I scrape my nail over my jeans in a figure eight pattern to collect my thoughts.

Clearing my throat, I say, "I'm hurt. I'm sad that someone would go out of their way to hurt me." I lick my dry lips and think back to that night. I really believed he was nursing a heartbreak and was just upset, needed an escape like I did. Had I known he had a history of this, everything would've been different.

It dawns on me that I have horrible taste in men. And apparently, that I have a horrible trust radar. Because I've trusted multiple guys who have done nothing but hurt me in ways that I should've seen coming from the start. I trusted Tom, too, only for him to hurt me the exact same way he did the first time. But I'm done being the dumb girl. I'll get my career back, and this is just the first step.

I've worked my ass off for years, and I'm not going to let one incident overthrow it.

She gives me a pitying smile. "I really am so sorry you went through that. Do you plan to focus on the new non-profit at *Young Americans?*"

"Yeah, definitely."

Grace nods. "How has your boyfriend Tom Walker reacted to this? He'll be at *Young Americans* as well, right? I heard the two of you are doing a Q&A together."

My face is frozen. I don't even blink, because I forgot that no one knows we broke up. And I was planning to ask for separate Q&As. But I can't bring that up *now*. "Uh, yeah. Yep. For sure. Tom has been...really...um, really supportive."

Dread pools in my stomach. Why did I say that? No, no, no. I should...well, I should what? Say, *actually, we're not together anymore. I can't seem to keep a guy!* Or how about, *all men suck and apparently he's sleeping with someone else.* I don't want Tom and Jake compared in an interview, or even mentioned in the same interview in a bad light, because though Tom may have broken my heart, he's still a person who's worked hard for what he has.

I want to preserve my image, as well as his. Every time I blink, all I see are Tom's tears trailing down his face after the baseball game. In the eight years I've known him, I don't think I've ever seen him cry.

"Candy?" Grace's voice cuts into my thoughts. "Are you okay?"

I clear my throat. "Yeah, sorry. What'd you say?"

She tilts her head to the side as if she's trying to pick up on something. Something I'm desperately trying to push down. When she does (or doesn't) see what she wants, she flips a page in her notebook. "I was just saying that I met Tom the other night."

My ears perk up at that. "Oh yeah? Where?" I casually ask, but my throat is tight with anxiety. Is he already at parties? Acting as if our relationship meant nothing?

"His apartment. I was hanging out with Ethan Hamilton."

Now it's my turn to study her. She has a slight blush on her cheeks. "Oh, that makes sense. You're the new bird."

"Huh?" She rears her chin back.

I lick my lips and smile. "Nothing. Forget I said anything. Ethan's a great guy."

She nods. "Yeah, he's a good friend. Uh, back on track." She hides a smile. "Do you and Tom have anything special planned for *Young Americans?*"

Do we? I didn't plan on going together anymore. But I guess I just fumbled that with this interview. I panicked, but I'll have to deal with the consequences of my choices once again. I take a deep breath and plaster on the world's fakest smile, hoping it comes off as semi-genuine. "It's a surprise. But we're pretty excited about it. We can't wait to talk to the kids about fighting for a better future."

Grace reaches across the table and unlocks her phone, pausing the recording. "I think that's all I have for you. If I haven't made it obvious enough by now, I can't wait for more meetings with Making Our Mark."

My mind is elsewhere, but I grip my bag tightly and give her a genuine smile. "Yeah, me too. And thanks for not giving up on me." I pack up my things and cheers her with the rest of my iced tea. "Have a good day, Grace."

"You too," she replies, connecting her iPad to a keyboard before settling into the beanbag deeper.

A weird fog comes over me as I walk out of the Union building. I grab out my AirPods and go to our roomie playlist, where Rykard, Les, Carter, Jared, and I contribute songs for our game nights. The first song is Marshmello's "It's OK Not To Be OK," but halfway through the song, I can't listen to it anymore. I go to the next song on shuffle, which is "Years" by Astrid S.

I haven't heard it, but from the drama of it all, I'm guessing it's one of Les's contributions. I listen to it as I walk through campus, which is fairly dead thanks to classes being in session. Zoning out, I keep walking, unsure if I want to head to the library or my car, so I just look at the ground as my feet shuffle against the concrete, unsure of everything.

I've now committed to being at the event with Tom. But I can't even talk to him to get closure because the second I see his face, I fall apart. I really am so stupid.

Chapter Twenty Eight – Candy

The West baseball team wins another game. And then another, and another. Each time, I'm there. And each time, I ignore the feelings that swirl in my gut, congratulating Carter and leaving right after so I don't have to see Tom.

I finally released the video yesterday, and it's gone viral. My following has grown by nearly 10%, so while I'm still not where I used to be, I'm on the climb. Which isn't to say I haven't had backlash. I have. People say we're slandering, others are threatening lawsuits, and more. But so far...Jake hasn't made a statement.

In fact, the whole Marx family has been silent. I hunker down at my house, go to class, and avoid people as much as possible. I'm thrilled that my following has grown and that there have been positive responses to the video. I've talked with some of the girls, and we've all become friends. United against a common enemy and all that.

But still, I just feel stuck in a rut.

The days go by quickly, and I binge every episode of *Gossip Girl, Buffy,* and *Emily in Paris.* I spend too much time playing Among Us on my phone, and I focus on my assignments.

I should be overjoyed with everything happening, but it all feels...stilted somehow. Like I'm the biggest imposter or something. I also keep thinking that I'll have a breakdown over Tom. But the tears don't come.

I've just been numb. After the night of rage karaoke with Les, I sort of pushed it out of my mind. I guess I'd rather be numb than a crying mess, though.

Now I'm sitting in my politics class where the professor going on about our midterms that we took last week. I hear a soft snore beside me, only to find Ethan dozing off.

I nudge him with my pen and he startles awake, scrubbing at his face.

"Late night?"

Ethan clears his throat. "Yeah, you could say that."

"Even with the finals coming up, huh?"

West's basketball team made it to the Elite Eight for the NCAA playoffs. Everyone's been buzzing about it. He raises a brow as if he's surprised I know about his sport. I glare at him.

"Yes, even with finals. There was a party last night, and things got a little out of control to say the least."

I briefly wonder if Tom was at the party with him, considering they're housemates and all. But I shake the thought from my mind. "You worried about Arizona State?"

"Nah," he says. "I've got this."

"Good. How's *Grace*?"

He gives me side eye and taps my desk. "I don't know. She ditched me at the party."

"Hmm,. Did you screw something up? I like her. We're getting brunch together next week."

"Who knows. Haven't talked to her in a couple days."

The professor glares at us, so we quiet down and listen for the rest of the class. My phone buzzes with a text.

Kira: *How are you holding up?*

My face scrunches, but I reply.

Candy: *Alright, I guess. You?*

Kira: *Want to catch lunch? Let bygones be bygones? I have to turn in an application for law school near you.*

This is the weirdest thing. Kira and I have always hated each other. But...women solidarity and all, I guess.

Candy: *Sure. I'm open next week. Want to meet then?*

Kira: *Yes! I'll come to West so you don't have to drive up here. I've got a meeting down there.*

When class ends, Ethan gives me a hug goodbye and jogs to the athletic building. I'm three steps past the library when Carter and Les bounce out from behind a tree, pull my arms, and start running.

"Um, *hola* to you too. What is going on?" I screech as Les squeezes me.

We get to the parking lot, and Carter yanks his keys from his pocket. Les opens the door and shoves me inside, buckling my seatbelt while I shout I'm being kidnapped.

She and Carter jump in the front seat, and Carter peels out of the *parqueadero.*

"Where are we going? I'm two seconds away from calling Mom."

Carter looks at me from the rearview mirror. "Don't do that." He glances at Les. "We're going to cash in our birthday gift."

I'm wearing leggings, the weather is a brisk sixty-eight, and I'm so not prepared for this. "You didn't." I reach up to Les and grab her shoulder. "Tell me he's lying."

She shrugs and smiles. "We're going skydiving!"

I lean back into my seat and sigh. "Why?" I whine.

Les turns around. "One, because I got you it for your birthday and we have yet to go. Two, I scheduled it three weeks ago and forgot to tell you. Three, you've been in a funk, and skydiving is going to be the rush of adrenaline you need to get you out of it!"

Carter turns right and heads to the freeway. "Just don't tell Mom, Dad, or Coach. They'll kill me if they know I'm about to go skydiving during baseball season."

Les clucks. "You'll be fine, babe."

"Says the woman who hardly ever disobeys her own mother," I mutter so she can't hear.

Carter hears though, and his lips quirk on one side. "It'll be a blast. *Nos sentiremos chingonas. Salte de tu cabeza.*"

I'm silent as we drive through Downtown Sacramento, passing the streets that I walked with Tom not that long ago.

Closing my eyes, I can almost see myself in front of the capitol, standing side by side with him.

But those memories are tainted, now overshadowed by Jake Marx. I keep thinking back to that TikTok and everything else he's done to the other girls that came forward. I feel so... violated. It's just an icky, gross feeling, and I'm pretty close to asking Les for her therapist because I might need to talk to someone about this all. I don't know. Life just feels heavy. The only good thing is Jake's now uninvited to *Young Americans*, so I won't have to worry about running into him there.

Just about running into Tom, my "fake" boyfriend. How am I supposed to tell him that I panicked in the interview with Grace?

I don't want him to take it the wrong way, but I also need him to play along for the sake of my reputation.

Not wanting to think about it any longer, I start a game of Among Us on my phone, calling out red because red is always sus. We're voting on the imposter when Carter pulls into a dirt parking lot with a hangar and a few skydiving signs.

I wouldn't say I'm bougie by any means, but that airplane looks like it's one flight away from breaking down. It's dull metal with some rust around the door. The hangar is open, showing everyone inside. People are suiting up in navy jump-suits, smiles on their faces.

"Mi mejor amigo y mi hermano están tratando de matarme." I end the game and unbuckle my seatbelt. "Hear me out. This has always been Carter's dream, not mine. So, how 'bout I stay on the ground and take pictures. I'm a great photographer." I wiggle my phone, trying to sell it.

Les laughs. "Nope, you're doing this." She glances wist-fully at the plane. "I haven't been since I went with my dad. It's been...two years now? I need my best friend for support. I brought some of my dad's ashes, and I'm going to sprinkle them on the plane."

I'm pretty sure I look at her crazy. "Well, you're going first then. I don't need someone's *ashes* sprinkled on me on the way down."

She reaches back and squeezes my knee. "I'm kidding. Just trying to lighten the mood," she replies as if it's the most normal thing to joke about.

Carter shrugs. "Your humor is a little dark sometimes, *cariña*."

She opens the door and jumps out of the car, wiggling her whole body in some weird dance that makes me question if she's full-on white girl wasted right now. "*La amo, pero los odio a los dos ahora mismo.*"

Carter flashes me a grin. "*Sí, lo sé.* If it helps, I'm a little nervous too, *hermana*."

I mock-gasp. "Big, strong baseball player is scared? Oh, don't tell your girlfriend that. She might try and comfort you. The horror."

He slaps my arm, and I hit him back. "Let's go, turd. I want to get this over with."

I get out of the car, and he shouts over the hood, "You're supposed to enjoy this!"

Plastering on a creepy fake smile, I give him a thumbs up. "Maybe if the parachute doesn't open, I will."

He softly bumps me on the head and pulls me into his side. "Stop it."

"Okay, *Papi*."

Carter rolls his eyes but lets go of me as we trail behind Les. She marches to the front counter with the assurance of a pro. Two minutes later, I'm signing my life away and telling the hot scruffy guy working the counter that I'm a size medium.

After getting suited up, my skydiving instructor, Andy, explains everything that we'll have to do while up in the plane. My eyes seem to widen with everything he says, and by the time he asks if I'm ready to get on the plane, I'm looking at him as if he (or maybe I) belongs in some sort of asylum.

We board the plane, and I'm just short of hyperventilating. The plane rickets and bumps as it goes down the runway, and Les and Carter's cackles filter into my ears.

Why are they so calm? Are they serial killers? It's unacceptable to be *this chill* while riding in a freaking airplane that doesn't even have a regular door or seats. Instead, it's jostling us around as if we're clothes in a dryer.

Andy tries to make casual conversation, and I gruffly respond to each of his questions. I find out he graduated from West two years ago and now works full time as a skydiving instructor. He's jumped over a thousand times, in places like Hawaii and India, and tells me I have nothing to worry about.

Which makes me mad because now he put that out into the universe and when you say nothing is going to go wrong, everything goes wrong. I said this year was going to be my year. Now look how that turned out.

The pilot says we're at altitude, and people begin standing. I'm white-knuckling the seat when Andy helps me up. He does a final gear check, and I'm praying to *Madre Maria* that I'm not going to die. I may have joked about it earlier, but I have way too many plans for this earth to go out early.

A few people we don't know go first, and then Les and her instructor jump. A moment later, Carter whoops as they dive out of the plane. Andy gets us hooked up to the door, and I make the dumb mistake of looking down to see clouds floating below us.

I'm about to say absolutely not when Andy counts, "One...two—"

And jumps on two. Who jumps on two?!

I scream as we tumble out of the plane. The air rips open my lips and plows down my throat. I quickly close my mouth, squirming around like a crazy person. But then Andy taps my shoulder and points to the other skydivers, and suddenly, we're freefalling.

The wind whips around us, but as we fall, I'm weightless. It's loud and silent at the same time, and the feeling is so peaceful that my fears leave my mind. I view the ground below us, perfectly grid-like from this high, and it seems stupid, but being up here, like this, it makes me feel as if I could do anything.

It's as if we're flying, not falling. Before I can truly appreciate it, Andy pulls the parachute, and we fling upward as it catches enough air to inflate. He laughs and asks how it was, and I give him a thumbs up.

We float down to the ground for a few moments, and I take in everything I can on our slow descent. The cold air, the way everything smells fresh, and how the mountain peaks can be seen above the clouds in the distance. As we descend, a calm feeling comes over me.

Life has been crazy, and I haven't been processing it. I've been numb, which felt nice for a while, but what I just felt skydiving? It was adrenaline, and excitement, pure bliss, and sensory overload.

The last thing I want to do after experiencing that is go numb again. I want to feel it all, even if that means some things hurt. Our lows only show us how good our highs are.

I may not have wanted to come, but as we land, my heels touch the ground and I'm almost disappointed. Carter was right...it did get me out of my head. I think it's time to process my lows so I can look forward to the highs. It's not normal to be numb all the time. I need to talk to someone. Or, I *want* to. And I know just the person.

Chapter Twenty Nine – Tom

I pull into the driveway of Candy's childhood home. It seems like forever since I've talked to Candy instead of just a few weeks. Still haven't gotten a word in with her. I've texted, called, even left a few more notes. I saw her video and everything about her new non-profit. I'm mad proud of her, and I know that she's gonna change a lot of lives.

I wish I could tell her that in person. Wish I could be a part of it, too.

It's time for another Spanish lesson with her dad, and I'm afraid Candy's talked to him. Maybe he'll see me and kick me to the curb. If anything, the DeLeóns are always fair. But, if I had a daughter, I wouldn't think twice about beating up the guy that cheated on her.

I scrub my face and stall, scrolling on my Buzzfeed app while listening to some of the songs Candy downloaded to my Spotify. "Quite Miss Home" by James Arthur plays, and I can't help but agree with it. Candy was always my home, and I freaking miss her.

Apparently, I've turned into some sap of a human being.

The top article on Buzzfeed makes me pause.

Jake Marx Makes First Public Appearance Since Damning Videos Were Released

The article recounts the video and talks about Jake's mom's campaign for senate this year, and how this sheds a bad light on the entire Marx family. Jake hasn't made a comment about the video, but he was seen leaving the gym with a hat and sunglasses on. However, a "close friend" to Jake Marx claims the videos are taken out of context and he plans to sue.

Good luck with that.

How can one video where he straight up says he was willing to rape a girl who he thought was too drunk to consent and then a dozen videos of girls explaining what Jake did to them "taken out of context." I put my phone away and take a deep breath.

It's time to face Candy's dad.

I knock on their door. A few barks come through as their dog, Oreo, jumps up and paws against the side windows. Candy's mom smiles as she opens the door. "Tom! How are you?"

She gives me a hug, her blonde hair tickling my chin.

I breathe in the familiar scent of the DeLeón home, which smells exactly like Cinnamon Toast Crunch. "I've seen better days, not gonna lie, Mama DeLeón. Where's that *papi* at?"

When she pulls away, a frown graces her pretty lips. "I'm sorry to hear that. Girl troubles?" she asks lightly, winking.

I give her a grim quirk of the lips. "Uh, yeah. That'd be an understatement."

She doesn't pry, but instead responds, "Cisco's in his office. Come on."

The house is quiet, but Oreo follows beside us, jumping up on my thighs, begging for a pet with each step. I give the little spaniel a few pats.

"*Papi,* Tom *está aquí.*"

Cisco turns around in his desk chair and chucks a baseball my way. I catch it easily, and toss it from one hand to the other.

"Why do you look like you've been sniffing dog shit, kid?" Cisco laughs.

I roll my eyes. "Hey, watch it, old man."

"Let me know if you boys need anything. *Trata de comportarse, por favor,*" Mama DeLeón says as she shakes her head and leaves.

"*¿Estás listo?*"

"Ready as I'll ever be, " I reply.

He stands from his chair and grabs a light raincoat before heading outside to the backyard. The DeLeón's house has always been my happy place. Not that my upbringing was bad. It was great. But the DeLeóns have property, a pool, and lush vegetation lining the walkways. It smells fresher out here. A few minutes away from the city and it's as if it's a whole other world.

Not to mention that every time I'd hung with Carter, I watched Candy from the corner of my eye. She was absolutely my first crush. Thinking about her feels wrong, as if her blocking me was her way of saying that I can't have anything to do with her, not even in the past.

But her green eyes, lined with sorrow and tears, still reach into my mind on an hourly basis. I can't shake her.

I'm excited about the scout coming to my game. I'm excited that we have a good chance this year to go to the College World Series, which West hasn't done since the 90s. But everything I'm excited about is shrouded with the darkness that I'm gonna do it all without the girl I'm in love with.

She'll be there, showing up for Carter. And I can trick myself that she's there for me. But deep down, I know she isn't. And it's that knowledge that sucks. I want to crawl out of this dark hole, escape the situation I've gotten myself into. I'm living my life the same, as if Candy didn't take all the light with her, leaving me with a dark sky.

But even routine can't fool me.

I watch my feet as I follow Candy's dad. If only she knew how long I've been coming to her house on a weekly basis to learn Spanish. Would it change things? Make her see how much I care?

Probably not.

The sky is blue without a cloud in it. That feels wrong too.

"¿En que piensas, mijo?" Cisco asks.

What's on my mind? Your daughter and how I wish I could get her back. I'm not usually selfless. I should just tell her about Kira, the video from senior year, and damn our careers.

But her crushed face when she sees the it got leaked will hurt me even more than it hurts her. I sigh and toss him the ball. *"Nada. Béisbol, yo supongo."*

"¿Y que de Béisbol?" He tosses the ball back to me, with a little more force than I was expecting.

I take a step back and throw it to him, harder this time. He catches it, but winces and laughs. I open up to him about the scout at my game and how he's interested in me. Cisco glows with the proud look of a dad. We talk about the meeting with Coach, Maldon and his antics, and how nervous I am that I won't go in the first few picks of the draft. I've decided to declare this year.

He responds quickly, and I have to stop him a few times to explain some of the words in Spanish that I don't know. Our conversation stays on the surface, never touching the topic of Candy. After tossing the ball back and forth for an hour, we head to the porch and grab some water.

I tighten my Apple Watch and lace my running shoes as Cisco goes inside to change into basketball shorts. When he gets back outside, he stretches. I follow his lead, mentally preparing for our run. Every week for the past three years, I come to the house, throw the ball and learn Spanish, and then Cisco and I run five miles.

Candace says it keeps him young, which is why he agreed to it. I'm pretty sure he just felt bad for me when Candy left, and that's how it started. But even when I cheated on Candy, our Spanish lessons and running never stopped.

That first week after I cheated, I was terrified he was gonna kill me. But he never said a word. He's truly the best guy that I know, and I appreciate everything he's done for me more than he'll ever know.

"Okay, *mijo*, let's go."

We round the house and begin our run down the paved road. For the first mile, we don't say anything. The running tightens my calves, and I feel the cool air with each breath I take. But with every step, my chest gets heavier. It's as if something is stuck in my lungs, and it travels up into my throat.

I tap on his shoulder and slow to a jog before stopping completely. Placing my hands on my head, I twist and breathe out. "I screwed up."

He furrows his brows. "*Español, Tom. Sigue siendo nuestra lección.*"

Shaking my head, I place my hands on my knees. "*No sé cómo decirlo.* I screwed up. With Candy," I breathe out. "I did something, and some people are holding things over my head, and I can't tell her about it. I think I lost her for good this time."

Cisco pats me on the back. "*Lo siento,* Tom."

I don't know what I thought. That maybe he'd have the advice I needed so that I could get her back? I don't freaking know because I'm so lost right now. A choked sob comes from my chest, and this is officially rock bottom. I'm on a public street in Sacramento, crying, as an old man comforts me.

One day, I'll laugh about this. But not today. I right myself and rub my eyes. "What am I supposed to do?"

Cisco places his hands on his hips and glances at a car that whizzes past us on the main road. "*Es difícil decirlo sin saberlo todo, pero lo que debe de ser, va a ser.*"

What if what's meant to be gets screwed up by someone else? I kick the pavement, scuffing my shoes against the newly paved asphalt. "Why are y'all so nice to me? You have to know what I did two years ago. I'm tellin' you I screwed up again, and you're not killing me. *¿Por qué?*"

His brown eyes bore into me. A breeze comes through, cooling the sweat that's gathered on my back. Cisco's West U baseball shirt blows against him, and he pulls at the hem, tucking it into the side of his shorts. "*Si tú y Candy están juntos, soy feliz. Pero aunque no están juntos, todavía te amo. Todos cometemos errores. Eres como un hijo para mí y tambien para Candace.*"

His words replay in my mind. No matter what happens, he still loves me like a son. I don't know what I've ever done to deserve it, but I swallow back the tears and nod, pulling him into a hug.

"*Todo va a ser bien, mijo.*"

I don't really believe that everything will be okay, but I agree anyhow, and we resume our run. He brings up random things like basketball and how the Kings are doing this year. Pretty sure he's just trying to take my mind off of everything.

It works for a bit, then we talk about preparing for my upcoming baseball games. The last half mile, we slow down to a walk, and the sun begins to set. Flower petals fall thanks to the trees blooming.

"Hey, for the record. I wasn't crying back there. Just allergies," I say, pointing to the trees.

"Yeah, okay," Cisco replies. "*Es bueno que los hombres lloren.*"

I laugh, and he chuckles.

"Same time next week?" I ask.

Cisco nods. "*Sí. Agarra tus cosas del porche.*"

"Yeah, wouldn't want to forget my phone." I wave to him as he walks through the front door. I round the house to the porch and grab my things.

A few notifications pop up as I press my phone to see the time. I pick up the rest of my stuff and make my way back toward my car. Swiping on the screen, it opens to Instagram where I'm tagged in a new photo. Kinda weird, since I'm not tagged in photos too often. Unless it's from a game. I head to my profile and tap my tagged photos.

Up pops a photo of Candy in front of the WU block letters. What the hell? It's from the West News account. In the caption, it reads:

Candy DeLeón speaks out against the inequality of women, what she's doing next, and how her and @tom_walk3r are planning to change the world together.

I click on the profile and go to the bio link, ready to read—

I slam against someone. My phone drops to the ground, and I reach out to stabilize the person in front of me. Candy gasps as our eyes meet, and she wrestles out of my arms.

"*¿Qué haces aquí?*" She shakes her head and picks up my phone. Handing it over, she says, "Why are you at my house?"

My hands fidget as I bounce on my heels. "Uh, I came over to, uh…um…see your dad."

Three years and I've never run into her. And now it's finna be the one time she can't stand to see me.

"To see my *dad*?" Her voice hikes up at the last word as if it's laced with total disbelief.

Knowing more lies will only make things worse, I swallow the dread and fear climbing my throat. "He's been the one teaching me Spanish for the past few years. I come over, we work out, and he talks."

"*Esto tiene que ser una broma.* Seriously?"

I shrug. "Yeah."

She rolls her eyes and tries to bypass me, but I step in front of her. "Wait."

Crossing her arms, she bites out, "What? What could you possibly want, Tom?

I unlock my phone and show her the picture. "What's up with this article?"

She worries her lip and glances away from me. "I panicked, okay? *Lo siento, pero* I couldn't have people saying more about me. Jake already thinks I got together with you to try and draw away from the scandal. I didn't want to say we'd broken up already, right when I released the video of me and those other girls going against Jake. Especially after…" She brushes her hair out of her face and looks at her nails. "Especially after the Disney video of us was leaked. It would've looked bad."

So she said we were still together to save her ass? That makes me feel great. "You used our relationship to make yourself look better?"

"No, that's not what it was. I just didn't want—"

I take a step away from her. "You didn't want to tell the truth, that you'd broken up with me, because you didn't want it to look like you jumped from one dude to the next, yeah? Or am I missing something?"

Candy pokes her tongue into her cheek. "I broke up with you? You forced my hand!"

"Maybe if you'd listen to me, I could—"

She glares at me. "No. Can you just go with it? Please. It's the least you could do for me."

I laugh incredulously. "The least I could… Alright, whatever. So how long do you plan to act like we're still together in the public eye?"

"A month. Till we get through *Young Americans Changing the World*. After that…"

She's not wearing any makeup, and her eyes are swollen. The usual flush of her skin is gone, making her look sickly pale. Her hands shake as she tucks them into the sweatshirt she's wearing. When our eyes meet, she quickly diverts her gaze.

"Are you okay?" I ask, reaching out for her.

She pulls away. "I'm fine."

"Okay." I take a deep breath. "Listen, we didn't even get to talk. I know you're hurt, but I promise you, Candy, that pregnancy test wasn't for me. I didn't cheat on you. But the person it was for, they've got something on me." I lie, telling her only what she needs to know. "That's why I can't tell you who it was for."

It's silent for a moment, and then she slowly shakes her head. "You know what's sad? I can't even trust you. I legit can't trust you after a decade of friendship. I hate to say this, but I don't believe a word you said. I'm tired of the lies, Tom."

"I'm not lyin—"

"Just stop!" she cuts in. "*Para con eso.* You asked what happens after *Young Americans.* And I think we need a clean break. I need to figure some things out by myself."

A clean break? Isn't that what this is *right now*?

Her inhale is shaky as she fiddles with something at the back of her neck. A moment later, she holds out the locket I gave her.

It sways in the distance between us, catching the drifting sun. I shake my head. "No, that's yours."

I watch her throat bob as she swallows. Her eyes shutter closed. "I don't want it anymore. I mean it. A clean break. No more second chances, no more being friends. I need to move on, for good."

Panic seeps into my veins. "Candy, you just said we've been friends for a decade. You can't just—"

"Take the locket!" her voice rises, and it's as unstable as the ground that just dropped from under me. "I don't want it anymore, Tom. I want this to be over. Please, listen to me."

I don't move, so she grabs my fist, opens it, and pools the locket in the palm of my hand. A vise tightens in my chest, and I feel as if I was just cut off at the knees.

"How the hell are we supposed to fake it at *Young Americans* together?" I croak out.

She shrugs. "You're a great actor. I'm sure you'll manage."

"Candy—"

"See you there," she says, moving past me and disappearing into her house.

I don't know how long I stare at the locket, unable to move. But by the time I get to my car, the sun has vanished beneath the horizon.

Chapter Thirty – Candy

The hollow of my throat is now empty. Things feel even heavier now than they did with the locket on.

I walk inside my childhood home and shout, "I'm home! Mom? *¿Papi?*"

My mom comes out of the kitchen, rubbing her hands on a towel. *"Hola, mi amor.* What a nice surprise. What're you doing here?"

How do I say this? I went skydiving and don't want to be numb anymore, and I just had a run in with my ex-boyfriend, and I want to talk to my mom and maybe cry because my emotions are on overload right now?

Instead, I shrug. But because she's a mom, she frowns and pulls me into a hug. How she knew that I'm upset from a shrug, I don't know, but I groan into her chest while trying to hold back my tears as she rubs my back and shushes me as if I'm a tired newborn.

"Do you want food?" she whispers loudly, and it's so unexpected that I let out a breathless laugh. My mother is the best.

"Do you have any of those chocolate caramels from Costco? Please tell me you're still hiding them in your closet."

She snorts and nods against my head. "Of course. Go to your room. I'll sneak into the closet to grab them and meet you there. I don't want *Papi* to see."

Three years ago, *Papi* had eaten so many of the chocolate caramels that he was sick for two days. We all vowed to never eat them again, but only to his face. I walk down the hall, glancing at the photos on the walls as I head to my childhood room. When I open the door, it still smells like teenage me, all cotton candy and sugar perfume. Polaroids are taped up on the wall from high school dances, baseball games, and late summer nights. My bed is made up in pale blue sheets with a cream comforter, and I collapse onto the mattress facedown.

A few moments later, my mom comes in and quickly closes the door. She leans against it, panting, caramel container wrapped in her arms. "He almost caught me."

Despite how I'm feeling, I laugh. It's completely ridiculous that a fifty-year-old woman is hiding chocolate caramels from her husband and that I'm an accomplice.

She sits down cross-legged on the bed beside me and opens the container, proffering a few caramels to me. I take them and devour each piece, relishing in the salt on top, the dark chocolate, and the smooth but sugary caramel in the center.

With a mouth full of chocolate, my mom says, "Let me guess...boy drama."

I pick at a loose string on the comforter. "Everything drama."

My parents aren't on social media (which is ironic considering what I do), and I haven't explained anything that's happened. If they've seen me on any sites online, they haven't mentioned it.

So I explain everything. I start as far back as Mexico and tell her all the sordid details. We get to the parts that involve Tom, and my voice cracks. I tell her about the video I just released, and the new non-profit I'm starting. "I'm happy about the non-profit, and I'm happy that I'll get to help other people. But...I don't know. I just feel weird. I didn't go through half of what the other girls went through, so I don't want to act like I'm some victim. But...I just keep waiting for it to feel better. I either feel nothing or I feel everything, and both of those are too much."

Mom leans against the wall and spins her wedding ring

around her finger. "I understand."

Does she?

She looks at the ceiling with a slight squint to her eyes, which I know means she's thinking. When she speaks, her voice is calm as if talking to a scared animal. "If you weren't in the public eye. You didn't have to care about what anyone thought of you, what would you do?"

I mull the question over in my mind, but the answer remains the same. "I still don't know."

She clucks her tongue. "Honey, it's okay. Listen, what that man did to you and those other girls is absolutely horrible. You are doing an amazing thing, but I know that also puts a lot of pressure on you."

"*Sí*, I suppose."

"It does." She runs her thumb over my cheek. "And it's okay if you feel overwhelmed with it all. Candy, this is not a normal experience. It's not something that everyone has to go through. Have you thought about maybe doing something to help you work through this?"

"Like therapy?"

"I think that'd be a good idea, baby."

My eyes begin to water, but I push the tears back. "But what about Tom?"

She tilts her head. "What about him?"

I tell her how I just ran into him. "I love him, *Mami*. I don't know how to let go of that part of me when he's been holding it for years. I'm just…"

"Hurt?" my mom offers.

"Disappointed. I always thought that when enough time had passed, Tom and I would get back together. And we did. I had gotten past his mistakes. I'd moved beyond it. Maybe it sounds stupid to you because I'm so young, but I thought he was it for me."

I shrug again as a tear escapes my eye.

"Hey," my mom lifts my chin and wipes the tear, "it's not stupid, *mija*. You are young, yes, but I'd met your father at your age. And you've known Tom since you were kids. It is *not* stupid. *You* are not stupid."

I bury my face in my hands and fall into her side, sobbing. "I gave him the locket back. I told him we were through for good after the Q&A together. It's really over, and maybe one day I'll look back at this and be glad it happened, but right now, all I can see is that my heart hurts, I'm still in love with him, and he wasn't in love with me enough to not cheat. I literally feel so dumb," I get out between shaky breaths. "Now I have all this other stuff and just feel like I'm going to burst. Like I have so much on my back that I might just disappear from the weight of it all."

She squeezes my shoulders and rubs my back, as I cry it all out. When I lift my head, my face feels swollen and water-logged. I hate crying.

"It's okay if you don't know what to do, or say, or how to act, Candy. You don't have to be perfect. You're allowed mistakes." She brushes my hair as I lay in her lap. "Time will tell for all of this. You have no idea what the future holds, but *mija*, I know it's so bright for you."

I wipe the last of the tears from my eyes. "I feel like I'm that old meme with Joe Exotic saying 'I'll never financially recover from this' but it's just me saying, 'My heart will never emotionally recover from this.' Maybe I'll start memeing myself. Everyone already thinks I'm a joke. Might as well help them come up with content."

She laughs and rolls her eyes while running her fingers through my hair. "It will get better, Candy. God doesn't always give us the answers we want to our prayers, but he does give us the answers we need. Time will heal everything you're worried about, *I promise*."

It's been a while since I've gone to church with my parents, but her promise to me and her words give me the smallest flutter of hope.

Or maybe I just have heart arrythmia from crying too much.

∞∞∞

Over the next week, Grace texts a few times with appearances that Jake has made. He's yet to comment to any media outlet. His socials have been silent, and it's almost as if he's disappeared, other than the grocery store and gym visits.

My account has grown another 50,000, and I've even had people reach out for sponsorship opportunities.

I haven't responded to them. It seems inauthentic to try and push ads right now with things still so shaky. I went to a session with Les's therapist. It was my first time in therapy, and whew, I couldn't stop talking. Things haven't necessarily gotten better, but I do feel lighter. Not happier, just lighter.

Like my mom said, time (and some therapy) heals.

I walk into the casual eatery right at one o'clock, which is when Kira said she could meet for lunch last week. She's already sitting at a table, tapping away on her phone in sleek leather leggings and an oversized tee. It's weird seeing someone who looks so much like Tom.

Don't psych yourself out, I tell myself. She's just a girl who has gone through a similar experience with a guy cheating. The mean girl in high school who wants to make amends…although, I'm pretty sure she views me as *her* mean girl in high school too.

The funny thing is, we actually had some good times together. We went to a couple protests with other people who tagged along, and a couple times we even had a few moments of "normal," basically, when we had called a truce and didn't bite each other's heads off.

When she sees me, a big grin appears on her face. For a second, my heart falters. It looks so similar to Tom's smile. But I push the thought away, walk toward her table, and sit.

"Hey, girl. How are you?" she says, flipping her braids off of her shoulder. They're dyed a deep purple, and it suits her.

Makes her eyes sparkle and offsets the green in them.

I smile. "Good. You?"

"Good, good. I got us menus. If you haven't been here, the coconut shrimp is so—"

"Amazing!" I cut in, and we both laugh. "It's my favorite."

"Mine too." Kira smiles. "Well, I guess we both know what we're gettin', then. How've you really been?"

I sputter through my lips and feel the vibration. "I'm sure you've seen the stuff with the Marx family."

She nods. "What a douche canoe."

"Yeah," I breathe out. "I'm really excited about the non-profit I started. We actually got our first client, and the lawyers working for us are amazing."

"OMG yes, seriously, that video gave me chills," Kira cuts in. "When I graduate, you better keep me on your radar. Sounds like my dream job."

We chat a little more about Making Our Mark, which is a nice distraction. But when we hit a lull, she asks, "How are you feeling with the Tom situation?"

I purse my lips and lick some of the cherry chapstick off of them. "Kinda sucky, honestly. It's weird. Like, we weren't together that long this time, but I had this interview, and when they asked about me and Tom, I panicked and claimed we were still together. Like, who does that?"

Kira raises her brows and leans back. "Cap. Did you really?"

Burying my hands in my face, I helplessly chuckle. "I mean, they assumed we were together, and then I didn't correct them. So, yeah. But I've barely talked to your brother. It's so awkward."

"Rightfully so," she says and holds up her water in a cheers. "I'm pissed *for* you, by the way."

I bite on the end of my nail and hear my manicurist curse me out. "How is he?"

She shrugs. "I've been so busy, I've barely talked with him. I think he's sad, obviously. I don't think he expected y'all to break up. But lemme tell ya, when I see him next, I will kick his ass for you, okay hon'?"

I laugh off her comments as the waitress comes to our table and takes our order. When she leaves, I ask, "So, you said you had someone cheat on you? Was it recent?"

"Yeah. Remember Noah from the protest? Found out that night he was cheating on me. Went to his place to tell him I passed my LSAT, with amazing numbers by the way, and walked in on him with someone else."

She taps her claw-tipped nails on the table and huffs out a sigh. "I was so mad. Started screaming so loud, and the girl was scrambling around trying to get dressed. Straight disaster."

Ay Dios mío, that's way worse than mine. Seeing the guy in the act? Ew. "I am *so* sorry. I can't believe that. The audacity of men, I swear."

"That's what I'm saying. So even though it was my ho bro that did this to you, accept my condolences, please."

"Oh, I will."

We meld into comfortable conversation, and it surprises me as much as it probably surprises her. She talks about applying to law school at West, Stanford, Davis, and a few others. Her eyes light up over her career, which is admirable.

The waitress brings us our coconut shrimp plates and a glass of the hibiscus juice I ordered. I dive into the crunchy, mouth-watering dish.

A few bites in, Kira wipes her mouth and clears her throat. "Look, I just want to say sorry for whatever went down in middle school and high school. I'm honestly not even sure why we were so mean to each other."

I smile, just a half-quirk of my lips. "Yeah, I'm sorry too. Thanks for inviting me to lunch, as well."

Kira nods. "So, now that you've released the that video, how's twitter and Instagram going?"

"Ah, it's going a lot better. The Tiktoks that were released helped a lot, but after all those women came forward? People have been pretty anti-Marx family. I hope it goes beyond Jake, though. I mean, it's insane to think that California would have a senator like her, but the polls have been in her favor big time." I take another bite and drink some of my juice. "Good news is that *Young Americans* canceled Jake Marx's interviews."

Kira's fork clatters on her plate. "Good. And I'm glad that you're still going to that. I'll be checking out Loyola Law School that same weekend, so I get to come watch the interviews Tom and you have. You worried about your question thing? He told me about it."

Am I? Absolutely. But I'd rather not talk about it. Shrugging, I say, "Eh, it's high school kids. They're not going to get gossipy with their questions. I think most are just excited to be there, so I'm not too worried about it."

But high school kids are also all over TikTok, and a bunch have probably seen those videos. Hopefully a moderator will be there to filter out inappropriate questions.

I pick at my food. "I told Tom that after *Young Americans*, we were over for good. I think I just need a clean break, ya know?" I lean on my elbow and blow hair off my face. "How did you handle it with Noah?"

"Uh, well, let's see. I cut up his clothes and dropped off all his things in a box on his lawn while it was dumping rain. So... I'd say *don't* do what I did?" She gives me a sheepish smile.

My jaw drops. "Okay, that's kind of awesome, though."

Kira points. "See, I'm glad you agree. And it's not like there were electronics or anything. Just old, holey clothes and a lingering smell of bastard."

We go back and forth, talking and finishing our meal. We're laughing, joking, and it feels as if we never hated each other. After we're finished, we make promises to catch lunch again and plan to meet up at *Young Americans.*

If I can be civil with Kira, who I've hated for years, maybe I can be civil with Tom. I'm not going to reach out to him, but we do still have to travel to *Young Americans* together. So, I do my own form of surrendering. I unblock his number.

Chapter Thirty One – Tom

I grab my game bag from the closet and head to grab some water from the kitchen. Ethan sits at the table, rubbing at his forehead. A prescription bottle sits in front of him with a glass of water.

"What's up?" I ask and fill up my Hydroflask.

He glances over his shoulder and sinks into his chair. "Nothin'. Just...tired."

"You had a good game last night. Hit up an after party?"

He stares at me listlessly, then replies, "Yeah, thanks." After putting his meds up in the cabinet above the fridge, hidden behind his protein, he leans against the countertop. "There was an after party. Got a little crazy. Some shit went down, and I'm tired."

"Bummer, man. I'm sorry."

"Nah, it's all good," he tosses out. "But I didn't take my meds for a few days, so, now my mom and sisters are on my ass, and I'm worried about this finals game tomorrow."

"You got this." I hit him on his back.

He stands up from his chair, pushing the meds away. "Ah, my bad, bro. You got a game to go to, yeah? Good luck. I'll try and make it."

We give each other a handshake and I slide my keys across the counter. "Cool. Maybe we can hit up Anna's afterward?"

Ethan nods as he pulls his phone from his pocket. "Yeah, I could go for some West french toast."

"It's only the best dish. See ya, dude."

The sun beats down as I walk to my Jeep. In just a few

hours, we'll be up against UC Davis. Should be an easy win, but they have a tendency to surprise us. Last year, we were supposed to blow them out of the water only for them to steal two runs in the last inning.

It was the hardest loss of the year.

I pull into the athletics parking lot the same time Carter hops out of his truck. He waits as I grab my bags.

"You ready for today?" I ask, slinging my stuff over my shoulder.

"Yeah, I think so. Don't tell Coach, but I went skydiving last week, and I swear the harness did somethin' to my shoulder. Hurts like a mug." He stretches his arm across his chest and winces.

"You still pitching?"

"I'll be fine," he grits out.

We walk into the athletics building where the rest of the team is hanging out, getting ready for our pre-game routine. I give his arm a squeeze. "Just don't do anything stupid out there today. If AJ has to pitch, we're screwed. I need you for that Cal Poly game, man."

"Noted."

Our pregame routine is simple and to the point. Coach tells us exactly what we need to watch for on the Davis team, and we change into our uniforms and cleats before heading out to the diamond. Out on the field, Coach has us do short sprints and some static stretches.

I check out the Davis players, including Ramón, who is pretty much a guaranteed draft pick this year. He's an awesome pitcher, but I know I can hit whatever he throws me.

Like a tap on the shoulder, I feel a prickle underneath my skin. Glancing into the stands, I find the source. Les and Candy sit just behind the dugout, chatting and laughing. Candy is wearing round glasses, and her hair looks a few inches shorter.

But no matter how long I look at her, torturing myself, she doesn't catch my gaze. I shake my head and the thoughts of her go with it.

Davis is up to bat first, and as always, I'm on second base. A few players hit, getting to second and third, where Maldon stands. The game starts off civil, Davis running up four players and West getting five.

But it takes a turn in the seventh inning when one of Davis' fastest runners, Alec Trent, is up to bat with two outs on the board. I signal to Ben that we have to get one of these players out before Alec either steals bases or hits a home run.

Sweat beads on my brow as our catcher signals to Carter. I'm too far to see what he does, but I do see his hands move toward his right inner thigh. Carter nods and scuffs his feet on the mound before cracking his neck.

I glance into the crowd, like Candy is my life source, the one thing I need to see to keep going, which is dumb since she told me to piss off. I find her, sitting in the stands chatting with...*Kira?*

What the hell?

Ben shouts at me, so I flinch and turn toward him. He throws his hands out, questioning what I'm doing. I wave him off and get my head in the game. Carter throws a curveball, and Trent swings but misses. I huff out a breath of relief and check to be sure that Maldon is in line with me. Our best bet is me getting the ball before the Davis player on first base gets to me on second.

Between pitches, I glance again to the crowd, and Kira is sitting with Candy and Les. I'm gonna kill my sis, I swear. What the hell is she up to?

Carter throws another curveball, but Trent hits it in a perfect arc into the outfield. I ready my stance as one of our outfielders catches it and hesitates. Glancing over my shoulder, I see the Davis player halfway to second.

Agitated for multiple reasons, I shout to my teammate, "Come on, already!"

He throws the ball to where I stand three steps away from second base, but it scuttles around on the floor. I quickly scoop up the groundball just as I hear someone slide into my base.

"Dammit!" I shout.

I shake my head and throw the ball to Carter. Scrubbing down my face, I regulate my breaths. That should've been a given. If my outfielder didn't hesitate, I could have tagged Davis out. Instead, the announcer now talks about the failed block, the point Davis just got, and the fact that Trent made it to first base.

Another of Davis's star players is up to bat, and I mentally reprimand myself. If we don't get the last out right now, they'll rack another run, tying us up. Focus on the game, man. Just focus.

But it's hard when I can see the woman who destroyed my relationship chatting with my ex. The one she claimed wasn't good enough for me.

Focus. I hear my dad's voice in my mind shouting.

I peel my gaze away from the crowds.

Carter winds up and throws a fastball, arm lingering in the air with his leg kicked up. Davis hits the ball down midfield and Trent comes running from first base. Our outfielder throws the ball to me, and I tag Trent out half a second before he slides into first base. Relief floods my system as Trent cusses at me.

I ignore him and grin at Maldon, who gives me a thumbs up. On the field, we're a team. He nods toward the pitching mound. I whip my head that way only to see Carter on his knees.

Memories of three years ago flash in my mind. Carter on all fours, throwing up and shaking. The moment he was so sick that I thought I was gonna lose my best friend.

The moment that I had to call Candy and beg God to make her answer the phone, because we hadn't spoken in over a month because I ruined our relationship.

Carter's diabetes was so bad, so untreated because he never got a diagnosis, that I nearly lost both twins from my life. I drop the ball I'm holding, and time seems to still as

I search the stands for Candy. She's up from her seat, mouth agape, with Les beside her, hands covering the bottom half of her face.

West's announcer brings me back to the field as his voice booms over the speaker, "DeLeón, arguably West's best pitcher, seems to have been injured with his last fastball pitch. West's coach and medic are helping him up. That arm is limp, and he's cradling his elbow. He looks to be in real pain."

The umpire stops the game, and I run toward Carter. It's just an injury, I tell myself. Not ketoacidosis, not something that will kill him. But panic still rises in my throat. "Whoa, whoa, what's going on?"

"Get back in the game, Walker!" Coach shouts and looks at the dugout. "You're first to bat."

Carter glances over his shoulder and winces. *I'm sorry,* he mouths.

I throw my hat to the ground and curse. I don't care about the game when the guy I consider a brother is being escorted off the field. Assistant Coach Jenkins stomps toward me. "Come on, Walker. Enough with that. Let's go."

I glance toward the stands, where Les and Candy were seated. Their seats are empty, and I want to be done with this game. I should be there when Carter goes to the hospital. But it doesn't escape me that I also want to check on Candy.

"I'll text you," Carter calls out. He nods when I glance to him. "Go kick their asses."

∞∞∞

We win 7-6, and the second the game ends, I grab my stuff and haul ass to West's University Hospital. I text Carter, and Les responds, telling me where they're at.

The sun winds down below the horizon as I exit my car and head to the third story where Carter is getting X-rays. The DeLeóns, along with Candy and Les, sit in the waiting room on wooden plush chairs that are teal blue and seen better days. They're talking quietly, and when Les looks and sees me, she stands and gives me a hug.

"Sorry, I'm a mess right now." I look down at my jersey, which is covered in dirt. I only changed my shoes, and now I'm thinking that wasn't the best idea. It's not like Carter is dying. I didn't have to rush here.

But I also did have to, because I wanted to.

When I glance past Les, Candy quickly averts her gaze. Guess she was staring at me after all.

Les scoots over to the next chair, so I don't have to sit in the empty seat between her and Candy. It's awkward, and everything in me itches to hold Candy's hand, to tell her it will be okay, and just be there for her. I want so bad to be there for her. Being next to her, unable to even look into her eyes, is one of the worst feelings in the world.

I stand, not knowing where I'm going. Pulling at one of the curls that has fallen out of my backwards cap, I say, "Uh, have any of y'all eaten? Can I go grab dinner?"

Candace gives me a pitying look and turns her head to Cisco. A silent exchange happens in their eyes, and Candace nods. "How about all three of you go get dinner and bring it back? It'll be a while before Carter is through with X-rays. They had a few people ahead of him."

Les stares at her phone and taps on the screen. "Actually, Carter just asked for me to go back there with him." She chews on her lips.

"Candy," I choke out. "You down to come with?"

She pulls on the hem of her West baseball tee, which swamps her. It must be one of Carter's. "How about we grab something from the cafeteria. A quick snack we can bring up to you guys?" She glances at her parents.

"*Bien. Gracias,*" her father replies.

I give them a grim smile and walk ahead as Candy catches up. We walk in silence to the elevator, but each breath is filled with her perfume. I steal glances at her whenever she's not watching. She looks better than the last time we talked. Her skin is flush and golden, her back is straight, and she exudes the confidence she's always had.

I've seen Jake getting dragged in the news. People have posted too many videos on TikTok talking about his bad behavior, especially with women, and it's a movement alright. Candy's new non-profit has gotten a lot of attention.

I'm just glad she got her career back like she wanted. She's even posting on Instagram regularly, something that has gutted me each day when I see her photos. The troll comments aren't gone completely. But more good comments are coming through. I play my part of pretend boyfriend well. I've commented a few heart emojis, called her my queen, and complimented her every step of the way.

I haven't posted anything on Instagram. If I do, she'd undoubtedly comment, playing her part as well. And my desperate ass would try and read into each comment.

The elevator doors swoosh open, and she walks in first. No one else is in the cab with us, and a deafening silence blankets us as we descend to the first floor. When the doors open once more, she keeps walking toward the cafeteria, and I follow behind her like a dog on her leash.

There ain't a thing to say to her that will fix us, but I still want to try. I clear my throat as we wait in line at the hospital cafeteria with a couple of doctors and nurses ahead of us, chatting about their days.

"So," I start, "how're things?"

She glances at me for a split second and then stares straight ahead again. "Fine."

"Cool." The awkward silence stretches on. "I...I liked your photos on Instagram."

I'm feeling like I just took ten steps back toward middle school. The words are stuttered and choppy, and I swear my voice even cracks. But for the past ten years, I've never *not* known Candy. I'd been her friend or boyfriend.

Now, I ain't shit to her.

It's a great place to be.

She raises her brows once. "Yeah, I've seen. Another week, and you'll be off the hook. We can announce our breakup, part as 'friends,' and you won't have to comment anymore."

"Yeah...but what if I still want to?"

"Let's not make this harder than it needs to be," she says dismissively.

"Alright." I scratch at my scalp and muss my hair. "We still flying to *Young Americans* together?"

"Same flight. But I'll probably sit elsewhere."

"Cool," I choke out again. "Well, I'm looking forward to it."

Mentally chastising myself for saying something stupid again, I glance over the cafeteria's menu as a distraction. But then I remember... "Why were you talking to Kira earlier?"

Candy gives a cursory side glance. "It's really none of your business."

I'm about to say yeah it is when Candy pulls out her phone and swipes at the screen. "Oh no," she whispers, placing two fingers against her lip. Glancing to me, she gives me a pitying frown. "Guess my mom was wrong. Carter already got his results. He fractured his elbow. They also found a rotator cuff tear. Surgery's next Wednesday. He's out for the season."

I shake my head. "That's terrible. I hate that for him." Carter is one of the hardest-working pitchers I've known. Baseball has been so important to him. He's gotta be crushed. I know I'd be. "Dang, the team is gonna miss him as our go-to pitcher."

"Yeah," she mutters, typing out a text. "You know what's weird?"

"Hmm?"

She puts her phone back in her pocket. "You and I would be the one comforting him if this were a year ago. But now? All he's gonna want is Les. *Los tiempos han cambiado.*"

"Yeah, times have changed." I'm about to apologize for the hundredth time when it seems she realizes she just talked too much to me.

She clears her throat, and her easy friendship is gone. "Anyway...think this will affect you?"

I plaster on a straight-faced smile and lie. "Nah, don't worry about me. I'll be fine."

"Wasn't worried." She turns her gaze from me.

Carter being out of the game does affect me. It affects the whole team. It affects my morale too. 'Cause I used to pretend that Candy was possibly in the stands for me. But now?

She's not gonna be at the games since Carter's out. And it's selfish to even think about myself when Carter is the one injured, but the fact that she won't even see me or be there for me when I succeed sucks.

That's the last of our conversation, and as we wait to pick up some crappy cafeteria food, I'm gutted. I miss talking to her without having to worry if she hates me. Yeah, I miss her lips, and her body, but it's more than that. I miss the way her mouth would curve into a smile whenever we'd watch *The Bachelor* and Chris Harrison would say it's the most dramatic night yet. Or how she'd hum while washing her dishes. How she'd come out of the bathroom while "baking" her concealer, whatever the hell that meant, with white patches all over her face. I miss game night and watching her cheer when she'd win.

I just miss her.

Chapter Thirty Two – Candy

Jake Marx has been quiet. I've had two more interviews about Making Our Mark, and the days go by without any new drama. I'm starting to accept things. I've gone to therapy again, and it's been eye-opening to the experience with Jake.

Now, it's time to inspire some high school kids at *Young Americans Changing the World*.

The flight to LA is calming. The plane's constant humming energizes me as if it's electricity charging my battery. The ride to the hotel is smooth, and I walk into my empty room with a backpack and roller bag.

A queen bed is made up with a card and chocolate welcoming us as attendees for *Young Americans*. I've got an hour to refresh myself before going to the conference center and picking up my materials as well as meeting with some of the coordinators for the interviews tomorrow.

The interviews will be televised and recorded in a large studio conference hall. As for the Q&A with Tom, that will be in a smaller conference room that holds about thirty people. We're supposed to be talking about the activism that we've done together at West University, though I'm not so sure what we'll be saying since it's been nearly two months since we've done any activism together.

Basically, it'll be a large pile of lies, but at least it'll be lies that kids can believe. Lying for the good of the people. Ah, I'm a politician already.

I hop in the shower, blow dry my hair, and redo my

makeup before getting dressed in a black turtleneck with a rose satin dress on top. I belt it at my waist, put on a simple gold teardrop necklace, and slip my feet in my high heeled black booties.

The mirror confirms that I look like an absolute goddess (or it would if it could talk), so I grab my phone and head out the door. Thankfully, the conference center is attached to the hotel, so I walk just a short distance before meeting with a woman at the entrance to conference hall B.

"Name?"

"Candy DeLeón."

She rifles through a few dozen name tags until she pulls one out and hands it to me. "Place it around your neck and keep it on you at all times in the event center. Be sure you have your photo identification with you whenever you check in and pass through the doors."

I nod. "Thanks."

The door opens up into large, stadium-style seating with a stage in the center. Cameras line the sides of the stage as well as the front of it, and people are off in cliques talking. I hear a familiar voice, and my feet fumble.

Tom stands at the righthand side, chatting with a slender blonde girl with hair down to her waist. She's basically Rapunzel, and her voice is sweet and confident as it flits over to my ears.

Kate Bradshaw. We met last year at a fundraiser in Sacramento. She runs a non-profit for kids with cancer, and they do everything from making a dying kid's wish come true to helping kids reacclimate to school and social events after being gone for months or years in chemo.

She's basically a saint, and I couldn't hate her if I tried. She was also a lifesaver in helping me start Marking Our Mark since I had no idea what the legalities of it all would be. But watching her and Tom hit it off so easy, smiling at each other and laughing, well, it sucks. *He's not worth the heartache,* I repeat in my mind.

Someone behind me clears their throat. "Are we just standing around here?"

I move to the side. "My bad."

A petite guy with wavy red hair smiles awkwardly as he walks past me. I take a deep breath and move toward the stage, refusing to let my eyes go back toward Tom and Kate. Moments later, I'm seated and scrolling on my phone when a woman moves to center stage and announces, "Hello, everyone! I'm Alison. If you do not have an interview with me tomorrow, you are in the wrong room. Please go to conference hall C."

A couple people stand and walk out.

"If you *do* have an interview with me tomorrow, we'll be going over entrances, guidelines, and a quick schedule walkthrough. Any questions? If not, we'll get started with the first interview slot tomorrow. Brandon Hayes?"

As I watch the others go on stage and practice the walkthrough, my phone buzzes, so I quickly take it out of my pocket.

Kira: *Hey! I'm here and just wrapped up my school tour. Want to have a girls night out?*

The plans I had scheduled tonight were to watch a movie and order room service, but a girls night out in LA? That sounds *much more enjoyable.*

Candy: *Absolutely. Text me the details.*

A remix of "Without Me" by Halsey pulses in the club, syncing up to my own heartbeat. It's loud, crowded, and full of young sorority girls and frat boys if their Greek shirts mean anything. The DJ announces it's College Night, and the whole club seems to scream and whoop in tandem.

Kira volunteered to be the designated driver tonight, and she sips slowly on a club soda. "Ooh, that boy is so cute. Look at him."

I glance at the tan, golden-haired boy smiling over at us. "Yeah, for *you*."

She waves me off. "Come on, what about you? Don't you know the best way to get over someone is to get under someone else?"

"*Sí*, so again, do it! I'm not interested, though." The thought of being with anyone right now makes me sick to my stomach. Pretty sure I'll never do a one-night stand again. But even beyond that…

Honestly, I can't imagine being with anyone but Tom. I stir my drink and sigh.

Kira leans against the bar and colored lights reflect off her leather dress. "You're not really still hung up on my brother are you? I thought you two were pretending to be together for your platforms."

I shrug. "We are. I've hardly talked to him, and I've seen him like twice in the past month. Been focused on turning my career around."

"You didn't answer my question."

My breath comes out ragged and more like a groan. "It's stupid to be hung up on someone who cheated on you…two times." I sip my drink. "Do I look stupid to you?"

Kira laughs. "You want me to really answer that?"

"Alright, cool it." I quirk my lips. "I really loved your brother. Yes, that probably makes me stupid, but I can't just hump some frat boy and get over it. Doesn't work like that for me."

She's silent as her eyes rove over my face.

I raise my brows and lift my drink in cheers. "Sorry to disappoint."

Someone taps on my shoulder. I turn around and see the golden-haired Adonis smiling my way. Perfect timing. I'm about to say I'm not interested when Kira pulls me back. "Sorry, she's taken."

"By you?" His deep voice cuts through the music without

any issue.

Kira glances at me with a look of disgust, but then blinks twice and smiles. "Yes! Taken by me. Just can't resist the..." Her gaze roves over me. "The...booties."

Frat boy looks at us weird. "Aight, sorry. Enjoy your night, ladies," he says and marches back to where he came from.

I turn to Kira. "The *booties*? That was literally *all* you could think of?"

"I like men!" she counters.

"That doesn't mean you think women are ugly! The booties," I mutter. "*Very* convincing."

"Hey," Kira cuts in, "we were enemies for years. I'm trying here. I also like your..."

"For the love of *Madre Maria*, just stop. I'm not your type, I get it." I roll my eyes and sip my drink.

We both stew in silence for a minute before catching eye contact. Her lips quirk, and I suck mine in as a laugh begins in my chest. She smiles, and I lose it as we break into cackles.

"I'm...so...sorry," she gets out in between laughs. "I should've said your hair or something."

I wipe the tears that have leaked through my eyes. "It's the fact you couldn't find one thing about me that you liked."

Her shoulders shake as she laughs. "It's the confidence that I should've been able to find something to like about you for me."

My laugh turns breathless as my stomach burns. "It's the using we were enemies for years for me."

"It's the weird style for me."

"It's the e-girl dress you have on for me," I retort.

She lets out a sound akin to a horse snorting before saying, "It's the still being hung up on your ex for me."

"*Damn, amiga.* Shots fired," I concede, and our laughs filter down to soft giggles.

Kira tosses back the rest of her club soda like a shot and holds out a hand. "Let's dance and forget about our worries. Then we're getting you back to the hotel. You don't need to be drunk for your interviews tomorrow."

I gasp. "Kira Walker caring about *me?* You'd think you'd want to ruin my interviews."

She bites her lip and averts her gaze toward a group of guys. "Nah, what kind of person would I be if I did that? Come on, let's go."

As we make our way through the crowd, someone puts their hand on my shoulder. I turn, only to find someone who definitely shouldn't be here. Jake freaking Marx. His smile lights up on that pretty boy face of his, and his eyes flow with mischief. As his grin grows, his teeth show, lit up blue by the blacklight of the club. "If it isn't Candy DeLeón."

I shrug his hand off. "What the hell are you doing here?"

Kira's brow furrows, and she pulls out her phone as if she might need it to call someone.

Jake cocks his head. "Shouldn't I be the one asking questions?"

"Be glad you're not in jail...yet." I move to walk away, but he lashes out and grabs my wrist. When I glance down, he moves his hand down to mine and tightens his hold. I try to yank my hand away, but he has a vise grip on it.

"What the hell do you want? Take a word from the wise, Jake. You should leave, *now.* In a matter of minutes, this could all be uploaded."

"I want my damn career back. You took *everything* from me. My CEO position, my name, it's now gone and spoiled." He grinds his teeth together as he smiles.

Kira steps toward us. "Hey, it's time you leave."

"No," he replies, "it's not."

She looks at me and back at him. "I'm getting security."

With that, she pushes through the crowd and disappears.

"I can't give you your career back. Nor did I take it. It collapsed because of your decisions. Not mine." I stomp on his foot, and he lets go of my hand.

As I step away, he lifts the bottle of beer he'd been holding in his other hand. "You stupid bitch. You have *everyone* lying.

That's what people like you do." He takes a swig of his drink, and people begin staring as his voice rises.

He cackles at his joke. Clearly, he's drunk. "You know you still want me," he says, putting on a slimy grin.

"Burn in hell, Jake," I say and walk away.

But a step later, glass shatters behind me. A piece rakes across the side of my leg, drawing blood from a thin, long scrape. It travels from my thigh to my shin, and immediately, blood drips.

Not enough for stitches, but enough that I hiss as I hurry toward the club door. Kira stands with a large security guard, pointing toward the club floor. When she sees me coming, her chest collapses in relief.

I limp toward her, and she hurries out, "What happened? Are you okay?"

I gesture to my leg. "I'll be fine, but we need to get out of here." I nod my head toward Jake and talk to the security guard. "That guy is drunk, shattered a beer bottle, and cut my leg. I'm leaving, not pressing charges, but he needs to be kicked out before someone gets seriously hurt."

He nods and is already pulling out a walkie talkie as he walks away, speaking into it for backup.

"Let's go." I pull on Kira's arm as we half-walk, half-run (or half-limp in my case) to her car.

She gets in the driver's seat and her hands are shaking. "Okay, seriously, are you okay? We need to get something for that."

I open up her glove box, and thank the good lord that she's like her brother and stashes napkins in there. Pulling a few out, I wave her off and press them to the cut. "It's not deep. Really, just a surface scratch. I'll be fine."

Kira lifts up her hair and fans her neck. "Maybe we should call Tom."

My face scrunches, and I shake my head. "Absolutely not. I'm fine. I promise."

"Okay," Kira concedes. "Okay," she says again, quieter this

time. She starts the car and pulls away from the curb. Every few seconds, she looks over at me with a worried look.

"Kira," I chastise. "I am *fine*. Stop looking at me like that. I'm good. Please, just take me back to the hotel."

"If something would've happened to you, Tom would never forgive me."

"Please, *I am begging you,* stop bringing up your brother." Because he was the first person I thought to call, and I hate it.

My adrenaline slowly fades, and I'm left taking a few deep breaths to calm myself. Carter would lose his mind right now if he knew what had just happened. I sigh and place my forehead against the cool window.

My leg burns, but the napkins are barely saturated with blood. It really is a surface scratch. A shower and I'll be good. Granted, you'll see it in my dress tomorrow for my interviews, but oh well.

It's over, and hopefully I never have to see Jake Marx again.

Chapter Thirty Three – Tom

I slept like shit.

Waking up early doesn't affect me, but lying in bed until three, feeling unsettled and wondering what Candy was doing, does. I went by her room after I'd had dinner, and she didn't answer my knock.

Maybe she avoided me. Or she was out meeting the other "Young Americans" who are changing the world. I was gonna wish her luck and tell her I was looking forward to our Q&A, but oh well.

Now, I'm munching on a bagel backstage as they interview the girl before me. She's a freshman in college who created a solar panel small enough to fit in a backpack but powerful enough to power up an electric car on a daily basis.

Alison asks her about her plans for renewable energy, and the woman is amazingly well spoken. She talks as if she's been on TV a million times.

I sigh as I toss the bagel wrapper in the garbage. A man comes up to me and points. "Tom Walker?"

"Yep," I reply.

"Cool, let's get you miked." He puts on the microphone and tells me how to avoid creating background noise and what not to do while out there.

Moments later, they announce a commercial break before swapping solar-energy-girl out for me. I sit down in a plush chair and Alison shakes my hand. She's a young, attractive woman who made a name for herself on the *Today Show*. Now, she does side events like this in addition to her other work. "You ready?"

"Yeah, ready as I'll ever be."

She nods and turns toward the cameras. They give her a countdown and she begins. "Our next interview is college baseball star turned activist Tom Walker, from West University. Let's talk a bit about your baseball career. Why is baseball such an important sport for you? What got you started in it?"

I place my hands on my thighs, avoiding the mic lines. "I've always loved baseball. From the time I was a kid, you'd find me playing with other kids at the local parks and in my own backyard. As I kept playing, I realized that there weren't a ton of other baseball players like me. Baseball doesn't have a lot of Black representation, and knowing that under 10% of the players in the MLB are Black really pushed me. I want young Black kids to have a role model, one that they can watch on TV and think, *hey, I can do that, too.*"

"Is that where your activism started?" Alison asks.

I laugh, thinking of my first protest in high school with Candy. It's like a jab to the side, but I can't let it affect me. "No, uh, it actually started with turtles."

"Turtles?" She raises a brow.

I think of how Candy helped me start a social media campaign against plastic straws our freshman year. It brings a smile to my face, and I automatically look for her in the crowd. But, I don't see her as I reply, "Yep. I have a soft spot for turtles, and I started protesting against the use of plastic straws. But, one protest usually leads to another. Over the years, my interests have realigned, and though I'm still *very* passionate about sea turtles—"

Alison giggles.

"—I am more passionate about ensuring the equal treatment of minorities and future Black baseball players getting the opportunities they deserve in the sport."

She asks me a few more questions.

It's natural, and enjoyable. I like talking to the kids, and I hope the advice I'm giving is good enough that they'll want to do something with it. Their smiling faces make me remember the days I spent chasing dreams in high school, and chasing a certain girl. I don't know why I thought she'd be here for my interview. I scan the chairs, and she's nowhere to be found.

Before I know it, Alison is telling me that the time is up and thanks me for coming. She lets the audience know that I'll be available in the halls for a Q&A with another West U student.

As soon as I'm off the stage, I'm calling Coach. Today is pushing it close, but if I leave at the time I'm supposed to, I'll be back in Sacramento with more than two hours to spare before the Cal Poly game tonight.

The scout's coming, and it's gonna be an interesting game without Carter pitching. I know AJ worked his ass off this week to be ready for this game, and I just hope it paid off.

The phone rings twice before Coach answers with a, "How's it goin', Walker?"

"It's good. Just finished my interview. My flight leaves at three, so I should get in at five. I'll come straight to the stadium."

Coach harrumphs. "I'm countin' on you. This event should've never been approved on game day. 'Specially not with a scout coming to watch you."

"I know," I cut in. "And I appreciate you working with me. I promise, I'll be there."

∞∞∞

I've got twenty minutes before I need to meet in the small conference room where the Q&A with Candy will be. I pace the hallways, nervous that everything won't work out like I planned for today. If I'm not back in time for the game, if something happens, my baseball career is over.

Maybe there will be other scouts, but maybe not. I'm a

bundle of nerves 'cause I'm worried about sitting so close to Candy and acting like a couple too. I round the corner of the hall and there she is, leaning against the wall with her eyes closed, phone white-knuckled in her hands.

Something is wrong. Part of me wants to walk over to her and ask her if she's okay. The rational part of me says to stay back, she doesn't want you anymore. She didn't even show at your interview, so she probably doesn't want you talking to her.

The dumb part of me wins, and I reprimand myself as I approach her. "You okay?"

Candy's eyes open wide as she flinches. "You scared me."

"Sorry."

"Uh, how'd you find me here?"

"I was just walking around." I point to where she's white-knuckling her phone. "Are you okay?"

She shutters a breath. "No, not really. I thought all this drama was over with."

"What's going on?"

"I, um, nothing. I'm fine." She rakes a hand through her hair and blows out a breath.

I'm about to walk away when I glance down and see a large, swollen scratch on her leg. "What the hell happened there?"

Candy rubs her lips together and glances away from me. "I went out with some people last night, and, uh, I ran into Jake Marx. He was sorta out of control and drunk, ended up throwing a beer bottle and some glass scratched me. It's not a big—"

"The hell it isn't! Are you kidding me, Candy?" I kneel down and look at the scratch. It's ugly and swollen, with red creeping out from it. Yeah, it ain't deep, but it can still get infected. I'm livid. My hands ball into fists. "I'm gonna kill him, I swear."

She sighs. "That's not even why I'm upset. Someone took a video and uploaded it." Turning her phone around, I read the headline in front of me.

Jake Marx Has Drunken Row With Candy DeLeón.

I shake my head. "Well, were you involved? Were you drunk and fighting with him?"

"No, of course not," she says, pinning me with a beady stare. "But it doesn't matter. My name is still associated with his in the article, and it just pisses me off. I thought I'd gotten rid of him. *Él es un insecto.*"

I grab her phone and read through the article. "I don't think anyone is going to fault you for this. Was he arrested?"

She cocks her head and juts out her chin as if saying *what do you think?* "Obviously not," she confirms. "But still, it was scary, and I got hurt, and I wanted to call *you,* but I couldn't do that because you're *you,* which just made me more pissed, and maybe therapy isn't helping because my hands won't stop shaking, and they only stop when I'm around you, but I can't be around you. Just forget about it, I'm rambling, and it's not a big deal. I'm fine. Is it time for our Q&A?"

She turns from flustered to almost-professional in a matter of seconds. Grabbing her hand as she tries to flee, my fingers zing with little shocks of electricity as she grasps my hand back, but out of respect, I drop my hold and step away from her, saying, "Slow down, we're fine. We've got time. You've been going to therapy?"

She rolls her eyes and nods. "Yeah, well, I was freaking violated by a guy and then you broke my heart. So...anyway, *Vámonos. Vamos a llegar tarde.* I'm done rambling."

"You can ramble to me anytime you need to."

She purses her lips and gently crosses her ankles while leaning against the wall. "No, *I cannot.*"

"Yes, you can. Candy—"

"*Para con eso.* Can we not do this here?" Her big green eyes plead with me.

I shrug. "I'm not doing anything. I just want to say I'm sorry. I screwed up, I get that. And I'm sorry you were violated. I'm sorry if I played a part in that because you left me and found him. I get it. I'm not expecting you to forgive me. Nor do you have to listen to me justify things anymore. I respect your decision to end things." None of my justifications will help anyway. They only drive her further away. "And I'm sorry things with Jake are being stirred up again. I tried to help with the videos, and I'm sorry if I made things worse. But you can *always* call me if you need help."

She perks up like a dog with a bone. "The videos? Wait, what videos?"

Shit. I'm an idiot. Heat rises from my chest to my neck. "Y-yeah. The TikToks that were uploaded. I saw them on TikTok. Where they went viral." My heart beats in my chest at double speed. "That someone...up...loaded."

"Did you...?" Squinting her eyes, she seems to rip open my soul and eat every lie. But a moment later, she shakes her head and crosses her arms. "We should go get set up."

My watch buzzes with the alarm I set for the Q&A. "Yeah, we should. I'll see you there."

I begin walking away, but she calls out, "Hey, don't you have a game tonight?"

"Yeah." I nod. And because I want to tell someone, I blurt out, "A scout's coming to see me."

Her brows raise. "Wow, um, good luck."

"Thanks." But how can I tell her that *she* was always my good luck? Ever from the start, it's been her in the stands, cheering me on, that made me play well.

It's the first game Carter won't be in. The first game she won't be there for. When she left freshman year, I struck out every single game. Athletes are superstitious. It's in our blood.

A scout is finally coming to watch me, but the good luck charm I need won't be there. As I walk away and head to the Q&A table to sit next to Candy, I can't help but feel that same panicky feeling I did when she left to go backpacking alone freshman year.

Except, she was always planning to come back then.

She's not coming back now. I'll sit next to her at this Q&A, we'll pretend we're a couple, and then I'm supposed to say goodbye for good.

How am I supposed to look at the woman I love and know that I'll never laugh with her again? Never touch her or kiss her? Never stay up doing stupid things like watching *Love Island* or taking last-minute spontaneous trips. Never go through In-N-Out and have to recite her crazy long order because she always wants a double meat, single cheese, burger with extra special sauce, grilled onions, add pickles, take off the lettuce with extra crispy fries, two packets of ketchup, a side of special sauce, a Neapolitan milkshake, a hot chocolate if it's winter, plus a pink lemonade.

Eventually, I'll see her move on with someone else, someone that gets to learn all of these things about her, and it wrecks me.

So as I watch her approach the podium I'm sitting at, waiting for our Q&A to start, I ask myself again: How am I supposed to look at the woman I love and tell myself it's time to let her go?

Chapter Thirty Four – Tom

The crowd loves Candy and I. They ask follow up questions from my interview this morning, like what it is about sea turtles that I love and what BLM means to me. Candy plays the part of the doting girlfriend so good that I pretend for a moment that everything is fine between us.

She points to a small, skinny girl with bright red hair and round glasses who says, "You are the cutest couple. I'm a big fan. How did the two of you meet?" She gushes, hands clasped to her chest.

I glance at Candy, whose smile falters just slightly, but not enough that anyone else would notice. Didn't think we'd get a shipper at this event, I guess. But this is what we prepared for.

She looks to me, and I see the pain in her eyes behind the smile. "Tom's my twin's best friend. We met in elementary school when the two of them stole my notebook as a 'joke.'" She air quotes. "I know what you're all thinking…hilarious joke, right? Thankfully, their sense of humor has gotten better over the years. Right?"

"Yeah, I've graduated to making jokes about her ever-changing hair, now."

A few people scatter laughs, and I pick a boy whose hand is raised. "Are you gonna play in the pros?" he asks.

"I sure hope so, kid. You play?"

He nods. "Yeah. Saw your game on ESPN a few weeks back."

I smile, and Candy chooses someone else. The question they ask is lost as my focus zeroes in on the last person I expected to see. Kira walks hesitantly through the door and to a row of seats in the back. She holds up her hand to wave at me, and I can feel a scowl forming on my face.

"Tom?" Candy asks, her voice lined with urgency.

Tearing my gaze away, I look toward the crowd and where the microphone is. "Sorry, what was that?"

A smart-looking kid in a dress shirt and slacks repeats the question. "Do you plan on partnering with any organizations to help Black ball players?"

"Absolutely," I reply. "I see you, fam, and it's something I'm passionate about. Baseball can be an expensive game. People are shelling out thousands of dollars for their kids when the kid isn't even ten. Kids are recruited out of high school, but it's usually the kids who have spent the cash and had the opportunity. Drafting from college is becoming more popular, and there are more Black players in college now. Though the growth is small, it *is* there."

He gives me a smirk, and I laugh. "Yeah, it's not good enough. We have to make our voices heard, which is a big reason why I'm here. Coaches need to realize that they're only going to recruit the players they want to recruit. There are great Black ball players out here, and my hope is that they'll do what they need to do to find them. But in the meantime, I'm partnering with The Players Alliance."

The moderator cuts in, "We've got time for one last question. Candy?"

She picks another girl who immediately asks, "I've been keeping up with Making Our Mark. Could you talk a little about that? Do you have any updates on your cases?"

Candy begins talking about her non-profit, and her smile is genuine and pure. It lights up her face, and I can't help but watch her. "I obviously can't comment on open court cases, but we're currently helping ten girls and one man fight against their abusers, and it's been such a great experience. We hope to expand to creating preventive videos that companies and universities can show employees and students to lower sexual harassment. I'm just really excited to continue this, so thanks for asking about it."

A few of the young girls in the crowd nod their heads, but all I see when I glance that way is Kira sitting in the back, still staring at me.

The moderator nods and steps in front of us. "Thank you so much, everyone, for coming today. Replays will be available on our website. Candy," she turns toward her, "we'll see you later for your interview with Alison. Our next Q&A will be with Arizona State's media trailblazer, Erin Jones!"

As soon as the crowd noise overtakes the silence of the room, I turn toward Candy. I can feel Kira's eyes on me, and they burn like a brand. But I can't leave without Candy knowing how grateful I am to have met her. She told me we're over, and I have to accept it. Even if it feels like I'm losing the most important person in my life.

I grab her hand. "It was a good last run, right?"

Her brow furrows. "*Sí, sí, gracias.* I know it, uh, wasn't the most comfortable."

I nod. "You were amazing. I'm still shook anytime I see you so in your element. Straight fire." Heaving out an awkward laugh, I continue with my throat tight, "I wouldn't be here without you. You made me passionate about this. You even encouraged the sea turtle thing, which I know you thought was ridiculous."

"Tom—"

"*Por favor, escúchame,* 'cause I don't know if I'll get another chance to say it. I'm sorry I didn't live up to your expectations. The fact I had a few years with you is incredible, and Imma cherish those memories, even if you don't. I'm sorry if I tainted our good memories with the bad, but I need you to know that you're the most amazing person I've ever met, Candy. Never doubt everything that you deserve. I...I really do love you, so please do me a favor and take care of yourself. You're gonna change the world."

I give her a quick kiss on the cheek and leave before she

can process what I've said. Because I didn't say it for a re-sponse. I said it in hopes of closure.

But instead, it's ripped my heart wide open, and I bite my tongue to keep the emotion at bay.

I get to the door before my arm is pulled back. It's not Candy, but Kira.

Without stopping, I grit out, "Not now."

"Tom! Wait!" she says, running to catch up with me. Her loose-fitted pants sway with each step, and she keeps tapping my bicep. "I'm begging you, please."

I turn into an alcove and face her. "*What*, Kira? I don't want to talk to you."

"I'm sorry, okay?" She pleads with her hazel eyes. "I made a mistake."

"Yeah, you did." I clear my throat, which is lined with emotion. "But you got what you wanted."

Kira looks over her shoulder as she fidgets with one of her bleach-tipped braids. "No, Tom. I didn't. I've been talking to Candy."

Like at the baseball game. But about what? They've al-ways hated each other. "What do you mean?"

"I wanted to make sure you didn't tell her about the preg-nancy test, so I, um, I befriended her."

"You *what?* Kira, do you not realize how out of pocket that is?"

"I do. And I'm sorry. Because I was wrong. So wrong, Tom. She's great and funny, and I...like her. I like her a lot. And I'm sorry I thought she wasn't right for you." She reaches for me, but I shake her off.

"Too little too late." I try to walk around her, but she grabs my arm again.

"No. She cares about you, I know she does. It's not too late."

"Yeah. It is." I heave out a breath. "It's over."

Panic flares in her eyes. "It can't be. What can I do to help?"

I bark out a laugh. "Help? All you've done is hurt. Nothing

we can do from here on out will help."

"Tell her. Tell her everything," she offers.

"I already tried!" I rub at my eyes. "I already tried. And you know what she said? She couldn't even trust me. She didn't believe a word I said. It took me two years. Two years, Kira, to get Candy to trust me. And you destroyed that trust in two seconds because you never do anything unless it benefits you. But what benefit did you get from us breaking up?"

"Tom," she whines. "I'm so, so sorry."

"I don't even care." My watch pings with a text saying my flight leaves in two and a half hours. "I can't do this right now. I wanted to watch Candy's interview before I gotta head to the airport. Why are you even here?"

"I had to look at a few law schools," she says quietly while teetering on her high heels.

"Of course you did," I mutter. "Thank you for proving my point."

"But I came *here* for you and Candy." Her lip quivers.

"There *is* no me and Candy!" I bite out, but my voice cracks. "It's over."

Before she can respond, I take her hand off my arm and walk away.

Chapter Thirty Five – Candy

I head out of the bathroom to see Tom storming off ahead of me, oblivious to the fact that I'm watching him. His back is tight, shoulders taut against the tight coral-colored button up he wears. He scratches the back of his neck and pulls out his phone. For a moment, I stand there, curious about what he's doing and where he's going.

The last words he said to me sounded so...final. And it's what I asked of him. I have absolutely no reason to complain. But...I guess I just didn't think it'd feel like this. Like I'm still missing a part of myself. *Él es mi alma.*

I wish I hadn't been as stupid as I was to fall for him two times. Because even looking at the back of his head makes me wish he were mine. But I'm not willing to go through him cheating on me a third time.

Shaking the thoughts from my head, I check my watch. I have ten minutes until I need to be miked up. Sighing, I walk in the direction that Tom did toward backstage.

Three steps in, I run into someone else.

"So sorry!" I exclaim as I brush the hair out of my eyes. "Wait, Kira? Hey! You're here!"

She glances up with red eyes and lipstick that's slightly messed up. "Candy...hi."

"Are you okay?" I ask, offering a hand on her shoulder. She looks like absolute crap.

Tossing her hair over her shoulder but for one lone braid, she swallows enough that her throat bobs. "No, I'm not. I'm so sorry, Candy. I'm a horrible person, and—"

"Wh—"

"No," she cuts in, just like her brother did a few minutes ago to me. "I did something horrible, and I'm not even sure why. How pathetic is that, right? I don't even have an explanation as to why I did it."

"What did you do?" Nothing she is saying makes sense. What could she have possibly done that would involve *me*? I try to think of everything I've told her over the past few weeks, but nothing major stands out. Unless... "Did you release video of the club last night?"

She did have her phone out when Jake approached us.

"No, no, of course not." Kira rubs at her brow and her voice is a quiet whisper. "Remember in high school when we went out to that protest and blew up the cop car?"

I widen my eyes. "Please tell me that did not get out."

Flashes of the past few months cross my mind. If it gets out that Tom and I were there when a cop car was trashed, we're screwed. We made a dumb mistake. One that has *never* been repeated. But the media will run with it, so will the Marx family, and I don't have enough damage control to fix that.

She shakes her head, and I release the breath that built up in my lungs. "*Gracias a Dios.*"

"But," she bites her lip, "I used to have footage of it. And I used it to blackmail Tom."

"You...what..." My skin prickles as the night outside of my house comes into focus. *The pregnancy test wasn't for me. I didn't cheat on you. But the person it was for, they've got something on me.*

Ay Dios mío...he wasn't lying. Tom...he told the *truth*. I blink and my skin feels like it's on fire. "The pregnancy test. It was...for you? And you held the video footage against Tom," I mumble, putting it all together. Then the last few weeks replay in my mind. "Tom didn't cheat. B-but *why*? Why didn't you want Tom to tell me? I wouldn't have cared."

I take my hands off of her shoulders and step away from her. "You ruined my relationship. And then you went along with it knowing that Tom didn't cheat on me. You became my *friend*." I scoff. "What the hell?"

"I know, and I'm sorry. Tom didn't cheat, and I never should've told him he had to keep the pregnancy test from you."

I laugh. "You didn't tell him to hide the pregnancy test. You *blackmailed* him. Your own brother?"

Kira nods. "I don't know what else to say except I'm sorry."

"That doesn't change things. I...I have to go." I turn to leave, but she reaches out to grab my arm.

With tears lining her eyes, she says, "Tom thinks it's too late to fix anything. He didn't tell you about the pregnancy test because he knew you'd rather have your career than have him."

"Those aren't mutually exclusive," I mutter.

"I am so sorry, Candy. Once we talked longer for two minutes before tearing each other apart, I saw everything that Tom did. He's still in love with you." She lets go of me. "And I think you're still in love with him too."

I swallow through the lump in my throat and walk away from Kira. But five steps later, I turn back around. "What were the results of your test?"

She licks her lips. "Positive."

I glance down at her stomach, even though there's nothing there.

"I'm keeping it," she says.

"Well," I nod, "congrats. And for the record, it wouldn't have mattered whether you were pregnant, decided to keep it, decided not to keep it, or not pregnant at all, I wouldn't have told a soul."

"I know," she whispers and looks down at her hands. "I erased the video. It's gone. There's no more evidence."

Shaking my head, I walk away for good this time, head clouded with a thousand emotions. Tom should've just told me. I would've forgiven him if our careers collapsed on the stupid video that Kira posted. *Si lo habría perdonado, entonces él todavía sería mío.*

But he didn't. Instead, he experienced the same pain I did the past six weeks, all because he didn't want to ruin my career. He *didn't* cheat, but he let me think he did so I could get my career back. The thought stops me in my tracks again.

He didn't cheat on me, and he bought the pregnancy test for his sister. Everything he said after our Q&A was so final. I pushed him away, refused to believe him, and now he's given me the closure that I asked for.

I don't want it anymore.

I have to find him. I need to see him and tell him I'm sorry he thought my career outweighed us. Because he means so much more to me than what the public says. My heart beats at double time when I start running to the conference hall.

He went this way.

Was he going to watch my interview?

My body stills. The interview. I check my watch, and I was supposed to be getting miked five minutes ago.

"Shit!" I call out. I pull out my phone and text.

Candy: *I need to talk to you.*

But no three dots appear on the screen with Tom's name. It doesn't even deliver the text, and my service in this conference hall sucks. Please tell me he didn't block me.

I'm about to search for him when someone taps me. "Candy DeLeón? You're up next. Come on."

"Okay, one second, please." I glance around the audience, but it's too dark to see.

"Ma'am, we don't have that. I'm sorry, but we have to get you miked. You're going on any minute now," he says.

"Okay." I breathe out. "Alright."

I'll catch up with him after. I'll find Tom and tell him I know everything. Sending a silent prayer up to *Madre Maria,* I pray that everything will work out how it's supposed to.

But I barely focus as they put the microphone on me and explain what I have to do. I nod, I smile, but my mind is scattered.

Alison announces me, so I head out on stage, no doubt looking frazzled. As she introduces me to the cameras, I scan the audience, looking for Tom.

He's nowhere to be found. Maybe he didn't stay to watch my interview after all.

Alison smiles. "You've been in the media a lot lately, and you handle everything so gracefully. What would you tell these young kids about public image?"

Now is when I wish *mi mami* was into pageants so I could've had practice answering questions on the spot. Even if I was focused, this would've been a tough one. Now? With my mind equivalent to *chilaquiles,* I'm scrambling for words. I glance out to the audience again, where blank faces stare back at me.

Moving my sight toward the camera, I pause on a familiar face. Tom sits beside the cameraman, a small smile on his face. He nods when our eyes meet, and he's still here.

Él todavía está aquí.

He was passionate about my career, enough that he let me go completely, and he's still here. I'm in love with him. The way he laughs whenever I dance in the car, the way he pulls at one or two curls when he's focusing, the way his hazel eyes catch the sun, lighting them to gold. Or the way he carries me, which makes me feel safe. The way his nose crinkles when he smiles too big, the way he grasps his sheets while lowering himself on me, or how he knows me perfectly, knows exactly what to do to make me melt.

Like I said to my mom, I thought he was it for me. And now, I know.

I'm never getting over Tom Walker, and I need to make him mine.

But I'm on live TV, so it'll have to wait.

I take a deep breath and turn back toward Alison. "Public image is big because you want people to respect you, and one mistake can completely shatter that. But public image is just that...an image. It's a snapshot of who you are. I've made a lot of mistakes this year." I glance at Tom. "I don't think anyone would argue that. Many of them were documented publicly. The public doesn't see you in action very often, nor do they get to know you on a personal level. *For me,* I've learned that while public image matters, it's not the most important thing."

I meet Tom's gaze again and hope he knows what I mean. I lick my lips. "It's much more important to be a good person, on and off the camera. Do what's right, be kind, and fight for those who can't fight. And when you make a mistake, fix it. Fix it as fast as you possibly can."

Tom's face is blank, but I hope he knows I'm talking about us. Because breaking up was a mistake. Wanting him out of my life was an even bigger mistake. I need to fix it.

Alison asks me more questions, and I talk about my plans for the rest of the year, what students can do now to get involved before they can legally vote, and how we should focus more on the crowd of people rather than just the popular individuals. The entire time I talk, I steal glances at Tom, who never moves from his seat. Just a few more moments, and I'll speak to him.

"What's the biggest lesson you've learned this year?" Alison asks, setting down her cue cards on the small table next to her chair.

I let out a small *hmm* while I think of what to say. Turning toward her, I cross my ankles and reply, "Women are not weak. We don't deserve to be called weak, and I'm here to show that I'm fighting back against anything, and anyone, who says differently. Women, especially minority women, are tired of being told we are not strong and don't belong in politics. We are here. *Estamos aquí,* and I'll be raising awareness and demanding change. But mostly, I learned to not give up. Never give up on the things, or people, that matter most to you."

My throat is thick with emotion as I glance toward Tom and silently beg him to stay there so I can talk to him.

Stay there, please.

Finally, Alison ends the interview and announces a commercial break. I breathe a sigh of relief as a stage crewmember comes out and begins to un-mic me.

As they work, Alison says, "You did a great job. The kids here absolutely love you."

"Ah, thank you." I feel a blush rising in my cheeks. "I've had a lot of fun being here. Thanks for the invite."

But I fight the urge to scream *can you undo the wires faster, please?*

Alison stands and hands me a business card. "My boyfriend is a reporter for Buzzfeed News. I mentioned you, the scandal, the unfair treatment between you and Jake Marx, and your new non-profit. He's interested in an interview with you."

My jaw drops. "I—Thank you. *Ay Dios mío,* thank you, Alison."

She nods. "Of course. His contact information is all there, but you should hear from him by the end of today to set up the interview. I know he's looking forward to it. Enjoy the rest of the convention, Candy."

"Thank you again. I really appreciate it," I say, looking down at the business card in my hand.

Maybe this year wasn't a total waste.

The stage crew unclips the last wire, so I thank him and run off stage as fast I can. Intermittent music plays, and the song "18" by One Direction begins playing. I smile thinking of the throwback, which sends me straight back to high school and Tom.

Every step feels like it's leading me to the future, and I can't help but feel a rising excitement in my chest. Going straight to the audience, I find the row where Tom sat.

But when I get to the center where he sat, he's gone. I glance around, but he's nowhere to be found. I pull out my phone and call him. It goes straight to voicemail. I call again, but it wasn't a fluke. Straight to voicemail.

Who the hell turns off their phone?!

Storming out of the conference center, I rack my brain trying to think of where he could be. His room? I'm halfway across the hotel lobby when I see Kira.

"Have you seen your brother?" I rush out.

She shakes her head. "No, he won't be here."

"What do you mean?"

"He had to take the first flight out for his game."

No. *No.* He's already gone? "But he was just here. I just saw him!"

I dial Carter's number. It rings twice. "Hey, *hermana.* What's up?"

"What time is the game tonight?"

"Uh...it's in...at seven."

I shake my head at what sounds like a drunken answer. *"Gracias."*

Hanging up the phone, I look to Kira. "Ready to earn your forgiveness?" I'm already on Google, booking a flight for three hours from now. "I need you to drive me to the airport."

Chapter Thirty Six – Tom

It's the bottom of the ninth inning, and I'm up to bat. West is down one run to Cal Poly. Considering Carter's out, we've done exceptionally well. But now we're two outs in, and if we don't get two more runners through, we'll lose.

Meaning, if I don't hit well, the game is over.

Cal Poly's pitcher throws a curveball. I swing my bat, but it collides with the ball too late and arcs over toward the crowd.

"Foul ball by West's Tom Walker," the announcer says. "Strike one in a game that looks as if it might end with Cal Poly keeping their undefeated streak."

I clear my throat and kick the dirt, rolling my shoulders before getting in position. The pitcher throws a fastball, and I miss.

"Strike two," catcher says.

"Yeah, got it," I snap.

"Walker!" Ben shouts.

I turn toward where Ben stands , hands cupped over his face. "Look to your right!"

Quickly, I whip my head over to the stands where Ben points. I scan through the large crowd until I see the stadium lights shining down on pink hair.

Candy holds a giant poster in the air and Carter stands beside her with his arm in a sling, whistling between his fingers with his other hand. The poster reads *Te amo, idiota!*

Everything in me stills as she shouts or mouths the same thing over and over.

Candy is here. At my game. Holding a poster that says I love you.

Is this a dream? A nightmare? I'll wake up to realize I'm the world's biggest fool? But Coach shouting, "Walker! What're you doing?" brings me back to the moment like a pinch on the arm.

I shake my head and laugh. Candy is *here.* I don't know WTF that means, but I'm grinning like a boy on Christmas morning. Filled with energy, I kiss two fingers and raise my fist in the air. Candy nods and kisses two fingers. *I love you,* she mouths one last time.

My lucky charm is here.

Lifting my bat, I take a deep breath and focus. Cal Poly's pitcher scrapes his cleats against the pitching mound before reeling his arm back and chucking the ball my way.

It barrels toward me, and I feel my smile growing bigger as I swing the bat. The ball clanks against the metal and soars high above. I jog to first base as it keeps going, past the outfield, and over the fence.

A home run.

The crowd cheers, and my face breaks into an impossibly-bigger grin as the two runners before me cross home and I run the rest of the bases, securing our win.

I sprint toward my team, and we end up in a pile of bro-hugs as we celebrate knocking Cal Poly off their undefeated pedestal.

"You pitched great, AJ," I say to the new pitcher, who has had a ton of pressure put on him now that Carter's out. I give him a hug and turn toward Ben, who punches my shoulder before pulling me in and slapping me on the back once. "Good game, bruh."

"Thanks," I say, raising a brow as I get out of our hug.

"Don't worry, we'll go back to our regularly scheduled hate-fest tomorrow."

I nod. "Aight, fam. Sounds good."

White people are so weird.

The swell of winning the game is nothing compared to when I look back behind the dugout and see Candy standing as close as she can possibly get in the stands. For a second, we just stare at each other.

She holds the sign over the dugout's wall, and shrugs her shoulders. I walk toward her, unable to tear my gaze despite my team members calling my name.

When I get five steps away, I slow and nod toward the sign. "You mean it?

She looks down at me from the stands, a few feet above me. "*Sí.* Kira told me everything. I'm sorry I didn't believe you. Granted, you should've told me, but it doesn't matter now. I was wrong. So wrong. Careers recover. Hearts do not. I've been walking around with a giant hole in my chest. And Tom, I'm not over you. I don't think I'll ever be over you because I am so in love with—"

I close the gap, reach up to her, and pull her lips to mine, cutting off what she said. She lets out a startled *oh*, which just serves to open her mouth to me. I kiss her like I should've been the last month and a half, frantic and without limitations. She drops the sign and grabs my cheeks, pulling me closer.

A camera flashes, and someone throws a water bottle at my thigh, so I break the kiss to flip two of my teammates off. They snicker and make a whipping motion with their hands. Grace holds up her camera, winks, and walks away without saying a word.

Candy bites her lip and reaches down to wipe lipstick off of my mouth. "Since you so rudely interrupted me...I'm so in love with you, Tom."

I reach underneath my jersey and pull out the locket I've kept hidden in an inner pocket since she gave it back to me. "Will you put this back on?"

She snatches it away from my hand and quickly clasps it around her neck. "You kept it with you? I felt naked without it on."

"Hmm, we might need to take it back off and test that

later. And of course I kept it."

I stand up on my tiptoes to bring her face back to mine. "Can you go back to being my girlfriend now?"

She smiles against my lips. "*Sí*. I love you. Don't you ever leave me again."

I chuckle. "*Te amo*, Candy."

Epilogue – Candy (One Year Later)

Les, Carter, and I sit in the stands of the Las Vegas Ballpark as we wait for Tom to finish showering. He was just promoted to the Las Vegas Aviators, the final stop before the Oakland A's. I couldn't be prouder, and watching him live out his dream is more fulfilling than I ever imagined.

"Where did your parents go?" Les asks, glancing around at the emptying stands.

I shrug. "Who knows. They probably went back to the hotel. They've been dying to go to the strip."

Carter chuckles. "You mean *Papi*. After last night, *Mami* was pissed that he gambled away twenty dollars."

Les snorts then pales. "Oh, wait? For real?" She hits my arm. "You said we were setting a hundred dollar limit."

I pull out my phone and smile at the background photo, Tom and I kissing at the Cal Poly game. Grace had taken it. I posted that photo immediately after Grace showed me it to Twitter and Instagram, and it's my most popular post to this day.

"Yeah, *we*. Not my parents. My mom is a hardcore no-gambling person. So let's not repeat the hundred dollar limit in front of her, *por favor*." I'm in my head scrolling through photos of Tom and I in Vegas last night when two thick arms wrap around my shoulders.

I yelp as Tom laughs, squeezing me from behind.

Turning, I tell him, "Good game, babe. You crushed the River Cats."

He kisses me and nods. "We sure did. Thanks for coming,

you guys."

I stand, and he wraps his arm around me as we walk out of the stadium with Les and Carter behind us. Tom squeezes me to his side. "I've missed you, *cariña.*"

My nose crinkles with my smile. "I've missed you too, *amor.* You gettin' along with the boys here?"

He nods and turns his baseball cap backwards. "Yeah, yeah, they're cool. Not nearly as cool as my famous girlfriend, but…"

I laugh. "Not famous."

"You are famous, Mrs. Today Show." He bumps my side with his hip.

"Okay, it's really cool, I'll admit." This year has been amazing. With all the drama stuck firmly in the past of last year, and Joanna Marx failing to secure a senate seat, it's been stress-free. Our non-profit has exploded, and we've helped over a hundred people to this day. The lawyers and paralegals are amazing, and West University has been supportive with their yearly donation. Grace has been a lifesaver with running it, and I know when I graduate, she's going to be even more help.

Jake Marx's foundation was taken over by someone else, and he's currently on trial against ten of the women who came forward. How it'll end, who knows. But I'm holding out hope for the women winning. Therapy helped me a lot, and I've been working hard with school. I doubled classes and enrolled in the summer, so I graduate in just a month.

Besides the fact that my boyfriend lives in another state, everything has been perfect. Tom's finishing up school online while playing baseball.

Once I graduate, I'll be moving to Vegas to help an amazing woman with her campaign for Nevada governor while still helping to run Making Our Mark. It'll be a lot, but I'll be closer to Tom. Though we still haven't talked about what we're going to do. Are we getting an apartment together? Am I doing my own thing?

We haven't lived together since before we got back together, and though it's been nice exploring each other while also being independent, I'm curious as to where we'll go from here.

Carter flicks my arm. "Hey, we'll catch you later. Gonna grab some dinner and then hit the strip."

"*Badios, amigos.*" I wave them goodbye, not really sorry to see them go. I could use some alone time with Tom. Preferably behind closed doors.

As soon as Les and Carter are out of earshot, I turn toward Tom. "Take me to your place."

He chuckles, his white teeth shining against the lights in the parking lot. "Damn, girl. You thirsty or somethin'?"

I glare at him.

"I'm playing. But, I have other plans." He nods toward his Jeep and unlocks it. "Come on."

"Ugh, *los hombres son lo peor.*"

"Huh?" he asks.

"Nothing," I sing-song, smiling sweetly.

He opens the car door for me, and I hop inside. We drive toward the strip, and I watch the lights sparkle against the dusk sky. He bypasses the strip completely, and I slide the locket on my neck back and forth, listening to the calm humming sound it makes. "Oh, I forgot to tell you, I went and babysat Isaac the other day. He's getting so big."

I pull out my phone and show him the picture of me holding Isaac as he yanks on my hair. Kira's baby is adorable, but it also makes me glad I'm not a mom. As soon as he starts crying, I'm ready to hand him back.

Tom smiles at the picture. "Little cutie. I miss him, too."

I put my arm over the seat and tickle Tom's neck. My nail catches on his gold chain, and I pull it slightly. Memories of our past fill my mind. "Hey, didn't you say we were matching?"

He pushes my arm off of him, and laughs. "Yeah, well, we are."

I look down at my own locket. "You know, I never did get

it open. I nearly took a hammer to it when we broke up, but then I couldn't do it. *¿No abre, verdad?*"

Tom pulls into a parking lot with a few scattered cars. "Hmmm."

He grabs the nearest spot and gets out of the car.

"Hmm?" I say as he closes his door. "That's it?" I shout.

I hear him laugh as I open my door. "Tell me how to open it!"

"You really want to know?" His button up practice jersey hugs his frame, and I'm tempted to rip it open.

"*Sí, claro.*"

He grabs my hand and pulls me toward a large area of neon, lit up signs. I glance around us. "*Ay Dios mío,* what is this place? I love it."

The pink and purple lights shine down on us, making our faces abstract paintings. Tom keeps walking me through the different signs, and not a soul is here.

"It's empty."

He chuckles. "It's the Neon Museum. Kinda cool, right? Figured you'd like it. Lots of Instagram-worthy shots here."

I roll my eyes but a giggle slips out. "Well then, Mr. Photographer. Get started. You're the one who takes the best photos of me."

"I thought you wanted to see how to get your necklace opened," he chastises.

"Oh, right. That first, then the pictures."

He reaches around his neck and fiddles with the slim gold chain around his neck. It comes unclasped, and he holds it out to me. "See that key?"

I nod, holding up the tiniest key I've seen. It's part of the clasp, and you'd never notice it without him taking the entire chain off.

"It unlocks your locket."

His eyes shine with something unknown, and he licks his lips. "You can open it."

I take my necklace off and fiddle with the key for too long

because of my nails. But I finally get it into the small opening on the side of the heart locket. When I push it in, the locket pops, opening ajar. I take the key out and hand him back his chain before I fully open the locket. Angling it against the pink neon sign, I read the words engraved into the gold.

Marry me.

I drop the necklace and yelp. But Tom's already on one knee and picking it up, holding it back out to me with a ring in his other hand.

All coherent thoughts exit my brain and I blurt out, "But you gave me that locket when we weren't even together!"

He laughs and hangs his head low while still proffering the ring and necklace. "Thank you for reminding me that I'm a forever simp. I had it made before you left to travel freshman year. I was gonna give it to you at the end of our backpacking trip."

But he never came. "You mean...you've wanted to marry me for *that* long? *Ay Dios mío,* boy you are insane. *Pero, te amo. ¿Estás seguro?*"

"Yes, I'm sure. Just answer the damn question already, my knee is hurting on these rocks." He glances up at me and smiles his panty-dropping smile. "Are you gonna marry me or not?"

"*Sí, mi amor.* Yes, of course!" I squeal.

He stands and lifts me into the air, and I wrap my legs around his waist. I lean in and kiss him, and now I'm really ready to tear his baseball jersey off. But he pulls back and sets me down. "Ready for the ring and your locket back?"

I nod, my hands in a prayer in front of my mouth. He clasps my locket back around my neck and holds out the ring. It's a slim gold band with an emerald cut diamond right in the center. I slip it on my finger and hold it up against the pink lights. It sparkles and catches the light in every facet.

"It's beautiful. You know I'm obsessed with you, right?"

He chuckles. "The feeling's mutual. I love you, Candy."

"I love you, too," I whisper. "When do you want to get married?"

I'm staring down at the ring, tilting my hand back and forth as it catches the light.

Tom clears his throat, and I glance up at him. He takes off his ballcap and musses his hair. "Well, we're in Vegas. How about tonight?"

My breathing stops for a full five seconds. I glance down at my white satin tank top and jeans and shrug as I let out my breath. A smile grows on my face. We've always been spontaneous. "Let's do it."

He sighs. "No cap, I'm out here sweating. Thought you were gonna say no."

I grab his hand, and we walk through the Neon Museum, stopping to take pictures with different signs. We walk for a few minutes before I see a row of chairs set up in front of a large sign that says Lady Luck. I glance toward Tom, who kisses my forehead. "Surprise," he muses.

Mom, Dad, Les, Carter, Tom's parents, Kira, Rykard and Jared, all turn their heads as we walk closer. Standing up at in front of the sign is Ethan, holding a sheet of paper.

"Is—Is this for real?" A blush creeps up my neck and a bubble of laughter escapes me. The lights shine down on us, and it's perfect. Completely spontaneous, full of adventure, and all me and Tom.

Tom shrugs. "If you want, yeah. Otherwise, we can just pretend this is an engagement party. I told them all to prepare for either one."

I squeeze his hand. "No way. We are getting married. *Me voy a casar contigo y luego te voy a follar en el hotel.*"

His eyes widen. "Not so loud, our parents are here."

But then he smiles with those full lips of his, and I stand on my tiptoes to kiss him.

"Hey!" Ethan barks out. "No kissing the husband until I announce it."

I pull away from Tom and raise my brows at Ethan. "*You're* officiating us?"

He nods. "Yep. Got my certificate online. But it's legit, I

305

promise. Oh, and here's your license. We'll have Les and Carter be witnesses."

I bury my head in my hands. Are my parents mad my wedding is going to be like this? *"Mami, Papi, ¿estas en acuerdo de esto? ¿No estan enojoados que no voy a tener una boda grande?"*

My dad's brow furrows. *"Mija, casi gastamos todo nuestro dinero con su quinceañera."*

Mami slaps his arm. "It did not bankrupt us. But no, honey. Of course not. Carlotta had a big wedding, and I'm sure Les and Carter will as well."

Carter clears his throat. "Alright, alright, no one's talking marriage, aight?"

Les drops her jaw and he pulls at the collar of his shirt. "I didn't say we weren't getting married. Just…like…not now, *señorita. Ay Dios mío,* can we just focus on the other twin?"

Les rolls her eyes, and I send a thought down our twin telepathy of *good luck getting your foot out of your mouth with that one.* Carter glares, and I pretend to reapply my lipstick with my middle finger.

I walk toward Rykard and flick his head. He's holding hands with Jared, and I squeal. "Happy for you," I whisper in Jared's ear.

"You too, babe," he replies.

Tom's parents hug me, and I'm touched they flew out here for a "maybe" wedding that they weren't even sure would happen. I turn toward Kira and give her a side hug. When I glance down at Isaac, I nearly die from cuteness. "Noo, he's our flower boy? This is the cutest thing I've ever seen."

He's passed out asleep, but Kira puts his little hand in the basket of flower petals and makes a couple float to the ground below.

Ethan claps. "Let's get it started."

He grabs a Bluetooth speaker and plays "Conversations in the Dark" by John Legend.

I bite my lip and skip in front of the chairs where Ethan Stands. Tom follows behind me, hands twitching the entire time.

Ethan reaches into his pocket and pulls out a bowtie and his phone. Attaching the bowtie to his shirt with a clip, he says, "Hold up, let's take a selfie of my first marriage officiation."

Tom rolls his eyes as I get in a selfie with Ethan and pucker my lips.

He snaps the pic and nods. "Good one. Alright. Welcome to the wedding of the soon-to-be Mr. and Mrs. DeLeón."

Tom turns toward Ethan and gives him a look. "Dude, I'm keeping my last name."

"Oh, my bad. Welcome to the wedding of these two. You guys wanna exchange vows or nah?"

I laugh and cover my eyes. "Here, I'll start. Tom, *te amo.* You are the person I want to go on vacation with, the calm to my storm, the sporty to my non-sporty, and the guy who is always down for an adventure. I cannot wait for this next adventure, and quite frankly, I'm just glad I'm getting into the marriage without a prenup since you signed that big contract with the A's."

"So romantic," Tom cuts in.

My smile grows on my face. "But really, I couldn't imagine marrying anyone else in jeans and a tank top. I can't imagine a more perfect place, time, and person. No one could love me quite like you do, *y estoy emocionado de pasar el resto de nuestra vidas juntos.*"

Tom, the giant sap he is, rubs at his eyes and clears his throat. "I'm not cryin', I swear. Candy kicked up some dust around here when talking."

Ethan rubs Tom's back and squeezes his shoulder. "I got you, dawg."

"You sound so white, bro." Tom shakes his head, but everyone laughs. Then he looks into my eyes and holds my hands. "You've had my heart for a decade. From the time I stole your school folder to now, I never stopped loving you. And I won't stop now. *Para mi, eres perfecta.* You are stunning, beautiful, kind, fun, and crazy. Who else would agree to a last minute surprise wedding? My heart has always belonged to you. And I don't ever want it back."

I squeeze his hands and bite my tongue as I smile to keep from kissing him right then and there. "Say the words, Ethan."

"Okay, I'm getting to them, hold on," he says, flopping his blonde hair in his face. He scans over a piece of paper.

"Say the damn words, Ethan," Tom echoes.

Ethan laughs. "Ah, it doesn't have to be exact. By the power vested in me by some online company, I now pronounce you two lovebirds husband and wife. You may now kiss the husband!"

I jump on Tom, and he catches me as our lips collide. Everyone I love, the family that has seen Tom and me through everything, cheers as we give a kiss that's probably a little too much. But I don't care. The man I love just became my *husband.*

When I pull back, our foreheads stay pressed together, and the moment, surrounded by loved ones, painted in neon lights, is picture perfect. Every moment it took to get here was worth it. *Cada. Momento.*

THE END.

Ready for Grace and Ethan's book? Read the first two chapters of the upcoming enemies-to-lovers book, Grace Isn't Given. The book will have you laughing so hard you'll cry.

Grace Isn't Given Preview

Chapter One - Grace

Balls are always in my face.

I'm the soccer goalie for West University's soccer team. But right now? I'm visiting my dad—who just happens to be the coach of West's boys' basketball team. And the ball in my face?

Hard, orange, straight to the nose, basketball.

I fall into an undignified heap, and it's possible I scream like a monkey. My head hits the floor, and my hands fly up to my nose where warmth gushes across my face.

"Grace!" my dad yells, running across the gym floor. He blows his shrill whistle and the bouncing balls around me stop.

But then two dozen college boys swarm into a circle around me, so again: Balls are always in my face.

I glance around the circle, viewing everyone who has a ball. Though I'm not sure why because I *know* who to blame for this.

Ethan freaking Hamilton.

If looks could kill, I just burned him alive on the spot. For once in his life, he has the audacity to look sorry. My dad holds out a hand, I grip it, and he helps me up (shocker). But my gaze never leaves the stupid blue eyes of Ethan.

Classic all-American boy. Blond, slightly-wavy hair, six and a half feet tall, muscles that make the girls swoon, and lips that most girls get fillers to have. He's the type who associates with girls who look like they came straight off of a Brandy

Melville ad.

I hate him.

He hates me.

Though I'm not sure why because he's the most pompous, stuck-up, backstabbing, idiotic—

"I swear I didn't mean to hit you," he says.

I narrow my eyes and take my hands away from my nose.

Ethan retches like the drama king he is. "Oh shoot, you gotta do something about that."

Getting up in his face, I say, "You wanna reset my nose? Because mean it to or not, I'll bet that it's broken."

"Grace," my dad chastises. "Leave 'im alone. Gus, grab the team doc, will you? The rest of you take a water break."

Gus, an actually decent guy who I call a friend, runs to the back of the gym and into the locker rooms. My dad ushers me to sit down, and I pinch my nose to try and keep the blood from flowing. But my white shirt is definitely ruined, my new jeans are probably unsalvageable, and my nose pulses in tune with my heart.

Worst. Monday. Ever.

I lean forward, still gripping my nose. "I came to tell you that Cynthia's car broke down up in Truckee. She couldn't get ahold of you."

Which is a problem, because then she called me, and I'm not a fan of my dad's new blood-sucking girlfriend. Fine, wife. Whatever.

He huffs and scratches at the stubble on his chin. "My phone is in my office. I told her not to go up there for a girls' trip. She never downshifts right," he mutters, walking toward his office.

"Cool! Yeah, Dad! I'm good! I'll just stay here until the team doc comes!" I roll my eyes.

Someone hands me an ice pack, and I nearly say thanks until I see who it's from. "Please get away from me. I don't need my face having any more damage due to being in close proximity to you."

Ethan scowls. "Yeah, totally did that on purpose. Because my sole goal is to be near you. Get over yourself."

I throw the ice pack at him, and it falls to the ground.

He gives it an impassive glance and shrugs. "Your loss."

And that phrase triggers anger in me. He *knows it.* "You're such a pompous ah—" I swallow the curse because my dad is walking over here and has a strict no-swearing-in-the-gym rule "—crobat."

Ethan cocks a brow and folds his arms. "Pompous acrobat?"

"Yep." I pop the 'p'.

He leans in closer, getting near my ear. My breath doesn't catch, I just take a quick inhale because I don't want to smell his BO. From my peripheral, I see him smirk.

"Pretty sure you were the acrobat that night," he whispers and steps back. Giving me a wink, he turns on his heel and marches away as if he's just won the freaking Battle of Gettysburg.

My dad is inches away from me, but I don't care. An angry blush crawls from my chest and into my cheeks. "Screw you, Ethan Hamilton!"

Ethan flips me off without turning around. "You already did, Grace!"

My gasp can probably be heard across the gym, but as I stomp toward Ethan, I'm pulled back by my dad. Dad grabs my arms, but I wrestle away from him.

"Sit your butt down! Now!" His voice echoes, and I flinch. He nods his head toward where the team doctor walks up with a small first aid kid. "Doctor Richards is gonna check you out, and I don't want to hear another peep. We clear?"

My gaze has officially annihilated two people in the past five minutes. "We're clear, Daddio."

He nods and walks away, like always, because that's about the only thing he's good for.

Now that I'm alone, I let myself feel the pain. My eyes water as Dr. Richards presses gently on the bone. He hums. "I won't have to move it much to reset it. I have a syringe here to numb you." Picking up the syringe of clear liquid he says, "You'll feel a little pinch."

The shot burns, but within a few seconds, the throbbing pain disappears. It's a welcome feeling, and the doc moves my nose slightly, applying pressure that I can feel, but the majority of it is numb. Packing my nostrils with gauze, he places a splint on my nose and tapes it up. It's so thick that my eyes have to close slightly.

"Tell your coach you'll be out of practice and workouts for at least two weeks. Take ibuprofen and ice your nose for four hours over the next forty-eight hours. You may need to sleep upright, and don't touch the gauze until you check in with me. Any questions?"

I shake my head. "Nope." My voice is nasally as if I have the flu. "Thanks for the help."

Standing, I grab my phone off of the bench and put it in my pocket. It looks like I stepped right out of a murder scene. Everyone from the gym is gone or in the locker room, I guess—including my dad. Maybe he called off practice to go get Cynthia.

Precious, perfect-princess, Cynthia. Ew, kill me now, she's legit five years older than me. So gross.

With a final look around to make sure I didn't miss my dad, I head out of the gym. I get a few steps away from the athletic facility before I hear the slap of someone's shoes running behind me.

"Hey, wait up." Ethan's voice does give me goosebumps, but they're hate goosebumps. Not like wow-you-have-a-sexy-voice-come-home-with-me goosebumps.

Now it's my turn to flip him off backwards, but stupid college athlete that he is, he catches up with me and walks beside me, gym bag thrown over his shoulder.

"What could you possibly want, Ethan? You broke my nose, forcing me out of practice for two weeks, not to mention providing a world of pain. But now, you're following me. You have an MO? 'Cause I'd like to get on my way, my man." I stop walking and cross my arms.

He grips the strap of his bag and taps his foot. "I'm sorry, aight? It was a bad throw, but I didn't see you there. Trust me, I wouldn't have purposely done that."

I scoff. "Well, I'd hope not. That'd mean you're not only a jerk but a psychopath as well. Apology not accepted. Anything else?"

Fishing around in his pocket, he pulls out his keys. "Can I at least drive you home? You can barely see with that stint."

"My dad asked you to drive me, didn't he?"

He shakes his hair free from his forehead and nods. "Yeah."

I roll my eyes. "Out of all the players, he asks the one I can't stand," I mumble under my breath. "Fine. Let's go."

Ethan walks ahead, and I follow behind him feeling like a dumb kid. Dad doesn't drive me home himself because he's probably already on the freeway picking up his precious Cindy. I have half a mind to call my mom and break into tears over this day, but she's probably working, and she's too far away to do anything for me.

A Denali truck lights up when Ethan presses his keys, and it's on-brand for him, so my eyes get another dose of eyelid. I open the passenger side door and climb in, not saying a word.

He starts the car and turns out of the parking lot. "So, how's your gas?"

I slap his arm. "Shut up, Hamilton. People now only refer to me as Gassy Grace thanks to you."

"Well, everyone still calls me JR Smith, so..." He leans back in his seat as he drives, and the sight of it makes me want to hurl my shoe at him.

"Yours is warranted. You dribbled the ball when you could've had the winning shot of the championship game. That's all on you, not me."

He glares at me as we stop at a red light. "You're the one who published it in the school paper!"

"Because no one would've known about it otherwise?" I throw my hands up.

"I'm sure they would've, but no one else created a viral meme of me missing the shot with my teammates' reactions in slo-mo." He guns the car the second the light turns green, and I hold out a hand on the dashboard to brace myself.

I press on my cheeks, which are still numb. "Wow, I'm so sorry I took a meme-worthy opportunity and exploited it. You, on the other hand, just freaking blew up TikTok with videos of me fake farting. Who does that?"

We sit in silence, both of us steaming, I'm sure. First of all, it was a horrible shot. He gave away the championship game. No one's fault but his own. Second of all, I'm over West's online newsletter and paper. Journalism is my degree. How could I *not* publish one of the dumbest mistakes a West player has ever made? Third of all, that was, what? Nine months ago? And judging by my nose, he's still making bad shots. Lastly, the jerk deserved it.

He should really only be angry with himself here.

Ethan grips the steering wheel harder than he needs to, clenching his jaw. "I do not like you."

I cluck my tongue as he pulls into my dorm. "Aw, the feeling's mutual hon'." I bat my eyelashes as he looks over at me. "Dare I say, I may have even *stronger* feelings!"

He parks the car and lays his forehead on the steering wheel. "You are so annoying."

"Funny. Because 'that night,' I remember you saying something much different."

Lifting his head, he says, "I don't get you."

"Well, it's a good thing I'm not your mystery to solve." I shrug and open the door.

Right as I'm closing the door, he says, "But you should've been."

The door slams, and for a second, I wonder if I made it all up. But when our gazes linger on each other for a second too long, I know he truly said it. And if there's one word to ever describe Ethan and I's relationship, it's *should've*.

Chapter Two - Ethan

Even the way she walks infuriates me. Her red hair cascades down her back, and it's as if she thinks everyone is watching the way her hips sway, but I know it's not on purpose. In fact, she doesn't even notice anyone looking at her. And it pisses me off more.

I stare until she disappears into the stairway of her apartment building before letting out a breath. When I blink, I see her warm brown eyes. You know, the ones lined in tears because of my dumb mistake. And of course, it had to happen to someone who loathes my entire existence.

Why does Grace Brooks hate me? Who knows. We were friends, turning into something more. I even liked her. My stomach heaves at that thought. Not anymore. One night we were together, and the next, she ignored me. I don't need anyone else screwing me over.

Shifting into drive, I grab my phone and press my sister's contact.

It rings a few times as I turn left toward where I live.

"What's up, little bro?"

Squeals of toddlers running in the background echo behind her, and it eases the tension in my shoulders slightly. "Hey, Mae. Just…having a day."

It sounds like she closes a door, and the ruckus silences. "You want to talk about it?"

The road noise as I drive soothes me, but it's not enough. "Not really, no." Guilt crawls up from my stomach, so I heave out the words, "I forgot to take my meds a few days ago, and—"

"You can't do that, Ethan," she whines.

I hold up a hand even though she can't see me. "I know, Mae. I've been slammed between school and practice and hitting extra workouts. And then today…"

"What happened today?"

She's going to kill me. Women do this. They don't even know each other, but they're ready to fight to the death for one of their own if a man does her wrong. "I accidentally broke my coach's daughter's nose."

"You *what?* How does that even *happen?* That poor girl! How old is she? What did you do?"

To stop her twenty questions, I butt in, "It was an accident! I made a bad throw, and she was in the way."

"On a basketball court? How is someone just 'in the way,' Ethan? You're trying to go pro, and you mistake her nose for the basket?"

I sigh. "No, she was coming through the door, my ball rebounded, and it hit her in the nose. She's the same age as me. Look, I feel bad, okay? I feel really bad. And I already felt bad before this. So, no, this isn't helping."

Mae clucks her tongue. "Okay, okay. Well, Leah agrees with me, and—"

I groan. "How did you contact Leah? We're still on the phone."

My two older sisters are always ganging up on me.

"Meh, I'm texting her. Should I add her to the call?"

"No!" I shout, slowing down as the stoplight in front of me turns from yellow to red.

She laughs. "Well, we have both decided you're responsible for her nose job should she need one."

The stoplight turns to green. "Let's hope she doesn't."

For a few seconds, it's silent. She's probably texting Leah more.

"Ethan? I gotta go, I just heard some sort of crash from the kitchen. The kids probably broke something. Listen, I love you. Like you said, it was an accident. If you feel bad about it, do something for her. But I'm sure it's just more of a low than anything. Especially if you were already feeling down beforehand. Promise me you'll take your meds as soon as you get home?"

I pull into my complex's parking lot. "Yeah, I'm almost

there now. I will."

"Trey! Erin!" She shouts. "What did you do?"

Hanging up, I chuckle and lay my forehead against the steering wheel as I turn the car off. Talking to Mae usually makes me feel better, but something gnaws at me. I shouldn't have said what I did as Grace left the car. Maybe she didn't even hear it. But if she did...

Stupid.

I let out a breath and get out of my truck, grabbing my gym bag from the truck bed. A few people pass as I walk to my apartment. We nod at each other.

The apartment is empty. My roommates, Tristan and Scott are both out, probably at class. I head over to the cabinet above the stove where I keep my vitamins and medication.

Taking one of each, I swallow them with a swig of water. I glance in the fridge, but nothing looks good. I know I need to eat, but my appetite is shot. Classes are done for the day. Practice was cut short, and agitation pumps through my veins.

I could go for a run.

Maybe a boxing studio or something. I need to get this feeling out.

I rub at my temples. Maybe a run will help me focus.

The last thing I need are thoughts of the girl I hate, clogging up my neuropathways.

Catch the rest of Grace & Ethan's story in Grace Isn't Given, which releases in June 2021!

Sweet As Candy Playlist

Starting Over - Niykee Heaton
Losses - Tjay
Because of You - Kelly Clarkson
I Hope - Charlie Puth
Without Me - Halsey
Yo Perreo Sola - Bad Bunny
quiero mas - Ozuna
18 - One Direction
Conversations in the Dark - John Legend
Come & Go - Juice WRLD
Years - Astrid S
Lasting Lover (Acoustic) - James Arthur
Dusk Till Dawn - Sia
Are you with me - nilu
Me Gusta - Anitta & Cardi B
Exile - Taylor Swift
It's OK Not To Be OK - Marshmello
Quite Miss Home - James Arthur
Be Like That - Swae Lee
You Got It - Vedo

Note From The Author

Though the stories presented in this book were fiction, these things happen on a daily basis. My own experience with cyberbullying inspired the idea behind this book. As someone with a small platform, people comment horrible things about my family, my parenting, or my writing on a daily basis, and I can't even imagine what it's like for an actual influencer. Let me make one thing clear: No one, and I mean no one, gets a say in another person's life. Be kind to each other and think before you post a comment that might hurt someone.

Now, without further ado, I wanted to bring light to a few different, but even more important, issues in this book. Many of the non-profits mentioned throughout the book were completely fictional. That being said, I encourage you to research and support these organizations that do so much good in the world:

People Power
The Players Alliance
Cybersmile
EROC
RAINN

Acknowledgements

Where do I even start? I'm so happy that I have an amazing support system that helps me write books.

First, a huge shout out to my writing group. They are all guys who write things about dragons and aliens and wizards, and how we got paired up is beyond me, but they willingly read romance for me. Jim, you always catch my weird sentences and crazy grammar. Dave, you ship my characters like they're your own, and your comments give me life. Vale, you let me know when my characters are being too dramatic or annoying, giving me balance so the whole book isn't full of kissing, lol.

Second, Ryan, you give me inspiration with your jokes, your athleticism, and so much more. You're the coolest dad, and I literally only wrote about baseball because you played. Love you <3

Third, Mom, you're always so supportive and truly believe I'm the coolest writer (which is a lie, but I appreciate it nonetheless). Danielle, you probably think my books are crazy weird because you don't have time to read, but you take photos of them that look beautiful, and you're my best friend. Kate, you always share my stuff and support my writing. Anna, you are a lifesaver to me, and you read my books, which gives me all the heart eyes.

Fourth, all my Instagram influencer friends. You guys hype me up and share my stuff out to the world, which is more helpful than you even realize. You are all so special to me, and

I can't imagine doing this without you all because you're so much cooler than I am.

Fifth, all my sensitivity readers. You went through each and every line, let me into your cultures, and trusted me with your worlds. I'm so thankful for everything, and I can't say enough how much you mean to me.

Sixth, Sarah, you made this gorgeous cover, which brought my favorite character to life! You deal with my forgetfulness and crazy deadlines.

Seventh, Lisa, I could not, seriously, could not have done this without you. Without your translations, the book doesn't exist.

Finally, ALL MY READERS! You're my favorite people in the world. You spread the word about my book, which means so much, and I love connecting with you all. I promise, the next book is going to be funny, heartwarming, and the best one yet. Xoxo.

Books By This Author

Les Is More

www.ingramcontent.com/pod-product-compliance
Lightning Source LLC
Chambersburg PA
CBHW051954240626
47153CB00005B/1749